About the Author

Melissa Hill is originally from Cahir in Co Tipperary, and now lives with her husband Kevin and their dog Homer in Co Wicklow. She is the author of bestselling novels, *Something You Should Know*, *Not What You Think* and *Wishful Thinking*, all published by Poolbeg.

For more information, visit the author's website at **www.melissahill.info**

Never
say
Never

Also by Melissa Hill

Wishful Thinking
Not What You Think
Something You Should Know

Never say Never

MELISSA HILL

POOLBEG

Published 2005
by Poolbeg Press Ltd
123 Grange Hill, Baldoyle
Dublin 13, Ireland
E-mail: poolbeg@poolbeg.com

© Melissa Hill 2005

The moral right of the author has been asserted.

Typesetting, layout, design © Poolbeg Press Ltd

3 5 7 9 10 8 6 4 2

A catalogue record for this book is available from the British Library.

ISBN 1-84223-221-5

Typeset by Patricia Hope in Palatino
Printed by Litografia Rosés S.A,
Spain

www.poolbeg.com

Acknowledgements

As always, huge thanks and lots of love to Kevin for everything. It is impossible to put into words how much I appreciate all you do – especially the driving bits. I'll pass the driving test eventually . . . maybe.

To Homer, who takes me for walks and gets me out of the house now and again.

Thanks to Mam and Dad, who give terrific support and encouragement – and not forgetting the other two, who have been relentless in promoting me and who get their own special mention in this book.

To Fiona, Breda, Aine and Lisa who – if I were so inclined – could keep me in storylines for good (don't worry, you're all safe enough)! A particular mention to new mammy Maria (who incidentally, is nothing like the new mammy in this story!) and a big welcome to baby Cathal.

Thanks to Ger Nichol, who continues to give me wonderful advice and assistance. To Poolbeg – Kieran, Brona, Claire, Lynda and especially Paula, who as always have been terrific. I really couldn't wish for a better publisher. To Gaye – for being such a good-humoured and patient editor.

To all at AP Watt – particularly Tania, Linda, and the truly wonderful Sheila Crowley for being so enthusiastic about my work. Thank you so much for having me.

Huge thanks to all at Eason, Hughes & Hughes, Argosy, Dubray and the Byrne Group, and to booksellers all over the country for the tremendous support you give my books – I really appreciate it. Thanks in particular to my local bookshops – Bridge Street Books Wicklow, Dubray, Bray; the Wexford Bookshop; The Book Nook, Cashel and Eason, Clonmel.

Likewise to Dolan's SuperValu for being so good, and also to friends and neighbours in Wicklow and my home-town of Cahir, who have been terrific in their support of me and my books. Thank you all – it means a lot.

To Tony Butler, Lynne Glanville, Tipp FM, East Coast FM, and all the print, radio and TV journalists who continue to give me great backing.

Thanks to Sarah Webb for arranging all those enjoyable events, days out and lively dinners with the Irish Girls – we'd be lost without you!

Well done to Colleen O'Neill, who earned herself a very special place in *Never Say Never*. Colleen, I really hope you like it. Thanks to everyone who entered the competition – I'd love to include you all, but if I did, the book would go on forever!

Finally – massive, massive thanks to the readers. I can't express how grateful I am to everyone who buys and reads my books, and to those who send me great feedback and lovely messages of support at my website **www.melissahill.info**. It means so much, and I love hearing from you.

I very much hope you all enjoy *Never Say Never*.

To my terrific sisters Amanda & Sharon
This one's for you

PROLOGUE

Late Nineties

'Man Plans – God Laughs.' Robin couldn't help thinking of that old Yiddish proverb as she listened to the discussion going on around her. For some reason, she'd always felt uncomfortable talking about 'the future'.

It was a mild evening in late May, and Robin and her friends, all soon-to-be graduates of UCD, were sitting on the grass by the lake in St Stephen's Green. They were having a 'where will we be in five years' time?' conversation.

"Andrew will be our big sports star," Amanda declared, positioning herself comfortably against her boyfriend's broad chest. She pushed a fair curl away from her pretty face.

Kate rolled her eyes. "You worked overtime on the crystal ball for that one," she said caustically. After graduation, Andrew was poised to sign with a well-known Irish rugby club.

Amanda gave Kate a withering look. "No doubt

1

you'll end up in politics, lecturing the rest of us as usual," she replied.

There had never been any love lost between Andrew's girlfriend and Kate. The two of them always managed to rub one another up the wrong way, and, Robin thought with a grin, neither tried to hide it.

"So what about you, hon?" Andrew asked, turning the attention back to the person who craved it the most. "What'll you be?"

Amanda tittered. "Famous, of course," she answered confidently. "I'll either be a big name in music or modelling, or perhaps make it big on TV." Again, she flicked her hair out of her face.

"Yes, I can see it now, *The Amanda Langan Show*," Peter piped up with a laugh.

Kate snorted and Amanda flashed her another look.

"And what about you, Peter?" Kate asked him.

Peter was studying radiology and took a keen interest in the environment – an interest he had acquired from his long-time girlfriend and Robin's close friend, Olivia. He was arguably the better-looking male in the group, his lovely dark eyes, sculpted jawline and sallow complexion making for a breathtaking combination.

"You'll have to ask the wife about that one," Peter replied, winking at Robin.

Amanda's head shot up and she looked at him, aghast. "You haven't proposed?"

Robin hid a smile. If any couple in this group would go down that road, Amanda was determined it would be her and Andrew. No way would she let plain ordinary Olivia Dunne and Peter Gallagher steal her thunder by getting engaged first!

Peter laughed, apparently reading her thoughts. "When and if I do, I guarantee you'll be the first to know."

Her startled blue eyes wide as saucers, Amanda sat back and nestled closely into Andrew. Robin looked at Kate and knew that she too could see Amanda mentally working out some way to get a proposal out of Andrew before Olivia and Peter pipped them to the post. They exchanged a grin.

"So, that's settled then," Andrew said, sitting forward and recapping the conversation on his fingers. "Amanda's going to be the TV star, *I'll* be the sports star, lovebirds Peter and Olivia will save the world, Kate will help with the paperwork . . ." Much to Amanda's chagrin he winked at Kate. "And, of course, Leah will probably end up owning her own restaurant."

Robin smiled proudly. Her good friend Leah was studying for her qualification in catering college, and was a wonderful pastry chef. Passionate and hardworking, Leah was the one who, in Robin's opinion, was the most likely to do well in her chosen career.

"So, who's left then?" Andrew went on, and Robin tried not to let her discomfort show. This was exactly why she hated these conversations – they always seemed to highlight her lack of talent, her lack of personality. She wasn't attractive like Amanda, talented like Leah or caring and motherly like Olivia. She was just the odd one, she supposed, the quiet, weird one that faded into the background.

Just then, Peter's girlfriend Olivia approached, followed closely by pastry-chef-in-waiting Leah.

"Hey, it's about time!" Peter said. "Where did you two get to?"

"We went shopping for goodies," Leah said, her mouth full, as she sat down.

Robin smiled. Leah never seemed to stop eating – as a trainee chef, she had no choice – but maddeningly never seemed to put on an ounce. "Chocolate, anyone?" She waved a Snickers bar around. "Oh, sorry, Robin, I almost forgot." Leah moved the bag of goodies away. "Better keep those away from you."

"Thanks," Robin grinned.

"I'll have some," Amanda said reaching for the bag. "I'm lucky in that I don't have to worry about my figure."

"So what have we missed?" Olivia asked, trying to get comfortable on the grass.

"Well, Amanda's dusted off the crystal ball, and is making predictions as to what we'll end up doing in the future," Kate informed her, another roll of her eyes leaving no-one in any doubt about her thoughts on the stupidity of the exercise.

"Oh, I *love* conversations like this!" Olivia sat forward, warming to the subject immediately. "Let me guess, Andrew will be big in sports, Leah will be – oh, I don't know – a really famous TV chef or . . . what?" Seeing Amanda's poisonous glare, she stopped short. "Well, what's wrong with that? Out of everyone here, I can certainly see Leah being a big star." She winked mischievously at Robin, fully aware of the effect her remarks were having on a miffed Amanda.

"And Robin will be . . ." Olivia paused then and turned to face her. "I can definitely see you going on to surprise us all. You're the most kind-hearted and sensitive by a mile, so I could see you doing something that involves helping others."

Robin was touched. Kind-hearted, sensitive? How wonderful that Olivia would think so highly of her. Whatever about the others, Robin was certain that she, Olivia and Leah would always be great friends no matter what they ended up doing.

"So what did you say about me and Peter? Hold on, let me guess, I will be . . . the settled one," Olivia declared. "Yes, I'll get my veterinary degree, work for a few years after we marry?" She looked at Peter for affirmation. "Then I'll be quite happy to stay home and rear all our kids," she added with an impish grin.

"Marriage, kids – no way!" Peter feigned terror.

"Good luck to you, mate," Andrew chuckled, moving slightly away from Amanda.

Olivia ruffled Peter's dark hair. "Well, after all these years, I don't think you're going to find anyone else to put up with you, are you?" she laughed.

Olivia and Peter were so easy together, so comfortable, so – perfect for one another, Robin thought. There was no doubt that those two would be together for a long time to come.

"I have an idea," Andrew announced, sitting up sharply then. "We should place a few bets with the bookies. See if Amanda *does* become a TV star, or Leah a famous chef, or you and Peter end up getting married ..."

Peter guffawed. "Typical Andrew, any excuse for a flutter!" He lay back and rested his head on one hand. "It's an idea though. We could do it, and then arrange to all meet up sometime later and see how it's all panned out – or not."

"I think it's a great idea!" Amanda enthused, undoubtedly having visions of herself returning to the fold replete with designer clothes and glamorous lifestyle. "It would be great fun seeing how it all turned out, how everyone's getting on ..."

Ever the sceptic, Kate shook her head in exasperation.

"It *would* be fun," Olivia added enthusiastically. "There's a chance we might not all stay in touch, so this would be a good excuse as any to catch up – why not?"

"I don't know," Kate said. "People make these stupid promises all the time at graduation, but they don't always work out."

"Well, I think it's worth doing – what do the rest of you think?" Olivia asked and everyone bar Kate nodded in agreement.

Realising she was outnumbered, Kate held her hands up in mock surrender. "OK, OK, whatever you want," she groaned. "I still think it's a silly idea though – we'll all be leading different lives, and might not even *want* to know one another. And by then, things could be completely different and we could be tempting fate. What if one of us dies or something?" Almost as soon as the words were out, she winced.

"Kate!" Leah and Olivia chorused. "Don't say something like that!"

Robin's stomach gave a little leap. Was she imagining it, or were all eyes turned on her just then?

"I'm sorry but it's true, you just don't know what could happen – to any of us."

"Well, look if something *does* happen, then obviously our meeting won't come about," Olivia said, her tone a little too bright. "But, if we're going to do this, we all need to make the effort, so are you in or not?"

In the end, Kate sighed. "I'm in."

"Great!" Olivia sat back on her heels, eager to start organising. "So we'll meet up where . . . in the UCD grounds?"

"Why not here in St Stephen's Green?" Robin ventured.

"Yes! That would be ideal," Olivia said approvingly. "Well?" She looked to the others for signs of assent. Kate shrugged and the others nodded.

"OK, then, that's settled. Same place here by the lake," Olivia bit her lip. "When?"

"Oh, late afternoon, I think, then some of us can do a bit of shopping on Grafton St beforehand," Amanda said airily.

"I think she meant *when* – as in what *year*?" Kate said through gritted teeth.

"Oh, I'm not sure . . . maybe five years?" Amanda suggested.

"Five years – is that too long?" asked Olivia.

"Not long enough," Kate said under her breath and Robin giggled.

"OK then," Olivia announced gravely. "We all graduate next week, and then go out into the big bad world and do our own thing. Chances are some of us will stay in touch, chances are some of us won't." She gave a sideways glance at Amanda and Kate. "Nonetheless, for the sake of our friendship and the fact that we've shared a lot, all seven of us plan to meet here in five years' time . . ." She checked the date on her watch. "Well, let's say same time, same place. May 28th at 3pm just to make it handy."

"To May 28th five years from now!" Leah raised her glass in the air, and the others duly followed, their expressions happy, and full of the promise of things to come.

All with the exception of Kate, who still looked sceptical.

Amanda glared at her. "Lift your bloody glass!" she ordered.

"It'll never happen," Kate muttered with a shake of her head, although her eyes twinkled as she grudgingly raised her drink in a toast with her friends. "Five years from now – all seven of us still friends and together? I'm telling you, it'll never happen."

She was right.

CHAPTER 1

Seven Years Later

Robin stood awkwardly in front of the security guard. Her heart hammered nervously as he asked – no *ordered* – her to hold out her arms. She did so, crucifixion-style.

He began to pat her down quickly and impersonally, and again Robin wondered why she always felt so guilty in these situations, when it was likely that it was just some loose change in her pockets that was setting off the scanners.

Ben stood on the other side laughing at her. Her boyfriend just sailed through every time. And even if Robin did manage to get past the scanner without incident (which didn't happen very often) the guards nearly always spot-frisked her anyway. With her shoulder-length auburn hair and light complexion, she looked as Irish as the next woman, so why did JFK airport security always peg her as a possible international terrorist? Oh, well, she thought, sighing inwardly, it surely was a sign of the times. Only a few years ago she and the rest of America had been able to board aeroplanes like buses and nip from city to city unchecked and unnoticed. And look where that had led. She supposed she should be relieved they were being suspicious.

The inquisition over, Robin joined Ben on the other side in Departures.

He shook his head. "Same thing, every single time," he joked. "Now come on, we'd better get a move on."

Robin quickened her step and the two of them hastened towards their departure gate. They'd been lucky to reach the airport in the time they did, she thought, the Friday afternoon traffic across Manhattan beggaring belief. She had lived in the city for nearly seven years now, and she still couldn't get used to the unbearable traffic. The taxi-driver had driven like a man possessed to get them to the airport in time for their flight.

"Have you got the boarding cards?" she asked Ben as they approached their gate.

"Me? I thought you had them," he replied seriously, although she knew by the mischievous glint in his eyes that he was only teasing. Hopefully.

"Not the time to be joking around, Ben," she scolded. "Not when this plane is about to take off."

"Ah, they'd never leave without us!"

"They would too," Robin said and, smiling at the cabin-crew member, asked him, "Wouldn't you?"

"It's another ten minutes till take-off, ma'am," the

crew member informed her, "but according to regulations –"

"It's OK – we're here now," Ben interjected.

"Passports, please."

Robin and Ben duly produced their Irish passports and waited for the next question.

"Visas, please." The man studied the visas, passports and Robin and Ben closely.

"Jesus," Ben said to Robin on the way down the gangway, "do none of these guys have a sense of humour any more? I know that things have to be tight, but it's only a bloody short hop down the road."

"Well, would you prefer they weren't so particular?"

"No, but –"

"Well then, button it, and let's start enjoying this little break of ours."

As they reached the door of the small intercity aircraft, Ben hugged her to him. Robin was really looking forward to this. She and Ben hadn't had a holiday in ages. OK, it was only a short few days in Washington, and they wouldn't get to do or see all that much, but still she was really looking forward to her first visit to the capital. Manhattan could be claustrophobic sometimes, and things had been so hectic at work for both of them they could do with this break.

Yet, Robin felt a familiar feeling of discomfort as she handed in her boarding card.

"Straight down on the left-hand side – seats 10B and C," the stewardess informed them pleasantly. Robin smiled as she passed by, relieved the girl hadn't made any comment. Still, she remembered then, it was unlikely there was any indication on her boarding card.

She and Ben made their way slowly down along the aircraft, bumping past people who were shifting their luggage about and trying to get settled.

Robin reached Row 10 and was about to take her seat and let Ben stow their bags overhead – as was their routine – when a familiar scent hit her nostrils. Instantly, she turned around and motioned for Ben to follow her back up the aisle.

"What is it, hon?" Ben asked but, with a quick glance at the seats directly behind theirs, he soon saw what was bothering his girlfriend. "Ah – not again," he said, his voice tinged with annoyance. "Don't these people ever listen to a bloody word?"

"You sit down for a minute – I'll talk to them," Robin looked around for a stewardess.

"Are you sure? I'll go with you if –"

"No, I don't want to make a big fuss," she said grimacing.

Seeing a stewardess approach from the other end of the plane, Robin waylaid her. Trying to keep her tone low so as not to be overheard by the passengers in the immediate vicinity, she outlined the problem.

"Let me look into it, ma'am," the stewardess said a little warily, "but, as you can see, the aircraft is almost fully boarded – it might be difficult now to reassign the seating."

"I understand that, but when I made the booking, I specifically asked that a provision be made –"

"Yes, but you are seated a row in front – surely it couldn't cause that much of a problem?"

"Look," Robin said softly, trying to sound reasonable, "I know it's probably difficult for you to understand but, yes, it *can* cause that much of a problem. Please understand that I'm not blaming you, but I did make the request at the time of booking and I was assured . . ." She trailed off, spotting a woman seated in the row next to them blatantly trying to eavesdrop. "Look, if you could just take a look at the seating arrangements, and find out if they have earmarked a zone for me, I would really appreciate it. Or perhaps we could just change seats with someone else?" Robin smiled graciously, hoping her polite approach would work.

"OK, I'll see what I can do," the stewardess said, heading for the top of the aisle.

Robin felt all eyes on her as she stood there waiting for the other woman's return, and despite her protestation that she could deal with the matter herself, she was relieved when Ben joined her.

"What's happening? Are they going to move us?"

"We'll soon find out," she said, seeing the stewardess approach. But by her expression, Robin knew immediately that her booking request had been ignored. It was the same old story.

"I'm afraid that an area hasn't been assigned, ma'am," the stewardess said apologetically. "I really don't know what happened in our booking office. Obviously they didn't pass on the request to the check-in desk. And as this is such a small aircraft . . ." She trailed off as if to imply that in such a cramped space, an assigned zone might not make much of a difference anyway.

"I can't believe this!" Ben interjected. "It's the same thing every time we fly with this bloody airline – how come AA can get it done, Delta can get it done, but your crowd –"

"Ben, calm down," Robin soothed, although she was just as frustrated as he was. Trust her bloody problems to ruin their weekend away – again! She really didn't know how he put up with her sometimes. "Look," she said to the stewardess, "I specifically requested it when booking and they assured me it would be fine." She said the last bit through gritted teeth, out of the corner of her eye once again spotting the old biddy earwigging.

"I think they may have misinterpreted things," the stewardess said. "Look, what if I just ask the passenger in question to put them away for the duration of the flight? We don't serve them as a rule anyway these days. Would that help?"

Robin hated the way people looked at her as if she was an over-hysterical hypochondriac of some sort – the way the stewardess was looking at her now. But people didn't realise that she wasn't just looking for attention or some kind of special treatment. This was serious.

"That's all we can do at this stage, I suppose," Robin said wearily, but one look at Ben as they followed the stewardess back down towards their seats told her that he was fit to burst. Robin kept her distance as Ben and the stewardess approached the occupants of the seats behind Row 10.

"Excuse me, ma'am," the stewardess said pleasantly to an overweight woman, accompanied by what must be her husband and their young son. "Really sorry to inconvenience you, but I wonder if I could request that your son put his snack away for the duration of this flight, or if maybe we could move you all to another seat near the front? We have a particular passenger onboard today –"

"Whaddya mean?" The woman's eyes narrowed. "I booked this seat 'specially, 'cos with my kidneys I have to be near the little girls' room. Anyway, what's the problem? National security mean no-one's allowed eat on these things any more?"

"No, no, that's not it at all, ma'am," said the stewardess soothingly. "We'll be serving a variety of refreshments once airborne, and some complimentary snacks, so if you could –"

"They better be complimentary – and not at those darn New York prices!" the woman's husband butted in rudely. "Anyway, the engine hasn't even started runnin' yet and my boy here is hungry." He glared at the stewardess. "I don't see any signs around here saying you shouldn't eat when you're hungry." With that, he reached forward and took a packet of peanuts out of his seat-pouch. Instinctively, Robin shrank backwards.

"I'm just making a polite request for you to put those away, sir," the stewardess repeated her plea. "I understand your confusion, but you've refused to move, and we have a passenger with a medical condition seated in front of you today."

The man leaned forward and looked up at Ben. "What, you addicted to junk food or somethin'?" he sneered.

"No, my girlfriend's allergic to peanuts," Ben announced loudly. "Your peanut dust can bring on a reaction, and the airline," he said, turning to the stewardess, "like most airlines these days, is *supposed* to provide a peanut-free zone for sufferers like her."

"Ben, calm down," Robin said, mortified, as everyone in the immediate vicinity turned to look. Further down the plane, heads began to pop up here and there, trying to see what all the commotion was about. Sensing an escalation of the scene, another stewardess moved towards them.

"Well, I ain't offering her no peanuts, am I?" the man asked, puzzled.

"That's not it," Ben explained. "She's hypersensitive. She can be affected simply by being as close to them as I am now."

"Well, it ain't my fault if people can't control themselves," the man went on, unmoved by Ben's pleas. "I paid my fare, same as everyone else here, and nobody's gonna tell me what I can and can't do." As if to prove his point, he opened the fresh bag and put a handful of peanuts in his mouth.

"Please, sir, we're about to take off and again, I'm really sorry for the inconvenience but –"

"Hey!" he said, raising his voice and looking nastily at the stewardess.

Ben reddened in anger, and Robin could see him struggling to control his temper.

"Me and my family ain't had nuthin' to eat since this morning and we're *hungry*! We're not movin' and I ain't puttin' away no peanuts, my wife ain't puttin' away no peanuts, and my son ain't puttin' away no peanuts for some stuck-up Central Park lady – so there!" He sat back, and his wife looked at him approvingly, apparently satisfied that her husband was the right man to put these troublesome city-slickers in their place.

"She could have a serious reaction, you idiot!" Ben hissed at him, unable to keep his temper in check any longer.

"Hey, who you callin' an idiot, son?" the man said, standing up and dwarfing Ben with his huge frame.

Ben didn't flinch. "You heard me!" His chest rose as he squared up to him.

"Sirs, I really must ask that you –"

"Ben, leave it, please!" Robin was upset now, having experienced embarrassing scenes like this many times before, although none as confrontational as this one.

"No, Robin, this guy is totally out of order. Who the hell does he think he is?"

"It's not his fault." She looked at the man's wife imploringly, but was afraid to come any closer for fear of what she held in her hand. "I'm sorry – I know it's not your fault."

The wife seemed to see the genuine fear in Robin's eyes, and immediately she closed the bag of peanuts and put them away. "Sit down, Max," she said sternly

17

to her husband, who amazingly, after a few seconds, complied, though he and Ben were still glaring angrily at one another.

"We didn't mean any harm," the woman said to Robin and then to the stewardess. "But my boy here, he gets antsy when he's hungry and so does Max. We got these peanuts in the airport. We really didn't mean any harm. And with my kidneys, we really can't move seats."

"That's OK, ma'am, but we need to take off soon. Now if you and your husband could just put those away, there shouldn't be any more problems."

"If you people had assigned a peanut-free zone like you were asked, there wouldn't *be* a problem," Ben said, his voice shaking with anger. "But you just don't care, do you? You just pack in as many idiots as you can fit – who cares if one of them becomes seriously ill because of your negligence?"

If there was one thing that struck fear into the heart of every airline, it was the suspicion of negligence.

"Sir, I appreciate your distress," the other stewardess spoke up then, "but really we must get going –"

"But really nothing!" Ben was in full flight, which is more than could be said for the rest of the passengers on Flight Number 81268. "It's totally unacceptable and I won't have it."

He stood up and, to Robin's horror, opened the overhead locker and removed their luggage. "Come on, Robin. We're going,"

"What?"

"Sir, if you could just –"

"I said, we're going! I've had enough of this – why should we have to put up with it? She made a request, she explained the danger and they ignored her. So forget it! You can bet this is the last time I fly with this bloody airline!"

Robin looked from Ben to the stewardess, to the peanut-crunchers, and back to Ben again, but at that stage she didn't care where they went as long as it was out of here, away from all the staring, the pointing, the whispered remarks.

"Come on, love," Ben said, leading her along the aisle towards the doorway. "We don't have to put up with this kind of carry-on."

"Really, sir, there's no need . . ." The voice of the stewardess trailed off as she realised that Ben wasn't to be placated.

"I'm so sorry," Robin said, mortified, as another stewardess had to be called to open the aircraft door. "I'm so sorry."

Providing a peanut-free zone for passengers like Robin was at the discretion of the individual airline, so really Ben had no right to be so hard on them. But she suspected he was tired of the fact that the condition could be so all-pervading when it came to their lifestyle.

Sitting in the taxi on the way back from the airport to their Lower East Side apartment, yet another weekend ruined, Robin smarted with the embarrassment of it all.

"I made it clear when I made the booking, Ben,

really I did," she said, looking miserably at him and trying to convince herself more than him.

Ben turned to her and took her hand in his. "Hey, don't you be feeling guilty about this. It was my decision to get off that plane. Anyway, I didn't want all those people to be staring at us all the way to Washington, did you?" he grinned. "So don't be silly," he added, ruffling her hair. "There'll be other weekends, and anyway it's not your fault."

But, Robin thought sadly, there was no getting away from the fact that without her allergy, there wouldn't have been a problem at all.

So of course, it was her fault – it was *always* her fault.

Chapter 2

A week later, Robin slung her bag over her shoulder, and headed north on Broadway. It was early April, but already the air was thick with a humidity that she reckoned only hardy, seasoned New Yorkers could tolerate. She still hadn't got used to the high spring temperatures, let alone the choking heat of midsummer. She had just left the air-conditioned cool of the office for the day, but already her face was red and perspiring and her light cotton shirt superglued to her chest and back.

Long strands of auburn hair were plastered to her face and neck and, not for the first time, she wondered if she should just bite the bullet and chop the whole bloody lot off. Still, it had taken so long to grow and, most of the time, it was quite manageable and needed little styling – days like today excepted, when she looked like someone who'd been trapped in a jungle for months on end.

It wasn't about to get any easier, she thought wryly, as she reached Wall St Station and began to descend the steps. The subway was tough going at the best of times, so on a day like today, she would be lucky to take in a single breath of air, let alone a fresh one.

She was just about to insert her travelpass into the ticket barrier, when her cellphone rang. "Nice timing," she muttered to herself, and quickly stood back as a throng of hassled-looking commuters hastened towards her. Two seconds later and she would have been out of range in the tunnels. She glanced at the caller display and was disappointed when she recognised Ben's cellphone number.

"Ben, hi," she said, her tone flat. A call at this time of day usually meant that Ben was working late – something that lately was happening more often than not, and another reason why the planned trip to Washington would have been a welcome break.

It was such a pity, because on an evening like this one, it would have been nice to throw open the apartment's old sash windows and eat dinner while watching the world go by. Ben, like Robin, loved to take advantage of the good weather – a result, she thought, of their Irish childhoods when a fine summer's day was a rare event and treated as such.

But Robin was wrong.

"Robin, it's little Kirsty – she's had a bad attack and Sarah's had to take her to hospital."

"Oh no, not again! Poor thing, is she very bad?" Ben's four-year-old niece Kirsty suffered from chronic

22

asthma and this wasn't the first time the little girl had been hospitalised.

"Bad enough, according to Sarah. She forgot to use her inhaler again. They've put her on the nebuliser."

Robin shook her head. "She's in St Vincent's?"

"Yeah, same as last time."

"OK, I'll meet you there. Does Sarah need anything?" Ben's poor sister would be up the walls.

"Just some peace of mind," Ben answered grimly. "But no, Brian's away, so I left work early and promised Sarah I'd go back out to their place to pick up a couple of things. I'm on my way from there now, so I'll see you soon, OK?"

"OK, see you later."

Sarah and her husband Brian lived about an hour's drive away from the city. Brian was obviously off on some business trip or another. Sarah had met her American husband while on a working holiday in New York one summer. She'd fallen so much in love with both him and his native country that she settled there for good, and the two had been living in New Jersey since Kirsty was born.

The hospital was close by, so rather than risk the stifling heat of the subway, she decided to walk. Still, with the choking dead air of the city, by the time she reached the hospital she was so short of breath she could only imagine how poor Kirsty was feeling!

"Robin, thanks for coming – again," Sarah said when Robin entered the ward, and Robin noticed that she had lost an awful lot of weight since she'd last seen her.

"You know it's no problem," she said, giving Sarah a warm hug before turning to Kirsty, who looked frail and even tinier in the hospital bed. Although, thankfully, Robin noticed, she was now off the nebuliser.

Robin held one hand behind her back. "Hi, darling, look who followed me here to see you!"

Kirsty grinned and her eyes lit up when Robin produced a small alligator beanie-bag. She had picked it up in a toy store on her way, and while she knew the fearsome-looking alligator probably wasn't the best choice for a four-year-old girl, she was loath to get something stuffed or furry, fearful that it would exacerbate Kirsty's asthma.

"She's much improved now, thank God," Sarah said, motioning Robin towards a chair alongside Kirsty's bed. "But on the way here in the car . . ." She trailed off, shaking her head.

"It's been so humid today," Robin said softly, fearful that Sarah was blaming herself. Sarah always blamed herself, feeling somehow responsible for failing to teach Kirsty the dangers of forgetting to use her inhaler. "I've had trouble taking breaths myself, so I can only imagine what it's been like for her."

"It's just been getting worse and worse since she started school," Sarah said quietly, "and I think she's too embarrassed to use her inhaler. But on days like today, when the air is full of pollen . . . I don't know . . ." She patted her daughter's forehead using a damp cloth. "Honey, we spoke before about always using your inhaler when you start wheezing, didn't we?"

24

The little girl nodded, her breathing now steady but her eyes tired and fearful.

"It's hard for her to get used to having to do it in front of everyone, I suppose," Robin said, reaching across and stroking Kirsty's little hand. "She probably hates drawing attention to herself. I was the same when I was younger." She smiled, remembering how her own mother had been equally as protective and worried about her peanut allergy. "And, of course, kids will be kids, and at school they can talk you into doing anything . . ." She smiled again, this time at Kirsty. "She's a good girl though – she'll remember next time, won't you, pet?"

Kirsty nodded, hugged her none-too-cute new alligator toy and grinned at Robin. She adored her and Ben, and Robin decided that they really should make a bit more of an effort to visit Brian and Sarah out in New Jersey. She felt guilty that lately the only time they saw Kirsty was when she was ill. But because they both worked long hours, Robin as a financial controller for a company in the financial district, and Ben for a graphic-design firm on Lexington Avenue, they tended to just chill out at weekends and go for dinner or a movie.

Lately, Ben was taking on some additional freelance work at weekends, in the hope that they could move out of Manhattan and get a place in the suburbs.

"It's either that, or move back home," he had said one evening over a pizza, and the wineglass Robin was holding had almost cracked in her hand.

"Back home – to Dublin, you mean?" she had said, her heart in her mouth as she waited for him to clarify.

She had no intention of moving back to Dublin – not now, not ever. She loved her life in New York, and since the 9/11 attacks had felt a deep love and allegiance towards America that she had never felt at home. She fitted in here, she belonged here, and up until then she had thought Ben felt the same way.

"It would be brilliant, wouldn't it?" Ben said, his dark eyes shining. "A complete change of lifestyle, something slow and easier than all this mad rushing around."

Robin felt exasperated. What was it about the Irish abroad that made them see 'the old country' through rose-tinted glasses? It was as though Dublin had never moved into the twenty-first century and everyone was still working at a snail's pace and travelling along boreens on horses and carts! Robin spoke to Leah on a regular basis, and from what she could make out, Dublin was now equally if not more manic than Manhattan. Everything was notoriously expensive, and lately they had introduced some kind of mad tram service, which meant that neither man nor motor could get around the city without sitting in painfully slow traffic. Robin had read on the *Irish Independent Online* only the other day that an ill-fated underground metro service had run into some kind of trouble with planning, and would be delayed for another few years.

"But what would you do?" Robin asked, wondering if Ben was being serious or if it was just wishful but harmless thinking. "I mean, would you seriously contemplate giving up your job – after working so hard to get where you are?" Ben held a management position at his firm.

"Work isn't everything," he said meaningfully, and Robin knew he was again hinting at the 'why don't we start a family' conversation.

"Ben . . ." she began, but luckily the waitress arrived with their pizza and the moment passed.

Now, as Robin studied Sarah's tired and anxious expression while she softly stroked her daughter's hand, she wondered how anyone could do it. So much worry, so much anguish – what was it that made people want to put themselves through all that? She adored Kirsty – in fact Robin adored most children and, funnily enough, they seemed drawn to her in return – but she knew in her heart and soul that she herself would not make a good mother. She just didn't have it in her.

"How's she doing?" The arrival of the paediatrician interrupted Robin's thoughts and she moved away from Kirsty's bed to give the doctor some room. He scanned the little girl's medical chart. "This has been her third visit in five months, Mrs Freyne," he said. "Why hasn't she been using her inhaler?"

The implied accusation was obvious to Robin and indeed Sarah, who looked ashamed. How was that fair? Robin thought, annoyed. Surely it was impossible to teach a child as young as Kirsty the importance of measuring her breathing and using her inhaler. She was barely a toddler, for goodness' sake! And Robin could safely assume that Sarah didn't enjoy having to rush her child to a hospital an hour away, or paying the healthy bills for the use of the ventilator. The way the doctor was behaving, it was as though Sarah, or indeed Kirsty, were being purposefully neglectful. How dare he? She had a good mind to ask him when was the last time he was solely responsible for a delicate child twenty-four hours a day, and how did he cope when the child was out of his sight. Bloody patronising doctors – Robin had come across enough of them back home when she was a child, and they were all the bloody same!

She made a mental note there and then to give Ben's sister more of a hand with looking after Kirsty. The very least she and Ben could do was to baby-sit the odd weekend and give Sarah and Brian some time to themselves. It would do them, and indeed Kirsty, some good to let someone else share the burden.

Yes, Robin thought – seeing Kirsty's expression light up as Ben entered the room – that is exactly what they would do. Although hopefully, she thought then, Ben wouldn't get the wrong idea and start thinking it was some kind of sign that she was ready for motherhood. Well, if he got that idea, she would have to nip it firmly in the bud. Robin was certain she wouldn't be ready for motherhood for a long time yet.

If ever.

Chapter 3

Leah took a deep breath – a very, very deep breath. This was easily the most terrifying experience of her life. She had done many frightening things over the years – bungee-jumping in France, white-water rafting in Belgium, not to mention going through the very scary motions of setting up in business in Ireland – but this, this was the most terrifying of all.

The night before, she hadn't been able to sleep, she was so sick with nerves, and she had spent much of the night in her kitchen experimenting with new recipes for her handmade chocolates. It hadn't been a wasted night either, she thought with a grin, as she'd come up with a raspberry and fluffy white chocolate truffle combo that was absolutely delicious – *Berrylicious* actually, which was just what she intended to name the new creation.

She took another deep breath and sat for a few moments more in her little Fiesta before getting out.

You can do this, she told herself. You've succeeded in your career and you will succeed in this – you can do it. Unfortunately, the message wasn't being relayed to the butterflies in her stomach.

Despite her student ambitions to become a pasty-chef, Leah found that time abroad after her degree had unexpectedly led her catering career in a totally different direction.

Having qualified, and eager to further her knowledge and experience, she had spent a few years in France working under the stewardship of a renowned Belgian dessert chef and chocolatier. Her own speciality at college had been pastries and desserts, but working alongside such an artisan and master of his work, Leah unexpectedly fell in love with the intricate handmade chocolatier craft. In order to hone her growing skills, she spent a further eighteen months away in Brussels. While there she approached with gusto the challenge of marrying delicious and unusual flavours with the finest chocolate, the sheer pleasure of creating something that looked irresistible and tasted like pure heaven.

By the time the initial apprenticeship was over, and her own skills were polished to perfection, Leah was hooked on the artistry of chocolate-making. There was no doubt in her mind as to where she wanted to go with her career, and when she returned to Ireland she immediately set about going into the confectionery business.

At the time of her return, two years earlier, the country was still in the throes of the economic boom and, following a huge leap of faith (and an equally huge start-up loan from her bank), Leah began her own specialised handmade chocolate company. She named the business Elysium, the Greek translation of which meant 'a condition of ideal happiness', which she felt went some way towards doing justice to her handmade creations.

She did her research beforehand and discovered that while the handmade chocolate business was a thriving Irish industry, there was little in the way of high-end artisan gift chocolates. Having experienced various selling-methods and chocolate boutiques during her time in Belgium, she eventually decided that the packaging and presentation of Elysium chocolates should be equally as important as the chocolates themselves. Her signature use of rich purple and gold-coloured ornate boxes, beautifully covered in beaded silk, and wrapped in delicate muslin, soon became hugely popular with card-and-gift stores and tourist retailers.

From humble origins in her own kitchen, to eventually securing a tiny shoebox in the local Enterprise Centre, Leah worked hard to supply her growing number of trade customers. It was true what they said about finding something you loved and never working a day again, she thought, because she absolutely adored her work. Josh, her boyfriend, often complained that she worked way too hard, but as far as she was concerned it was the best job in the world.

Recently, she and Josh had set up home together in a one-bed luxury – but, unfortunately, rented – apartment

MELISSA HILL

on Dublin's Southside. Their relationship was going great, the business was going great, Leah was a few months away from her thirtieth birthday and life was great.

But, she thought, finally getting out of the car, if she could just get today over and done with, then life would be even better. As Josh had pointed out before leaving for work that morning, all she could do was her best. Unfortunately, Leah knew from experience that her best would probably not be enough.

She jogged up the steps and into the building, her dark ponytail swinging as she went.

She felt strange wearing her hair like that outside of the kitchen, always thinking that the style looked particularly childish on her, probably because of her huge brown eyes and round face. The ponytail had been Olivia's suggestion – apparently, it never failed. And seeing as the ponytail trick had evidently worked for Olivia, Leah was prepared to take her word for it. She was prepared to try *anything* if it helped her through today's ordeal.

She gave the rather dour-looking receptionist a friendly smile. "Leah Reid," she said by way of announcement when the other woman didn't reciprocate. "My appointment's at ten o'clock."

The receptionist gave her such a look of derision that Leah wondered if she had somehow inadvertently announced to the girl that she was the Queen of England. It was one of those 'if you think I give a damn about who you are and why you're here, then you've got another think coming' looks – the ones that were so prevalent when it came to what passed for service these days. Leah immediately regretted being so friendly. 'Smile and the world smiles with you,' her mother used to say, in the hope of instilling manners into her children. These days, it was more like 'Smile and the world thinks you're a nutter,' Leah thought, with a self-effacing grin.

From the receptionist's eventual curt nod towards somewhere behind her, Leah deduced that she should take a seat on one of the plastic chairs lined up along the wall. She sat back and, despite herself, began nervously wringing her hands together. Then she stopped herself, realising that at a time like this, greasy, sweating palms were exactly what she didn't need.

She picked up a magazine and was about to check her horoscope when she realised that that particular issue was almost three months out of date. She turned instead to the problem pages, thinking that troublesome spouses and illicit affairs were always in vogue.

"Leah Reid?" She looked up, startled, to see a small, middle-aged man with a clipboard and, more importantly, what seemed like a kindly face, looking questioningly at her. His face reminded her a little bit of the TV presenter Pat Kenny, despite the fact that he was almost completely bald. She nodded.

"This way, please." He made towards an office doorway.

Leah stood up, relieved. This guy looked like a bit of a pussy-cat. Maybe things were looking up and maybe, just maybe, this mightn't be such a disaster after all.

But, the questions were an absolute nightmare. Leah had quickly scanned *The Rules* the night before but had been unable to concentrate. She was too busy worrying about the main event.

"Great day, isn't it?" Leah babbled as she followed him inside, habitually falling back on the great Irish conversation starter. Well, it was either that or the Dublin traffic and Leah could hardly start moaning about that with him, could she? Certainly not in the circumstances.

Two minutes in the room with him, and all Leah's hopes about this guy being a pussy-cat were cruelly dashed. He asked to see her driver's licence and, when Leah handed it to him, he recoiled as if he'd been burnt.

"Take it out of its plastic sleeve, please, Ms Reid," he ordered, his expression po-faced as Leah obliged. Uh-oh. It seemed she'd already got off to a bad start.

Nonetheless, she steeled herself and tried to act confident – but not too confident – as he began the questioning. The first question was actually quite simple for her, something about the correct situation in which you should dip your headlights.

"Well, I very rarely drive at night," she answered, pleasantly, "so that question doesn't really apply to me."

He looked at her. "Can you answer the question please, Ms Reid?"

Leah thought for a second. "Well, when another car is coming towards *you*, I suppose, otherwise you'd blind him. Not that it makes any difference, people just tend to blind you anyway, which is exactly why I avoid driving at night."

He said nothing and went straight on to the next question, this one about the right of way on roundabouts.

Leah was pleased – this was one she knew very well. The rules were very simple really.

"When you approach a roundabout, you have automatic right of way."

He looked at her. "Explain further?"

"Well, when you approach a roundabout and you're not planning to go round it and you just want to go straight through it, then you are automatically free to do so."

"I see." By his face, Leah wondered if she had said something wrong. But no, roundabouts were her thing, the one driving situation where she was completely confident she was in the right. The problem was with the other drivers who didn't know how to use the thing properly and, Leah thought wearily, there was always one. She hadn't the heart to beep her horn at the poor eejits (usually men) who didn't know what they were doing, but the problem was *they* always beeped at *her*.

Leah sat back in her seat, feeling better already and confident that she had aced that bit at least.

A few minutes later it was time for the main event, and Leah walked out of the building ahead of the tester, leading him to where she had parked the car.

To her utter surprise, he then asked her to walk around the car, ostensibly checking for broken mirrors and lights, etc, and refused to entertain Leah's protests that of course everything worked fine, wasn't the car only two years old? Then he mortified her by asking her to recite the car's registration. Why would anyone need to know that, Leah thought, when, if she had forgotten where she'd parked it, the car could easily be found by pressing the alarm-button on her keys and following the sound? She knew it was a two-year-old Dublin registration but that was about it. God, the embarrassment!

Would something that simple mean a fail? she worried, as she moved up a gear and drove towards the main street. She had just about remembered to put up her 'L' plates beforehand, Olivia having reminded her that not displaying her plates would definitely mean an instant fail. It had taken her close to an hour to find a place that stocked the stupid things, and nearly another one trying to stick them to the blasted windscreen.

Leah cast a quick eye towards the tester in the passenger seat, being careful not to swing her ponytail too much – the more elaborate swings, Olivia warned her, were only for checking her rear-view and side mirrors. He was marking boxes and, as far as Leah could see, wasn't watching her driving at all. That's a bit rude, she thought. Despite herself, she began to get annoyed. All these months she'd been dreading taking the bloody test – for the third time – and hardly sleeping these last few days thinking about it, and then your man couldn't even be bothered to test her properly! It was true what they said about them deciding in advance how many they were going to pass or fail, she thought, remembering an article she had read about the nature of the testing process, and how it was all down to luck, or the mood of your tester. It had nothing to do with your driving, or your ponytail-swinging or whether or not you knew the blasted reg of your car!

Leah looked up and quickly slammed on the brakes when she realised she had just been about to drive right through a zebra crossing – with, of course, the obligatory mother and buggy directly in her path. Shit! She gripped the steering wheel and smiled beatifically at the tester. "Well, I suppose you could consider that great reflexes and reaction time, couldn't you?" she said, a little unnerved by her own forthrightness. It must be the adrenaline making her giddy, she thought, checking her rear-view mirror before moving off again.

The roads were crazy this morning – the traffic was crawling at a snail's pace and it was as though the entire population of Dublin knew Leah was sitting her test and were out to make things hard for her. Take this person, she thought, spying a woman in one of those huge SUVs coming towards her, probably on her way back from the morning school run, a determined look on her face that suggested she wasn't going to stop for anyone. As she came closer it became even clearer that this particular woman *wasn't* going to stop or give way to anyone, Leah included.

She mentally recited the rules of the road. The other driver's side of the road was obstructed by parked cars and Leah's was clear. Which meant Leah had the right of way, didn't it? It meant that she was perfectly entitled to keep going, and the other driver had to stay out of *her* way, didn't it? Right, so she would keep going and Missus would just have to wait until she passed and the road was clear.

So Leah did keep going and . . . oh blast her, Missus kept going too. They were getting closer and closer, each eyeing the other, neither willing to give an inch, until, finally, in sheer desperation, Leah edged up on the kerb and onto the path. Of course, Missus drove past with a face on her that would sink the *Titanic* and not a wave, a nod of thanks, nothing! Leah steered to her right and the Fiesta's two wheels toppled none-too-gently back onto the road again.

Leah's heart pounded. Blast it, blast it, blast it . . . would your man see that as initiative or would it be an instant fail? She wasn't sure. No, no, no, nobody was supposed to drive on the path, surely? There was nothing in the rulebook, mind you, but . . . Leah groaned inwardly, just wishing she could open the door and tell the bloody tester to feck off for himself. This was *not* going well. First, she'd been a bit vague on the questions for the oral exam, then she couldn't remember the Fiesta's registration, not to mention the close call with the zebra crossing and now this! Was there anything else could go wrong at this stage? Anything at all? Well, she might as well keep going and hope for the best.

But, no sooner had Leah made her brave decision to proceed, than one of the 'L' plates she had so painfully positioned on her windscreen earlier, came unstuck from the glass, and fell neatly into her lap. Well, she'd definitely failed it now, hadn't she?

The look of pure horror – or was it terror? – on the tester's face answered Leah's unspoken question all too well.

Chapter 4

That same morning, Olivia was cleaning her bathroom and wondering how Leah was getting on with her driving test, when the phone rang.

"I'm really sorry to disturb you like this," she heard Alma, her manager, say with genuine regret, "and really, if I could have avoided phoning you, I would have, but if we don't operate soon, I think the poor little mite could die."

Olivia's insides tightened. "Oh, no – what's happened, Alma? Which one is it?"

"He's just been brought in. By the looks of things, he was run over, then some kind-hearted soul," she said with heavy irony, "tossed him into the ditch to die. I don't know how long he's held on but he was found by someone this morning out walking their dog." Her voice softened. "I don't even know if we can save him but –"

"Right. I'll be there in ten minutes," Olivia said decisively. By the sounds of it, Alma's patient mightn't have long left. On call or not, the very least she could do was try.

She put the phone down, grabbed a coat from the cupboard under the stairs and hastened back into the living-room.

"Let's get your coat on, pet. We've got to go the Centre," she announced. A veterinary surgeon by profession, Olivia worked part-time at the local animal shelter.

She hated having to drag her four-year-old all the way down there but there was simply no time to organise a baby-sitter. Ellie normally loved 'helping out' but this evening neither Alma nor Olivia would have much time to humour a little girl.

"It's not Angel, is it, Mummy?" Ellie asked, her eyes wide as Olivia helped her into her coat. An elderly abandoned dachshund, Angel had been at the Centre for sixteen months, and the little dog and Ellie had formed a special bond within seconds of setting eyes upon one another.

Olivia knew that Ellie would have mixed feelings should poor Angel ever be rehomed. As would Olivia herself. Every dog, cat, pony and ferret had a special place in the hearts of all the employees and volunteers of Paws & Tails Refuge Centre.

"No, this little fella has just been brought in," she explained, closing the front door behind them and hurrying Ellie towards the car. "Alma thinks he was hit by a car."

This poor little dog wouldn't be the first, or indeed the last, hit-and-run victim upon which Olivia had operated. She'd been working at the Centre for years, having gone there not long after graduation and originally intending to spend some time there before something better came along. But having witnessed the incredible dedication of the staff and volunteers, as well as the unfortunate condition of the abandoned and neglected animals, she had been unable to leave, despite Peter's insistence that she would never make any money. That wasn't the reason she'd become a vet in the first place, Olivia had argued. Yes, she could make a fortune in private practice but why not use her skills on those poor animals that really needed it? Wasn't that what vets were for at the end of the day? Peter, who at the time was struggling on his junior radiologist wages, couldn't believe that she could be so unaffected by money – or, in this case, the lack of it. But knowing Olivia, it could never have been any other way. As Peter had said many times himself over the years, if she hadn't continued working at the Centre, she would have been "taking in and fostering every Tom, Dick and Fido that looked any way miserable".

Once Ellie had come along though, Olivia had had to reduce her hours and now worked only a three-day week and occasional emergencies when Rick, the full-time vet, was unavailable. This was one of those times.

"You'll save him, Mummy. I know you will," Ellie said, her tone revealing utmost confidence in her mother's veterinary skills. "You always save them – every one of them."

Pulling out onto the main road, Olivia bit her lip, and marvelled at the blind and innocent trust of four-year-olds. Because Olivia knew well that, for all her talents, she hadn't been able to save every one of them – and for all her medicinal know-how, she certainly hadn't been able to use it when it mattered the most.

There had been an emergency that day too, Olivia thought sadly, her mind recalling that heartbreaking evening all those years ago. In fact, if there hadn't been an emergency, she would have been home on time and things might have been totally different. If only that poor Labrador hadn't swallowed that chicken bone and needed an emergency operation to remove it. If only she'd been home when she thought she'd be. If only, if only, if only . . .

That day she'd been feeling utterly shattered. Her feet had been killing her and, even though it was only early afternoon, she was really looking forward to getting home. Especially on that day.

It had all gone wrong from the second she arrived that morning. Unusually for Olivia, she'd arrived at the Centre ten minutes late – but, although she wasn't sure of it at the time, she'd been late for a very good reason.

A short visit to her doctor at lunch-time confirmed her early-morning suspicions and from then on in, Olivia might as well have been on a different planet.

Alma, the manager at the Centre, noticed it immediately.

"Well, spit it out," she challenged Olivia soon after helping her administer worming tablets to a particularly skittish Alsatian.

"Spit what out?" Olivia laughed, trying desperately to keep her news to herself but annoyed with herself for being so bloody transparent. An open book, Peter always called her, and he was right. She could rarely keep a secret or her feelings from anyone. Her open face and particularly her wide, expressive blue eyes, always gave her away.

"Whatever it is that's got you beaming like a Cheshire cat all afternoon," Alma teased. "Although being married to a hunk like yours would probably be enough," she added with a wink. "But you've been married a good while now, so what's different?"

"Nothing," Olivia said, unable to stop grinning and unwilling to look Alma in the eye. "I'm just in a good mood today, that's all."

Just then the telephone rang, and as their budget couldn't stretch to a full-time volunteer, and Olivia was closest to the door, she went out to answer it.

"Paws & Tails Refuge Centre."

"Hi, love," Olivia heard Peter's familiar voice and she grinned even more broadly.

"Hi, yourself," she replied evenly, although she was dying to blurt it out there and then, dying to share it with the world. "What's up?"

"Nothing really, just checking that you're definitely on the eight to four shift today, right? You're not on a split or anything?"

"Nope – I'm out of here by four. Do you want me to pick up something for you?"

"No, no – just checking. I could even be back home before you yet, but I'm not sure – it depends on how things go here."

Olivia could tell by her husband's weary tone that he was up to his tonsils – again. She hoped he would get away from the hospital that bit earlier today, not just because she had something to tell him, but also because he was working way too hard. He hadn't been himself lately, and tended to be tired and a little moody, the stress of working all those long hours obviously taking its toll.

"Did you get yourself seen to by any of the doctors yet?" she asked him. "About those palpitations you had last week?" It was probably a result of the stress he was under, but still Olivia didn't want him taking any chances. And working as he did in a hospital, he was in the best place possible to get himself checked out. It was probably fine, but still –

"It's nothing, Olivia," Peter replied, a little testily, and Olivia thought she'd better not push it, and just let him get back to work. The sooner he did that, the sooner he'd be home!

"Right, well, take it easy, love, and I'll see you at home this evening."

"OK, great. Talk to you later then."

Most definitely, Olivia thought, smiling softly to herself as she put the phone down. Hopefully, Peter *would* be home before her, because this particular evening they had plenty to talk about.

She glanced up at the clock. Time for a quick afternoon tea-break. Olivia didn't normally bother with tea-breaks, viewing them as a surefire way to unhinge her attempts at keeping her figure. Still, her tummy was rumbling, she'd had very little for lunch and, in fairness, she wouldn't have to worry about her figure for too much longer. And starving herself surely wasn't good for the baby.

Olivia's heart leaped. The baby! She was actually having a baby. She and Peter, her college boyfriend, the long-time love of her life, after all these years they had finally, finally conceived. It was weird, she thought, it still wasn't quite real to her, not until she told Peter anyway. Even though the doctor had congratulated her on the news and given her the due date, to Olivia it wouldn't be true, it wouldn't be real until she told Peter. After three years of marriage, and two years of trying, it had finally happened. It had *actually* happened! She and Peter were about to become parents! He would be ecstatic. Olivia mentally hugged herself as she tried to imagine what their baby would look like. The doctor had told her to come back in a few weeks for the first ultrasound and she couldn't wait to see Peter's face when they heard the heartbeat for the very first time – oh, this was just amazing news!

The next hour passed without event and Olivia managed to get through a much overdue pile of paperwork. She sat back in her chair and yawned. "Great, nearly time to go home," she sighed, relieved.

No sooner were the words out of her mouth, than

Susan, one of the Centre's many volunteers, came into the office. "Olivia, bit of an emergency – someone's just brought in this poor Labrador – he's going into convulsions . . ."

Without a second thought Olivia leapt into action and twenty minutes later her hands were buried deep in the dog's abdomen, trying to remove the dangerously sharp pieces of bone that had most likely come from a cooked chicken. Judging by his condition, the dog was probably a stray who, starving, had come across the chicken carcass in someone's refuse and, unable to believe his luck, had gone through it with relish and amazing speed. But now, the poor thing could lose his life because of it. Shards of bone had punctured his stomach and upper colon and Olivia knew that he was lucky to have been discovered when he did.

At last, the extractions were done and Olivia completed the final phases of surgery.

Then she looked up at the clock. Her eyes widened as she caught sight of the time. It was after five.

"Blast it, Alma, I didn't realise the time! I told Peter I'd be leaving here at four!"

"Go! Go on, off with you!" said Alma. "I'll finish up here. And sorry – I didn't notice the time either –"

"My fault, Alma," said Olivia wryly as she rushed to remove her scrubs.

She hastily cleaned herself up. Then she rang Peter's mobile but only got his answer service. Perhaps he was still driving home . . . She tried the house but got the answering machine. In her haste to get to work that morning, she'd left her own mobile at home on the kitchen table, so if Peter thought she'd already left and was trying to contact her on that, he wouldn't be able to. Finally, she left the Centre and hurried to her car.

Almost forty minutes later, she drove into their housing estate in Shankill, her heart plunging towards her stomach as she saw the ambulance parked there.

A small group of people were standing around on the path, their faces grave as they saw her car approach. Among them was her mother, turning a stricken face towards her. There was her next-door neighbour Cora and her new neighbour Deirdre with her little boy – Alex, Olivia remembered his name was, and then wondered why all this stupid trivia was running through her mind. It was a delaying tactic, she thought, simply a delaying tactic. Because one look at her mother's face and Olivia knew that something terrible had happened.

Her body racked with fear, her movements almost zombie-like, she got out of the car and went to her mother. "What's going on, Mum?" she asked, her voice shaking. "Where's Peter? Is he here?"

Eva's eyes brimmed with tears and she shook her head. "I'm so sorry, love," she whispered hoarsely. "He didn't make it."

"What – what do you mean?" Olivia barely got the words out. Her mind whirled. "Did you – who – ?"

"No, love, I only just arrived now – Cora from next door phoned me. She couldn't get you at work or on the mobile. It was that new neighbour of yours, Deirdre, who –"

"Oh God, no!" Olivia's heart stopped then as, behind her mother, she spotted the paramedics lifting something no – *someone* – into the ambulance on a stretcher.

A covered stretcher.

With a cry she made to run towards the ambulance, but somehow Eva stopped her. "There's no point, love," she said, holding her daughter in her arms. "It was a massive attack. He's gone."

"No," Olivia's words were barely a whisper, and it was as though all the breath had somehow departed from her lungs, all the blood had left her body. She felt as though she was no longer part of herself, as if she were somehow floating outside it.

"There was nothing we could do, pet," her mother continued sorrowfully. "By the time the ambulance got here, it was too late – we were *all* too late." She tightened her embrace. "I'm so sorry, love. But he's gone."

"But how . . . what . . . what happened?" Olivia's legs had turned to jelly and she began to sway.

"They're not fully sure yet, pet. Look, you need to sit down. Let's go – let's go next door to Cora's, OK?"

Shocked and bewildered, Olivia let her mother lead her away. A million and one emotions coursed through her, but strangely, at that moment she could only make

49

sense of one. "Oh God, Mum, I could have done something . . . I should have been there!" she blurted hoarsely, overwhelmed with remorse.

"There's no point in saying that, love. There was nothing anyone could have done."

But that wasn't true, and Olivia knew it. They might have been helpless but *she* would have known what to do.

But Olivia had been too busy doing something else, too busy being the big saviour for her animals . . . and now it had cost her everything.

Chapter 5

To make her feel even worse, Olivia thought, as she drove home from the Centre having successfully operated on the little hit-and-run victim – today would have been their wedding anniversary. She shook her head. It was inevitable that she would think about it, she thought about it every time, but still, for Ellie's sake, she had to try not to let it upset her too much.

She let herself and Ellie in the door of the modest semi-detached house she had moved into not long after her daughter was born. It had been a difficult time, trying to raise a new baby so soon after losing her husband, but Olivia thanked Heaven every day that the strain and pressure of it all hadn't affected her pregnancy. Ellie was all she had now, and although her mum, Peter's parents, Leah and her other friends were great, Olivia still felt lonely sometimes. Without Peter it was as though she was no longer a complete person.

The two of them had been together so long, had thought they'd be together forever, and then, one moment of forgetfulness – of *stupidity* – had taken him away from her. Everyone told her it wasn't her fault that she'd been late, but Olivia blamed herself for what had happened. Yes, maybe she couldn't have saved him . . . but now she would never know, would she? And for a very long time, the guilt had nearly been harder than the grief.

Still, that had been nearly five years ago now, and with the exception of significant anniversaries or birthdays, Olivia was getting on with it. She had good friends, family, a nice house in a nice quiet area and, of course, she had Ellie, who was her pride and joy. Her mum looked after Ellie when Olivia was at the Centre and, luckily, Alma never minded her having to drag Ellie along whenever there was an emergency. All in all, she supposed she'd coped quite well.

She made herself and her daughter a small snack.

"Mum, can I do some painting after lunch?" Ellie asked.

"Yes, but only if you stay in the kitchen this time," she said, ruffling her daughter's fair curls. Her hair was way too long and probably way too thin, but Olivia couldn't bring herself to cut it and part with those beautiful little ringlets – not just yet.

Later, Olivia had just finished cleaning the bath when she heard her mobile phone beep from somewhere. She stood up, red-faced from exertion, and went to hunt for the phone.

When she did find it, she didn't recognise the

number, but that was nothing new. She hated mobile phones and only kept one so she could be contacted by the Centre or by her mother when she had Ellie, if necessary. Otherwise she couldn't be bothered.

It was a text message. *"Nailed it!"* proclaimed the sender.

Olivia smiled. It had to be Leah. Her friend had taken her driving test this morning and, by some miracle, must have passed it. She must have had to change her phone number again too, she thought. Leah was forever losing her phone or leaving it behind in places, and had changed her phone four times this year alone, which was why it was a question of 'pick a number – any number' when you wanted to get Leah on the mobile. Luckily, her mobile phone didn't feature on any of her business literature; otherwise she would never have any customers!

"I don't believe it!" Olivia wrote back, meaning it. Leah was the scariest driver she had ever come across.

"Please – you should never doubt my amazing abilities!" Leah shot back, and Olivia grinned. Her friend was obviously thrilled with herself.

"So are you out celebrating tonight then?" she enquired, thinking that Josh would probably take her out somewhere. Painfully slow at inputting text messages, this was a long sentence by Olivia's standards, and it took her ages to complete it.

"Definitely! Do you fancy meeting up later?"

Oh, Josh must be working late or something then. Olivia thought about it. At that moment, a few drinks and a chat with Leah sounded wonderful. She hadn't realised just how much she'd missed her friend until Leah had returned from Belgium.

It was wonderful to have her back permanently again, and although Olivia had made lots of friends over the years, there were none like those who knew you best. With Leah, she never had to avoid the subject of Peter, never had to answer awkward questions about her single status. Not that it was anyone else's business, but Olivia only felt comfortable talking about Peter to those who knew him. And considering the day it was she could do with some cheering up. Yes, she'd love to see Leah tonight, she thought smiling.

Despite the fact that she hated leaving her, she knew she could ask her mother to look after Ellie for an hour or two. Her mother loved having her and Ellie adored being spoiled by her grandmother. Eva wouldn't mind; she was always on at Olivia to get out and about more. Having been on her own for quite some time now, Olivia knew her mother would like her to move on and maybe try to meet someone else. She met Leah and hunky Josh for a drink the odd Saturday night, but it had been ages, months actually, since she and her friend had been out on their own. And Leah passing her test was a great excuse for a celebration.

"Will see how land lies and get back to you," she texted again very slowly and then, using her fixed line phone, dialled her mother's number.

"Mum, would you mind looking after Ellie for a few hours this evening? Leah passed her driving test and wants me to meet her for a drink to celebrate."

"She passed it?" Eva, who knew Leah well, sounded surprised. "Did she bribe the tester – or did she try the short-skirt trick?"

"I'd imagine it was something like that, or else the poor guy was so terrified he didn't know what he was doing," Olivia said with a smile.

"Probably! But, of course, I'll take Ellie. I'll be here all evening so drop her over whenever you want."

"Thanks, Mum."

"And be sure and enjoy yourselves and don't worry about coming back early or anything," Eva soothed. "It's a Friday night, after all."

"Don't worry, Mum. We're a bit old for the Temple Bar thing – well, I am anyway," she added wryly, trying to remember the last time she was on a rip-roaring night out on the town. Not that she missed it.

"Just take your time and enjoy it – that's all I'm saying," Eva said. "Ellie will be fine with myself and your dad."

"Well, I'd better start getting her ready then, not to mention myself. See you later, OK?"

"And tell Leah I said congratulations, won't you? Although make sure she gets a taxi home. I don't want that friend of yours trying to prove to everyone what a good driver she is after ten Barcardi and cokes!" Her mother's infectious laughter trilled down the line and Olivia smiled. Eva knew Leah only too well – and it would be just like her to try something like that. She'd better phone her friend and make sure she wasn't driving. She read Leah's mobile number from the text

MELISSA HILL

message and tried phoning but the line was engaged. Leah was no doubt swinging from the grapevine at this stage, telling the good news to all and sundry. She might as well just send her a text then. *"Celebrations good to go. Meet you later. Say where and when . . ."*

It was a few minutes before Leah replied. *"Great! See you in Pearson's on Baggot St around six? Champers on me!"*

Olivia's eyes widened. Champers? Leah really was going all out tonight. Pearson's was a strange choice though – she'd have thought her friend would choose somewhere local rather than head for town. Still, Olivia couldn't give a damn where they went – she was just looking forward to getting together with her friend for what would undoubtedly be a great night out.

Leah's mobile rang just as she was putting the key in the front door of her apartment.

"Hi, Eva," she answered warmly, seeing the number displayed on the screen. "How are you?"

"I'm fine," Olivia's mother said cheerily. "Olivia told me about the test and I'm thrilled for you. I just wanted to say enjoy yourself tonight, but also to make sure Olivia doesn't worry about Ellie –"

"Thrilled?" Leah interrupted, startled. "Eva, I failed miserably! There's nothing to be thrilled about!"

"What? But why on earth did you tell Olivia you passed it then?"

Leah frowned, confused. "I haven't spoken to Olivia

56

since last night when she rang to wish me good luck with the bloody thing, but good luck must have gone on holiday." She rolled her eyes. "What on earth would make her think I passed it?"

"But she said the two of you were going out for a celebratory drink. She said you'd sent her a text telling her you'd passed the test, and would she go with you for a drink this evening. She wanted to know if I could look after Ellie for a while. She wouldn't have made it up, surely?"

"She said I sent her a text?"

"Well, I'm not completely certain, but I think she mentioned a text."

"Eva, I've been on a different planet most of today, but I'm one hundred per cent positive that I did not send Olivia a text asking her to come out for a drink tonight." Although it sounded good, now that Leah thought of it. She could do with drowning her sorrows.

"Where did she say she was meeting me?"

"She didn't mention that. But, Leah, I'm a little concerned now. I know Olivia is a grown woman and she can do what she pleases, but why would she lie about meeting you?"

"Maybe she has a secret lover on the go?" Leah said dramatically, although she dismissed the thought as soon as she said it. Olivia wouldn't have a secret lover; her friend wouldn't have a lover full-stop. Peter had been the love of Olivia's life and the only man she had ever wanted in her life. Still, it was all a bit strange.

Then Leah's eyes widened as she thought of something. "Maybe she just *presumed* it was me!" she said, her mind racing as the possibility hit her. "Olivia never updates her phone, and I've changed my number since – maybe she got some kind of message and thought it was from me?"

"What?" Eva pondered this. Then her voice changed. "But, Leah, if that is the case then Olivia –"

Leah finished the sentence for her, her eyes wide. "Olivia has got the wrong end of the stick and has made arrangements to meet someone else – someone who definitely isn't me!"

When five thirty came and went and there was still no sign of Leah, Olivia wasn't unduly concerned. Her friend was a dreadful timekeeper and it was likely that she'd popped back to check her messages at the office, or, Olivia thought smiling, maybe she was wearing a crucifying pair of high heels, which were undoubtedly gorgeous to look at, but by nature of their height prevented the wearer from walking at any great speed. Olivia couldn't understand her friend's obsession with her height. Petite and just over five foot tall, Leah never went out in anything less than a four-inch heel, while Olivia never went out in heels full-stop. Looking good in high heels was the last thing you needed when you had to run around after a skittish four-year-old.

Just then Olivia's mobile beeped. It was Leah.

"Where are you?" the message read.

"Where? I've been here for the last half-hour," Olivia replied. *"U r late"*

"No, I'm here – waiting for you."

Olivia looked around. Admittedly the pub was busy, but it would've been impossible for the two of them to miss one another. She was sitting near the entrance and facing the door. Unless there was a side entrance she didn't know about, she thought, craning her neck around – and Leah had come in that way. Still she could see no sign of her.

"Can't c u – where?" Olivia replied eventually.

"Bar."

Olivia looked over and, while there were plenty of people standing by the bar, none of them looked anything remotely like her friend, unless Leah had grown several inches and cut her hair since she'd seen her last. Confused, she sent another message. By now, her fingers hurt.

"U r here? In Pearson's?"

"Yes – can't see u either, busy here. Meet u outside?"

"OK."

Although Olivia was loath to give up her table, the only one that had been available, she dutifully went outside to wait for Leah. She stood casually against the wall of the pub, trying to assume a disinterested posture amongst the group of ostracised smokers gathered around the doorway. The door of the pub opened again, but it wasn't Leah, rather a tall and dark-suited man – a businessman, Olivia deduced. The man glanced briefly at her, looked left and right and then he too leant against the wall. Where the hell was Leah? Olivia thought, now feeling a little concerned. She stole a quick glance at the man, who looked as though he might be waiting on someone too and was at that moment deftly keying his mobile phone. Then, her own phone beeped again.

"Am waiting outside now – where r u?"

Blast it! Olivia thought. She *definitely* had the wrong place, because wherever Leah was waiting, it definitely wasn't here. She'd better just ring her, she thought, hitting the dial key. Thinking of it now, Olivia didn't know why she hadn't thought about doing that a long time before. Besides her snail-like speed, this was the main reason she hated texts – there was so much blasted ambiguity!

Someone wanting to speak to the other man must have had the same idea, because almost as soon as she dialled Leah's number, his phone rang.

"Hello?" Olivia heard him say and her blood ran cold when she realised that she could hear his voice not only alongside her, but in the earpiece of her phone.

"I can't understand it," Olivia said, reddening, when the realisation of what was happening had dawned on both of them. "I was supposed to meet my friend – we were going to celebrate – she passed her driving test you see and –" She was aware that she was babbling but she couldn't help it. How embarrassing! But the man in the suit was smiling – in fact, not just smiling but laughing, a big hearty laugh that would normally make Olivia smile too, only she was so mortified. And he was taking it all so well and without embarrassment that Olivia warmed to him immediately.

"I thought I was meeting my business partner," he said. "I had just clinched a deal and we were supposed to be celebrating but, in my excitement over it all, I think I must have punched in the wrong number. My old phone was stolen and all my pre-programmed numbers are . . ." He trailed off, laughing again.

"Oh!" Olivia exclaimed, understanding. "You sent a message to me by mistake and I automatically assumed it was my friend and . . ." She reddened again. "I'm sorry, I should have made sure but –"

"No, *I'm* sorry," said the man, his greyish blue eyes twinkling. "I would normally ring, but Frank had some kind of family do on today and I knew his wife wouldn't appreciate the interruption, so I sent him a text. I should have known there was something up when he – or should I say *you* – suggested going for a drink."

"Oh dear!" Olivia now saw the funny side, and how easily they had both been confused.

"I'm Matt Sheridan," he said, extending a hand.

"Olivia Gallagher," she replied, taking in his open friendly face, and deciding that in a way he reminded her of Kate's husband Michael, but was much better-looking.

"Nice to meet you, Olivia, although I think this will probably go down as one of the strangest making of acquaintance I've ever experienced!" He chuckled. "And here we both were, thinking we were out for a night of celebration." He looked at her, and just then and for reasons she couldn't quite fathom, Olivia almost hoped he would suggest they go inside for a drink anyway.

But Matt obviously wasn't thinking the same thing. "Oh, well. I suppose it's a good thing after all," he said, his mind elsewhere. "For once I'll have a clear head when I take my son to Saturday morning football practice."

Olivia smiled. "Ellie, my daughter, plays football too – well, the four-year-old version, anyway. She loves it."

"Adam's four too, so I doubt he's much better!" Matt replied. "But I think it's good to get them into sport at a young age, isn't it?"

Olivia nodded, and unconsciously repositioned her bag on her shoulder as if to move away.

"Can I give you a lift anywhere?" he asked. "Well, I should say, do you want to share a taxi? I left the car back at the office."

"No, it's fine – I'll nip home on the Dart," she said, realising it would only be a short walk from here to Lansdowne station. "Well, it was nice to meet you, Matt, and sorry again for . . . well, for the confusion."

"You too," he said, with a friendly grin, before heading off down the road, and leaving Olivia feeling something akin to disappointment as she walked away in the opposite direction. So much for her girlie night out with Leah, and trying to forget significant anniversary dates.

Chapter 6

A few days later, having just about got over her embarrassing 'blind date', and having received a right telling-off from her mother (despite the fact that she was thirty years old), Olivia received a phone call from Leah.

"Have you seen this?" her friend cried in disbelief. "Please tell me you got one too!"

Olivia laughed, knowing exactly what she was referring to. "Yes, it came in the post this morning."

"I cannot believe she is doing this! I mean, she made enough fuss about being pregnant but, Olivia, have you ever heard of anyone having an 'Expectant Mummy' party? Where does she get these ideas?"

Olivia giggled. She had thought the very same thing upon opening the post and finding that she had been invited to their old college friend Amanda Clarke's 'Expectant Mummy Party'. It seemed it wasn't necessary for the guests to be expecting or mummies, but, of course, it helped. Andrew and Amanda had defied the critics (namely Kate) and had stayed together throughout university and beyond. They married the previous year, and in true Amanda-style she had gone all out with her wedding preparations for her Big Day. Now, it seemed another, even bigger day was imminent.

"Well, you know Amanda, any excuse for a party."

"Any excuse to show off, you mean," Leah said wryly. "And it's not all that long ago since she went overboard at that wedding. Poor Andrew must be doing his nut with all this fuss. I must arrange to meet up with him and get him out of the house for a while."

"Ah, don't be nasty."

"You think I'm bad – what will Kate say once she hears about this?"

Leah and Kate were still great friends, and Kate was now also pregnant with her first child. Olivia could only imagine the nuggets of sarcasm she would come out with about Amanda's latest attention-seeking exercise. The two girls still disliked one another intensely.

"I spoke to her the other day and she's still in shock after the fuss and pomp of the Clarke wedding, so God only knows what she'll make of this," Leah said.

Kate, who had been married herself in a small ceremony two years earlier, had spent the entire day open-mouthed in astonishment at the lavishness of Amanda and Andrew's wedding. Leah had spent the day proclaiming that silver service and personalised dinner plates were all very well and good, but what was the point if you 'couldn't feel the love'?

Olivia smiled at the memory.

Leah and Andrew had always been very close, and Olivia knew they had kept in contact through phone and email all the time Leah had been away on her apprenticeship. The two of them had always had a rare friendship, in that there had never ever been an attraction between them – they were just very good friends. Amanda had always been a little jealous of Leah and Andrew's friendship, probably a little threatened by it, but she need never have worried.

Olivia didn't see much of the newly-weds these days, but she felt much the same way about Amanda as she had throughout college, and took her attention-seeking with a pinch of salt. The girl was still as spoilt, silly and immature as ever. She would never have been Olivia's choice for a friend, but because she was Andrew's girlfriend she had always made the effort. She'd particularly disliked the way Amanda had always been a bit nasty and dismissive of Robin but, as a group, they had little choice but to put up with her.

A faint sadness stirred inside Olivia as she thought of Robin. Her close friend had moved to the States not long after graduation, and it had been ages since they had heard anything from her – or at least it had been ages since *she* had heard anything from her, she thought wryly.

"I still can't believe Amanda invited *us* to this," Leah said chuckling. "I mean, I could understand the wedding because, well, she was always great for showing off but –"

"Yes, but you're still quite close to the two of them, aren't you?"

"To Andrew, maybe. But, Olivia, you remember what Amanda was like in college, all jealous and spoilt and she could never get Andrew away from us quick enough."

"Ah, that was just silly immature stuff, Leah – we were all immature back then." She paused slightly, remembering. "Didn't we make that silly promise that time? That silly reunion pact?" Olivia's stomach twisted when she thought about it now. Kate had been right about their tempting fate.

"I know." Leah was quiet, probably thinking the same as Olivia – that, despite the fact that the group had kept in touch for the most part, fate had intervened in their great plans for a reunion. "I suppose Kate was right – we were a bit naive really, weren't we?"

"At the time it was a good idea," Olivia said, shaking her head at the memory. "Anyway, we see so much of each other now that there's little point in meeting up to see how we all got on, is there?" she said, trying to keep her voice light. "We all know."

"Yeah . . ." Leah went uncharacteristically silent.

"So, are we going to this party, or what?" Olivia asked, purposefully changing the subject. "I'm very interested in seeing what happens at one of those affairs."

"Ugh, I don't know," Leah replied. "But actually, she's given me a bit of a brainwave now. Do you think

I should think seriously about a new range of chocolates for Expectant Mummies?"

"It's an idea!" Olivia laughed, feeling a familiar pride in Leah's achievements. Out of everyone in the group, talented Leah was always the one most likely to succeed. Her gift-chocolate business was doing very well, and having tasted some of her friend's more recent concoctions, Olivia could see why. Her friend had always been a terrific cook, but no one was more surprised than Leah when she had gone abroad to perfect her pastry-chef skills, and returned as a trained chocolatier. "Are things still as busy as ever with you?"

"Yes, but it's calmed down a little since Mother's Day, thankfully."

"You'll have to think about taking on someone else soon, Leah. You'll work yourself into the ground otherwise."

"I wish I could afford to – but I'll have to do a bit better before I can think about taking on some poor misfortunate that I can boss around!"

"Like you do Josh, you mean?"

"Exactly!" Leah laughed. "Listen, I must go, I want to catch Robin before she heads off for work. It should be around sevenish in New York at the moment, shouldn't it? I'm dying to find out what she makes of all this."

"Do you think Robin will be invited to this thing too?" Olivia asked, suspecting that even if she were invited, Robin would hardly come home for it. She wasn't so good at keeping in touch, although Leah seemed to know a lot about what was going on with her.

"Hardly, but it's an excuse to have a good old bitching session, isn't it?" she said wickedly. "No, I was planning to ring her anyway. I haven't spoken to her in a while, and I'm dying to find out how things are going with this boyfriend of hers."

"She's still with him then?" Olivia asked, once again feeling a little hurt that she knew so little about Robin's life now. "He's not American, is he?"

"No. All those handsome, loaded New Yorkers, and Robin had to go and find herself a Irishman from the 'Wesht'!" She laughed. "Listen, I'll go – I'll tell her you were asking for her, will I?"

"Do – and tell her to give me a ring sometime."

As she replaced the receiver, Olivia felt vaguely saddened that she and Robin, having been so close throughout university, were hardly in contact at all these days.

It was a pity really, Olivia thought, going into her living-room and slumping down on her sofa. Back then, the two of them had been friends from the very beginning, right from their rather unusual first meeting, all that time ago.

It was late one Friday afternoon and Olivia and Peter were grabbing a quick coffee and a few moments together at the cafeteria in the UCD Arts Building.

"What do you fancy doing tonight?" Peter asked, his

dark eyes even more striking than usual in the afternoon light.

"Don't know if I fancy going out at all," she said with a grimace. "I've still got loads to do on this paper and, even though I don't feel like it, I'll really have to make the effort. You go out, though. I'm sure the others will be up for it."

"Nah, I'll stay in with you and ferry food and coffee to you like a good househusband," he said, eyes twinkling.

She and Peter had recently moved into a small apartment in Clonskeagh and they were still very much in honeymoon mode. Initially, Olivia did have her reservations about moving in with him, especially as they were both so busy, but so far things couldn't have been better. Far from being a distraction to her studies, Peter often was a great help.

"Well, you might get bored with that very quickly!" she teased, draining her coffee mug. "Seriously though, if you want to meet the others . . ." Then, she trailed off, as something at the table just behind them caught her eye.

"No, I'm not in the mood tonight, I think I'll . . ."

Olivia barely heard his reply, and her heart began to thump in a heightened state of alert as she tried to take in what was happening. Sitting at the table behind them was a petite auburn-haired girl who seemed to be having some sort of difficulty breathing. Olivia's first thought was that she must be choking on something, judging by her dangerously red complexion and the fact that she was seriously struggling for breath. But, strangely, at the same time she was groping for something on the floor beneath the table, but in her panicked state was unable to get to it. The girl was on her own at the table, and all around them no one other than Olivia seemed to notice that something was wrong.

"Peter, look!" she said, getting up from her seat.

"What?" Peter looked around and immediately jumped up and went towards the girl.

"Are you OK? Can I help you?" Olivia asked her, feeling rather stupid, as it was pretty obvious she was far from OK. But then she realised that, no, she wasn't choking – in fact the girl seemed to be having some kind of seizure.

Then before she knew it, Peter had cleared a space behind them and had swiftly placed the girl in the recovery position on the floor. Well done, Olivia thought, impressed. At least somebody knew what to do. Olivia wouldn't have had the first clue. At this stage, people had begun to gather and stare.

But soon it was clear to both of them that lying the girl on her side was making little if any difference, as by now she was desperate for breath. Olivia's heart pounded. Shit, what was wrong with her?

"Get her an ambulance or something!" Olivia called out to one of the counter staff, who was standing there shell-shocked along with everyone else in the room – the students and staff of the café unused to such drama on a normally quiet Friday afternoon.

"Shit!" Peter said, looking around wildly, as if trying

to discover the root of the problem. He grabbed the girl's wrist. "Her pulse is going ten to the dozen so she must be having some kind of attack. Olivia, quick, check her handbag, see if there's an inhaler or something in there."

Handbag? Spying the bag under the table, Olivia realised that this must have been what the girl was trying to reach earlier. But because the handle was caught under a leg of the chair, the poor thing's frantic attempts had been in vain. So, Olivia deduced, there had to be an inhaler or something in there – something that could help.

Moving as quickly as she could and trying to control her own rising panic, Olivia emptied the bag's contents onto the table. Hairbrush, wallet, make-up, a pen and notebook, some lip-balm, lots of old bus tickets . . . but nothing resembling an inhaler.

"Peter, there's nothing here!" Olivia wailed, full of dread. On the floor the girl was still struggling. Olivia knew this wasn't a normal fainting attack: the girl's face was full of colour, way too much colour and Olivia had fainted herself enough times to know that when you fainted, you lost blood to the head, not gained it.

"There has to be something!" Peter said, clearly panicked now. He stood up and started frantically checking through the contents of the girl's bag, going through her books, checking if maybe there might be something written down somewhere. Then he stopped suddenly, as if realising something. "Shit."

"What, what?" Olivia asked, and then frowned as

Peter's gaze rested on the remains of the girl's lunch – a barely-touched chicken bap. "Food poisoning?" she offered hurriedly.

"More like an allergic reaction." Peter was again urgently searching through the girl's things.

"Reaction? To what?" Olivia urged him, her heart now beating almost as quickly as the poor girl's, she suspected.

"Not sure yet, but this should help," he said, immediately seizing what Olivia had dismissed as an oversized ink pen, but which she could see now was actually a narrow tube holding a syringe of some sort.

Lying on her side on the floor, her eyes wide, the girl was now gesturing with an arm as best she could. She seemed to be pointing at her leg.

And then, before Olivia could take in what was happening, Peter had broken open the packaging and was back on the ground alongside the girl. He shook the syringe and squirted a little liquid out in a way that Olivia had seen million of times on TV but had never thought she would witness in a real-life situation like this. Then, he sat the girl up and carefully placed the syringe in her hand, helping her guide it towards the correct spot – somewhere on her calf. Then, and Olivia didn't know how he did it, but somehow – under the girl's panicked direction – Peter began to crudely administer the injection. After what seemed like an age, the girl stopped shaking but within a few minutes more her colour had returned to normal.

Panic over.

"What was it?" Olivia asked Peter later, once the ambulance arrived from nearby St Vincent's, and the girl had been safely loaded into it. Still shaken from the drama of it all, the two of them had forgone the remaining afternoon's lectures and had stayed drinking very strong coffee in the cafeteria. "What was in the syringe?"

"Adrenaline, according to the paramedics," Peter stated flatly. "Apparently allergy sufferers carry supplies around with them, in case this kind of thing happens."

"What *did* happen?" Olivia asked him. She had barely heard what the paramedics had to say, although she did overhear something about some kind of shock.

"She was allergic to something in that sandwich," Peter said. "She took one bite, had a serious reaction and began to go into shock – anaphylactic shock, the paramedic said."

"Anaphylactic shock, from an ordinary chicken bap?" Olivia couldn't believe that something so innocuous could have such an effect. She had heard the term 'anaphylactic shock' before and knew that this was something that could happen to people who were allergic to penicillin or some anaesthetic drugs. Strangely, she also recalled the term being used in that film *My Girl* after poor Macaulay Culkin's character was stung by bees.

"Jesus, Peter, she could gone unconscious or died or something, couldn't she?" she said, more to herself than to him.

He nodded. "They reckon that if she hadn't got the adrenaline in time, she would almost certainly have gone into a coma." Peter shrugged. "Yes, I suppose she could have died."

"Oh, wow," Olivia said, her eyes widening as the realisation hit her. She put down her coffee cup and lovingly squeezed his arm. "Well done, love – you actually saved that girl's life!"

Peter shrugged again. "I suppose I did," he said, with a proud smile.

A week later, the girl was waiting for Olivia outside one of her lectures.

"Hi!" Olivia said, recognising her immediately. "How are you feeling?"

"Fine, thanks to you and your um . . ." she looked around, as if expecting to see Peter appear behind her. She seemed quite shy, Olivia thought. Her blue eyes were darting here and there and she appeared almost afraid to look directly at Olivia.

"Oh, it was all due to Peter," Olivia said easily. "I hadn't a clue what to do. I'm really glad you're OK."

The girl smiled, as if unsure what to say.

Olivia looked at her watch. "Listen, I don't have another lecture till two – do you have time for a coffee?" When the girl looked startled, Olivia grimaced. "Oh, sorry – can you drink coffee?"

The girl's nervous expression finally broke into a smile, and she fell into step beside Olivia. "No, I can drink coffee – it's just a few things I have to be careful with."

"Really? Like what?" Olivia was fascinated. Imagine

having to live your life not knowing whether something you eat could kill you? How did she manage? "Oh, I'm Olivia, by the way," she said, realising that she didn't yet know the girl's name.

"Robin." She smiled softly. "And I suppose I just wanted to thank you and your friend for helping me the other day. If you hadn't found my adrenaline kit . . ." She trailed off as they reached the cafeteria.

"Scene of the crime, eh?" Olivia said, trying to lighten the atmosphere. It was obvious the poor girl was shy and very embarrassed about her attack. Again, her gaze kept shooting here and there as if people would recognise her as the silly girl who made a scene here over a week ago. Well, Olivia decided, if she had her way, Robin would have forgotten all about it by the time their little chat was over.

"So, what can I get you?" she asked as they stood at the counter. "Tea, coffee . . . and oh, good, they have those chocolate brownies back in again – want one?"

Robin looked uncomfortable. "Sorry, chocolate is a big no-no most of the time," she said, apologetically. "Anything with possible traces of peanuts in it is a big no-no."

The poor thing, Olivia thought, trying to imagine not being able to eat *chocolate* of all things. No wonder she was so shy – she was probably used to being made to feel like the odd one out. "Probably better off," she said with a grimace, putting the brownie back on the shelf and, in an attempt to relax Robin a little, added, "No wonder you're so slim!"

"Not by choice, unfortunately!" Robin gave a little laugh, and Olivia delighted in this small achievement.

They took a table near the window where they could look out at the comings and goings in the Arts Building.

"So, listen," Robin began quietly. "I really don't know how to thank you enough. Most people don't know what to do . . . some of them think I'm coming down off Ecstasy or something." She shook her head sadly. "It's mortifying sometimes."

Olivia shook her head. "Ah, some people just don't know how to react to these things," she said, sitting forward conspiratorially. "When I was in primary school, one of my classmates was epileptic. As you can imagine, at our age, we were afraid of our lives of her, but at the same time, we all wanted to be her. Imagine, getting all that attention because you were sick. We thought it was great!"

Robin looked at her, a faint smile playing about her lips. "I used to hate being the odd one out in school like that, and I was so frustrated about not being able to eat what I wanted."

Olivia nodded, eager to hear more.

"And then, of course, being a child and forgetting how much something could affect you, I used to be a bit brazen. I'd take a bite out of a bar of chocolate, just to see what happened, just to see if my mother was only kidding me." She smiled. "The funny thing was, the only time I got attention from the other kids was when I did something like that – it was the only time they'd notice me. So I tended to do it a lot." Robin shook her head. "Most of them were terrified of me, but to be honest there was more reason for me to be afraid of them!"

"Really? Why?"

"Well, you know the way kids swap lunches and share sweets and things at lunch-time?"

Olivia nodded, understanding immediately. Many's the time she had swapped her mother's boring ham sandwiches for Louise Rooney's altogether more exciting tuna and mayo ones. And Mrs Rooney always gave Louise orange squash, instead of milk like Olivia's mother gave her. If Robin had to stay away from foods that could kill her and yet she innocently swapped lunches with her classmates . . .

"I could never do that," Robin went on. "So, as you can imagine, I wasn't the most popular child in school."

"Kids don't understand, I suppose."

"At that age, I didn't really understand either, which was why I kept eating the wrong things." She gave a lopsided smile. "So, understandably, the kids were freaked out, the teachers nearly had heart attacks, and my mother was furious. In the end, I spent most of my primary school lunch-times in class on my own. It's different these days though, and they've banned nuts in most schools now."

How sad it all was, Olivia thought, yet how easy to imagine. As a child, knowing she was different and trying to prove herself to the other kids meant that Robin was a danger to herself. Yet being kept inside at playtime obviously didn't help her social skills or her friendships. No wonder she was so ill at ease with herself, and so embarrassed about the attack.

"Well, you must have been the most intelligent one in the school, then!" Olivia said jokingly, trying to lighten the mood.

Robin smiled and rolled her eyes. "Another reason for my classmates to tease me," she laughed.

"So tell me, what's it like now? How do you manage now – with the nut thing?"

"It's not too bad," Robin replied. "I still can't touch nuts, or anything that might contain nuts. As for last week, the doctor reckons I reacted to the oil that they used to coat the bap – it may have been some derivative of peanut oil."

"Something you couldn't possible know," Olivia said, beginning to realise just how dangerous the allergy could be.

Robin nodded. "There's lots of hidden stuff," she said. "I have to avoid some packaged foods like the plague, as they're often processed in the same factory or on the same line as products containing nuts. Same with most standard chocolate bars."

"Gosh, how do you do it? I can't imagine what it would be like not being able to eat chocolate."

"It's not a big deal really. You don't really miss what you've never had. You can get special nut-free chocolate, but I'm not that bothered. It's still taking a chance because you just never know. Human error and all that."

Olivia couldn't get her head around it.

"So what about when you eat out? *Can* you eat out?"

"Sometimes, but I have to be careful. You just can't be a hundred per cent certain that the staff know the ingredients of each and every dish. Chinese or Oriental food is totally out because they use a lot of nuts. I've never actually eaten Chinese food – how's that for an admission?"

Olivia smiled. She adored Chinese food.

"But I've heard some horror stories though," Robin went on. "I remember hearing about a fellow-sufferer who was assured in a restaurant that satay sauce didn't contain nuts – imagine! Luckily, the person didn't take any chances, but still you'd have to be sure you came out with your adrenaline kit that night."

"So how does that adrenaline thingy work then?" Olivia enquired.

"It's called an epinephrine pen and most allergy sufferers carry one around with them all the time. Say, if you eat something, and have a serious reaction like I did the other day, a shot of adrenaline takes you out of it, and stops you losing consciousness. It's easy enough to use normally, but I was so far gone the other day that I really needed help. It's a total lifeline."

"A lifeline," Olivia said, the reality of what Peter had done only now truly sinking in. "So, you really could have died?"

"I was heading for unconsciousness, definitely. After that, who knows?" She shook her head. "It's been a while actually. I thought I'd finally learned to control it. But I think it's the kind of thing you can never fully control – you just have to live with it."

"I must say, I think you're amazing," Olivia said. "I really can't even imagine what it must be like. It's like every day could be . . . well, you just never know. Sorry," she said, shaking her head, "I don't mean to sound morbid."

"I know what you're saying," Robin said, laughing now, "but it's been a part of my life forever, so I don't know what it's like to be 'normal'. You do learn to live with it. I think it's harder on parents – I know my own mother had a really terrible time with me. She only had the one child, probably because of my allergy and the difficulties in dealing with it. I don't think she had a day's peace once I started school." Then she grimaced slightly. "Sorry, I've just remembered I hardly know you, and I'm already boring the face off you about this thing. You must be ready to explode."

"Not at all," Olivia said smiling. "I think it's fascinating, and I know Peter will be dying to hear every detail. Tell you what – why don't you pop over to our place tonight for dinner?" Then she paused. "Now, I don't want to put you under pressure or anything and don't worry, I'm a very plain cook, so I could make anything you like . . ."

Robin laughed. "I'd love to, but I don't want to put you out. Cook what you like and I'll bring a sandwich or something."

Olivia didn't push it. "Great, I know Peter would love to meet you."

"Peter's your boyfriend?"

"Yes," Olivia smiled when she thought about him.

"It's a sad story really – we met here on registration day – and we've barely been apart since."

"Oh – I thought you meant sad as in sorrowful."

"No, as the rest of our friends keep telling us, it's just 'sad'." She laughed. "But he's great – from day one we just connected and – two years later we're still together."

"But that's lovely – good for you! Although, I'm not surprised. Not only are you really attractive but you're nice and friendly with it."

"Ah, shucks, thanks," Olivia teased, secretly pleased by the compliment.

"I mean it. You and your boyfriend were great to me that day. I don't think I could ever find a man like that – not one that would put up with me anyway."

"Ah, don't be silly – you're like my friend Leah. She reckons most of the men around these days are complete nutters, but I just keep telling her . . . what?" she broke off, as Robin burst out laughing. "Oh, right, 'nutters', yes, I see what you mean."

The two girls laughed together easily, and both realised that this was the beginning of what could be a great new friendship.

Chapter 7

"I have a surprise for you," Ben said, his eyes mischievous as he led Robin along Lexington Ave.

"What kind of surprise?" she asked, intrigued. She loved it when Ben did things like this, although at the same time she was a little concerned as to what he had up his sleeve this time. He'd rung her at work earlier and, full of obvious excitement, had asked her to meet him outside his office building when she'd finished for the day.

Although, knowing Ben, he most likely wanted to go and do something tacky and touristy, she thought with a smile. The two had met shortly after he moved to New York, and in the very early days he was like a child in a sweetshop, eager to experience all that this magnificent city had to offer. Robin was a million miles away from being jaded – in New York she didn't think it could happen – but at that stage, having lived in the city for years, she had already done most of the touristy things.

Back then, Robin hadn't intended meeting anyone. Still feeling the effects of a particularly disastrous fling with a totally unsuitable man – one she'd tried her utmost to forget – the very last thing on her mind was meeting a man, least of all an Irishman, and certainly not at a New York society wedding.

Robin's close friend and workmate, Anna, was marrying her high-school boyfriend, a lovely, gentle – and loaded – man called Burton Greene. Robin had been thrilled when the two announced their engagement, but was even more thrilled when she discovered that they planned to hold their wedding in the Plaza Hotel. If there was one place in New York that held special memories for Robin, it was the Plaza.

Many years before, on her very first visit to the city, she and her American cousin Fiona had one night sneaked into the foyer while the doorman was helping one of the hotel guests out of a limousine. Robin still clearly remembered her absolute awe at stepping inside the luxurious hotel for the very first time. *Home Alone – Lost in New York* was one of her favourite Christmas movies and, as this particular visit occurred over the holidays, it seemed as though she was reliving parts of the story herself. Earlier that day, she and Fiona had chased squirrels in Central Park, gasped in appreciation at the toys in FAO Schwartz, admired the skating rink at the Rockefeller Centre, and then, to complete the most memorable Christmas Eve she had ever experienced, stood open-mouthed in wonder at the most amazing and truly beautiful Christmas tree in the Plaza foyer. The hotel's famous and overly elaborate crystal chandelier almost paled in comparison to the magical, fairytale-like tree standing majestically above them. It was probably right there, staring at the tree's decorations twinkling brightly in the light, that her love affair with New York truly began – which was why the Plaza was one of her favourite places in the city.

And on Anna and Burton's wedding day, the hotel – or more likely, the wedding co-ordinator – didn't disappoint. Robin had decided to wear an understated but sexy Robert Cavalli minidress for the occasion and, in such sumptuous surroundings, she felt almost justified in blowing most of the previous month's wages on the delicate wisp of jade-coloured silk. Her lack of funds for groceries as a result of her splurge had done no harm in helping her fit into it either, she thought wryly. The style here today was utterly spectacular, and Robin hoped desperately that, as one of Anna's pauper friends, she would be able to hold her own in the fashion stakes alongside Burton's megabucks relations. Making an impression was of the utmost importance in Manhattan, but never more so than at a society wedding. In truth, Robin found it all terribly shallow.

Speaking of impressions, she thought as she sat down, that very cute guy with the warm chocolate-brown eyes sitting across from me at the table is definitely making one on me. He had caught her eye on a number of occasions and twice she had to look away from the weight of what she hoped was his interested gaze. Despite herself, and unused to such obvious flirtation – especially in this town – she had to smile. He was sitting alongside Robin's date Gary, another work colleague, and was chatting away easily to him.

Just then, Gary looked across at Robin. "Hey, you two might know each other. Ireland's a small country, isn't it?"

"Sure, we're probably related," the other man said, in a highly exaggerated 'Oirish' accent, before Gary could make the introductions. "You look terrible like my cousin, Eileen Dooley, so you do." With this he gave her an almost imperceptible wink.

Robin's eyes widened in mock-surprise. "Not Eileen Dooley from Letterkenny?" she replied giddily, immediately getting into the swing of things, the few glasses of wine she'd already consumed helping considerably. "I'm her second cousin – twice removed!"

"Go 'way out of that!" he replied laying it on thick. "Jaysus, 'tis a terrible small world all the same, so it is!"

"Wow!" Gary sat back, impressed. "So you two are actually cousins then? It *is* a small world. I've never travelled further than New Jersey but you Irish – you guys get everywhere, don't you?"

Robin and her 'cousin' exchanged a mischievous smile.

"Well, look, why don't I let you two catch up," Gary said, sensing that he would have little to contribute to a conversation between two long-lost Irish relations.

Unfortunately, his own crowd had originated in France, so he couldn't even *pretend* he knew who or what they were talking about, more's the pity.

"Aye, thanks."

Gary turned to speak to the person sitting next to him, and Robin raised an eyebrow. "Isn't 'aye' supposed to be a Scottish expression?" she said, taking the opportunity to have a good look at him. He was remarkable in that he had exceptionally clear skin, not a mark, not a trace of acne, nothing. It was as though he had come straight from a beauty salon before the wedding, and knowing some of the men in this town, Robin thought wryly, perhaps he had.

"Scottish, Irish – I think it all sounds the same to these 'guys'," he shrugged and Robin couldn't help but notice what a remarkable smile he had, leading her in turn to wonder whether or not those Tom Cruise teeth were natural. There was also a very good chance that his deep brown eyes might simply be the result of a good pair of contact lenses. The only snag was, she'd noticed earlier that he kept tugging at his collar, a sure sign he wasn't comfortable with wearing a suit. It was highly unlikely then, she deduced, that he would go to all that trouble with his appearance, and something instinctively told her that he wasn't the type.

"What?" he asked then, his expression amused.

"Sorry?" Robin sat back, startled.

"You were making some kind of judgment, weren't you?"

"Judgment about what?" she said, unnerved that

someone she'd just met could read her so easily. She was generally a cagey person, and, as she'd been told many times before, often difficult to get to know.

"About me."

"What? What makes you think that?" she replied defensively.

He smiled. "You were, weren't you?"

"I was not."

"Were too," he said, feigning a sulking, childish tone, and Robin couldn't help but laugh. He was lovely.

"You big kid!" she said, warming to him more and more, irrespective of his alarmingly good looks.

"Tell me what you were thinking," he asked, sitting forward and resting his chin on his hand.

"I was . . ." Robin thought quickly, "I was just wondering how you know Burton and Anna."

"Don't know them at all," he said, glancing towards the head table. "Apparently one or other of their dads – possibly Burton's, I think – is a major shareholder in my boss's company. Jeff, my boss, couldn't make it today so we went along in his place."

"Oh." At the mention of 'we' it suddenly hit her that he must have a date.

"What about you?" he asked in return.

"Anna's a work friend." She followed his gaze towards the top table where Anna was beaming from ear to ear.

"She seems a bit cracked to me," Ben said. "Spending good money on those fancy ice sculptures that'll end up as plain H2O in a few hours' time."

Robin looked at him. "I haven't heard that one in ages," she said with a smile.

"Heard what?"

"That expression 'cracked'. I have a friend back home – Leah – she used to say it all the time."

"Leah – pretty name."

"Yes, it is," Robin replied, and at the mention of her friend's name, she felt an uncharacteristic bout of homesickness. She wondered what Leah was doing now, what everyone was doing now. Probably in bed fast asleep, she thought wryly, remembering the time back home and trying to snap herself out of it. She really should ring her soon.

"Do you know – you seem to spend an awful lot of time daydreaming," she heard him say.

"What?"

"Well, I've spent the last ten minutes trying to chat you up and you keep looking dreamily into the distance."

"You're trying to chat me up?" Robin smiled at his directness.

"Well, why else do you think I begged your man to swap places with me?"

"What man?"

"The one sitting over at that table, joking and laughing with all my workmates. He seems to be having a right old time."

She looked at him. "You're telling me that, before dinner, you sought out the person sitting across from me and asked him to switch places with you?"

"Yep."

"But . . . but what made you think I was fair game?" she asked, feeling a little bit put out. "I mean, didn't you stop to think I might be here with a boyfriend, or a partner or –"

"Didn't matter," he said, with an indolent shake of his head.

"What do you mean – it didn't matter?" she repeated, stunned at the size of his ego. Yes, he was good-looking but . . . "You can't go around assuming that every woman you like the look of is willing and available to fall at your feet at a quick flash of that smile – that's just so – so arrogant!"

"You like my smile? Cool," he said, annoying her even further.

"Look, I really don't know who the hell you think you are," she continued, having had it up to there with men like him. Good-looking men were all the bloody same – so full of themselves and cocksure that they could pick any girl up at the drop of a hat. "But if you think you can just –"

"Oh, I'm sorry, let me introduce myself," he said pleasantly, cutting her off. "My name's Ben McKenna, I just moved here a couple of weeks ago and, assuming I play my cards right, I fully intend to be the man you'll be spending the rest of your life with."

Thinking back on it now as she followed Ben down Lexington Avenue, Robin couldn't help but smile. Even funnier, he had thought it was such a killer line, and the poor thing couldn't understand it when right afterwards she had simply burst out laughing.

"What? What did I say?" he asked, when Robin had recovered.

"You idiot!" she grinned, hardly able to speak for laughing. "What made-for-TV movie did you get that from?"

"What? That came right from the heart!" he said, looking hurt as Robin's shoulders continued to heave with laughter.

"Was it really that bad?"

"It was absolutely brutal."

But the fact that Ben had genuinely assumed it to be a romantic overture had been one of the most endearing things about him, and the main reason they began seeing one another after that wedding.

It was difficult not to be endeared to Ben. He had such a childlike, almost naïve, sense of wonder about everything in the city, that with him it was as though Robin was living her earlier days in Manhattan all over again. For the first few weeks of their relationship, he and Robin behaved liked tourists and did everything from carriage rides in Central Park, trips across the river on the Statten Island Ferry, theatres on Broadway, shopping on Fifth Avenue, and Ben's favourite – viewing the city from the top of the Empire State Building.

But sadly, for Robin, there was nothing that could ever beat the view from atop the Twin Towers. That day on the Empire State with Ben, looking out at the panoramic view of the island below, Robin's gaze drifted across towards Battery Park and she felt once again the gaping void the destruction of the Towers had left deep in the hearts of everyone living in this wonderful city.

She'd been on her way to work that terrible day and, like many others working in the financial district, had been deeply affected by the tragedy – and possibly more so by the fact that she was still alive. Immediately afterwards, she began to question whether or not she had done anything worthwhile with her life so far, and in this regard she found herself sorely lacking. She hadn't done anything meaningful, other than have the usual things like work, friends and a good life in New York. But there was nothing in particular that she could be proud of. Yes, she'd been doing well in her career, had learned to live successfully with a life-threatening allergy, and had lots of friends. But, her New York friends weren't the same as the ones she had left behind.

Feeling particularly lonely at one stage not long after the attacks, Robin half contemplated leaving Manhattan and heading back home to Dublin. Yet, she knew in her heart of hearts that she wasn't ready yet, if ever, to do that. No, Robin's life was in New York and now that she had Ben, New York was home.

Now Ben was practically dragging her along the path on the way to – from what Robin could make out – Grand Central Station.

"Seriously, Ben, where are we going?" she asked,

struggling to keep up with him, especially in this heat. "Why are you bringing me here?"

"I told you – it's a surprise."

Robin knew better than to ask any more questions, especially when he was in a mood like this. Her interest was very definitely piqued though, when they entered the huge cavernous train station and Ben headed immediately towards the ticket office.

"We're going on a train – at rush hour?" she said puzzled, trying to grab the ticket off him.

"Oh, no, you don't!" Ben put the tickets in his trousers pocket, hiding them away from view.

A few minutes later, the two headed down to one of the platforms, where a virtually fully boarded train awaited departure. Almost immediately, Robin understood.

"Ben, why are we going to Bronxville?" she said, seizing a free seat in one of the carriages.

He winked at her. "Just wait and see."

Fifteen or so minutes passed after the train moved away from the station, and as Robin silently watched Uptown Manhattan rush past them, she thought she could guess what Ben was up to. Bronxville was a very charming English-style village located some fifteen miles north of Midtown, and Robin knew Ben wasn't planning on going there today simply for a guided tour. She sighed, wondering how on earth she was going to get out of it this time.

"You've been house-hunting again, haven't you?" she challenged him.

Ben smiled boyishly. "OK, I admit I couldn't resist it. But this one is just perfect, Robin – it's just half an hour's train journey from Grand Central, it's in a really nice area and it's even got a back garden and a study – a small one, mind you, but –"

"Ben I told you, I don't want to move. I love the place we're in now. What is so important about having a house? We don't need one – we've already got a great apartment that anyone would kill for, so why –?"

"Just take a look at it first before you say anything, OK?"

She could sense his irritation but wondered why on earth he kept doing this when he knew how much it annoyed her. "OK." Robin didn't have the energy to argue. She would humour him – again – by going through the motions of taking a look at this house, with its lovely garden and its perfect study and all the rest. Then, she would do as she always did and tell him that the apartment they had was perfect, and why would they want to move all the way out here?

Granted the Lower East Side apartment was leased, and she and Ben earned enough to pay a mortgage on a house of their own but . . .

The object of Ben's affection was a spacious two-storey house which sat on a corner site with an attractive wooden porch all the way across the front. It had obviously been very well looked after by the previous owner, the two bedrooms were spacious and nicely decorated, and the tiny garden that Ben had been so enthusiastic about was admittedly a welcoming oasis of calm, something that was difficult to find in New York at the best of times.

Despite herself, Robin began to imagine Ben and her sitting out in the garden during the spring and summer, relaxing in the warm evening sun after another tough day in city. For once, she could understand why Ben seemed so anxious to move away from Manhattan, away from the noise, honking horns and hectic lifestyle. Yet the buzz, the constant stream of activity, the traffic, the smells – the fact that the place was so full of life was what Robin had always loved about living in the city.

Still, she thought, looking around the attractive, contemporary and – compared to their apartment – very spacious house, she could actually picture herself living here. The village itself was idyllic – a lovely spot nicely nestled alongside the Bronx river, full of towering lush trees and charming and stately Tudor, Victorian and Colonial houses. It had been a short train journey out, and an even shorter walk from the station. Despite herself, Robin had to admit that this might be one of Ben's better ideas.

"Well, what do you think?" he asked, although Robin could tell by his expression that he knew she was impressed.

"It's not bad," she said, giving nothing away.

"You like it – I knew it!"

"I said it's not bad."

"Not bad? Robin, it's perfect. You saw inside – there's nothing to be done to it. The studio would be perfect for the work I bring home –" he nudged her, "no more giving out about leaving my drawings all over the place and look," he indicated out the window, "how could you not want to live in a house with a garden like that?"

She nodded. "I know, but our apartment . . ."

"You and I both know that we can't stay there forever. We're getting older now, Robin, and although we're not quite geriatrics it would be nice to put down roots somewhere – especially since you've made it quite clear that you're not prepared to do that at home."

He was right. God knows she had gone on enough about how her life was here now, and that she couldn't see herself ever wanting to move back to Ireland. Still, buying a house was one thing but buying one with Ben was a different kettle of fish altogether.

She looked at him, her thoughts going a mile a minute. "Look, Ben, I do like the house. It's just I'm not sure . . ."

"What aren't you sure about, Robin? What are you afraid of?"

"I don't know . . ."

"Is it me – us? Are you not sure how you feel about us?"

"That's not it, Ben. You know I love you very much. It's just –"

"Just what? Just that you're still thinking about that idiot, is it?"

"*What?*"

"Are you worried that the same thing will happen again? Because I'm telling you, Robin, that won't happen. I wouldn't ever leave you – I wouldn't hurt you."

He looked at her, his dark eyes honest and open, and in her heart Robin knew he was right. She did love Ben and she knew that he wouldn't hurt her. The problem was that she had the power to hurt him, and hurt him very much. He might love her now but if he were to –

"Look, Robin, we've been together a while now, and I do think it's time we took things to the next level," Ben said, interrupting her thoughts. "We love one another, we're committed to one another, and we're already living together, so why not take the plunge and get a place of our own?"

"I suppose . . ." She knew it wasn't fair to keep him hanging on like this and, yes, she did love him as much as . . . well, as much she could love anyone. Maybe he was right. Maybe she should just make the commitment, get the mortgage and buy a place. God knows, Ben had certainly proved that he loved *her*, despite the frustrations and inconvenience that went with her allergy. She knew that there weren't – *hadn't* – been many men that could put up with that and all its associated inconvenience.

"OK," she said, feeling a burst of adrenaline – for once, not from a syringe – but as a result of a natural high. Positive and negative emotions rushed through her all at once, but she tried to concentrate on the positive. "Let's do it! Let's get a place of our own – let's buy this house!"

Ben's eyes widened. "Are you sure?" he asked,

coming forward to give her a hug, a huge grin on his face. "Are you absolutely positive?"

"I'm absolutely positive," she repeated, before she could change her mind again.

Ben was already tapping numbers into his cellphone. "I'd better tell the realtor we'll take it, otherwise a place like this will be snapped up in no time."

But later, on the way back on the train listening to Ben's excited chatter, Robin couldn't help having second thoughts about what they had just done. She'd just made a decision to commit herself to this man for a long time – a very long time. And although she loved him dearly, Robin wondered how on earth she was going to tell Ben that buying a house together was the closest thing to full commitment she could ever give him.

Anything beyond that was impossible.

Chapter 8

Olivia was late, unbelievably late. She was on duty at the Animal Centre in little under an hour, and it seemed as though the world was conspiring against letting her out of the house. Ellie wasn't any help either. She had picked today of all days to be contrary, and was at that very moment standing in the middle of the hallway in a pair of pyjama bottoms.

"Ellie – what are you doing?" Olivia asked.

"Don't want to go to Grannie's house," her daughter said sulkily. "Don't want to go with you – want to stay here on mine own."

"Honey, you know you can't stay here on your own without Mommy. Anyway, don't you want to see Granny? She'll be very disappointed – she might cry."

Ellie giggled. "Grannies don't cry," she said, and Olivia thought that if Ellie's humour lifted that easily she might just get away in time. At the best of times, her

98

daughter was as stubborn as a mule and if she didn't want to go, then she bloody well didn't want to go. Sometimes she was so like Peter it hurt.

"She would cry," Olivia continued, "and she'd cry even more if she saw you wearing your pyjamas instead of those nice jeans she bought you, remember? The ones she got you for your birthday with the pink flowers on them?" She crossed her fingers behind her back, and then exhaled a sigh of relief when Ellie turned and started up the stairs – hopefully now willing to change.

Ten minutes later, they were finally ready to leave. But the gods definitely weren't with her today, Olivia thought, furiously searching for her car keys. Blast and damn it, she said silently to herself as she opened cupboards and drawers, lifted newspapers and magazines, until finally she spied the elusive keys sticking out from under a pile of newly dried washing.

"OK, let's go!" she said, buttoning Ellie's jacket and heading outside.

Then, Olivia's face fell. A Land-Rover, probably belonging to someone visiting next door, had partly blocked her entrance. In fairness, there was room for her to reverse out, but she would have to be painstakingly careful. Great, more time lost!

She settled Ellie in her car seat and proceeded to inch her way past the other car's tailgate. It was a bit nerve-wracking though, because she was reversing blind out onto the road and couldn't see if there was anything else coming. She couldn't take any chances either with Ellie in the back.

Olivia's was the last in a row of semi-detached houses, and her gateway was at the corner of the green – a corner that cars entering the estate tended to take very quickly. She prayed that at this hour of the morning, things would be that bit quieter.

Beep! Beep!

Olivia jumped. So much for it being quiet, she thought, moving the car forward and craning her neck behind to try and see what was happening. Some drivers just wouldn't give an inch, would they? And because she couldn't see a thing over that monstrous Land-Rover, she was *never* going to get out of here!

She was just about to release the handbrake and try again when, in her driver's wing-mirror, she saw someone – a man – who appeared to be waving her on. Well, thank goodness for that, she thought – must be the Land-Rover owner. But why the hell didn't he move the bloody thing?

Soon, thanks to her saviour, and much to her relief, she was safely out on the road. She looked across at the man, and was about to wave her thanks and move off, when suddenly surprised recognition dawned – and not just for Olivia. The man, the 'text man' as Leah laughingly called him, looked equally surprised to see her.

"Oh! Hello again," Olivia said, winding down her window as he approached.

"Hello again, yourself," he said, his grey-blue eyes as warm and lively as she remembered. "You live around here too?"

Too? Olivia repeated silently. Surely he couldn't be one of her neighbours? She would have noticed if someone that cute had been living in the vicinity and, if she hadn't, then Trudy from down the road certainly would have. Sixty-year-old Trudy had some kind of radar for spotting attractive, male neighbours that might be suitable for 'misfortunate' and manless Olivia.

He must have just moved in.

"Yes, this is my house, and if it wasn't for that army tank there," she added wryly, "I'd be out of the driveway and gone in no time."

"I was on my way back from the corner shop and I saw you struggling, so I said I'd give a hand. I had no idea it was you though," he said with a grin.

"Thanks, I could have been there for ages."

"Hey, speaking of struggling – did your friend pass her driving test that time?"

Olivia shook her head ruefully. "No, poor Leah. She had a terrible time that day, so there would have been no celebrations anyway."

"That's a pity. But, you'll be pleased to know that I've been extra careful with my text messages since. No more making arrangements with complete strangers!"

"Me too." Olivia blushed slightly at the memory.

"That was mad, wasn't it?" he said, shaking his head. "Two eejits sitting in a pub waiting for one another and neither of us had a clue." He laughed. "And your face when I answered the phone – it was an absolute picture!"

"Would you blame me?" Olivia laughed too. "For a

second there I thought I had been set up by one of those hidden camera shows or something."

"Mommy! I want to see Granny!" Ellie wailed. Strapped into her car seat, which she hated, she was getting impatient.

Matt peered into the car, having spotted her for the first time. "Hello," he said, easily. "What's your name? Oh, don't tell me," he added before Ellie could answer. "I bet it's something like Britney, 'cos you're very pretty and have lovely blonde hair – just like Britney Spears."

Ellie giggled. "I'm not Britney," she said, delighted at being described as pretty. "I'm Ellie."

"Pleased to meet you, Ellie." Matt reached in to shake her hand and Olivia nearly fell off the seat when Ellie offered her own little hand in return. Not at all used to men other than those in her family, she often viewed them with suspicion. Olivia had had one or two dates since Peter, but none of them had gone any further than just that – a date. Probably because Ellie had caused such a ruckus and behaved like the child from hell when they called to collect Olivia beforehand, she thought wryly.

But Matt was obviously well used to, and very comfortable with children, and just then Olivia remembered him mentioning before that he had a young son. Which of course meant that . . .

"Matt, breakfast!" a woman called faintly from the door of one of the houses across the green and confirmed Olivia's slightly deflating conclusion that, of course, Matt was married. No wonder Trudy's radar hadn't detected him – there was no point. But if he lived across the green, he hadn't lived there that long, otherwise Olivia would definitely have noticed him before now.

Matt turned towards his wife and put a hand up in the air as if to signal he was on his way. Then, he turned to Olivia and grimaced. "I'd better go," he said. "Catherine can be dangerous with a frying pan!"

Olivia smiled at him. "Thanks again for helping us out."

"No problem." He stood back as she went to move away. "Nice seeing you again,"

"You too," Olivia said, moving away from the kerb.

"Bye, Brit– I mean, Ellie!" Matt gave her a little wink and, thrilled, Ellie waved happily at him.

Driving along the green, and casting a quick glance at Matt's departing figure in her rear-view mirror, Olivia couldn't help thinking that it was a very rare man who could put a beaming smile on the faces of both Gallagher women.

Across the green, Catherine stood at the doorway and watched Matt fawning all over that woman. Who the hell was she? she wondered, her stomach plummeting as she began to feel an all-too-familiar suspicious niggle. And why on earth was Matt being so friendly towards her?

She couldn't believe it when she'd looked out the window a few minutes earlier and had seen him leaning casually against some strange woman's car, chatting and joking as if he'd known her forever. How *did* he know her? He couldn't have got to know the residents here already, could he?

Or was it like in the apartment building, where Matt seemed to be on friendly terms with everyone on the same floor – especially that good-looking brunette who lived down the hall?

No, Catherine didn't like this at all. She'd thought that moving out of the apartment and into a nice quiet mature estate like Cherrytree Green would be ideal. Ideal for getting Matt to settle down, and concentrate less on work and more on Adam and family life – concentrate on the important things.

The last thing she needed, she thought – as Matt approached the house – was the love of her life concentrating on smiley women from across the green.

The following lunchtime, at Olivia's invitation, Leah called over with an armful of Sunday papers and a rumbling tummy. Josh was working Sundays at the DIY store he managed, and Olivia was glad of the opportunity to get Leah on her own. Although she often asked her best friend over for lunch, this time she had a particular motive – she desperately wanted to confide in someone about Matt.

So, over a leisurely lunch, she confessed all.

"So, what are you going to do about him?" Leah wanted to know.

"Leah!" Olivia blushed.

"What? You're the one going around with the glazed look in your eyes!"

She blushed. "I just can't stop thinking about him. He just has this lovely way about him and he's so friendly –"

"But he's married," Leah interjected. "He might be lovely, he might be friendly, and Ellie might have taken to him, but he's married."

"I know," Olivia sighed. "It's just typical, isn't it? The only man who has made my heart beat faster in years and he has to be taken!"

And it was true. Olivia couldn't remember the last time she had even looked at a man with anything other than a passing interest. The few men she'd been out with recently hadn't really appealed to her all that much – she'd gone out with them more for the sake of moving on than anything else. But Matt Sheridan was different. There was a definite attraction there and, despite the fact that he was probably very happily married, Olivia suspected that it wasn't just one side-sided. She remembered the way his eyes lit up when he recognised her in the car. And how he had said "See you again sometime" before she drove away. There was meaning there, definitely. Matt wasn't just being nice to her – he liked her too.

When she mentioned this to Leah, she wrinkled her nose. "If that's the case, he doesn't sound like such a nice guy to me. Chatting up and flirting with other women – would you like to be married to a man like that?"

"It wasn't like that, Leah," Olivia insisted, although she supposed she was right. Still, who knew what his wife was like? She might be an awful cow and poor Matt could very possibly be stuck in a loveless marriage. Why else would he be chatting up other women? "He just seemed really, really nice, that's all."

"This *really* isn't like you."

"What?"

"Going all gooey-eyed over some balding, aging and married Lothario!"

"I told you – Matt is *not* a Lothario and he's definitely not aging – about thirty-five, I'd say. And he's not bald!"

"Which means that he probably hasn't been married long enough to use the old 'my wife doesn't understand me' line."

"Leah, he hasn't used any line!" Olivia's heart sank. She'd been out of the game too long to even recognise any such line. Anyway, Matt hadn't exactly said anything remotely like that, had he? He had just been friendly because he recognised her – end of story.

"Oh, I suppose you're right – I am being stupid," she admitted. "I mean, the man is probably just being nice because he feels sorry for me and then I, desperate, lonely idiot that I am, immediately want to jump on him!"

"Is he *that* good-looking?" Leah asked, surprised that she was even having a conversation like this with Olivia.

Olivia imagined Matt's sparkling eyes and his open,

laughing face. "Yes," she said, dreamily, "he is." Then, aware of how stupidly childish she sounded, she burst out laughing.

"Oh, dear – you definitely have it bad then."

After lunch, they decided to have coffee in the living-room.

"So Andrew's in good form then?" Olivia asked, putting a plate of chocolate marshmallows on a tray and then remembering that Leah, who was surrounded by delicious handmade chocolate on a daily basis, would have no interest in high-sugar mass-market choco-mallows.

"Mmm, I love these," Leah leaned against the worktop while waiting for the kettle to boil, "but I'm stuffed after all that lunch."

Olivia wondered how on earth someone who never seemed to stop eating and was surrounded by such temptation every hour of the day, could manage to stay so slim. Not that Leah was stick-thin, but she had a nice figure, and could still get away with wearing a white T-shirt with slim jeans, unlike Olivia who these days looked as though she was wearing an inflatable swimming-aid around her middle.

"Yes, Andrew was in flying form," Leah answered. She had met up with him the previous night for a drink, and as was so often the case with Leah, 'one' had turned into much more than that. "We had a great old chat – and he was asking for you."

"Was he?" Olivia was pleased. She and Andrew had always got on well at college, although they were never particularly close. She remembered him phoning her once or twice after Peter, and although she was sure it was just a polite duty call, she appreciated the gesture. Some of her and Peter's so-called social circle had all but ignored her afterwards and Olivia would never forget it. Back then, Leah had been away, Robin had been away and she and Kate had kept in fleeting contact, but by then both had their own lives. It was only when Leah returned that the three of them had become friendly again. Leah was somehow the heart of the group, the one that kept them all connected even after all these years. She supposed it was different too, because she and Peter had been so close back in college that no one else had ever really got a look-in.

"So what does he make of this Expectant Mummy party?" Olivia asked with a slight grin. She and Leah hadn't quite made up their minds as to whether they were going to attend Amanda's little soirée, but as neither of them were expectant mummies – nor likely to be, Olivia thought wryly – it was unlikely.

"Taking it all in his stride, as usual," Leah answered. "Oh, she overdoes the helpless kitten act and all that but, you know Andrew, he doesn't take the blindest bit of notice of her."

"Is he still so easy-going then?" It was still hard to believe that Andrew had done so well. Unfortunately a knee injury had prematurely ended his hopes of becoming a professional rugby player. However, his computer studies had served him well and he was one of the few people who had actually made any money out of the dot-com boom at the time. He was a rare technological entrepreneur in that he had a real business idea and the wherewithal to follow it through, rather than having just a fancy website and catchy buzzword. Andrew had come up with a web-based business-to-business software solution. Like all the best ideas, his was simple and easy to operate and he had few problems in raising venture capital for it. He also showed great vision, as he had sold the company for a small fortune, just before the tech bubble burst. Since then, he had wisely invested his money in various tax-incentive properties across the city, earning him a comfortable living with little effort. Which is exactly how Andrew Clarke liked it. Now it seemed he was quite happy to just sit back and enjoy life. Which was nice work if you could get it, Olivia thought.

"So what else is new with him?" she asked now.

Leah grimaced guiltily. "I'm not too sure. We were so out of it I can't remember much to be honest. He kept buying rounds of tequila, which is why I was so twisted last night."

"Oh dear," Olivia smiled, trying to remember the last time she had been 'out of it', "were you that bad?"

"I must have been, because Josh barely spoke to me before he left for work today. Apparently, I nearly woke up the street coming home last night. Olivia, I can barely remember getting home. Andrew was just as bad."

"But Josh knows that Andrew's an old friend, doesn't he? He doesn't think –"

"Oh, no – Josh knows it was nothing like that – he was just annoyed that he had to clean up after me this morning!"

"Oh dear," Olivia said again, thinking she sounded like her mother. Leah's exploits were beginning to make her feel positively ancient and there was only a year between them. She really should start getting out and about more.

"I'd say Amanda wasn't too impressed with Andrew either – he was worse than I am." Then she put her head in her hands. "Oh my God, I've just remembered!"

"What?"

"Oh, I'm such a gobshite!"

"What? What did you do?" Olivia asked again, getting worried.

"I starting shooting my mouth off about work, about how it was impossible to get anywhere in business here in Ireland because it's impossible to qualify for a grant, and all sorts of rubbish like that." She paused. "And then Andrew . . ." She trailed off, shaking her head in embarrassment.

"Andrew what?"

"Andrew offered to help me out. Well, no, knowing me I probably *asked* him to help me out. And we had this long conversation about him putting money into the business, and I told him all about my dream of opening a shop and basically plans for world domination!"

"You didn't?" Olivia laughed.

"Oh God, I hope he didn't think I was serious. He's

probably sick to the teeth of friends going on at him looking for a leg-up."

"Don't be silly. Andrew's your friend – he knows it was only the drink talking. Anyway, if the two of you were as drunk as one another, then chances are he won't remember either."

"I hope not. I'd hate him to think I was being a leech."

"He won't think that. Don't be silly. Anyway, if I were you, I'd start worrying about what you're going to say to that poor boyfriend of yours. I don't think he signed up for cleaning up your sick when you two set up home together!"

Leah cringed. "I know. I'm lousy really. I told Josh we were going out for one or two. Then I arrive in at all hours of the morning twisted and telling him I'd left a present for him in the fireplace!"

Olivia couldn't help but giggle. "Oh, Leah, how does he put up with you?"

"I don't know, and at the same time I don't know what I'd do without him either." Her voice grew serious. "You know, I never could see myself settling down, Olivia, particularly not with someone like him."

"What do you mean?"

"Well, I don't know. I just thought I'd spend the rest of my life chasing after the same sort of unsuitable bastards that I did all throughout college. The unattainable ones, the dangerous ones, not the normal, down-to-earth good ones, like Josh."

Not to mention bloody good-looking, Olivia

thought, picturing her friend's extraordinarily attractive boyfriend. "Yes, but you guys are a partnership – you've both brought something to the relationship. He's lucky to have you too, Leah. Not every girl would be as understanding as you've been."

"I know, I know." Leah's face clouded slightly and she turned her attention to making the coffee.

She put the two mugs on the tray with the chocolate marshmallows and followed Olivia into the living-room, where Ellie sat playing with her toys in the corner.

"Which house did you say Matt lived in?" she asked, setting down the tray.

Olivia went over to the window. "Well, I'm not really sure now. It's either the one with the green door . . ." she pointed to one of the redbrick semi-detached houses across the green, "or that one with the hanging basket."

Although Olivia had lived in Cherrytree Green for years, she had kept herself to herself and knew only a handful of her neighbours. The area was a quiet, mature little mews, and a lot of the residents were older and settled with grown-up families. They liked their privacy, and generally didn't interfere with one another – which was exactly why Olivia liked living there.

Leah gaze followed in the direction Olivia was pointing, and as she did, the green door opened and Matt stepped outside.

"That's him!" Olivia exclaimed, jumping out of sight and feeling immediately foolish for doing so.

"Hmm," Leah continued peering out the window.

"Not much of a Lothario, I suppose – no gold medallions and, as far as I can tell from here, he does seem to have all his own hair."

"Leah!"

"What? I'm just telling you what I think. Now, he's getting into – oh, nice car – he's obviously worth a few quid."

Olivia stole a look as Matt steered his Volvo out onto the road and around the other side of the green, to exit on the farther side from her house.

"He's not bad, although it was hard to tell from here," Leah continued a running commentary. "I wonder why the wife wasn't with him? Judging by the get-up, he looked like he was going off somewhere nice – for Sunday dinner perhaps?"

Olivia didn't answer. She was too busy thinking how handsome Matt looked in his dark suit. Oh, stop behaving like a love-struck teenager! she scolded herself.

"Oh – there's someone else coming out now," Leah said, beckoning to Olivia to come and have a look. "Must be the wife."

"We shouldn't be doing this, Leah – we're like a pair of children spying on people!" Olivia was trying to stay sensible although she had to admit she was interested in getting a look at Matt's wife – very interested.

"Don't be stupid – this is better than *Coronation Street* – here, take a look. She's got the kid with her too."

"What's she like?" Olivia looked over, expecting to see a stunning blonde with a perfect body and an equally perfect face, and she saw, her heart plummeting, that the woman coming out of Matt's house fitted the bill exactly.

The son looked about the same age as Ellie, and was rather cute, dressed all in denim and running way ahead of this mother to chase after something in the air – a butterfly, Olivia decided.

They had definitely just moved into the area, as Olivia was certain she had never seen either of them before.

"I wonder why they've not gone with him?" Leah moved away from the window. She sat down on Olivia's sofa and began spooning sugar into her coffee. "He must be one of those workaholic business types – off into the office on a Sunday or something."

"I doubt it." Matt didn't come across as a workaholic type. He came across as someone energetic and fun, someone who enjoyed life. But then again, what did Olivia know? She had met him – what, twice? And it was hardly a proper meeting either time. How could she possibly make any assumptions as to what type he was?

Feeling strangely saddened, she joined Leah on the sofa and picked up one of the newspapers, hoping to take her mind off the image of gorgeous Matt's equally gorgeous wife innocently out for a walk with her son on a Sunday afternoon – completely unaware that some slattern across the road had taken a fancy to her husband.

All of a sudden, Olivia felt ashamed of herself. Matt

Sheridan was *not* interested in her and certainly had not been flirting with her. He was simply a decent, happily married family man, who was reasonably chatty to strangers and silly women who had problems reversing out of driveways, so there was no point in wasting her time thinking about him any longer – no point at all.

But trying to forget about Matt wasn't proving easy. The following Thursday evening it was lashing rain and, having discovered she'd run out of milk, Olivia made a quick trip to the corner shop, and went in leaving Ellie waiting in the car. It would take forever to get Ellie organised to go out in this weather, and she'd only be a minute or two at the most. She was chatting pleasantly to Molly, the shop's proprietor, when Matt walked in.

"We must stop meeting like this," he said, shaking his wet head out of its hood, and flashing Olivia a broad smile, which, of course, had the instant effect of turning her insides to mush.

Bloody hell, she thought, berating herself for getting carried away simply by the sight of a decent-looking man. If she heard any of her friends were carrying on like this with a married man she would murder them. Although having thoughts about carrying on wasn't exactly the same as *actually* carrying on, but still.

"Hello," she said easily, praying that the heat in her cheeks wasn't blatantly obvious – but whether it was or not, she knew well that the shopkeeper's keen interested eyes were taking in everything.

Molly was a lovely woman, but there was something about women in corner shops that ensured they had access to an information network better than most government agencies. She was a chatterbox who seemed to know everything, and like most women Olivia knew at that age – with the exception of her own mother – Molly was constantly offering her introductions to Mrs Murphy's son or Paddy Kavanagh's nephew, or whoever she thought might be suitable for the "misfortunate young single mother". So, Olivia tried her very best not to let her true feelings be known, especially where Matt was concerned. And, for all Olivia knew, Molly might already know Mrs Sheridan, who she was certain wouldn't be at all pleased to hear that the neighbours were making eyes at her husband in the corner shop, good-looking and all that he was.

But, judging from Molly's apparent interest, and blatant appreciation of Matt's good looks, she was as yet unaware of the newcomers to Cherrytree Green.

"So, how are you?" he asked, paying for his newspaper. "Did you get to where you wanted to the other day?"

"Yes," she answered and wondered why it was that the mere presence of Matt Sheridan made her monosyllabic. "Yes, I mean – thank you for helping us out – it was very good of you."

"No problem. How's Ellie?" he asked, and Olivia marvelled at how friendly and easy he was when her own insides seemed to be melting. "A dotey little thing," he said, nodding towards Molly in order to

116

include her in the conversation. Once again Olivia couldn't help thinking how lucky his wife was to have ended up with such a charming, friendly – oh, sod it – *yummy* husband.

"Lovely, just like her mother," Molly said, with a slight smile and a definite meaning in her tone. At this Olivia tried to flash her a look.

Matt laughed. "You're right about that," he said, studying Olivia closely and in that moment she knew that she wasn't mistaken. It *hadn't* been wishful thinking, Matt *did* seem attracted to her, and as much as she knew how wrong it was, Olivia couldn't help feeling warmed by the thought of it. God, it had been ages since she'd felt like this. Sod's Law it had to be a married man.

She laughed in what she hoped was a carefree manner. "Ellie would be thrilled to hear that!" she said to Molly.

"What age is she now?" Molly asked easily. "Four, isn't it?" She raised her eyes to heaven theatrically. "Which means it's four years, God love us, since –"

Beep! Beep! The loud sound of a car-horn from outside cut her off.

"Oh, I'd better go," Olivia said hurriedly. "Ellie's in the car on her own and she could be up to all sorts." She snatched up the milk from the counter and, smiling a quick goodbye at them both, hurried out of the store.

"Oh, look, she forgot her change," Matt commented and Molly went to the door and called after her, but it was too late. Olivia's car was already halfway down the road. "Poor thing," Molly shook her head sadly and went back behind the counter. "Having to bring up that child on her own."

"On her own?" Matt murmured offhandedly, before picking up his own change and putting it in his pocket.

"Yes, and an absolute shame it is too," Molly continued, obviously bursting to tell him all about it – whatever 'it' was. "The husband died suddenly while she was pregnant with Ellie," she informed him, leaning forward conspiratorially. "Just took a turn and dropped dead one day after coming home from a hard day's work, apparently." She sighed dramatically. "Isn't it terrible the way the young people are under so much pressure these days with work and big mortgages and everything? It's the stress that does it, if you ask me. And him a radiologist, if you please, practically a doctor himself – but that didn't save him. So she moved here not long afterwards – to make a fresh start, I suppose." She sighed dramatically. "It's not easy thing bringing up a child on your own, but I'll tell you one thing, father or no father, you won't find a better-behaved young one than Ellie Gallagher and that's no easy claim these days. A lovely little thing, so she is."

"She is indeed," Matt replied.

"But it's an awful shame," Molly went on, apparently determined to fill Matt in on Olivia's misfortune. "Such a young couple, and married only a short while when tragedy struck. God love her, it was a terrible thing to happen to anyone but especially to someone so young."

Matt nodded. "I'd better be going," he said, putting

his newspaper under his arm and heading for the door. "Thanks again," he smiled at a visibly disappointed Molly.

But, despite his own curiosity, Matt was unwilling to partake in idle chit-chat about a woman he hardly knew, yet a woman who had occupied his every thought since he'd first laid eyes upon her.

Chapter 9

At the weekend, Robin and Ben met Sarah and Brian for dinner in a trendy restaurant on the Upper East Side – Brian spending a rare few consecutive days at home. Robin adored Ben's sister, and although lately she and Ben had been making more of an effort to visit her and little Kirsty in New Jersey, in Robin's opinion they didn't socialise enough together. The reason being, she suspected, the brash and opinionated Brian, who she hadn't liked from day one.

Now she studied the menu the waiter had given them with habitual caution.

"So, how's Kirsty?" Ben asked genially, and instantly his sister tensed.

"Don't mention the war," Brian said, rolling his eyes as he set down his menu. "It was hard enough convincing Sarah to come out tonight as it was. For some reason she seems to think that the child will spontaneously combust if she's not around."

"Brian, don't start, please," his wife whispered, embarrassed. "I'm just a bit worried after that last stay in hospital," she added by way of explanation. "The baby-sitter is new and we haven't been using her all that long. She doesn't really know how to handle Kirsty if anything –"

"Seems no one knows how to handle Kirsty, other than her mother, of course," Brian interjected dryly.

"Brian, it's not like that. We just can't possibly expect her to know what to do . . ."

Just then, the waiter arrived to take their order, and the rest of her sentence trailed off.

Robin felt sorry for Sarah. It was obvious that Brian felt she was being unrealistically overprotective of Kirsty's asthma, yet Sarah couldn't be blamed for worrying.

"I know what you mean. It's a big responsibility, isn't it?" she said with a warm smile. "It's hard to rely on someone else to know what to do if she gets an attack."

Sarah nodded gratefully. "It is – and to be honest, I'm not just worried about Kirsty. As she gets older she's learning that she needs to take her inhaler, but it's not fair to the baby-sitter. She knows Kirsty's asthmatic but still . . ."

"Sarah, you can't wrap the child in bloody cotton wool!" Brian said. "Honestly, the more you fuss over her the worse she gets!" He looked at Ben and Robin, exasperated. "You should see the way Sarah won't let her out of her sight. It's not good to molly-coddle a kid like that."

121

Robin and Ben exchanged awkward glances. The way Brian spoke about her, you'd swear that Kirsty was just some troublesome 'kid' and not his four-year-old chronically asthmatic daughter. But Brian was away most of the time, and just didn't understand the worry and stress poor Sarah had to endure.

"Look, I'm sure the baby-sitter will manage just fine," Ben soothed. "Does she have your cellphone number?"

Sarah nodded, red-faced and embarrassed at her husband's lack of etiquette and, Robin suspected, hurt by his lack of understanding. Her own father had been the same.

"Well, then, I'm sure she'll ring if anything happens, won't she?"

"I suppose," Sarah bit her lip. "I feel guilty leaving her though – it's so humid and the pollen count is high and –"

"Oh, for goodness' sake, Sarah – will you give it a rest! The kid will be fine, which is more than I can say for myself! This is my first weekend at home in ages – we're supposed to be out for a relaxing dinner, and already you're giving me heartburn! Forget about it!"

For a long moment, an awkward silence descended on the table. Then the waiter returned with their first course and Brian turned to Ben. "So," he asked, purposefully changing the subject, "how's business?"

"Good, very busy actually," Ben answered, equally anxious to change the subject, but more anxious, Robin thought, to take the spotlight off poor Sarah.

Robin didn't know how her kind, gentle sister-in-law put up with such an ignorant oaf for a husband. "She'll be fine," she mouthed, giving Sarah another encouraging smile, before taking another sip of her wine. The others had begun making inroads into their starters but, as she was unfamiliar with this particular restaurant, Robin had declined to order one herself. She glanced at Sarah's green salad and Ben and Brian's deep-fried shrimp, and while everything seemed innocuous enough, it was just too much of a chance to take. She had taken chances on the basis of doubtful assurances before, and while she lived to tell the tale, Robin knew too well that it just wasn't worth it. Anyway, she didn't want to ruin the meal for everyone else by throwing caution to the winds, and particularly not for Ben, who, if the worst came to the worst, would have to administer her adrenaline. Poor Ben, she knew the entire process terrified him, and he had nearly keeled over at his first few attempts. It was very important that friends and family of a nut-allergy sufferer be able to inject the adrenaline properly and Ben, while only too happy to do so, had found it terribly difficult in the early days. The shot was very user-friendly, but because it required a very quick jab in the fleshy part of the leg, rather than a slow, easy injection, Ben was very hesitant.

Eventually though, Ben learned that a sudden jab was the lesser of two evils, and after several attempts could now administer the injection easily, although he only had to put his skills into practice a couple of times.

While it was embarrassing, and Robin hated having to put people in the position, both Ben and her friend Anna at work were experts with the kit, and could be called upon if the need arose. Despite this, by being extra careful in her day-to-day living, Robin went out of her way to ensure the need didn't arise.

Tonight, although ravenous to the point of pain, Robin wasn't about to take a chance on deep-fried shrimp she knew nothing about – no matter how delicious they looked.

"Aren't you having anything, Robin?" Brian asked her. "Oh, I just remembered, you're another one of these fad dieters, aren't you?" He shook his head. "What is it with women these days? You should hear some of the crap the girls at the office come out with – if they're not on Atkins, they're in some 'Zone'," he made quotation marks with his fingers, "or else they've talked themselves into believing they've got some kind of wheat or dairy intolerance!" He laughed derisively. "But seriously, Robin, you don't need to lose weight – you look great!"

At this Ben lay down his menu and gave his brother-in-law a look that could cut him in two.

"Brian!" Sarah gasped.

Robin gave a tight smile. "It's fine, Sarah. And thanks, Brian," she said pleasantly, though inwardly annoyed that he had drawn attention to her problem, "but I can assure you, what I'm on is far from being a fad diet." She hoped Brian would drop the subject. Sarah was already a bit edgy.

"Oh, shit, yeah – I forgot about that whole nutty

thing," Brian said, biting down hard on his shrimp. "Nutty being the operative word! Are you sure it's not all in the mind, Robin? I mean, what did a few peanuts ever do to you?" He laughed as if he'd made a particularly witty comment.

"They almost killed her – twice," Ben answered flatly, and Robin kicked him under the table. Ben had no patience with cynics when it came to Robin's allergy, and he knew only too well how hard it was for her.

Still, there was no point in getting upset about it, Robin thought, and this was supposed to be a relaxing evening for all of them. Brian was just an idiot who couldn't help putting his foot in it.

"A load of baloney, as far as I can tell," Brian went on as though Ben hadn't spoken. "When we were kids there were no such things as nut allergies and pollen allergies and God knows what else these drugs corporations are imagining up these days. You do know that that's all it is, don't you, Robin? The big pharmaceutical guys are brainwashing America and our children, preying on people like you and Sarah. They get us all worked up about our health and our kids, and then we go and dutifully pay them lots of money for drugs that help ease our worries and our conscience." His point made, Brian went back to the rest of his shrimp.

Things had been tense all evening, but it seemed that this was the last straw for Sarah. "Brian!" she whispered harshly, her voice a mixture of embarrassment and outrage. "How dare you paint Robin as some kind of raving hypochondriac! What do *you* know about worry and conscience, when you spend the whole time off on your bloody road trips? When was the last time you had to rush Kirsty to hospital after an asthma attack? When was the last time you had to listen to her struggle for breath, and wonder if her little lungs were going to give out?" Tears shone in her pretty eyes. "And then you have the cheek to sit here and accuse *me* of being overprotective! Of course I'm being overprotective, you silly bastard, because I need to make up for both of us!" With that, she stood up and grabbed her handbag.

Robin put a hand on her arm. "Sarah, please don't worry – it's fine."

"No, it's not fine, and I really hope that both of you can forgive my husband's stupidity."

"I don't mind really."

"But I mind, Robin," Sarah replied, "and I'm sorry but I really have to go. I know that tonight has been ruined now, but I can't listen to his bullshit any longer. I'm going home now – home to where I should be, back to my child who needs me – because it's fairly obvious that her idiot father doesn't give a damn!"

"Sarah, please calm down. It really is fine . . ." Ben soothed.

"No, it's not bloody fine," Brian retorted. "What are you trying to prove here, Sarah?"

His wife reached for the light cotton shawl she had brought with her. "I'm not trying to prove anything – I'm going." As Sarah reached across to give her a hug, Robin noticed she was trembling.

"I'll phone you tomorrow," she told her, and Sarah nodded silently.

"Well, so much for a pleasant evening!" For once, Brian looked flustered – obviously, Robin thought, unused to Sarah standing up to him like that. Good for her – it might do him the world of good.

Although, catching sight of Ben's hard stare as his sister and brother-in-law exited the room, Robin knew that doing Brian good was the furthest thing from her boyfriend's mind just then.

"He's such a prat!" Ben said, when they returned to their apartment later that evening. "Lecturing you like that – who the hell does he think he is?"

They had left the restaurant soon after, the thought of dinner no longer quite so appealing. Robin had been relieved in a way. She had ordered something simple, and something that shouldn't be at all dangerous, but kitchen utensils could be switched and chefs could be careless, and you just never knew. Instead, they had picked up a pizza from a reliable place near the apartment – the proprietor of which often joked that, of course, he'd make sure it was safe for Robin – hadn't she been keeping him in business these last five years?

"It wasn't so much that – it was the way he lectured Sarah that annoyed me," Robin answered, taking a huge bite out of her pizza. "Honestly, you'd wonder why the likes of Brian ended up having children at all – he's never there for Kirsty and she adores him!"

Ben fiddled with a strand of her hair. "She adores you too, you know," he said, "and wouldn't you wonder why the likes of you and me don't have children, when it's obvious you'd be a terrific mother?"

Robin moved his hand away. "Don't, Ben."

"Don't what?"

"Don't start this whole kids thing again."

"Robin, it's just that I can't understand why you're so against having children when you're obviously a natural with them. Kirsty adores you, *all* kids adore you and despite what you say, I know you love them too."

Robin shook her head. She couldn't *believe* this had come up now. Wasn't it enough for him that she had agreed to settle down and buy a house together? Why did he have to bring up the kids thing again?

Ben took her hand. "Look, I know how you feel about it, and, of course, I'm not going to push it, but you know I've always thought your reasoning is crazy."

They had been over and over this many times before and still Ben couldn't understand it. He just didn't get it. It wasn't about not wanting to have them, it was about what they would have to go through if they did.

"Do you have any idea what it would be like trying to bring up a child suffering from my allergy?" Robin said. "God knows it's bad enough as it is – like tonight when I can't go to a restaurant, or we can't even eat at a friend's house without there being a big fuss over what I can and can't eat. Imagine what it would be like with a *child* like that!"

"Yes, but there are no guarantees that the allergy will be passed on –"

"But there is, Ben." She had tried to explain this many times before but he just wouldn't listen. "There is every guarantee that it will be passed on. The condition is hereditary, and because mine is so severe, I'd say there is a nine out of ten chance that it would be passed on."

"But what about that ten per cent then? Don't you think that having a child of our own would be worth taking that chance? It's not as though you don't like or want kids, Robin, I know you do, so why let this ruin your chances of becoming a mother? As you said yourself, it takes over so much of your life, so why let it extend to this?"

"Ben, it's very easy to say that now, but you can't possibly have any idea of what it would be like. You can see it with Sarah and Brian, how Kirsty's asthma has put that relationship, that marriage, under severe pressure."

"Yes, but that's because Brian is an insensitive prat who doesn't realise –"

"It's not that, Ben. Of course he realises! He realises but he doesn't really understand." She shook her head. "It was the very same with my parents. My mother had a terrible time with me and, as you know, was fiercely protective. My dad, although he knew that my allergy was very serious, still thought that Mum was overly cautious and hysterical."

"I know all this," Ben said, "and I know that sometimes your dad wasn't cautious enough."

Robin nodded. When she was six years old, her father had one day during the summer holidays taken her on a trip to Tramore Strand as a treat. After a pleasant day in glorious sunshine, with Tom helping her build sandcastles and teaching her to swim in the sea, Robin was ravenous. Her father, innocently but rather carelessly, Robin thought now, had bought them each a portion of chips from a roadside caravan, not even thinking to check what cooking oil they used. Robin had taken one bite of a chip, had an immediate reaction and within minutes started going into anaphylactic shock. Luckily, her dad had remembered to take some adrenaline with them, but had left it in the boot of the car. In the time that it took for him to go back and find it – leaving poor Robin lying in a semi-conscious state outside the chip-van, a crowd of horrified onlookers surrounding her – his daughter had almost died.

"Mum went crazy. Understandably she blamed him, and it eventually drove them apart." It was something that Robin had always felt guilty about, despite the fact that her mother assured her it wasn't her fault. Robin knew it was, yet there was little she could do about it. She wasn't about to take that chance with a child of her own. It was too much of a burden.

She turned to look at Ben. "No matter what you might think, that of course you'd protect the child and make sure that nothing ever happened, you'd always feel as though you're sitting on a time-bomb. Someone said that to me once and I thought it was the most appropriate description I'd ever heard. It changes your routine, your relationships – your whole life."

"Robin, I'm not being funny, but surely parents of so-called 'normal' children could say the same thing? Children will change your life, no matter what. There's always the chance that they could run out in front of a speeding car, or pull a boiling saucepan down on top of themselves or . . ." He trailed off, exasperated. "I think you're imagining the worst-case scenario here, and after what you've been through yourself as a child, I can completely understand that. Still, I don't think you should deny yourself or me the chance to become parents simply because you think it will be hard work. It's hard work anyway. And look, there's always that chance that a child of yours might not inherit the condition, isn't there?" Ben caught her hand, and looked her in the eye. "Isn't there?"

Robin sighed deeply before looking right back at him. "For me," she said, "that small percentage is way too much of a chance to take."

Chapter 10

A few days later, Leah was sitting in her workshop going through a supplier catalogue when the phone rang.

"Hey," Andrew's cheerful tones came on the other end, "how's the head?"

"Oh, you're a bad influence on me, Andrew Clarke!"she exclaimed, recalling their recent heavy night's drinking. "Josh is barely talking to me – still!"

"I'm surprised he's still with you, considering. Anyway, I was in the same boat – Amanda was livid that I stayed out so late."

"What time was it?"

"It must have been four or five by the time I got in. I can't believe they stayed serving that long."

"Well, why wouldn't they, when you put your gold card behind the bar and kept buying rounds for everyone?"

"Ah feck it, don't tell me I was in flash-git mode that night, was I? That was your fault for making me out to be some hotshot businessman."

"But you are," Leah teased him, knowing Andrew did tend to lay it on thick but only when he was drunk. Anyway, why not? He was a successful businessman so why shouldn't he show off a little?

"Give it up. Look, I can't talk long but I'm meeting with the accountant soon about what we talked about that night. Can you give me some sort of idea of how much you need?"

"What?" Leah's heart stopped. "Andrew, I was only joking – please don't think that I was begging or anything . . ." She trailed off, mortified.

"What are you on about, you eejit? Wasn't it my idea in the first place? Anyway, I made some enquiries about a premises this morning and –"

"What?" Leah squealed. "A premises – what for?"

"For the shop, of course. Leah, I know we had a few that night, but don't tell me you've forgotten the entire conversation!"

"But I thought it was just a joke. I didn't seriously expect you to –"

"Look, you have the basis of a very good business there, but in order to go further you need to expand. You said yourself that your stuff would fly out the door if you had a retail premises. Well, that's what we're going to do."

"Andrew, I just couldn't take –"

"You're not taking anything from me – I expect a

good return on my investment. I know a good business when I see it, Leah, and I trust you to make a go of it. Despite the fact that you lot think I'm just a jammy bastard who got lucky a few years ago, I do know what I'm talking about. Anyway, you're a good friend and I'd rather put my faith in you than some fresh-faced business graduate that doesn't have a clue about the real world. You've been working in this kind of business for a while, you know what it takes. And if you're willing to take me on as a business partner, a silent partner, mind – I don't want to stand on your toes – then I think we can make a real go of this."

Leah was speechless.

"Well, are you going to get me some figures or what?" Andrew went on.

"I'm just . . . I'm just amazed at all of this. What'll Amanda think?"

"Leah, I've invested in a couple of ventures over the years – you're not the first one."

"Oh, I know that – I didn't mean . . ." It was weird – all of a sudden Leah felt as though she was taking to her boss, not her mad old college friend Andrew, Andrew who could drink her under the table and who used to let her cry on his shoulder whenever her latest bastard dumped her.

"No," as if sensing her thoughts, Andrew spoke softly, "what I mean is, that I make the business decisions. Nine times out of ten Amanda doesn't know what I do with my money and, to be honest, she doesn't want to know. As long as there's enough in the joint account or on the credit card to keep her stocked with clothes and shoes, that's all she cares about."

"Andrew – are you absolutely sure?" Leah was feeling a curious mixture of fear and adrenaline. With Andrew on board there was no telling what she could do. She could take on staff, and spend more time on her chocolate recipes without having to worry about accounts and suppliers. And an outlet – an actual store – wow, imagine how things could go then? Anything could happen!

"Of course, I'm sure. Look, I know it was a drunken conversation, so I can understand that you find it a little weird but, Leah, I promise you, once I put up the money, there'll be no interference from me. It's still your baby and I trust you completely. If you've any doubts in that regard, don't, 'cos I don't want anything to do with it – unless you'd prefer that I did, in which case I'd have to withdraw the offer as I just don't have the time –"

"No, no – that would be perfect! I mean, that's exactly how I'd prefer it too. I'm just finding it so hard to get my head around it but, wow, I haven't even said thank you. Andrew. Thank you, thank you, thank you!"

"You're welcome. Now, do you think you could stop thanking me for a second and get your ass down to Blackrock and have a look at this premises I have in mind?"

"Blackrock? You don't mean Blackrock, Dublin, do you?" Leah knew that in that trendy upmarket village, her produce would literally run out the door.

"No, I mean Blackrock, feckin' Cavan, where else?

Anyway, I'm meeting with the estate agent about another place at two, and then I was hoping we could pop out there for a look – what do you think?"

"What do I think?" Leah repeated, exhilarated. "I'll be there!"

"Seems a bit sudden, doesn't it?" was Josh's response when later on that evening Leah told him the good news. "I mean, you haven't seen this guy since his wedding, and then all of a sudden he wants to make a huge investment in your business?"

"But he's an old friend," Leah said, her spirits dampened slightly at his less than enthusiastic reaction. "We've both been very busy with our own lives, you know how it is, but we've always been close and if Andrew Clarke has enough faith in my talent to invest his money there, well, I think I have a right to be pleased about it." She knew she was sounding petulant but she didn't care. Sometimes, Josh got a little bit funny about Leah's work, probably because he had always worked for his father, who ran a popular chain of DIY stores. Josh hated working there and was always looking for any excuse to get out of it, yet the pay was good and the hours were flexible and, having done nothing more than an Arts degree in college, he wasn't qualified to do much else.

"So what's he planning?"

"He isn't planning anything, Josh. It's entirely up to me. But we went out this afternoon to have a look at the premises he had in mind for the shop and oh, it's just perfect! Blackrock, can you believe it?"

Kate certainly couldn't when earlier over the phone Leah had told her about Andrew's offer. "Blackrock is just perfect, Leah, such a busy little area, and upmarket too, just perfect for Elysium! And," she added, with a laugh, "it passed the cappuccino test a long time ago!" Kate was a huge fan of the television show *Property Ladder*, which often advocated that a good indicator a particular area was on the up-and-up was the prevalence of coffee and cappuccino bars springing up here and there.

Leah knew well that Blackrock had always been on the up-and-up, and indeed was one of the most desirable places to live on Dublin's Southside. The affluent and discerning inhabitants of the village and surrounding areas would be the ideal clientele for her. It would be a terrific start and she couldn't contain her excitement at the prospect.

"So what happens now?" Josh asked her. "Are you going to go for this place or what?"

"Well, Andrew is hammering things out with the estate agent about the lease, but based on the figures we went through this afternoon, we should be well able to manage things. I'll need to take another look at my range, see how I'm going to manage fridge displays and all that, so I'm going to take a pop into town tomorrow to check out some of what will soon be my competitors!" She hugged Josh delightedly. "Can you imagine me, with my very own store? Honestly, Josh, I knew I was doing OK with supplying trade, but retail will just take the business to a completely different level!"

"I know it will love, congratulations," Josh returned her hug, but decidedly half-heartedly.

Leah hugged him even harder, trying to get her enthusiasm to rub off him a little. She knew it was hard for him knowing that she would be working a lot more than usual to get the shop set up, but the way Andrew was driving forward, it shouldn't take much longer than a few weeks before they were open for business. Yes, she would have to work like a demon between now and then to satisfy existing suppliers and come up with new stock for the outlet, but at least things were moving forward. If Leah had her way, the business would get to the stage where maybe Josh wouldn't need to work with his dad any more, and she would be able to support both of them – well, not *she* – she knew Josh wouldn't like the sound of that – but the business certainly would. Her margins were terrific as it was, and once she started selling direct to the public there would be no stopping her. Yes, she would have to sacrifice a lot of her home and social life to get there, but wasn't that what all business people had to do to be successful? Then when everything had settled down and the business was more or less running itself, she and Josh could slow down and take things easy, maybe go on a nice holiday to the Caribbean or go and visit Robin in New York or something. Josh would get used to it – it might be weird at first but he *would* get used to it. He'd have to, wouldn't he?

"September," Leah decided then, her eyes shining at the thoughts of it. "I'm determined to have the very first Elysium chocolate boutique up and running by my thirtieth birthday."

Chapter 11

It was the night of Amanda's famous Expectant Mummy Party and Leah was just about ready to climb the walls. The fact that Andrew was now investing in Elysium meant that she had to speedily rethink her decision not to attend, as it would appear very rude not to. Thankfully Olivia had come along to give her some moral support. Which at that moment in time Leah badly needed. She wondered again what someone like her was doing in a place like this.

Amanda seemed to have invited all her new-mummy friends, and if Leah didn't know better she could have sworn that the girl had also raided the nearest maternity ward, there were so many heavily pregnant women in attendance. She was trying her level best to ignore the sight of them sitting on the sofa, gazing at and lovingly rubbing their expanding bellies. The room had been decorated with baby balloons, and

Never Say Never

Mother & Baby and *Your Pregnancy* magazines were strewn all over the coffee table. Although there wasn't a child in sight, Leah could almost smell the baby powder.

As usual, Amanda had gone way over the top, but judging by her apparent glee at falling pregnant in the first place, this wasn't surprising. Leah recalled the strange phone call she'd received from the girl a few weeks earlier. She and Amanda weren't close so to say it was a surprise to hear from her was a complete understatement.

"Leah – hi, I'm so glad I got you at home!" she shrieked.

"Why, what's wrong?" Leah hadn't been able to tell by her high-pitched tone whether the girl was excited or upset. And, with Amanda, it was always hard to tell.

"Well, I have some amazing news!"

"Oh?" Leah waited for the impending announcement that Brown Thomas had had a last-minute 'day only' sale and that Amanda had secured an impossibly gorgeous Jill Sander dress for some one of her fancy dinner parties, or something similar.

But she was wrong

"I'm pregnant!" Amanda announced breathlessly. "Now, I know what you're thinking – and it *is* a bit of a surprise, seeing as me and Andrew have only been trying for a few months or so – but still, it's happened!"

Leah gulped, images of Amanda and Andrew 'trying' coming unbidden into her mind. Ugh, what a horrible expression – why couldn't people say something less graphic like 'hoping to have a baby' or something? "Oh," she said, then quickly added, "it's fantastic news – congratulations." Inwardly, though, she couldn't help feeling slightly deflated.

Not another one.

"Thanks, Leah! Imagine me – pregnant! It's hard to believe, isn't it? I can hardly get used to it myself, especially when I've just found out. We're supposed to keep it a secret and not tell anyone until the twelve weeks are up, but I just can't wait – I'm five weeks pregnant and want to tell the world!"

"Five weeks!" Leah repeated, taken aback. That was a little early to be shouting about it. "So, how are you feeling? Have you been sick, or anything?" she asked.

"Oh, Leah, you wouldn't believe it." As if to demonstrate, Amanda's tone all of a sudden sounded like that of a frail old lady. "It's been just awful – I'm so tired all the time and weak as a kitten. And then, each morning I'm like Mount Etna, throwing up on everything, over and over again. It's simply *dread*ful."

"You poor thing." At this, the slight envy Leah had been feeling ended quickly. She could only imagine what morning sickness must be like.

"But, you know me – easy-going as anything. I'll just take it all in my stride."

Leah couldn't help but smile. Amanda was probably one of the least easy-going people you could meet. Always quick to take offence, she would start an argument with anyone who looked at her sideways. She and Kate had always been at loggerheads throughout college, no-nonsense Kate having little time for what she described as Amanda's pathetic childishness and Amanda more than once calling Kate "a humourless cow".

Leah idly wondered what a heavily pregnant Kate would make of Amanda's news.

"Well, look, Leah, I've tons of people to phone, but obviously I wanted to tell you personally – before word gets out." She put it so dramatically that, despite herself, Leah had visions of shrieking newspaper headlines proclaiming Amanda's pregnancy to the world. "So, I'd better go – I still have a whole list of people to get through!"

"No problem. Pass on my congratulations to Andrew. I take it you two will be breaking out the champagne?"

"Oh, no celebrating for me," Amanda said, piously. "From now on, I'll have to be *very* careful – no alcohol."

"You can have a glass, surely?" Leah said surprised. At only five weeks, was a total ban on alcohol absolutely necessary?

"Oh, no!" Amanda was adamant. "Anyway, Andrew wouldn't allow it – he's treating me like a china doll as it is! Honestly, Leah you should see the way he looks at me, as though I'm the most fragile and precious thing in the world!"

And don't you just love that, Leah thought, rather uncharitably. Amanda adored being the centre of attention, and, of course, being pregnant meant that Andrew was undoubtedly waiting on her hand and foot. No doubt she'd milk the role of delicate mother-to-be for all it was worth. Lucky old her.

"Well, tell him congrats from me, won't you?" Leah said.

"I will. Oh, be sure to tell Josh the news, won't you?" Amanda added.

"Of course – he'll be delighted," Leah said, ringing off and thinking privately that pregnancies and children were so far down her boyfriend's agenda, it wouldn't register with him even if Amanda was having a litter of kittens.

Now, someone with a very similar agenda to Amanda, one of her party guests in fact, was droning in Leah's ear, the woman's nasal tone piercing her brain. "Becoming a mother changes your life in ways you couldn't *possibly* imagine."

"Oh, it changes you completely, Grainne!" Another guest joined them, and Leah was sandwiched in between the two.

Having nothing to contribute, she silently beseeched Olivia, who was standing at the other end of the room for assistance, but in vain. Her friend was deep in conversation with someone else.

The woman who was called Grainne had strolled in earlier dressed to the nines in designer gear, accompanied by a put-upon nanny, and Leah immediately decided that, even if this woman had ever *seen* a nappy in her lifetime, she would almost certainly not know what to do with it.

"Don't you find that you look at life completely differently these days?" Grainne went on.

"Of course!"

Amanda, her blonde hair styled to perfection, drifted towards the group to join the conversation. Stuck in the middle of all this, Leah felt decidedly uncomfortable. "Sometimes I feel as though I didn't know what life was really all about until I discovered this new one growing inside of me." Dressed in over-the-top designer maternity wear, Amanda pushed out her non-existent tummy and bestowed a beatific smile at Leah, who smiled politely back.

Grainne nodded gravely. "The thing is, you really don't understand true pain or suffering until you've experienced childbirth," she declared, and Leah noticed Amanda's dreamily serene expression deflate slightly at this. "Nor, until then, can you truly understand what it is to be a woman."

"But, of course, absolutely." Amanda nodded gravely. "As a woman, pregnancy and motherhood completes you."

"What?" Leah asked, her hackles rising slightly at this. "What do you mean, 'completes you'? You're saying that up until becoming pregnant, your life has been worthless?"

Grainne nodded. "Well, not worthless, but certainly nothing I've done is as important as having my daughter."

"But what about all your achievements in life so far – your degree, your career, your relationships?" Leah asked, feeling slightly threatened.

"Yes, of course, but all those things become superficial once you have a child." Grainne spoke as if motherhood had helped her achieve some form of Zen state. She and Amanda exchanged patronising smiles. "You'll understand when you have one of your own."

Leah's heart skipped a beat. "*When* I have one of my own?" she repeated. She felt so uncomfortable with these conversations, hated people's quick assumptions. Granted, Amanda didn't know about her situation but still . . . " And what on earth makes you think I *will* have one of my own?" she asked Grainne, unable to prevent the rise in her tone.

At this, it was as if all conversation halted in the room, and everyone turned to look at them. Out of the corner of her eye, Leah saw Olivia approach, and soon after she felt a protective hand on her arm.

"Oh Leah, I had no idea, I didn't realise . . ." To her credit, Amanda looked genuinely perturbed.

"Me neither." Grainne shook her head sadly, and assumed a sombre expression. "You must think we're very insensitive."

Insensitive? Idiotic, more like, Leah thought. But really, she decided, she shouldn't let this kind of talk get to her so much. "It's fine," she said, relaxing a little, "but, sometimes I *do* find it difficult to –"

"You know," Grainne went on as if Leah hadn't spoken. "I sometimes wonder if there's something in the air these days – something *literally* in the air, from those nuclear power plants or something – because so many of my friends are having similar problems." The other women nodded in agreement.

"Problems?" Leah repeated, her eyes widening.

"Well, you know what she means . . ." Amanda actually looked embarrassed as she indicated somewhere in the direction of Leah's tummy.

"Fertility problems," Grainne finished.

"Leah," Olivia began, "why don't we go and sit down –"

"No," Leah shrugged her off, blood rushing to her face as she faced Grainne. "I'd like to know why Ms Earth Mummy here seems to think that I have a fertility problem."

Grainne frowned. "Well, seeing as you said you couldn't have children, I just assumed –"

"You assumed wrong. And I didn't say I *couldn't* have children – I just choose not to."

"Oh!" The shocked disbelief on the other woman's face was a picture.

Leah sighed inwardly. *Same reaction, every time.*

"But, but why? I mean, why not?" Grainne blustered.

"Why should I?" Leah replied sharply, momentarily enjoying the other woman's discomfort.

"But, but . . . it's what people *do*, Leah!" Amanda protested. "What we're *supposed* to do."

Leah bristled. She was sick of this argument, sick of having to always defend her choices. "Why?" she challenged. "Is it written down in some life manual that in order to live a full and healthy life, all women are *supposed* to have children?"

"But – but why would you *not* want them?" Amanda said, looking at Leah as if she had gained another head. "I mean it's only natural, isn't it?"

Leah's heart tightened and, for a moment, she couldn't think of a reply.

"So, who will look after you when you're older then?" Christine, another expectant mummy piped up. At this, the other women murmured and nodded in approval.

Leah recovered from her momentary lapse. "You think that having a child will guarantee you'll be looked after when you're older?"

"But of course – who else would do it but your own flesh and blood?"

Leah shook her head, having heard this argument many times before too. "I'm sorry but have any of you visited a nursing home lately? Do you think all the residents are there because they have no family to look after them? Of course not. Chances are most of them do have children of their own – children who for one reason or another cannot, or *choose* not to look after them. It guarantees nothing."

"Well, *I* think that people like you are terribly selfish." Christine laboured the point. "You *do* realise that it'll be *our* children – the taxpayers of tomorrow – paying your pension when you get older, don't you? So, *our* children will be looking after you."

Leah bristled. "You're calling *me* selfish, when the only reason you could give for having a child is someone to look after you when you get older? Give me a break."

"Amanda, Leah and I have to get going soon," Olivia said softly, trying to be peacemaker.

"I think you're all missing the point," Grainne went

on, ignoring her. "What about all those poor couples who can't have children? Isn't it incredibly selfish and unfair of you not to have children, when you can?"

That particular accusation really annoyed Leah. As if her own, *personal* choices were made out of spite!

"I feel desperately sorry for anyone who wants a child and can't have one – of course I do," she said, "but my having a baby, simply because I can, won't help those people. And even if I did do that – even if I *did* bring a child into the world, but knew well I wasn't fully committed to motherhood – then surely that is even more unfair to the child?"

Grainne didn't respond and the two women glared at one another.

"How, then, can you call me selfish?" Leah persisted.

"Look," Christine said then, "I respect your choice, as long as you don't have anything against children. Because, personally, I think anyone who doesn't adore children is just plain weird."

At this, Leah's stomach gave a little jump.

"OK, I think we should end this conversation here and now," Olivia said a little more firmly this time.

"No, this is interesting actually," Leah went on. "So tell me then, why *did* you decide to have children, Christine? What made you come to that decision?"

"Well, I suppose I've never really thought about it all that much, and I didn't come to a decision – as such." She looked around at the others for support. "It's just what you do, once you get married, isn't it?"

The other women nodded in agreement.

"Amazing," Leah said, shaking her head. "I'm standing here in a roomful of educated, successful career women, and you're all saying that you made this decision – this immensely important decision to bring another person into the world – because 'it's just what you do'? Another human being that needs constant looking after – not just now but for the next twenty years or so? Crazy!" She shook her head in bewilderment. "Put it this way, if child-rearing was considered a job you'd have to stay with for all those years with no pay, would you be so willing to sign up without thinking strongly about it? I don't think so – so why this?"

"You're looking at all of this very practically though, aren't you? What about love? What about that wonderful, amazing feeling of absolute adoration for your child? Not to mention the love they will give you in return?"

Leah looked from one woman to the other. "So you'll all love your kids no matter what? And you think that no matter what, you will always have someone to love you back?"

"Yes!"

The women nodded in unison and Grainne smiled, sensing she had won the argument.

"You think that's a good enough reason for creating another life – just to have someone to love you? And you lot think *I'm* selfish?"

The other women looked at one another, unsure how to answer that.

Grainne broke the silence. "You'll understand it all when you have one of your own," she said dismissively. "Until then, you really haven't got a clue."

Chapter 12

"You know that kind of judgemental attitude really gets to me!" Leah said later, when she and Olivia had left Amanda's and were sitting in Leah's apartment eating a fish and chip takeaway. *"I think you're terribly selfish,'* she mimicked Grainne's patronising tone. *"Motherhood completes you* – what in God's name is all that about?" Her hands shook as she spoke, annoyed that once again, she had let people's – *women's* – disparaging attitudes get to her.

"Leah, they are spoilt, pampered biddies, that's all," Olivia said softly. "Between the nanny and the housekeeper, they all have plenty of time on their hands to sit back and think about the 'psychology' of motherhood. I'm willing to bet that Grainne one has never had to clean up after a sick child, or been kept awake all night with a screaming baby. It's a warped view of motherhood, a rose-tinted Hollywood version, and as a mother myself I can tell you from experience that it's nothing like that."

Leah's shook her head. "I'm sorry, but sometimes those sorts of comments really upset me. I hate being made to feel like I'm a leper just because I've made a decision not to have any children. I mean, what's it got to do with any of them?"

Olivia was silent for a moment. "Leah, you shouldn't let them upset you like that," she said kindly. "Look, you and I both know that what they're saying about motherhood being all sweetness and light is utter crap. I love Ellie to bits, but most of the time I'd be lucky if I actually got any time to ponder over how 'wondrous'," she made quote-mark signs with her fingers, "the whole experience is! As it is, I'm torn between one minute wanting to hug her to bits, and the next wanting to shake her to bits!" She laughed. "You know all this anyway, and you shouldn't be letting Amanda's stupid cronies get to you."

"I know, but I've been hearing a lot of this lately, and it's driving me mad. People always assume that Josh and I are childless either because we're waiting to have them in the future, or we can't have them at all. They can't bloody accept that we are child*free* by choice. And the problem is, I always seem to end up having to defend myself – as if I've committed some kind of crime or something!" She shook her head. "God knows there are enough messed-up kids around these days, and maybe if their parents had thought a little bit more about whether they actually wanted them or not, instead of just having them because it's 'what you do' . . ." She trailed off and shook her head. "Why is choosing not to have children such a taboo, Olivia? Open the papers and all you see is people talking about how childcare is too expensive, and how much strain and pressure they're under trying to raise them properly. Yet when some of us decide *not* to put ourselves through it all, they call us self-obsessed and heartless!"

Olivia nodded, but for a long moment an uncomfortable silence hung between them.

"It's just so bloody frustrating!" Leah said then. "As women, we're supposed to have all these choices and in this day and age I – stupidly, it seems – thought we were free to make them. Yet, when I'm honest about *my* choice not to have children, I'm made feel as though I've done something wrong!" She shook her head. "And to be honest, what with Kate's pregnancy and now Amanda's, I seem to be feeling the pressure more."

"I'd imagine it is frustrating for you," Olivia said carefully.

Again there was a strained silence, until eventually, her heart beating quickly, Leah looked at Olivia. "Do you mind if I ask you something?"

"Of course not."

In truth, Leah felt guilty about it, and was loath to push it, being very aware that reawakening memories of a very difficult and lonely time in her friend's life could be very hard for Olivia. Still, and especially after tonight, she needed to ask.

"What *is* motherhood like?" she asked her. "What was it like in the early days – the really early days, when you knew nothing about babies, nothing about looking after Ellie, or feeding her or all that?" She watched Olivia closely for a reaction. "Was it anything like you'd imagined?"

Olivia gave a wry smile. "To be honest, I'm probably the wrong person to ask, really. It wasn't quite the same for me."

"I know that, and I really don't want to bring it all up again for you but –"

Olivia waved her away. "No, no, don't be silly, I don't mean that. It's just obviously I wasn't myself at the time. I was still grieving, so I wasn't your typical new mother. I had other things on my mind, so I think I went through it all on complete autopilot. I had no other choice. I had to decide whether I would fall to pieces over losing my husband, or be there for our daughter. As well as that, I had a lot of help from my mum." She smiled. "Actually, I think she's the one you should be asking about this, Leah. She did most of the nappy- changing and night-feeds back then."

Leah remembered how devastated her friend had been after the funeral, and how Olivia's mother had thrown herself into caring for her eldest daughter and then, a few months later, her new granddaughter.

Olivia had come through all the heartbreak eventually, but Leah knew she was today a completely different person to the one she had been back at university. Back then, Olivia had been a planner, a perfectionist and everything from study time to nights out needed to be organised and planned down to the very last detail. Peter had been the same – hardworking, diligent and equally fastidious – so the two of them as a couple had been so perfectly matched it was incredible.

Thinking back now, Leah suspected that this very fact might have been part of the reason for their short break-up after graduation. She knew that Olivia had struggled a little then, the lack of routine and structure that suited her so well in college life having completely upended her in the 'real world'. Trying to make sense of what she wanted to do with her life, and unsure of all the plans she had so carefully laid, both professionally and in her relationship, Olivia panicked, and out of the blue finished with poor Peter. Leah had been in Paris at the time, and couldn't believe it when she heard that the 'perfect couple' had broken up, yet she suspected that it wouldn't last long.

She was right. After a short while, the two were back together and, if anything, their time apart galvanised them into action and made their relationship stronger. Peter proposed, they made plans for their wedding, began looking for somewhere to live and from then on in it seemed there was no stopping them.

But tragically, as Olivia had eventually discovered, there were some plans that couldn't be fine-tuned to the last detail, some things that just couldn't be controlled.

"Earth to Leah," Olivia teased, and Leah smiled, realising she had spent the last few minutes deep in thought. "Look, don't worry – you shouldn't feel as though you have to justify your decisions to anyone."

"Oh, I suppose, I'm worse. In fairness, I should just let them think what they like, or that I *do* have fertility problems. But at the same time, I don't see why I should do that. I don't see why I have to lie and cover up about it because I might insult someone who has chosen differently. I totally respect any woman's choice to have a child, so why can't they do the same for me?"

Olivia looked sideways at her. "Leah, what's brought all this about? Are you and Josh OK?"

Leah sighed and shook her head. "No, we're great. Granted we haven't seen all that much of one another lately, what with work being so busy over the last few weeks, and he's not all that excited about all the work I need to do to get the shop going." She rolled her eyes. "Still, we'll be fine."

"You should take it easy. Work isn't the be-all and end-all of everything, you know."

"I do know." Leah smiled. It was still strange hearing something like that come out of Olivia's mouth, when she herself had thought the very opposite a few years ago.

"Nah, things will be fine, he knows what I'm like – and once we get the shop opened and I take on some staff, things will settle down. It's just . . ." She took a deep breath.

"What?"

"It's not . . . it's not just tonight that's got to me. It's *all* this talk of pregnancy and motherhood, with Kate

157

too. I don't mind admitting that lately I feel a bit . . . weird. I'm not quite sure how to handle it." She looked embarrassed.

"Weird?"

"Well, for a start, I worry that I'm not giving Kate the necessary support. We've always been close, and I suppose I'm afraid that our friendship will suffer because we can't share all this pregancy and new mother stuff."

Olivia nodded. "I suppose it must be strange, because in college you were the one who wanted children, Kate insisted she didn't, and then she went off and got pregnant on you." She laughed, seeing Leah's expression. "You know what I mean – Kate was probably the last one of us you could picture as a mother. Then, Amanda – look, she's just being Amanda – looking for attention, and getting lots and lots of it. I mean, whoever heard of a party to celebrate your pregnancy?"

Leah rolled her eyes. "I know."

"But look, it hasn't happened to *us*, has it? I've been a mum for years now and you and I are still as close as ever."

"But that was different. I was away for most of your pregnancy and for Ellie's early days. Other than sending her presents on her birthday and hearing about it all on the phone, you couldn't really say I was involved."

"But you don't really have to be involved, Leah. You can still be a good friend; you still *are* a good friend."

Leah nodded and looked away, although she still

wasn't quite sure how to get her feelings across without sounding silly. "It's just . . . oh, I know you're going to think I'm crazy, and after all this time, it's not as though I can do anything about it but –"

"But?" Olivia waited patiently for her to continue.

Leah grimaced. "At Amanda's tonight, I don't think it was just the comments that bothered me."

"Go on."

"I mean, the talk about how motherhood 'completes' you drives me up the wall, of course. But then, there's the normal day-to-day pregnancy stuff that Kate is excited about, and I can't join in. I feel like such an idiot when I try to, because obviously I haven't a clue what I'm talking about and then . . ." She paused and looked directly at Olivia. "I suppose it might be getting to me a little now that I won't be able to join in – ever."

Olivia reached for her hand and squeezed it. "I thought it might be that. I did wonder actually, but I didn't want to say anything. You've always been so decisive about it that –"

"I'm . . . I think I'm a little jealous, actually," Leah blurted. There, she had finally admitted it. She saw Olivia give her an encouraging smile. "I never thought I'd say that, I swore that it wouldn't matter. After all, I've made my decision, my business is my baby as such, and I have other fish to fry. So, it didn't matter – not at the time – but now, when it seems that I'm the only one of the old gang not settling down and having babies, I'm not so sure. I think that's what made me so tetchy tonight. I'm feeling left out."

"Look, I can completely understand that. You were bound to feel that way at some stage and now, with Kate, one of your closest friends, going through pregnancy and your being forced into a roomful of happily pregnant women tonight, it's inevitable that you'd question things. But having doubts about your own decisions doesn't necessarily mean that they're wrong. You had to make some tough choices, Leah, and it's only natural that sometimes you'd question them. I'm sure Josh, in his quiet moments – if he has them, that is – would possibly question them too."

"It's a little too late for that now though, isn't it?" Leah said sadly.

Olivia squeezed her hand again. "I suppose it is."

Despite her friend's protestations that the decision never to have children didn't bother her, Olivia had always wondered about that. She had always wondered if some day the time might come when Leah would regret her decision, and regret the fact that she had to choose between losing the man she loved with all her heart, or becoming a mother sometime in the future.

She remembered how, when Josh and Leah started going out first, Josh had blown them all away by his gorgeousness and the fact that he seemed almost too good to be true. They all got on like a house on fire and he obviously adored Leah. Yet, only a few months into their almost fairytale relationship, Josh had dropped a bombshell that shocked Leah to the core.

Leah hadn't been in a serious relationship for some time, so it wasn't as if the subject was foremost in her mind, but one evening Josh took her out to dinner and told her that he loved her very much, that he could easily see himself spending the rest of his life with her, but that he didn't – *couldn't* – ever see himself wanting children.

Leah had laughed at the time, thinking he was joking, wondering why on earth he had even begun such a stupid conversation. She'd recited it word for word to Olivia afterwards.

"I've had some problems in other relationships with this," he'd said. "And I just wanted to come clean and let you know exactly how I feel about it before we go any further."

Then, by his face, Leah had known that this was no joke: Josh was deadly serious. His face was solemn, his clear blue eyes thoughtful, as he tried to explain his feelings.

"It's something I've known for a long time – something I've always known, actually. I like babies and kids and I love my nephews and my little niece, but I also know for certain that I don't want a child of my own."

"But how can you possibly make a decision like that at this stage? You never know, you might feel differently in a few years' time."

Josh shook his head. "I'm not getting at you in particular, but why do people always assume that you don't know your own feelings about something like this – that you might change your mind? From as young as seventeen we're all expected to make decisions as to what university we'll go to, or what career we'd like. If you can be trusted to make a life-affecting decision like that at such a young age, then why not this?"

"Yes, but that's completely different. You could easily change your mind and –"

"Leah, I won't," Josh took her hand and looked deep into her eyes. "I've had many conversations like this with various women over the last few years." He smiled when Leah raised an eyebrow. "I know how that sounds too. But this is the reason why. I care about you a lot, I think we could have a future here, and I think it's only fair that you should know everything about me, so that you can make an informed decision."

"Decision?"

"Yes. Because if you keep going out with me, thinking that my feelings will change, then you'll be kidding yourself from the word go, and there's little point in our going any further with this. I won't change my mind, believe me."

Leah breathed deeply. "Wow, this is a strange conversation, I must say, but look, Josh, it isn't a massive thing for me either, to be honest. But I don't think I could tell you here and now that I never want children, because I really don't know."

"But I do, Leah. That's the thing – I do."

"You're really serious, aren't you?" she asked. "But why?"

He shrugged. "I don't really think there is a reason as such. Cowardice could be one of them. Another is the fact that I enjoy my life and I enjoy my lifestyle. I've never had any great desire to repopulate the universe. I don't buy into the fact that's it something we all 'have to do'."

"And what about your parents – your own upbringing?" Josh's dad had worked hard at building up his business and as a result he now owned one of the most successful DIY chains in the country. Leah knew that the two didn't exactly see eye to eye at the best of times, but still that didn't really give Josh enough justification to never want a child of his own.

"OK, I hate this psychology shit, and I suppose if you think deeply enough about it, you could say that all of this stems from my background. You know I'm adopted, and that me and my adoptive dad don't have a terrific relationship. But, Leah, I honestly don't think that's it, I don't think that I'm trying not to repeat the 'sins of the fathers' or anything else like that. I'm just making a lifestyle choice, in the same way that some people become vegetarian. Surely I'm entitled to do that without having to justify it?"

"Well, I don't know if it's quite the same as vegetarianism," Leah said with a grin, "but I suppose you are entitled to make your own choices."

"Exactly."

Josh said nothing more for a moment and Leah thought about what he had said earlier.

"So, some of your previous relationships haven't gone well as a result of this?" she asked.

Josh gave a wry smile. "That's putting it mildly. My last girlfriend, Sharon, knew about my feelings on this right from the beginning. It would be unfair otherwise. So, she accepted it from the outset but I suppose, like yourself, she thought that maybe over time I'd change my mind." His eyes fixed on Leah's. "But I didn't, and I haven't, and I can't see myself changing my mind – not over time, not now, not ever. I'm certain of that."

"I see."

"So what I'm asking you to do is go away for a while and think about it. Think seriously about whether or not it is enough for you just to have me in your life, or whether you want something more."

"That's not an easy decision to make, Josh. I mean, I don't know where we're going. I care about you a lot too, but we haven't been together all that long and . . ." She trailed off.

"I know that, too. But I'm mad about you, Leah, more than I've been about anyone in a long, long, time. We have a great laugh together, we like the same things, you're strong, independent, you know your own mind, you don't take shit from anyone . . ."

She laughed. "Glad you realise it!"

Josh reached for her hand across the table. "Seriously though, this is important. If I had some sort of medical problem or something like that I would have to tell you straight away. This isn't a medical problem – as far as I'm concerned it isn't a problem at all – but it is something that will affect you and your future. If you're the kind of person that can live with that, well and good, but if you find you can't, well . . . I wouldn't like to hold you back."

"So what happened, the last time, with that girl Sharon? Did she try and change your mind?"

"Not exactly. For the most part she accepted it and we were fine for a long time. Towards the end though, occasionally I would spot her looking lovingly at a cute child in the street, or she'd been watching some sentimental TV show about childless couples or something and then I could almost read what was going through her mind. We were together nearly three years when she decided she couldn't take it any more. It was as though she hadn't really thought about it when we got together first – after all we were very young, but then when one of her friends had a baby and she realised she couldn't ever have one of her own –"

"She realised she couldn't make that sacrifice," Leah finished. Josh nodded and she took a drink from her glass. "At the moment, I couldn't tell you that what you've said bothers me one way or the other. I care about you a lot too. I really enjoy our time together, and I could also see us enjoying the same things, and having a good life if we did stay together. But I suppose it is easy to say that now."

"So you'll have a think about it then?" he asked. "A good think about it too – don't be afraid to get another point of view or discuss it with your friends or anything like that. Don't worry about breaking my confidence, Leah, because as far as I'm concerned I've nothing to hide, and I stand by my decision."

She nodded. "OK, thanks for being honest with me. And I promise that if I choose to go along with your decision, I'll be faithful to it, Josh. I *won't* change my mind. If I decide to respect your choice never to have children and still stay with you knowing what I know, then it'll be my choice too."

But, looking at Leah now, sitting on the couch, confused and upset after having yet again to justify that choice to others, Olivia wondered if those words still held true.

Chapter 13

The following Friday evening was hot and sticky and Robin cursed the fact that the air-conditioning unit really picked its moments to give up and stop working. She wasn't long home from work, the heat was putting her in bad form and she debated whether to make dinner or just phone Luigi's for a pizza. There was little point in cooking for herself when yet again Ben was working a late night. Last week and the week before, if he wasn't working late in the evenings, he was spending extra time at the office doing the American equivalent of a 'nixer' in the office.

Robin thought he was taking a chance doing this, as the management of Grafix Solutions would not be impressed to learn that a senior staff member was using company equipment and resources outside of normal working hours. But Ben was determined to complete whatever project he was working on, irrespective of Robin's warnings, or indeed complaints. They had been a bit cagey around one another since 'that' conversation, and Robin knew that Ben still couldn't understand why she was so determined not to take the chance on ever having a child.

Since then, things had been a bit tense, and Ben had said nothing more about looking for another house. The one they'd gone to see in Bronxville had been snapped up before they'd even had a chance to bid on it. Lately, he was being decidedly cool with her and as he was normally so happy and carefree, Robin didn't know what to make of it.

To make it worse, they'd visited Sarah and Kirsty in New Jersey the previous weekend and while Robin was playing with Kirsty in the living-room and telling her silly made-up stories, she overheard Sarah commenting to Ben in the other room about what a wonderful mother Robin would make. Ben had said nothing and quickly changed the subject.

Her head snapped up as she heard the telephone ringing. It had to be Ben, on his way home and asking if she wanted him to bring anything for dinner. Robin raced to answer it. Great, at least she wouldn't have to cook tonight. It had been a busy day at work and she really wasn't in the mood.

But the caller wasn't Ben.

"Hi, stranger!" Leah's sunny tones almost bounced out of the receiver. "How are you?"

"Leah – hi! Good to hear from you. What time is it over there?" A pointless question, Robin knew, but one she instinctively asked, just so she could picture Leah's surroundings and get an idea of what she might be doing.

"About eleven – Josh is out, and I'm here on the couch, stuffing my face with Pringles and watching a *Sex and the City* rerun, so obviously I thought of you and how I haven't been talking to you in about . . . oh, I'd say it's nearly two months now. Did you get my message from before?"

Robin felt guilty. She did get Leah's message – weeks ago – but in truth had completely forgotten to call her back. "I'm sorry, Leah – things have been manic."

"I can only imagine," Leah said dryly. "All the shopping, and the movies, and the theatre and all that . . ."

"Hey, it's not quite like it is on the TV shows, you know!" Robin laughed, "We do actually do the odd day's work here too."

"Don't ruin all the glamour for me!" Leah scolded. "But seriously, how are things? You and that fine Irishman still going strong? I've said it before, and I'll say it again, Robin Matthews – I really don't know how you manage it. Probably the only decent single man left in the country and you have to nab him."

"Ah, he wasn't in the country at the time, Leah!"

"I know, but it wasn't fair that we couldn't at least have had a crack at him first!" She laughed. "No, seriously, how is he?"

"He's great – working late a lot these days, though."

"Working late in *that* sense? That doesn't sound like Ben."

"No, working late in the *actual* sense," Robin said, feeling a bit foolish for mentioning it and allowing Leah to plant a previously un-thought-of idea into her brain. Not that Leah would be malicious, but now that Robin thought of it, what else would her friend say to something like that? There wasn't a chance that Ben would . . . was there? Robin shook her head, and resolved not to think about it.

"So how's everything with you?" she asked Leah, changing the subject.

"Great, we're all fine. Did you get those photos I sent you of Andrew's wedding, by the way?"

"Yes, Amanda looked amazing." Typically, Amanda looked every inch the radiant bride on the day and she and Andrew looked very happy together. Robin had been invited to the ceremony but she couldn't get the time off work. At least, that was her excuse. The truth was she just didn't feel right about it. She just wasn't ready to face them all again. "You looked stunning too – and I loved Olivia's red dress."

"Yeah, she's looking great, isn't she?"

"So are you," she replied. "And Josh is still as gorgeous as ever. How are things going with you two?"

"Fine."

Immediately, Robin sensed a slight hesitation in her voice. She knew, of course, about Josh's reticence to have children, and wondered if Leah was having second thoughts. Her friend had always insisted that she'd love a family, but then had settled for having the man of her dreams instead.

Weird, Robin thought, that she was going through a similar situation at the moment, although in her case she was being the reticent one. Despite his lack of paternal feelings, Josh seemed lovely and she hoped he and Leah were OK. It would be a shame if Josh's situation upset it all for them.

But when Leah explained all about Andrew's involvement in her business, and that lately Josh seemed a bit put out about that, and the fact that she would have to work around the clock to get the store open, Robin realised she'd been wrong.

"So, do you lot see one another much these days, what with Kate being pregnant and Olivia busy with her little girl . . ." she trailed off, wondering if the others were still as close as they had been all throughout college.

She was no longer part of the 'gang', no longer a paid-up member of the close-knit group that existed all throughout uni and afterwards. Leah kept her updated, but to be perfectly honest, Robin now felt very much detached from them all. They were once as close as a group of friends could be, but now, over time, distance and circumstance, the once-formidable strength of the friendship had been broken.

"Oh, I can't believe I almost forgot to tell you!" Leah cried, and Robin could almost picture her large dark eyes widening in anticipation.

"What? Tell me!"

"You won't believe it, but Amanda is pregnant too! I can't believe I didn't think of it when we talked about the wedding earlier and –"

"I don't believe it! Is she thrilled?" Robin knew without any doubt that Amanda would be.

"Well, of course, she is," Leah replied. "Sure, won't all the attention be on her now for the next few months or so, and you know our Amanda – she'll only be too happy to lap it up." She giggled. "You should see her, Robin – she's so funny. Barely a few months gone and she's walking around, supporting her back and waddling away like she's carrying a sack of potatoes. I'm telling you, she'll milk this for all it's worth."

"Oh, Leah, stop!" Robin burst out laughing, recalling how little patience Leah had for Amanda's theatrics. She could imagine Amanda doing just that, not to mention bending the ear off everyone she knew about how 'dreadfully wearying' it was being pregnant.

Despite her airs and graces, or even more so because of them, Amanda's antics could be hilarious. Robin could be much more gracious about how Amanda had treated her in college, now that she was thousands of miles away and it was unlikely she would have much to do with her any time soon.

"Well, tell her I said congratulations," she said. "And say hello to Kate." She paused slightly before adding, "And tell Olivia I was asking for her too, of course."

"Don't you have her number? I'm sure she'd love to hear from you."

"Oh, that's right, sure I have," Robin said quickly. "I might give her a call."

"Do. She really would be thrilled, Robin. She often

asks about you and I know she'd love to hear how you're getting on."

Robin bit her lip. "You should come over some time," she said, trying to keep her voice light. "You'd really enjoy it and I haven't seen you in so long –"

"But when are you coming home again, Robin?" countered Leah. "It's been years now. I know your parents have visited, but don't you miss home at all? Don't you miss us? We hardly know what's going on with you these days."

"There's nothing much going on at all, Leah," Robin said, laughing nervously. She didn't want to get into a conversation like this. "I'm sure your own life is a lot more interesting. As I said, Ben and I are working hard at the moment, but there's nothing much else happening."

"Well, try and keep in touch more often, OK? You might not miss us, but we miss you, me in particular."

Robin was touched. "Thanks, Leah. And believe me I do miss you, but as I said I have a life here now and this is my home."

"You don't think you'll ever move back?" Leah asked, and Robin knew she was faintly shocked at the thought that there was a good chance she might not.

"Certainly not at the moment, anyway." Then she added, hoping to lighten the tone, "I'm up to my eyes in credit-card debt!"

"I'm not surprised – with all that temptation!" Leah sounded decidedly envious. "Listen, now that I think of it, will you try and get a copy of the new Godiva catalogue? I need to keep an eye on what the competition are doing – I wish!"

"No problem," Robin answered. "I'll get on it straight away, and listen, I'll let you go. This call will be costing you a fortune."

"It is, but not to worry. You're worth it. Speak to you soon!"

Leah rang off and Robin replaced the receiver, a little sad that their conversation had ended, but at the same time relieved that Leah seemed to have forgotten her earlier enquiries about when she would next be returning home.

As far as she was concerned, it wouldn't be any time soon.

"Mornin', you!" The following morning Ben reached over and planted a light kiss on Robin's forehead, waking her up. She'd had a couple of glasses of wine the night before and had stayed up late watching crap TV. Suddenly she realised she couldn't remember going to bed or hearing Ben come in. He couldn't have been working that late on a Friday night, surely? Recalling her conversation with Leah, her stomach gave a fearful flip.

"Morning to you back," she replied before adding, tentatively, "What time did you get in last night?"

Ben swung his legs out of bed. "Not sure, sometime after one, I think. You were flat out on the sofa when I came in. I had to carry you to bed."

"Was I?" Robin couldn't focus on trying to remember – she was too busy worrying about what was keeping Ben out until one o'clock in the morning. "Did you go out after work with Dave, or something?"

"No way – I was shattered!" There was little sign of a lie or evasiveness in either his tone or expression. "I thought I'd never get it done in time, but luckily I did."

"Well, whoever he or *she* is, I hope they're happy," Robin couldn't keep the petulance out of her tone, "because I've hardly seen you this last week."

"Oh, I think she'll be happy," he said, cheerily. "In fact, I think she'll be over the moon when she gets a load of this."

Typical Ben, Robin thought, completely oblivious to subtlety – no, just completely oblivious full stop. Here she was, trying to let him know that she was teed off at him for all these mysterious late nights, and there he was letting it go right over him.

Robin tried a different tack. "What was so important that kept you in the office every night this week?" she asked, yawning as she pulled a sweater and some jog-pants out of the wardrobe.

"Come here and I'll show you," he said, his expression mischievous, and Robin suspected that whatever dumb presentation or corporate brochure it might be, she had better pretend be impressed.

But when Ben led her into the living-room and pointed out the slim booklet lying on the coffee table, she didn't have to pretend anything.

"Oh, my goodness – it's amazing!" she said,

studying Ben's work and his amazing computer-aided illustrations.

Kirsty had recently suffered another bout of severe hayfever, and last weekend while visiting, Robin had picked up the beanie toy she had given her at the hospital, and come up with a silly little story about an alligator that also suffered from hayfever.

She hoped it might help teach Kirsty about trying to control her exposure to pollen and to take her medicine. 'Atchoo' was a big, strong and very adventurous alligator, but he was always running into trouble as a result of his allergies. The moral of the story was that Atchoo could have lots more adventures if he looked after himself and took his medicine when he was supposed to.

Kirsty was fascinated by the tale, and made Robin tell it over and over again that afternoon. Upon their return from the house, Robin had written down the story from beginning to end, so that she wouldn't forget it between then and the next time she saw Kirsty.

Ben had obviously 'stolen' her scribbled notes for the story, had come up with some cute graphics and had reproduced the entire story from beginning to end in an attractive font, along with stunning animal illustrations.

"*Atchoo the Alligator* – cool, huh?" Ben was leafing through the pages. "It's a great story and Sarah was raving about it, so I thought, why not give Kirsty something she can keep, something to remind her of Atchoo's adventures? It might convince her that it's OK to take her inhaler in school, that it's cool to be a little bit different."

"Oh, Ben, this is just incredible!" Robin said, putting a hand to her mouth as her eyes wandered through the story. She marvelled at the amount of work he had put into the graphics. "This is what you've been working on all week?"

"Well, I knew we'd be going up there today so . . ." he shrugged as if it was no big deal, but by his beaming smile she knew he was delighted by her reaction.

"She is just going to love this," Robin cried, awed by this thoughtfulness. What a lovely, considerate, gesture! And here she was thinking he was out having it off with someone or other. She should have thought more of him, she should have known Ben was a far better person than that.

Again, Robin wondered what on earth she had ever done to deserve such a kind, loving, and gentle man like Ben McKenna. This was truly incredible.

They visited Kirsty that same day, and as expected, she adored her personalised copy of *Atchoo the Alligator*.

"I never knew I had such a talented brother!" Sarah was equally thrilled, and hopeful that Atchoo's experiences and the instructions in the book would help Kirsty feel more at ease.

"Hey, I can't take all the credit – it's Robin's story," he said, ruffling his girlfriend's hair.

Robin was secretly thrilled that the little rocky period she'd been imagining was over.

"Can I show it to the girls in school, Mom?" Kirsty asked.

"No, hon, Uncle Ben and Auntie Robin worked very

hard on your storybook. It might get ruined in school."

"It's not a problem," Ben said easily. "The paper quality isn't the best so it probably will get wrecked. In any case I've got it saved on the PC, so I can always print out another copy." He stroked Kirsty's dark curls. "You can show it to your class if you like, kiddo."

"Yay!" Kirsty cried happily.

Robin had to smile at Ben's so easily adopted Americanisms. She'd picked up a few expressions herself over the years, but compared to her, Ben had only been here a wet week. He was worse than those who went to London for a weekend visit, and then came back asking for 'arf a laager, mate'.

"Just be careful you don't get sacked for using company equipment, Ben," Sarah said, her face worried as the thought struck her.

"For printing out a teeny insignificant booklet like that? Not a chance."

But by the following weekend, Ben had to print out ten more copies of *Atchoo the Alligator*.

Robin had been at work one day mid-week when she got a call from Sarah.

"Hi, what's up?" she asked, feeling slightly concerned. Sarah usually called only if something was wrong with Kirsty. "How's Kirsty?"

"She's great," Sarah said cheerfully. "She's been using her inhaler properly ever since you and Ben gave her that little book."

"Great."

"But the thing is, well, you know she brought it to school with her?"

"Yes?" Robin suspected now that she knew the real reason for the call. The flimsy copy of *Atchoo* had already come apart.

But she was wrong.

"Well, Kirsty must have shown it to one of her teachers, because just this morning I got a call from the principal asking where they could pick up a copy."

"What?" Robin instinctively checked the date on her computer screen to reassure herself that it wasn't April 1st. Sarah, like her playful older brother, was no stranger to playing tricks on people.

"I'm serious. I explained the situation to her, and she wants to know how to go about getting more copies. She asked if you wouldn't mind giving her a call."

"She's looking for printouts of the story?"

"I think so. She thought it was a great idea. Will I give you her number?"

"Just let me get a pen." Robin was intrigued and also a little bit proud of the fact that the school had been so impressed. When Sarah had finished reciting the number, she rang off, and immediately Robin rang Kirsty's school.

"Hi, Robin Matthews here – Sarah Freyne asked that I contact you."

The principal was very friendly. "Robin, hi, thanks so much for calling. I understand you're responsible for that neat little storybook Kirsty brought to school last week."

"Yes, well, I wrote the story, but the illustrations were done by Kirsty's Uncle Ben."

"Well, I must admit it's very well written. Are you a children's writer by profession, Ms Matthews?"

Robin burst out laughing but she was pleased by the thought of it. "God, no – I work in finance."

"Well, you certainly have a way of getting through to children, especially children like Kirsty."

"She's been having a tough time of it with her asthma lately. I just thought this might help."

"It's difficult for children, and Kirsty's not the only one having problems. That's why I think this is such a great idea. Do you know I have at least three other children in Kirsty's grade alone suffering from asthma? Not to mention the kids in the other grades." She sighed. "Sometimes I think all that talk about air-pollution is correct. It can't be good for kids. Anyway, I asked Kirsty to let me keep the book for a day or two, and I brought it along to our most recent parent/teacher meeting. When I showed it to the parents of the kids with asthma, and told them the kind of effect it had on Kirsty, they went crazy for it."

"They did?"

"Yes, they all wanted a copy. So, that's why I called Mrs Freyne today. I wanted to know what bookstore stocked it, so I could tell the parents where to get it. But then she told me that it wasn't in bookstores, that it was just something you guys had done on computer."

Robin resisted the urge to laugh. It was nice, though, to think that something she and Ben had done would be so helpful to kids with asthma. Robin could have done with something similar when she was in school, as not only did it help take the stigma out of being different, it also meant that you had something the other kids couldn't get. Robin was pleased for the little girl.

"Well, look, leave it with me. I'll talk to Ben and see if he can get some more copies printed out for you."

"The parents are only too happy to pay you, of course."

"Oh, no, that won't be necessary!" Robin was embarrassed now.

"Believe me," the principal informed her, "if this little book can help parents and teachers educate these kids on how to control their asthma, it's worth anything."

"No, please. We'd be delighted to help. I'm sure it won't be a problem but I'll check with Ben and give you a call in a few days – OK?"

"That would be great, thank you."

The principal rang off and, as she hung up the phone, Robin couldn't help but smile.

Ben would get a right kick out of this – that was for sure!

Chapter 14

Leah jumped when the phone rang. She had been run off her feet all day trying to get a huge batch of product out to a regular supplier, and had been so immersed in her work that she had almost forgotten where she was. The chocolates needed to be ready for collection first thing the following morning, and with the way things were going, Leah thought, her face flushed from exertion, she'd be here till all hours trying to get it done.

The order had come in only that afternoon, but Bags' n' Bows were one of her best customers, and Leah had no intention of letting them down.

Still, at that very moment, surrounded by ribbon and tulle, Leah sorely regretted her decision to advertise her gift-boxes as 'hand-wrapped'. Why couldn't she have had generic boxes and be done with it? But Leah knew that much of her custom derived directly from the fact that the chocolate boxes looked so appealing.

She cursed inwardly as, partially-wrapped box in

one hand and ribbon in the other, she reached for the handset.

"Hi love, what time will you be home?" Josh asked cheerfully.

"I'm not sure – I'm really up to my eyes here," she answered, unable to keep the irritation out of her tone. She'd be home when she was home.

"Do you need a hand?" he asked, and Leah bristled. Of course, she needed a hand but there was no point in Josh coming all the way over here to 'help'. He had tried that before, and all he had succeeded in doing was to annoy Leah and slow her down. Not to mention the time he packed twelve full cases of chocolates, which Leah had first thought was terrific, until she realised that he had failed to include the protective bubble-wrap which kept the boxes from hitting against one another. The boxes had been squashed and completely ruined in transit, and the customer had been livid. Leah had spent almost a full day trying to calm the customer down, and the rest of the *week* replacing the order. Sometimes, Josh had absolutely no cop-on.

"I'll be fine, Josh, thanks, but look, I can't really talk – there's way too much to do here."

"Are you sure you don't want me to come over? I could bring a takeaway. It seems like I haven't seen you in days."

"Well, that's because I've been very busy." The shop would be fitted out and ready within a few weeks, and Leah was working flat out to get everything ready to move in.

"But you're always busy, Lee. I know things are a bit up in the air at the moment, but who goes in to work on a Sunday?"

"Josh, it's not as though I could get anyone else to do it, is it?" she answered testily. Yes, she had gone back to the workshop last Sunday, so she could get a head start on the following week's stock. Well, it was either that, or lounge around all afternoon on the sofa drinking tea and reading newspapers. If there was work to be done, then it had to be done, end of story.

"It could have waited. You need time for yourself too, you know – and for us."

Great, the last thing she needed was a bloody guilt trip about how hard she was working these days. Of course, she was working hard. Wasn't she trying to get everything ready for the shop, while at the same time trying to keep the day-to-day stuff running? Why couldn't he understand that this was a crucial time for her, and that she just didn't have the luxury of running home, just because he was bored and had no one to play with?

"Josh, I'm sorry but I just don't have the time for this," she said to him.

"Leah, it's half-seven in the evening. You've been in there since six this morning. You're killing yourself!"

Shit! Leah thought, checking her watch. It couldn't be! But it was, which meant that she would be home a lot later if she didn't get off the phone.

"Josh, I really have to go, OK? You get whatever you want for dinner. I'll grab something on the way home."

"But what time will you be –"

"I'll be home when I'm home, Josh, right?" Leah felt like a heel when there was silence at the other end. "Look, I'm sorry. I don't mean to be short with you. But you have no idea how much there is to do between now and the opening."

"What's the point of putting yourself in hospital in the meantime, love? Because with the way things are going, that's what will happen."

"I know, I know, and look I promise this weekend we'll do something, OK?" *Just please, get off the phone and let me go back to work,* she urged silently.

"OK?" she repeated, when Josh didn't answer.

"Yeah, OK. See you later then."

"Great." Still holding the chocolate box in one hand, Leah hung up and returned to her work-desk. Of course she was working hard – with all that was happening at the moment, what else did Josh expect? Andrew Clarke had put a lot of faith in her by investing all that money in her business, and in her talents, and Leah was determined not to let him down.

"He's just being so bloody childish about it." A few days later, Leah tried to explain her annoyance to Olivia. This time *Josh* was at work and, as she was up to date with her stock, for once she was at a loose end.

"From day one, he made it quite clear that he doesn't agree with the fact that Andrew's invested in Elysium," she told her friend. "He doesn't agree with

Andrew full stop. For some reason he just seemed to dislike him on sight and, to be honest, I'm finding it a bit of a strain. I mean, here I am, working my ass off to get everything ready for the opening, and all Josh does is spend the whole time moaning about Andrew and what he has to gain, and why doesn't he share some of the work."

"And do you think Andrew should?" Olivia asked. She knew that Leah was desperately looking forward to getting the store up and running, but she suspected that her friend was doing way too much on her own.

"No, of course not. I don't want Andrew involved; Andrew doesn't want to get involved. That's the only reason I agreed to do this in the first place. The business is mine and Andrew is simply a silent partner. Josh can't understand that. As much as he seems to dislike Andrew, he still thinks that he should be more involved, that he should help me more."

"Well, maybe he does have a point. I know how difficult it must be to run everything yourself. What about giving Alan some of the load?" Leah had recently taken on a part-time assistant, a shy quiet young man called Alan who went about his work diligently, eager to learn all he could from his boss.

"Alan is just an assistant – he doesn't really have the know-how when it comes to running a business."

"Well, maybe he might surprise you. You should give him a chance – that's what you're paying him for, surely?"

"No, it would take way too long to train him to do

everything," Leah said, dismissing the idea. "There's no point in doing that at this stage anyway. I'll get it done quicker by myself and that's the end of it."

Olivia knew that sometimes Leah found it difficult to let go of the business she had built up from the very beginning, that she found it hard to assign control to anyone else. She worried now, looking at Leah's tired and gaunt face and the determined look in her eye, that with this new store, she might be taking on way too much. Josh had every right to be concerned.

"Well, look, try not to worry about the deadline too much. Surely a week or two later won't make too much of a difference?"

Leah sighed. "No, I don't suppose it will, but at the same time this is the date that Andrew and I agreed. I don't want to let him down."

"I'm sure Andrew wouldn't mind one way or the other. Didn't he say that it's yours to run whatever way you choose?"

"You're starting to sound like Josh."

"I know, but like me, Josh doesn't want you running yourself into the ground over this. I can't say I've had any experience with building an empire, but I know the Romans slept sometimes too."

Leah laughed. "You're right. I do take it way too seriously sometimes. Things will be fine, and Josh is just teed off because I don't spend any time with him in front of the TV any more."

"You are making some time for yourselves surely?"

"It's very difficult." Leah shrugged. "I'm at the

187

workshop as often as I can, so now he's started to do some more shifts at Homecare. You know Josh – he's one of those people who hates sitting in on his own."

Olivia refilled her coffee mug. "Still, you two should try and calm it down a bit, go for a weekend away or something."

Leah laughed. "At the moment, there aren't enough hours in the day, let alone wasting time going away for weekends. But look, things will get better once the business opens. Josh just has to bear with me for a while, that's all." She looked at her watch. "Anyway, I'd better leave you alone to get ready for work. Do you want me to drop Ellie off at Eva's for you?"

Olivia was due at the Centre at twelve, and usually dropped Ellie off at her mother's beforehand. "Um, no thanks, we've got loads of time," she said, only too well aware of Leah's limitations as a driver.

"Right – well, I suppose the next time I see you will be at the launch party?"

"Probably. But look, try to take it easy in the meantime, won't you? I'm sure it's tough for Josh too."

"Don't worry, we'll be fine," Leah assured her.

As she closed the door behind her friend, Olivia really hoped that they would be. Then again, she thought, going upstairs to get Ellie ready for her granny's, she was probably just being silly in worrying about them. Leah and Josh had been through much tougher times than this and hadn't they come out of it all just fine?

Chapter 15

Through her front window, Catherine watched the silly cow from across the green trying to bundle her child into the car.

Pathetic, she thought, so pathetic the way she kept making big eyes at Matt, fawning all over him whenever they happened to bump into one another.

Which, Catherine thought, rather worriedly, seemed to be happening a lot lately. Only the other day, when Matt should have been tucking into the gorgeous beef stew she had spent all afternoon preparing, Catherine had again caught the two of them chatting easily at that woman's front gate.

She'd have to put a stop to that – and quickly. She didn't want Matt getting too friendly with the neighbours, especially unattached female neighbours. They'd had that problem before, and if it weren't for darling little Adam, she would have been none the wiser. No, there was no letting him out of her sight this time, that was for sure. She and Matt had been through too much together over the years to have it all ruined by some desperate slapper living across the road. No way.

God, didn't the woman have any shame? She shook her head in disgust as she watched her drive away. Laughing and flirting with him in full view of the green and all the while knowing that he had a family – that he had a son! The cheek of it! Catherine had a very good mind to just go over there some day soon and give the silly cow a piece of her mind! But Matt would go mad if she did that. He flew off the handle altogether over that last woman, didn't he? No, she would simply bide her time and see what happened, and if Matt showed any sign of straying, well then she would have to do something.

Her hands shook as she went into the kitchen and opened the cupboard. Why did he have to do this, she thought, taking out the ironing board. Why did he have to go looking for someone else – was she not enough for him? Did she not look as good, if not better than that bitch from across the road? Catherine had got one really good look at her one day while passing in the car. She and her little girl were out in the front garden, and yes, her eyes were a wide, deep blue and she was very striking. But there was no glamour, no character – and she was overweight for goodness' sake!

Catherine ran a self-conscious hand over her own flat stomach and tiny waist. Surely all those hours at the gym, not to mention the hours at the hairdresser touching up her highlights meant something!

But then, a lot of the time, Matt didn't even notice her hair or her slim figure or her salon tan. No, he was too busy organising his next business venture or fussing over Adam. If it weren't for Adam, Catherine wondered if he would bother with her at all. If it weren't for Adam, he might be long gone, gone off into the arms of some plump, boring, ordinary woman, a woman who could never give him what Catherine did.

She wrinkled up her nose. *Her* name was Olivia, apparently. Matt had mentioned that one day after Catherine had once again interrupted one of their little 'chats'.

"She's a lovely woman," he'd said. "Very friendly but a little bit shy too, I think. And her little daughter is just so cute – the resemblance is amazing actually."

Every word had cut Catherine to the quick and immediately she hated Olivia –

Olivia with her cute daughter and her big blue eyes and her bright smile. Olivia, who was obviously single and obviously desperate for a man – any man, to brighten up her boring lonely domestic routine.

Catherine knew all about boring and domestic routines – sometimes she wondered why on earth she'd ever given up her full-time job and agreed to spend all day doing housework and looking after Adam. But she didn't have to think too long about the answer. She did it to support Matt, and they both knew it wouldn't do for Adam to be looked after by some stranger, and being fed yellow-pack fish fingers every day for dinner. It wouldn't be fair on the child.

So, despite how bored she sometimes felt, Catherine was still glad she decided to do it. Still, at times like this, she wondered if Matt really appreciated the sacrifice she'd made. He'd given her a lot of support certainly, and this new and bigger house had been his suggestion – and mostly paid for by his wages – but still, it was hard not to be bored.

Then again, Catherine thought, reminding herself that this move had inadvertently put him in contact with *that* woman, being bored and stuck at home didn't give anyone an excuse to go off chasing other women's men, did it? Catherine wouldn't dream of doing something like that – no, she had enough respect for herself and indeed for Adam.

She sighed. At times she wondered why on earth she bothered staying faithful to Matt, let alone minding Adam in order to support him in his career. It's not as though she had any shortage of attention – she was always getting wolf-whistles and admiring glances when she was out and about.

She knew she had always been attractive; she had worked bloody hard to ensure she *stayed* attractive, and it was quite satisfying to find that even now, despite the fact that she was in her early thirties, she still had the power to make men go weak at the knees. Catherine smiled as a thought entered her mind. Like that *very* attractive guy at the video shop – the manager. He was young, but quite sexy-looking and always extremely well dressed. Yet, despite his best attempts at keeping a professional distance, Catherine knew he fancied her rotten. Didn't he redden up like a Spanish tomato every time she bumped into him at the store? It had all started a while back when she'd complained about a dodgy DVD she'd rented there, and the manager – Rory was his name – had to be called upon to placate her. He was so apologetic, and admittedly, so flustered by her good looks, that at the time, Catherine couldn't resist flirting with him.

Well, she thought, picking up the Disney DVD she'd rented yesterday for Adam, thoughts of Matt's 'friendship' with their unglamorous neighbour propelling her into action, maybe she might just take a trip down to the store and do some more flirting! What's sauce for the goose is sauce for the gander, she decided, going upstairs to choose an eye-catching and suitably flirtatious outfit, something that would make Mr Xtravision redden up even more.

Twenty minutes later, Catherine stood in front of the mirror and assessed her over-the-top but unmistakably sexy appearance. Matt was away this weekend, so this was the ideal opportunity to put her plan into action.

She smiled. By the time she was finished with him, neighbourly relations would be the last thing on Matt Sheridan's mind.

The following morning at 7am, Olivia was sitting in her kitchen nursing a mug of hot coffee and wishing that the caffeine-jolt would hurry up and do its job. She hated early mornings, had always hated them, and there was nothing she'd like more than to go back to bed and curl up under the warm duvet.

But there was little chance of that this morning. She'd brought home a few hours' worth of paperwork from the Centre yesterday, and although the work wasn't terribly urgent, she wanted to get a good head start on it before Ellie got up in a couple of hours' time. It wasn't practical to be going through patient files when her daughter was around – dangerous because her attention needed to be elsewhere, and difficult because Ellie in true toddler fashion made the very most of the fact that her mother's attention was elsewhere. Olivia had learned in the early days that when Ellie was quiet, it was usually because she was up to no good.

She went into the living-room, sat down by the window at the sideboard that doubled as 'her desk' and switched on her laptop, wishing that she had done the sensible thing and let it warm up while she was getting breakfast.

The bloody computer, which Olivia was convinced was running on the slowest, crudest operating system imaginable – probably based on Bill Gates' original Windows doodlings – took absolutely forever to get going. She gazed unseeingly out the window while she waited, her eyes tired and watering.

Olivia wasn't sure how long she had been sitting there when a small movement across the green caught her eye. Oh God, it was someone coming out of the Sheridan house again, she thought, guiltily averting her eyes. Anyone would think it was her *intention* to spy on the new family, and what if Matt himself noticed her light on across the way, and saw her sitting at the window, apparently spying on him on his way to work?

She went to move out of sight, but first gave a quick glance to ensure that she hadn't been seen.

As she did, Olivia's mouth opened wide. This time she didn't – she *couldn't* – look away. There was Matt's wife, barely dressed in a satin bustier-type combo that wouldn't look out of place in an issue of *FHM*, wrapped around some man – some tall, blond, *young*er man that definitely wasn't Matt! What was she up to?

Well, it was pretty bloody obvious what she was up to, Olivia thought, seeing the woman pull her beau closer for another kiss – she was cheating on poor old Matt!

But why? Why would anyone feel the need to cheat on a warm, wonderful man like Matt Sheridan? Why would any woman who was lucky enough to have a loving, devoted husband and a perfect little child – a perfect family – recklessly put it all in jeopardy for a fling with someone else?

Then Olivia berated herself. Who was she to judge? What did she know about that woman and her family? Who knows what goes on behind closed doors – isn't that what her mother always said?

She was a fool to presume anything; for all she knew Matt and his wife might have a terrible life together and lover-boy, whoever he was, was her only means of happiness. But still, what would poor Matt think when he realised that his wife was having an affair – and worse, flaunting herself and her fancyman all around the place!

Although it was hardly flaunting, Olivia thought now, trying to calm herself. It wasn't as though the woman expected the mostly elderly neighbours of Cherrytree Green to be spying on her at that hour of the morning, was it? Still, it was brazen enough of her at the same time.

Seconds later, Olivia heard a car drive away, and when she looked back at the house, the wife had gone back inside.

But where was Matt? His car was in the driveway – surely she wouldn't have been carrying on while he was asleep in another room, would she?

"Oh, for goodness' sake, it's none of your bloody business anyway!" Olivia said out loud, before striding purposefully towards the kitchen for a fresh caffeine fix. But this time it wasn't to wake her up – she was fully awake now. No, this time it was to calm her down.

What should she do? She and Matt were neighbours after all – even *friends* to some degree – should she say something to him?

No, it wasn't really her place, she didn't know him *that* well, and she couldn't exactly admit that she had been spying on his house, and that she knew all about him and his wife and their son and their so-called perfect life. She couldn't do it, she *wouldn't* do it, and it was absolutely none of her business. She would not be the one to tell Matt anything about his family or his wife that he might not know. She would not be the one responsible for breaking up a family because of her own selfish needs.

Not this time.

"Hi, Matt!" A few days later, Olivia smiled as Matt walked across the green towards her house, little Adam by his side.

She was outside, pulling weeds and vainly trying to make the garden look at least half as presentable as the one of the green-fingered couple next door.

"Hello, yourself!" Matt warmly returned her smile, and Olivia's heart went out to him. Such a lovely guy, happy and carefree and out for a walk with his son, and little did he know that his monstrous wife was cheating on him. Life just wasn't fair.

"Doing a bit in the garden, I see?"

"Yes, you know yourself," Olivia replied, removing her gloves and throwing a sideways glance at the garden next door. "Just trying to keep the place up to standard." She stood up.

"Good for you – I've always hated gardening and luckily my place doesn't need it." Olivia didn't have a chance to examine the state of his own garden across the way before he came through the gateway and introduced his son. "This is Adam, by the way. Adam, say hello to Olivia."

The little boy looked up at her with watchful eyes but said nothing.

"Hi, Adam, nice to meet you," she said, bending

down and offering her hand, remembering how Ellie had responded to Matt when he introduced himself properly to her like that. Obviously, little Adam didn't feel the same way.

"Want Mummy!" Adam squealed, turning away and ignoring Olivia.

Matt looked embarrassed. "I'm sorry about that. He can be a little bit wary of people he doesn't know."

"That's OK – Ellie can be the same," she said, hoping to make him feel better and trying to ignore the fact that the boy didn't look remotely like his dad. Matt had dark hair and was lightly tanned, whereas Adam was very fair, a smattering of freckles across his cheeks, and his not-so-friendly manner suggesting to Olivia that his mum's genes were the dominant ones.

Then horrified, a thought came unbidden into her mind. Maybe Adam wasn't even Matt's child. Maybe the wife had been carrying on behind his back for years and poor Matt knew nothing about it! Such a silly cow – anything was possible! Olivia put her gloves back on and tried to shake the horrible thought from her mind. With that, she got down on her knees and quickly resumed her weeding.

"Er . . . do you have something against flowers then?" Matt asked, looking curiously at her.

"No, why?" Following his gaze, Olivia looked down and realised she had been taking her frustrations with Matt's errant wife out on her poor Busy Lizzies, the one flower that returned year after year, despite her failings as a gardener!

"Oh no! I can't believe I did that!"

"Well, maybe we can still save them," he said, in the manner of one of those hunky doctors on *ER* and inwardly, Olivia swooned. "Adam, you stay there, while Daddy helps Olivia, OK?"

With that, Matt got down on his knees alongside her, and began replanting what was left of the unfortunate flowers, the hint of an amused smile crossing his lips.

Just then, Olivia realised that Matt must think her an awful ditz. On day one, she turned up for a night out with a complete stranger, the next time, she was having problems reversing her car out of the driveway, then she had run out of the shop that time without her change, and *now* for no apparent reason, she was merrily pulling up perfectly decent flowers in her front garden!

"Matt, it's fine, really," she said, cheeks red with mortification at the fact that once again, the mere presence of this man had turned her into a demented idiot. Wait until she told Leah about this – she would kill herself laughing.

At the thought of her friend's reaction, and the ludicrous situation in which she once again found herself, Olivia too couldn't help but giggle.

"What? What's so funny?"

"I'm sorry," Olivia said, trying to stifle a laugh. "I know you think I'm an absolute idiot, and I'm certainly living up to it now!"

"An idiot? What do you mean?" Now Matt was smiling too.

"It's just –" Olivia didn't care how it sounded, she

knew she had to come clean, otherwise every time she saw Matt, things would just keep getting worse. "It's just every time we meet, I seem to end up doing something stupid. I'm not sure why that is, but I can assure you that I'm not like this all the time. I'm not really any good with men . . . since my husband . . ." Then she floundered, horrified. "Not that I consider you a man in *that* sense, I mean, I know you're married and everything, so please don't think that . . . it's just . . ." Oh, God, she was really making a mess of this, she thought, heart pounding. So much for coming clean and trying to save face. "I'm sorry," she said eventually. "It's just, I suspect you think that I'm a complete ditz and really I'm not, but for some reason you seem to have that effect on me . . . I mean, I really like you and . . . " She trailed off then, realising that she was digging herself in deeper with every word. She was never going to able to explain it properly, and especially not now, not when Matt's truly mesmerising grey eyes were that close, his gaze steadily fixed on her face. Obviously trying to decide whether or not she should be committed to an asylum, Olivia thought, deflated.

"Olivia, look, I'm sorry if you thought that –"

"Hi, Matt!" Thrilled to see him, Ellie bounded out the front door, cutting off whatever Matt was about to say and, thankfully, sparing Olivia's deep embarrassment.

What had he been about to say? She didn't know but, from the wording and the apologetic look on his face, it could only have been some kind of brush-off . God, he must have thought she was coming on to him!

"Hey, Ellie!" Matt stood up, and seeing her daughter race into his outstretched arms, Olivia's embarrassment was swiftly replaced by panic. This was crazy. She couldn't stay friendly with Matt Sheridan like this. Not when her daughter had clearly fallen for him as much as she had. The guy was *married,* for goodness' sake!

"Hey, Adam, come to say hello to Ellie!" Now Matt was introducing the two children, and the earlier sullen Adam seemed much more receptive to her daughter. Great, that was the last thing she needed, Ellie becoming friendly with Matt's young son and having to be brought to Matt's house for birthday parties and days out and the like!

No, no, much better to just cut all contact with the man, for her own, and indeed Ellie's sake. Now that she knew exactly how she felt about him, and obviously Matt did too, there was no point in putting herself through what undoubtedly would end up as heartache. She'd had enough of that in her life already. Better just to cut all ties with Matt and forget about him. But to think that his brazen wife across the road was quite happy to carry on with some young fella, and here was Matt resisting Olivia's stupid attempt at explaining her feelings, putting his wife and child first without a moment's hesitation!

Yet that was why she liked him so much, wasn't it? Olivia admitted. He was a warm, charming, amiable man – in a way, a little like Peter had been. The attraction wasn't all one-sided either but it seemed that Matt was adult enough to see it for what it was. Anyway –

"Matt!"

Hearing a voice call loudly across the green, they all turned around. Matt's wife was standing in the doorway, waving what looked like a mobile phone in his direction.

"We'd better go," Matt said, with Olivia thought, a slight regret in his tone.

"Aw, can't Adam stay here?" Ellie asked, looking almost as disappointed as Olivia felt. Adam looked hopefully up at his father.

"Some other time, Ellie." Matt smiled warmly at her, before he lifted Adam up onto his shoulders. "Adam, say goodbye to Ellie and Olivia, OK?"

"Bye, Ellie, bye 'Liva," This time he gave a broad smile, and only then could Olivia see a clear resemblance between him and his father, right down to the tiny gap between his two front teeth.

"Bye, Adam, see you soon," Olivia said, still embarrassed about her earlier ramblings, and unable to even look in Matt's direction, let alone look him in the eye.

"See you soon." Matt's tone was unusually devoid of its characteristic warmth. Then, with Adam hoisted high on his shoulders, he went back across the green towards his wife, Olivia and Ellie staring silently at his retreat.

Chapter 16

"Be careful what you wish for, as you just might get it," Leah's grandmother used to say. Well, Leah did get it: she had a growing business, her first retail outlet – and Amanda bloody Clarke.

Stupidly, Leah hadn't seen it coming. She was just so thrilled at the scope Andrew's investment would give, thrilled at the idea that her ideas could really go somewhere, she hadn't even considered that Amanda might be interested.

But as the opening of the Elysium store drew nearer, Amanda had been spending lots and lots of time there, and lately this had begun to get on Leah's nerves. Only last week she had 'popped in for a look' but by the end of the visit had tried to commandeer control of the premises' layout and decoration. At the time, Leah had been so preoccupied with getting things ready and deciding on displays that she had just assumed Amanda was showing a friendly interest. Amanda had also insisted that the colour scheme Leah had chosen was "all wrong for the store's image". Leah's logo was simply cream with gold calligraphy lettering, something Amanda decided looked dated. With all the work Leah was doing to get the store set up, she had little time to tinker with her logo! But she held her tongue, simply because she hadn't the time nor the inclination to get into an argument over something trivial. Not to mention the fact that Amanda and Andrew were, in effect, Leah's landlords. So Leah had said nothing, assuming that once Amanda found something else to occupy her, she would soon get bored with the new store and leave Leah and her new assistant, Alan, alone to get on with the day-to-day running of the business.

But in fairness, Leah thought now, Amanda's social connections might be a bit of bonus.

Amanda insisted on Leah having an official launch party and "a chocolate-tasting evening" for Elysium. She had also suggested they issue invites to some of Blackrock's most prominent business people and some local media. Leah suspected that most of the attendees though would probably be more interested in a possible interview with hotshot entrepreneur Andrew Clarke, than supporting her new store.

Notwithstanding, the exposure would be terrific, and hopefully it would give Blackrock's newest retail outlet a timely boost. Then, after all the celebrations and excitement, it would be down to the tough task of growing turnover and making the business work, something Leah hoped she'd be doing on her own.

Still, she couldn't get away from the fact Andrew had made all of this possible, and as much as she'd like to sometimes, she couldn't turn around and just tell Amanda to butt out. She had made a deal with the devil or more aptly, the devil's husband, and now she had to take things as they came.

She sat down at the kitchen table and went through the invite list for the Elysium official launch party. She knew that RSVPs were largely ignored or forgotten about – by her own friends anyway – and she knew most of the gang would be going. Her new store was much cause for discussion and celebration – not to mention the fact that they hadn't had a decent get-together in ages.

It was such a pity that Robin wouldn't be around, but Robin had missed lots of reunions over the years, from Olivia and Kate's thirtieth birthdays, to Leah's homecoming and Amanda and Andrew's wedding. But Robin had her own life now, though she and Leah seemed just as close as ever, even if it was just over the phone.

When the new store was fully up and running, and she was sure she could trust her new staff to look after things, Leah resolved to take a few days off and she and Josh could visit her friend in the Big Apple.

The two of them would certainly be ready for the break at that stage. Although, these days he seemed to have thawed a little, and seemed to be making the effort. Once the launch party was out of the way and Leah started to find her own routine, she was sure that things would get back to normal. She and Josh were soul mates, weren't they?

Leah smiled. It was funny the way he seemed slightly jealous of Andrew. As if there was anything to be jealous about! Andrew was great but thankfully he stayed out of her way. No, it was Amanda who couldn't keep her nose out of things these days. But again, once they had the launch party, things should get back to normal. She hoped.

Leah sighed, remembering their college days. Sometimes it seemed like a lifetime ago. Back then they had nothing to worry about other than men, the occasional exam and whether they had enough money for a decent night out any given weekend. How had things changed so much in just a few years? Robin had moved away, Olivia was a single mother, Kate was pregnant and . . .

Speaking of Kate, she really should give her friend a buzz. She hadn't really spoken to her in a few weeks, and was eager to find out if she and Michael would be coming to the launch party, especially as it would be happening so close to Kate's due date.

"Hello, stranger," she said, when Kate answered. "How are you feeling?"

"Hello, yourself!" her friend replied, obviously pleased to hear from her. At this, Leah felt a little guilty. It was ages since they'd spoken, what with all the running around Leah was doing to get the shop organised. It seemed she'd had little time for anyone lately.

They chatted for a little while about Kate's

pregnancy, Leah's new store and Amanda's unwanted interest in it.

"You should tell her where to go, Leah. The last thing you need is someone like her under your feet all day. Anyway, I can't see her being much good to you in her 'condition'."

Leah had told her all about Amanda's Expectant Mummy party and her pregnancy-related neurosis. Kate wasn't having any of it.

"Since when is having a baby akin to having open-heart surgery?" she said.

Leah couldn't help but smile. At this party, poor Amanda wouldn't get away with pleas of pregnancy-related delicacy while sharp-tongued Kate was around.

Now eight months pregnant, Kate had only recently – and rather reluctantly – taken maternity leave from Russell & Rowe, the city-centre advertising firm in which she worked. As with everything in life, Kate had taken pregnancy in her stride.

"God love her, I don't think she even has to do any housework over in that mansion of hers in Booterstown," Kate continued. "I mean, what about all these pregnant women that go out and work in fields every day, with one baby on their back and another one on the way? I doubt anyone runs around after them, patting their poor brows and feeding them grapes on a chaise longue, do they?"

"Stop it! That's bitchy!" Leah couldn't help laughing at the image, but at the same time she felt disloyal.

Kate had no such problems. "Oh, come on, Leah!

What's wrong with the girl? Pregnancy does *not* mean that you give up your own right to a life, and simply become a host for your baby, does it?"

Leah giggled, enjoying this gossipy diversion. "Well, she did tell me she couldn't drink anything other than purified water until after the baby's born, and that it's only fair she gives up red meat, dairy products and potatoes too."

"What? You're joking."

"That's what she told me."

Kate exhaled sharply. "Honestly, if I didn't know better, I'd swear Amanda Clarke believes she's the next Virgin Mary – although the virgin part might be a problem," she added tittering.

"Ah, Kate, give her a break. She's just getting used to the idea. I expect all newly expectant mothers are the same in the early days." No point in including Kate in that category; she had treated her pregnancy in the same no-nonsense way she did everything else and Leah really admired her for it. "She's probably not sure what or what not to do," she said, in Amanda's defence.

Kate was unmoved. "I suppose, but if she's like this while pregnant, what'll she be like once she has the little sprog? You know how some mothers become about their little darlings."

"Well, that won't happen for a little while yet," she said, "but personally, I think it's just the novelty of it that's making her like this. She'll be fine once she gets used to it."

"Hmmm."

"So, do you think you and Michael will be able to come to the launch party?" Leah asked, changing the subject.

"Of course, we're coming! I wouldn't miss it for the world!" Kate enthused. "Not when I finally have an opportunity to show off my toned bod in that Halle Berry style leather catsuit."

Leah laughed. It would be just like a heavily pregnant Kate to turn up in something like that. She didn't give a damn as to what anyone thought of her. Having said that, though, she would probably still look great.

"How's Olivia? Is she going to your launch party? I'm really looking forward to seeing her – and you. It seems I haven't seen you all in ages."

"I know and I really feel bad about that, Kate. But with all the work I've been doing, I haven't been the best at keeping in touch lately." She grimaced. "That's why I hope there's a good turnout at this party – with the way I've been carrying on, I might not have any friends left!"

"And what about Robin?" Kate asked, her tone changing slightly. "Did you invite her?"

"She couldn't possibly come all the way home just for one night, Kate. You know how it is."

"She could arrange it if she really wanted to," Kate replied, unmoved. "Although, if she couldn't be bothered coming home for the funeral that time, at least for Olivia's sake . . ." she trailed off.

"I wouldn't expect her to come back just for this,"

Leah said, breaking the silence that followed. "Anyway, her life is in New York now."

"I suppose." Kate still wasn't impressed. "But the two of you were such good friends, and this is a big thing in your life. I really think she should make the effort."

"Well, you never know, she might surprise us." Leah said in effort to appease Kate, but at the same time she didn't hold out much hope. Robin had gone to New York not long after university and hadn't returned since. What were the chances of her coming back just for this small gathering?

Little or none, Leah decided glumly, thinking it would be a very long time before they saw Robin back in Ireland again, if ever.

Chapter 17

Olivia stood back and stared in awe at the newly-decorated facade of Leah's chocolate store. It was the evening of the official launch party, and Elysium Chocolate truly lived up to its name. She also loved the fact that, from the outside, the place looked for all the world like one of those old-style jewellery stores. Of course, Leah's confections were little jewels in themselves, she thought, running her eyes across the gorgeous glass-fronted displays inside – again continuing the jewellery-store theme.

Kate was already there.

"You look fantastic!" Olivia said embracing her warmly. "Not much longer to go now!"

"Thanks, but I know I look like the side of a bus," Kate replied wryly. "Still, I'm determined to make the most of tonight. It won't be long before I'm chained at home to the bottle-warmer!"

She sat down alongside Olivia, and the two chatted easily for a while until Leah joined them, bringing them two plates of food. Dressed in a simple, black shift dress, she looked great, her dark eyes lively and shining with pleasure. She soon had to leave them, however, in order to circulate among the guests and they saw her striking up an animated conversation with someone who was either a client, or shortly about to become one.

Josh, by contrast, seemed rather quiet tonight. He'd greeted Olivia briefly upon arrival but since then had sat quietly on his own in another corner of the room. No doubt he and Leah were both very tired, the strain of working all hours to get the shop going as well as trying to fit in a normal day's work obviously taking its toll on them. Hopefully things would improve soon. She and Josh were so well suited that Olivia would hate to see them break up. Still, it could happen to best of them, as she herself knew well.

She remembered how she and Peter used to fight like dogs just before their big break-up after graduation. She would get annoyed over stupid things like Peter not including her in a drinks round when she already had a full glass in front of her – Peter would be annoyed if she gave even a slight glance towards another guy. It was as though the two of them purposely engineered these arguments to bring some form of drive or energy to the relationship. At that stage they had been together so long they had been in something of a rut. But when finally things did come to a head and they spent some time apart, after which Peter proposed, they hadn't looked back. It was as if each of them then knew where they stood.

Olivia wondered idly if it would take a huge upheaval like the one she and Peter had experienced to get Josh moving on a proposal. She shook her head, thinking that she was beginning to sound like her own mother. Get him moving on a proposal indeed! There was Leah, an extremely talented, independent, successful woman celebrating her success with her friends, and the only thing Olivia could think about was that Josh hadn't proposed. She was definitely turning into an old biddy, she thought, trying to push the recent spying incident on Matt Sheridan's wife out of her mind.

Just then, Amanda floated across the room, looking healthy, tanned and – as Kate had pointed out earlier – very obviously designer-clad.

"But how can you tell the clothes are designer?" Olivia had asked. "I mean without physically lifting up her skirt and getting a look at the tag?"

"I have an eye for these things," Kate said, stifling a grin. "No, I don't actually, but whatever it is, it's expensive and I don't think the likes of Amanda Clarke – pregnant or otherwise – would be seen dead in anything other than haute couture."

Amanda did look great though, Olivia thought, and pregnancy obviously suited her. Her blonde hair tumbled in long layers around her shoulders, Claudia Schiffer style. The dress was a deep crimson red and with Amanda's tanned skin and highlighted locks the effect was doubly striking. And the shoes! The shoes were like nothing Olivia had ever seen before! They were almost too gorgeous, too elegant to be used for walking. If anything, they should be sitting in a glass case in some fashion museum somewhere. She wondered if they were designer too – if so they had to be Prada or Fendi or that guy the Americans loved, the one with the name that sounded like a cross between an Irishman and a toy train, Jimmy something . . .

"Olivia, Kate, how are you?" Amanda trilled, and as she bent to embrace her, Olivia caught the scent of expensive (probably designer too) perfume. "I'm delighted you two could come – it's been ages!"

Olivia smiled a dutiful smile. '*I'm* so delighted you could come?' Wasn't this Leah's party?

"I'm so sorry I haven't had a chance to say hello until now," Amanda continued in that weird faintly-out-of-breath tone that she affected now and again. Olivia knew that this drove Kate up the wall, and at that precise moment she could understand why. "This is exactly what it was like at my wedding, remember? Everywhere I went people were pulling and dragging out of me – but tonight it's all because of this." She caressed her stomach softly and laughed, obviously enjoying all the attention immensely.

"I heard. Congratulations." Kate plastered a smile onto her face.

Olivia bristled. Yes, the girl was pregnant, and it was only natural for her to be excited about it, but tonight was Leah's night. Just because Andrew had invested in the new venture didn't mean that Amanda had the right to try and steal the limelight with all her floating around and carrying on as though this was another one of her uppity soirées.

"Did you two get something to eat?" Amanda asked them, and, Olivia noticed, seemed a little put out that she and Kate weren't as enthused as everyone else seemed to be about her pregnancy.

"I'm fine, Leah got us something earlier," she said, indicating the empty plates on the table.

"Oh, Leah's been great at keeping everyone happy," Amanda gushed. "I just don't know what we'd do without her,"

"Without her? Isn't this Leah's launch party, Amanda?" Kate said aloud the words that had been right on the tip of Olivia's tongue.

"What? Well, of course – of course it is. I just meant that she's so good with people, you know? Of course, she's worked in restaurants for most of her life, so she knows how to deal with the *general public*." She emphasised the words in such a way that she might as well have been honest and said 'riff-raff'. "Me, I just can't deal with all these strangers wanting a piece of me, and all because I happen to be married to Andrew Clarke."

With that, she beamed regally, and Olivia thought she could see Kate physically struggling to hold her tongue.

"Anyway," she said, sitting down alongside Kate and patting her hand, "where's Michael tonight? And more importantly, how have you *been*?" she asked, obviously referring to Kate's impending motherhood.

"Michael's on his way. He had to work late," Kate said shortly, knowing full well that Amanda couldn't really give a damn where Michael was. She just wanted another male to fawn over. "And me? Well, I'm just fine – apart from the burning cystitis, crippling piles and constant farting." At this, Amanda visibly balked and Olivia had to bite down on her lip to keep from laughing. Kate had never been one to airbrush reality, and since her pregnancy she'd got ten times worse. Amanda should know better than to expect Kate to join her in gushing new-mommy sentiment.

"Oh! I haven't – I didn't expect – I suppose I'd better . . ." For once, Amanda was lost for words. "Oh, there's Grainne Fingleton. I'd better go and say hello." With that, she quickly made her exit.

Olivia and Kate looked at one another and burst out laughing.

"You wicked woman, Kate Murray!" Olivia said. "You've ruined the dream for her."

"Oh, come on, she was asking for it!" Kate took another sip of her mineral water. "Sitting down with her back to you, purposefully excluding you like that – God, I could strangle that girl sometimes!"

"I know. Many's the time I had to stop you!" Olivia laughed, thinking of their old college days.

Just then Leah approached, a glass of champagne in her hand, leading a dark-haired, attractive girl of about eighteen years of age.

"Hi, everyone – this is Colleen O'Neill, my cousin," said Leah. "Colleen, these are my good friends Olivia –

and Kate –" As they shook hands she went on, clearly delighted at her cousin's presence, "I haven't seen her in ages and she was good enough to travel all the way down from Derry to be here tonight – isn't she great?"

"Anything for my favourite cousin," Colleen quipped, her blue eyes lively. "And the fact that the room would be stuffed to the rafters with chocolate helped a fair bit too!" she added mischievously, and the others laughed.

"So what do you do yourself, Colleen?" Kate asked, smiling. "Will tonight tempt you to follow your cousin into the confectionery business, do you think?"

Colleen shook her head with a laugh. "No, I think I'd much prefer eating it to studying it, to be honest! I'm at college myself – in Belfast."

"Oh, I know the city – brilliant for shopping!" said Olivia.

"Definitely!" Colleen grinned, then spotted someone waving to her from across the room. "Excuse me," she said to Leah. "I must get back to the chocolates! There's a truffle over there with my name on it! I'll talk to you later, OK?"

"Sure – enjoy!" Leah replied. "But don't you dare leave without saying goodbye!"

"I won't, and congratulations again – it's a great night. Nice meeting you all!" With a little wave to the others she disappeared into the crowd.

Olivia knew Leah was thrilled that friends and family had taken the trouble to come – it was such a wonderful endorsement of her talents.

"So, it's going OK, isn't it?" Leah asked, looking

excitedly around her. "I can't believe there's so many people here! Lots of Amanda and Andrew's friends, mind you but . . ."

"Well, whoever they are, they seem to be enjoying themselves – and the chocolates." Kate looked across the room to where a couple were making serious inroads into a pyramid-shaped slection. "You should be very proud of yourself."

"At the moment, I'm too bloody nervous to be proud," Leah confessed, sitting down at their table. "But it is going well, isn't it? Amanda's great at organising these kinds of things – I wouldn't have known what to do."

Olivia and Kate looked at one another.

"So, is Amanda going to be permanently involved in this, or is she just helping you get started?" Olivia asked carefully.

Leah grimaced. "To be perfectly honest, I'm not quite sure. She pretty much organised this party – you know how she is, always loves to be in the middle of everything. I think it's a bit of a novelty for her at the moment so . . ." She trailed off and shrugged her shoulders. "Put it this way: I think me and my little chocolate store will be way down on her list of priorities once tonight is over."

Olivia wasn't so sure about that, not after the way Amanda had been so condescending earlier, but she said nothing. No point in saying anything to Leah tonight, not on one of the biggest nights of her life.

"I still can't believe that you and Andrew are in business together now," Kate said, shaking her head in wonder. "He was so lazy in college – he was the last person I'd have said would end up a successful businessman. It's weird the way things work out, isn't it?"

"Andrew was always a dote," Olivia said warmly.

"Shame about the wife!" Kate added with a grin.

"Ah stop that. Amanda's not that bad," Leah scolded. "You just have to know how to handle her, that's all."

"Mmm," Kate wasn't convinced.

Just then, a smile broke across Leah's face, and Olivia followed her gaze to see the beautiful Josh approach.

"Hi, you two," he said, smiling at Olivia and Kate. "Enjoying the night?"

"It's a great night," Kate said, beaming unashamedly at him.

One night over a few drinks, she had admitted to Leah that Josh Ryan was the only man alive that could tempt her to cheat on Michael. Leah's reaction to this was one of amusement tinged with more than a little alarm at the realisation that Kate was quite serious. But Olivia knew exactly what Kate meant. Josh was so attractive it was unreal. Clear blue watchful eyes, shiny tousled hair, a jaw-line made for snowboarding, and a tanned athletic body, he was most normal women's idea of perfection.

"You'd run away with him," her mother would say, and did when she met Josh for the first time at Olivia's, keeping him talking in a corner for most of the evening. But, despite Josh's obvious good looks, he was one of the most likeable men you could meet.

"Have you taken anything with that camcorder yet?" he asked Leah.

"No, I'd forgotten all about it. I suppose I'd better get some shots of the guests – and outside! Oh, Josh, we have to get a shot of the shopfront and all the balloons!" She leapt up out of her seat.

Josh was soothing. "Relax, hon. I'll do it. You stay there and enjoy yourself."

"Would you mind? I left it out back in the office – it should be underneath my jacket –"

"It's fine, I'll find it," he interjected, and with a grin, said to the others, "Andrew Clarke doesn't know what he's letting himself in for. This one would forget her head if it wasn't well screwed on."

"Josh Ryan!" Leah exclaimed. "I'll have you know that I'm well capable of remembering things, and it's Andrew that's getting the better part of the bargain. Now out you get and do a bit of work for yourself. All you've done all night so far is scoff all my hard work!"

"Well, that's your own fault for going out with a diagnosed chocoholic," Josh teased, giving her a quick kiss. Then he winked at the others. "Why else do you think I snapped her up?"

Leah feigned outrage but Olivia could see she was trying not to smile. Things had obviously improved between those two, and whatever rough patch Leah had thought they were experiencing must have been overcome. She was pleased.

"If you keep on like that you'll find yourself out on your ear one of these days," Leah said. "Now stop annoying me and go and get some footage before people start leaving."

"OK, OK, I'm going," he said, and with a final cheeky wink at Olivia and Kate – one that left them panting in his wake – off he went for the camcorder.

"Don't end up taking too much rubbish," Leah called after him. "Short clips of something are better than long clips of nothing." But Josh was already out of earshot. She turned to the others and shook her head. "He's a disaster with that camera. And I know that the fact he has a couple of drinks in him isn't exactly going to improve his camerawork. It's a terrible pity we don't have one of those LCD display things on it, then he might have some idea of the rubbish he's actually filming."

"He seems in good form," Kate commented. "He must be relieved that everything's finally up and running now."

Leah nodded. "Yeah, it's been tough on him, really. I've hardly been at home in the last few weeks. But I think things should settle down a bit after tonight."

"I'll say it before and I'll say it again: Leah Reid, you are one lucky cow," Kate said, shaking her head. "What I wouldn't do . . ."

"Hi, everyone!"

Kate froze instantly while, as if from nowhere, Michael sat down and put a protective arm around her shoulders. "Hey, congratulations, Leah, great party!" He took a sip of his drink, eager to get into the swing of things. "So, what were you saying, just then, love?" he asked his wife. "What wouldn't you do?"

Kate, Olivia and Leah looked at one another and promptly burst out laughing.

Chapter 18

Robin wasn't sure she had heard right. "Are you serious?" she asked, wondering if the oppressive humidity was making her imagine things. There she was, sitting in an eighteenth-floor office on Park Avenue with a view over Central Park most New Yorkers would kill for, and the scary woman sitting across from her had said that her and Ben's little booklet was "a brainwave, a money-spinner, a work of absolute genius".

"But – but it's not even a real book!" Robin interjected, stopping the other woman's enthusiastic rant. "I mean it was just a thought – just a joke, really."

This was all too surreal for words.

It had been weeks since she had provided Kirsty's school with extra copies of *Atchoo the Alligator*, but since then, the school principal had been phoning her on a regular basis to pass on compliments and thanks from some of the children's parents.

"The story's message is getting through," the principal told her. "These parents have been tearing their hair out for years trying to get the kids to help control the condition, and now this book is encouraging them to do it. They'll be forever grateful to you."

One particularly grateful mother had come in the form of Janine Johnston, an employee of Bubblegum Press, a small New York children's publisher with offices on Park Avenue. Immediately recognising the book's potential, and the fact that it had an immediate effect on her young asthmatic son, Janine arranged a meeting with the company's Acquisitions Editor. By the end of following week, Robin discovered that – without ever once having thought about it – she was to become a published author.

"It'll be huge," Marla, the publishing director had enthused, after informing Robin of her plans over the telephone. "The story is simple, accessible, and if we get a good illustrator on board, we could make a real killing here."

"Oh, you don't want to use the same graphics?" Robin had said, wondering how Ben would feel about all this. It was his book, after all. His idea and his hard work that had made the book what it was.

But as it turned out, Ben couldn't care less. "I just downloaded the stuff from some clip-art site on the web," he said, clearly unconcerned about it. "It's your story and if they want to bring in some hotshot illustrator to improve it even more, then all the better!"

Now, listening to Marla outline her plans for

publishing *Atchoo the Alligator*, Robin wondered if this was all a set-up, just another one of Ben's silly practical jokes.

"I've had to rearrange our list so as to get it out by the end of the year. Then we can make a quick killing at Christmas – and also before the rest of them get in on the act."

Robin looked at her blankly.

"The other publishers. If any of them get wind of this thing they'll be in like wildfire with one of their own."

"Oh."

"Now, in order to generate word of mouth we're going to heavily target schools, hospitals, support agencies, places like that. Once we've got a buzz going, then we'll think about blitzing general bookstores and . . ."

Robin let most of Marla's plan of action go over her head. She still couldn't believe that they were offering to publish her little book. How was it possible? Surely, there were hundreds, if not thousands, of children's writers, *any* writers, that were more suitable for this than she was? When she said this to Marla, the publisher laughed.

"Robin, in this game, most of the time, the writing doesn't matter. It's the big idea, honey, the *concept* – forget wizards in boring old boarding schools. This is the next big thing in children's publishing. I can feel it!"

"Well, you're the expert," Robin said, not quite sharing Marla's enthusiasm. *Atchoo* was a cute little story certainly, and Kirsty and her classmates seemed to love it but . . .

"There's more," Marla said, leaning forward and interrupting her thoughts. "David and I had a meeting this morning," David was Bubblegum's MD, "and he wants to take it further, corner the market before the competition jump on the bandwagon." She nodded sardonically out the window. "Once a trend starts on Park Avenue, it won't be long before every publisher on the avenue, and America, follows suit. Bubblegum are determined to keep ahead of the game."

The game? With all this talk of tactics and blitzing, Robin wondered whether publishing was actually some form of elaborate war-game.

She wondered what else was coming.

"We want you to do some more books," Marla said, "cover some more children's problems – things like say *Diabetes Deer*, or *Epilepsy Elephant* or *Asthma Ass*." She laughed, apparently at her own lack of imagination. "Hey, I dunno – you're the creative one here, but, Robin, do you know what percentage of American children suffer from one or other of those ailments I just mentioned? Take peanut allergies . . ."

Robin opened her mouth to speak but Marla plunged on, explaining that apparently the number of children with severe peanut allergies in the US had grown tenfold in a generation.

"It's the most common food allergy, and there's no cure and no means of prevention," she told Robin, who had given up trying to get a word in. "I read only yesterday somewhere that two and a half million Americans now are peanut allergic, and something like five per cent of all children under age six. Several hundred thousand are at risk for life-threatening reactions – talk about a target market! We're sitting on a fortune here, Robin!"

Robin was in two minds. Yes, the thought of writing more stories that might help some of those children appealed to her enormously, but she hated the way the publisher made it all sound so predatory. Marla and the others didn't really care whether the books actually helped – they were just thinking of their admittedly huge target market.

Still, she supposed, business was business, and if *she* didn't do it, then it wouldn't be long before they found someone who would. And this was really too exciting an opportunity to turn down.

"I suppose I could try out a few things and –"

"Great! Let me talk to David – we'll get going on the illustrator, and hopefully, get these babies sold before publication all over Europe, and possibly – hey!" She paused in mid-sentence, eyes widening. "China! That's something I never thought of! Imagine all those Chinese kids with peanut allergies – poor kids, what are they gonna do – don't they put nuts in everything there?" She slammed down the intercom button. "Hey, Bonnie, get me George in Rights on the line when he's finished that conference call – we gotta do something about getting this series to the Chinese!"

It didn't surprise Robin when later over lunch, Marla informed her that before working in the always-dynamic publishing world, she had worked in the even faster-paced New York fashion industry. Apparently, she started work at six-thirty am each morning and didn't leave the office until late that evening, having spent the entire day on the phone to editors, agents and publishers in different countries. Robin didn't know how the woman did it. Some days, Robin could barely summon up the enthusiasm to work nine to five.

"Now, about your advance," Marla began, "I think we're looking at twenty-five per book, and so far we've come up with four possible books, so how about a hundred?" She looked at Robin for affirmation.

A hundred dollars for a couple of evenings' work? Robin was hardly listening. A story about an epileptic elephant had already began to form in her mind and –

"And then say six, seven per cent on royalties, plus seventy per cent advance on any foreign rights, plus the initial hundred grand advance and . . . oh, I don't know, Robin, I think you'd better get yourself an agent." The publisher drained her coffee mug with a flourish.

Robin sat rooted to the chair. Did Marla say . . . did she really *mean* . . . were they seriously offering her a hundred *thousand* dollars for these simple little stories? This was *definitely* one of Ben's elaborate jokes.

But Marla didn't look at all like she was joking. She was now looking distractedly at her Rolex, apparently eager to get this meeting over and done with so she could flit off to the next 'big thing' in publishing.

"So what do you say, Robin?" Marla asked her impatiently. "Are you gonna come on board with us, or what?"

Chapter 19

If Olivia wasn't careful, she really was in grave danger of turning into a serial curtain-twitcher. But she just couldn't help it. How could she *not* look when the house was right across the green and the front door was plainly visible from her desk and her couch? It was only natural that any movement outside the window – be it at Matt's house or elsewhere – would catch her eye, wasn't it?

"Olivia, when did you re-arrange the furniture?" her mother asked, her brow furrowing as she sank into her favourite armchair, which was usually in a nice spot in front of the telly, but was now positioned back to the window – where the sofa used to be.

"Oh, I saw something similar on *Changing Rooms* and I just thought it might make the room a lot bigger."

"I don't think so, dear – in fact I think it makes everything a lot more cluttered. Why on earth would you put the sofa facing the window like that? I know there's only the two of you but . . ."

Olivia gritted her teeth. Shit, she'd have to move it all back – otherwise her mother would go on and on about it and typically, using her famous powers of deduction (and perhaps a quick chat with Ellie), would eventually discern that the rather odd realignment of Olivia's furniture was not some elaborate attempt at feng shui, but because she needed a vantage point for keeping an eye on the family across the green.

"I suppose you're right. I just wanted to try something different for a while, that's all."

Just then Ellie stormed through the doorway, Olivia's mobile phone clutched in her right hand. "A message, Mummy!" she declared excitedly.

A waste of time, more like, Olivia thought. No doubt it was yet another of those messages that would tell her that she was the lucky winner of a million euro, but in order to claim her prize she would need to phone this number and stay on hold until she was old and grey. They were the only kind of text messages she got. When Olivia wanted to communicate with someone, she preferred a good old-fashioned chat and most of her friends, having many times endured her painfully slow attempts at texting usually gave in and just phoned her. In fact, Leah was the only one who had sent her a text recently – apart from . . .

"Give it here, pet." Olivia reached for the handset, and her heart raced as she stared the number displayed. There was no mistaking it – Olivia had it almost memorised by now. It was him! It was definitely him! Matt had sent her a message!

Unless, she thought, panic rising as she thought about it, unless it was the wife warning her off! But how would the wife know anything? Even more, Olivia thought, what was there to know? Nothing really – apart from the fact that she had a stupid schoolgirl crush on her husband, it had all been totally innocent, not to mention that 'it' probably only existed in Olivia's own warped little mind.

"Is something wrong?" her mother enquired.

"No, nothing wrong," she replied, trying to keep her voice even. "Just one of those silly 'you've won a big prize' messages." She stood up, anxious to read the message in privacy – whatever it might say. "I'm making a cuppa – want one?"

"But we just finished one – Olivia, what is the matter with you? You really are behaving very strangely lately!"

"There's nothing wrong, Mum – I just fancy another cup, all right?"

"Fine, fine, sorry I said anything."

Phone in hand, Olivia almost pranced into the kitchen. Her hands shook as she pressed *read* and almost as soon as she had, the thought struck her that Matt might once again have mistakenly sent her a message, perhaps another one destined for his business partner.

That was probably it, she thought, her spirits deflating at the thought of it.

But then, her heart leaped as she read the words.

"Can I come over? Need to ask you something."

Olivia read and reread it at least five times. He wanted to come over! Shit, shit, how was she going to get rid of her mother? Eva would be terribly put out – it had been ages since they'd spent some time together and . . .

No, think about it, this *could* very well be a message to his business partner. She sent a tentative message back to him, which seemed to take her all of five minutes to type. *"Matt, Olivia here. Did you mean to send this to me?"*

Now, that wasn't too bad, was it? She hadn't said yes or no, hadn't referred to the message at all really, and if it turned out that he had indeed sent it by mistake, well then she hadn't gone and made an eejit of herself by gleefully answering back and coming across like an eager beaver. Now all she had to do was wait.

It was as though an eternity passed until she got a reply.

"Yes! Definitely meant to send to you but sorry. Can see why you thought that. Can I?" Then the phone beeped again. *"Please?"*

Olivia was grinning from ear to ear. She'd replied before she had time to think about it, her fingers dashing across the keys in an unusual display of text-dexterity. *"Give me twenty mins – c u soon."*

"Mum, I'm afraid I have to go out," she said, coming back into the living-room and trying hard not to betray the fact that she was almost delirious with excitement.

"Oh?" Eva raised an eyebrow. "Anything serious?"

"No – it's just – no – one of the mums from Ellie's

231

playgroup. Her daughter isn't well and she's asked if I'd do some shopping for her."

"Shopping? It's almost eight in the evening."

"Well, she lives near Cornelscourt. I can go there for late-night shopping." Good thinking, she thought, congratulating herself. "But I might be a while."

"Oh. Well, I'm in no rush home anyway – why don't you head away now and I'll look after Ellie while you're gone?"

"No . . . I mean, the thing is, she really wants Ellie to come visit her, so I'm taking Ellie with me."

"But it's almost Ellie's bedtime! And if the child is ill, I really don't think it would be a good idea to expose Ellie to . . ." Seeing her daughter's expression, Eva gave up. "All right then, I'll have to come and see you some other time. It's a pity really. I was looking forward to a nice evening in together, just the three us. I feel like I haven't seen you in ages."

Immediately, Olivia felt guilty. This wasn't right. She shouldn't be shooing her mother away so that she could make way for some man – a man that wasn't even a decent prospect. Her mother would be horrified if she thought that the one man Olivia had been able to think about romantically after Peter happened to be married to somebody else. As much as she knew her mother would love to see her settled, Olivia was very much aware that Eva, or indeed her father, really wouldn't appreciate this scenario.

"Look, why don't I call over tomorrow morning?" she said. "Maybe we can head into town and do a bit of shopping or something? I'm sure Ellie would enjoy that."

"Yes, do that," her mother said, and with some relief Olivia saw that she was getting up to leave.

Hopefully, Matt wouldn't arrive before she left, otherwise Eva would be very suspicious indeed.

But she needn't have worried. Matt arrived a good half hour after Eva left, and to Olivia's utter surprise presented her with a bunch of brightly coloured gerberas.

"What's this for?" Olivia said, blushing, and glancing worriedly towards the house across the way. What was he doing bringing her flowers like this? Wasn't he being a bit obvious? Then her heart sank. Obviously, Matt had no intention of taking Olivia in his arms and asking her to consider a raging affair, not when he was so casually arriving on her doorstep with a big bunch of flowers in full view of the entire green!

"You'd better let me in or people will start talking," he said, his eyes twinkling with amusement. If Olivia didn't know better, she could have sworn he had read her thoughts just then.

"Oh, of course." She stood back to let him into the hall and, as she did, the unmistakeable scent of Paco Rabanne XS aftershave assaulted her nostrils. In that instant, thousands of memories raced through her brain – it was the same brand Peter used to wear.

"So, where's Ellie?" Matt asked, looking around her living-room with interest. "Hey, nice room, although Catherine seems to think the sofa looks better against the window. I quite like it like this though."

"Does she indeed?" Olivia had no interest in the interior-design skills of his feckless wife, nor did she need reminding of her existence. Matt obviously wasn't here for a night of illicit passion then. "Ellie's in bed. So, would you like a drink or a cup of coffee or . . . ?" she asked him, feeling annoyed all of a sudden. If he wasn't here to persuade her into having an affair with him – and seeing how enticing he looked just then in a pair of dark Levis and a tightly fitting khaki T-shirt, he wouldn't have to do too much persuading – what the hell *was* he here for?

"A beer would be great, if you have one," he answered, and to Olivia's amazement he jauntily followed her into the kitchen. She rummaged in the back of the fridge.

"I don't drink beer myself but there should be something here left over from our last barbecue. My friend Josh drinks Carlsberg so . . ." She trailed off, sensing Matt's presence directly behind her and hoping that the cool of the fridge would help soothe her flushed cheeks. What was he doing here?

"Ah, there's still a few here," she said, locating some cans of beer. She closed the fridge door behind her and, without looking at him, offered him a beer.

"So, what is it that you wanted to ask me?" she said, leaning against the kitchen worktop and trying to keep her voice light. Sensing she might need it, she was about to open a can for herself when . . .

"Olivia, I think you and I both know there's something going on here," Matt blurted out.

"I'm sorry?" was all she could say, but her insides

leapt. She knew it! It wasn't her imagination after all – he did have feelings for her too!

Now he was moving towards her. "I don't really know how to say this, but I've never met a woman like you."

Olivia gulped, unable to believe what she was hearing.

"I haven't been able to look, to even *think* about another woman in the last few years, but with you – with you it's different."

Oh no, Olivia said silently. Don't do this. Don't ruin it with clichés about how your wife doesn't understand you, and how you think you married too young and all the rest of it. The feelings she was having for Matt – although clearly wrong – were still very real and she did not want to feel as though she was in an episode of some pathetic soap opera. Had Leah been right about him after all? Was Matt just another faithless married man, eager to hop in the sack with any poor misfortunate who happened to be taken in by his charms?

"I don't know, it was weird, but after that first time, after that stupid text message thing, I just – I just couldn't stop thinking about you." He shook his head. "God, I know that sounds pathetic, but it's true! And then when I realised you lived here I –"

"You thought, great – nice and handy to be able to just pop over the green for a bit of nookie when the wife's away? After all, if she's at it – why not you?" The words were out before Olivia could stop herself, and she barely noticed him shrink backwards, his expression shocked. For some reason, the way Matt – a *married* man – had expressed his interest so casually really annoyed her. Despite the fact that Olivia was clearly interested in him too, she was disappointed. Somehow she'd thought more of him – expected more of him. And then, she knew she had no intention of having a seedy affair with this man. Whatever about Matt's own circumstances, or the problems he might be having in his marriage, she just wasn't going to do it; she wasn't going to be part of it. The love she and Peter had had was much too important to be cheapened now by a seedy affair with a married man. Yes, she was attracted to Matt Sheridan, unbelievably so, but this wasn't right!

Matt was now sitting at the kitchen table, his face white. "I don't know what you're talking about. I never said anything about having an affair . . . while . . . while my wife's away . . ."

"What?" For a second, Olivia panicked. "But – but I thought – well, what was all that 'I couldn't stop thinking about you' business then?" She hadn't misread the situation, had she? Because if she had, she didn't think she would ever be able to show her face outside the door again. How embarrassing! But then, what did he mean when he said –

"Olivia, my wife is dead," he stated flatly.

She stared at him, shocked. Was there no end to his tricks?

"What? What are you talking about?" she said, her voice dropping to a whisper. "Didn't I see her before,

236

calling you from the house, telling you you had a phone call?"

Matt shook his head, and then he smiled slightly. "I suppose it could have looked that way but ... Olivia ..." He sat forward now, obviously understanding her earlier over-the-top reaction. "Catherine is not my wife. She's Adam's childminder, my wife's best friend. Natasha died two years ago in a car accident."

"What?" Now Olivia didn't know what to think. "You live with your childminder?"

Matt was smiling broadly now. "No, no, I don't live there at all. Adam and I have an apartment, not far from here, in Dundrum. We spent a lot of time here – well, because there isn't much space in an apartment for a child of his age to run around. I've been looking for a house, but work is so busy and ..."

Olivia's mind raced as she slumped into the chair across from him. "But – before, in the garden – Adam said he wanted his mummy ..."

"It's just something he says, usually when I speak to other women, strange women."

"Seriously?"

"Seriously. His mum's still very much a part of his life. I've made sure of that. She died when he was two years old but yet he seems to remember her. Of course, the apartment is full of photographs and we watch a lot of home videos ..." His voice trailed off, his green eyes full of emotion. "I'm sorry. It's still hard sometimes."

"I can imagine." This was awful – what must he think of her?

"Better than most, too," Matt said. "The woman in the corner shop, she told me all about you – and how you're alone now too."

"Did she?" Obviously, Molly was up to her matchmaking tricks again, although this time, Olivia thought with a smile, she couldn't say she was too upset.

"I'm sorry, I wasn't looking to pry or anything but –"

"It's fine," she said, waving a hand dismissively. "I know Molly has a bit of a mouth on her."

Matt spoke softly. "So, I know what it's like – I know it isn't easy."

"No, it isn't." She didn't want to talk about this, not here, not now, not with him. "But I'm fine now. I'm over it."

"It isn't easy on your own. Parenting, I mean."

Olivia shook her head. "It was difficult in the early days, certainly, but my friends and family were great – I don't know what I would have done without them."

"I don't know about you, but in a way I think having Adam to worry about helped me a little. I couldn't be selfish, I couldn't retreat into myself because I had him to think about."

"I know what you mean." She looked away sadly.

"Listen," Matt said, standing up and moving towards her. "I didn't come here so that we could stir up painful memories of our respective spouses."

She nodded and was about to say something, but before she could open her mouth, Matt had taken her hand in his.

"As I was saying earlier, I've been on my own for over two years now, and in all that time I haven't even looked at another woman. Yet, since I first met you . . ."

Olivia looked into his beautiful, earnest eyes and knew that this was something special. Everything she had wished for, had hoped for these last few weeks was now happening to her, and yet despite her exhilaration she felt – frightened.

But Matt seemed to understand. "Look, I could be making a fool of myself here. Maybe I've been misreading the signs, maybe you don't feel like I think you feel. But, Olivia, I think you do, and with all you've been through – with all we've *both* been through – I think that you're also a little afraid. But that's perfectly normal, because I feel that way too." With that, he reached upwards and tenderly tucked a tendril of hair behind her ear. "What do you think?"

That simple gesture, the faint touch on her skin, had at that moment the effect of removing all reason, all thought from Olivia's mind. "I think," she said, putting her arms around Matt's neck and reaching forward for a much-longed-for kiss, "I think we might be on to something here."

Chapter 20

"I'm so pleased for you!" Leah grinned. "He seems really, really nice."

The following Saturday, Leah had called over to Olivia's for lunch and Matt had been there when she arrived. She very quickly gave him the once-over, before deciding that he was perfect for Olivia.

All that week, Olivia had been walking on air and she couldn't keep the smile from her face. That first night, she and Matt had talked well into the night and it was almost dawn by the time he'd left the house.

From her doorway, Olivia had watched him sneak like a sixteen-year-old schoolboy across the green and back to Catherine's house. That was an odd scenario, that was for sure, she thought, closing the door behind her and heading upstairs, hoping for an hour or two's sleep before Ellie woke. She couldn't help feeling a mixture of guilt and relief at the fact that her daughter was a very heavy sleeper and it was very unlikely she would have heard anything. Hopefully.

Matt had told her that he, Catherine, and his wife Natasha had known one another for years, having all grown up in the same area of Dublin together. Catherine wasn't married, apparently.

"She's the type that's having way too much fun to ever get married!" he said with a laugh. "But she's been great – great to me, great to Adam. I really don't know what I would have done without her. I suppose she's the only one who understands what it's like. She loved Tash as much as I did. She was bridesmaid at our wedding, godmother at Adam's christening, you know the type."

"So, she looks after Adam while you're at work?" Olivia asked.

"Yes, she's great with kids, really great."

"She must be," Olivia said, impressed. "By the way, I never asked, what is it exactly that you do? I remember that day after the text fiasco," she rolled her eyes, "that day we first met, you had just clinched a major deal?"

"Ah yes, that must have been the Big One," he said, smiling at the memory.

"Big One?"

"Yeah, a new apartment complex – in Bulgaria. I'm a property consultant, an overseas property consultant. Not an estate agent as such, rather our agency helps find suitable investment properties for Irish clients overseas. We used to do a lot of stuff in Spain and Portugal but the market's saturated now and there's no value to be had there any more. These days we concentrate only on emerging markets." He smiled. "The Bulgarian developer had just given us sole agency in Ireland, which was a huge boost and . . . sorry, I'm probably boring you."

Olivia smiled. "Not at all. It's very interesting actually, although I always pictured you overseas property guys as small, heavy, and sporting a nice tangerine glow from all that time spent in the sun."

Now, Leah wrinkled her nose when Olivia told her this. "He seems nothing like those Costa del Dosh types."

"He's not. As you said yourself, he is really, really nice," Olivia beamed at her friend. Then she threw a short glance over her shoulder checking to see if Ellie was within earshot. "Although I still don't like saying too much in front of –"

"Mommy, where's Matt gone?" Ellie piped up from behind. She had run downstairs and was holding a still-wet colourful painting, the paint splattered all over her hands and cheeks.

"He had to go home," Olivia said, filling the kettle with water. "And he said to say goodbye, but he didn't want to interrupt you while you were painting."

"But I wanted to show him my picture," she cried mournfully.

Leah raised an eyebrow. "This Matt seems *very* popular."

"Don't worry – he'll be back later this evening," Olivia told her.

"Goodie! Is Adam coming too?"

Olivia grinned. "Yes, Adam's coming too. Now go and wash all that paint off your hands – we're having lunch soon, and then we'll go and put your picture on the grave, OK?"

"OK, Mommy!" Ellie dutifully rushed back upstairs to the bathroom.

Olivia rolled her eyes. "It'll take forever to get that stuff off her clothes, but she seems to love arts and crafts and, to be honest, it's great for keeping her quiet." She gave a faraway smile. "Peter was the same – always good with his hands."

Leah sat down at the kitchen table. "She seems to have taken to Matt in a big way. And judging by that silly grin on your face, her mum seems to have taken to him in a big way too."

"He's great," Olivia said with a smile. "And yes, Ellie is crazy about him."

Leah paused slightly. "And have you told him . . . about Peter, I mean?"

Olivia's expression clouded. "Not the whole story. Although, apparently Molly from the shop said something to him," she added, and Leah raised an eyebrow. "Ah, she can be a bit of a matchmaker, and probably thought she was doing me a favour. He's told me all about his wife and how she died, but I just can't bring myself to tell him my sad stories."

Leah shook her head. "I suppose it's a bit early all the same. Still, Matt seems lovely and I really hope you're not stalling because you still blame yourself. Despite what you think, you really aren't to blame –"

"Of course, I'm to blame, Leah – who else is there to blame for the fact that Ellie doesn't have her father?" Olivia stood up and looked out the window and into the back garden, her eyes tired and sad.

Leah grimaced, sorry she had brought the subject up. "I really thought you had come to terms with it all by now," she said softly.

"Oh, I had, in a way, but all this with Matt now . . . I suppose it just brings it all back."

"Well then, you should explain everything to him – and quickly."

"I know that, but it's still difficult for me to talk about it – and to a complete stranger as such. I've only known Matt for a little while. I don't want him to think I'm irresponsible, and I don't want him to blame me too."

Leah gritted her teeth. "Olivia, you are not irresponsible, and you're the best parent I know. You've done a fantastic job in raising Ellie without Peter and, unlike Matt, you don't have someone helping you out like he does with his friend Catherine – quite the opposite! Speaking of which, have you heard from Peter's parents recently?"

Olivia shook her head. "Not for a little while, but in a way, I'm glad. It only confuses Ellie. She goes up to Galway for weekends and when she comes back it's all Daddy this and Daddy that. She doesn't really understand."

"Still, as you said yourself, you can't pretend Peter never existed."

"I know that, but I'm the one that has to make all the excuses and explanations, while Teresa and Jim just spoil her rotten." Tears sprang to her eyes. "They've always blamed me too, you know."

Leah shook her head. "I'm sure that's not true and, if they do, they're idiots."

"Yes, but they loved him and now he's gone."

Leah looked sideways at her. "I haven't seen you like this in a long time."

"I haven't *felt* like this in a long time, to be honest," Olivia replied sadly. "But now, by getting involved with Matt, all the feelings I thought I'd buried are being forced to the surface again, whether I like it or not. When Matt wants to know what happened, I'll have to face it all again, won't I?"

"That would have to happen no matter who you got involved with – or when," Leah said kindly. "And I think you and I both know that no matter how much you loved and miss Peter, you have to move on eventually."

"But am I doing the right thing?" Olivia asked, panicking now, wondering if she was being silly thinking she could have a relationship with Matt Sheridan. He was a nice guy and, yes, it seemed as though they got on very well and had lots in common, but what would he think once he knew everything?

"I think you're doing the right thing," Leah said, standing up and putting a comforting arm around her friend's shoulder. "And I also think it's time you moved on. What you had with Peter is long gone, Olivia, you know that, and you've suffered enough. Now, you have to make the most of what you do have, and look to the future."

Olivia thought about it; she had thought about it many times over the last few days. She *did* have to move on and come to terms with the fact that Peter wasn't coming back.

"You're right," she said, brightening a little as she turned to face her friend. "You're so right. I've spent way too long suffering over this. It's about time Ellie and I moved on."

Chapter 21

Early the following week, Kate gave birth to a baby boy, and Olivia, Leah and little Ellie went to visit the new mum at the hospital.

Leah had been unprepared for the sight of poor Kate in the hospital bed. She looked ravaged, drained, and certainly not the sharp, lively Kate she'd been before and all throughout the pregnancy.

Kate watched with tired eyes as Olivia and Ellie cooed over baby Dylan, Leah standing slightly away and watching from a safe distance. Since she'd come to terms with the fact that she was never having any children of her own, she usually preferred to keep her distance. Otherwise, she might start feeling things she knew she shouldn't.

"I love the name," Olivia said, smiling at the new mum. "He's a beautiful little baby, an adorable little thing. And I can't believe how much he looks like you!"

"Yeah, he's gorgeous, Kate." Seeing her friend smile proudly at the compliment, Leah didn't want to admit out loud that, wisps of red hair aside, this baby looked like every other baby she had ever seen, red-faced, wrinkly, and she supposed, cute in a cabbage-patch-kid kind of way. She couldn't really understand how anyone could see a parental resemblance at this early stage. The child could have been Amanda Clarke's for all Leah could tell.

As if he could read Leah's thoughts, Dylan let out an ungodly wail.

"Oh dear," she said, stepping away from the baby's crib, resisting the urge to put her hands over her ears.

"Please tell me it gets easier, Olivia," Kate groaned, reaching across for him. "He hasn't stopped crying since he arrived."

"Look, let me – you take it easy for a while," Olivia said, deftly lifting Dylan out of the crib and leaning him over one shoulder. She rubbed his back gently. "Of course, it'll get easier. You two are just getting used to one another at the moment, that's all. Give it a day or two and he'll be fine."

As if on cue, Dylan stopped crying and Kate's eyes widened in disbelief.

"Wow, how the hell did you manage that?"

Olivia winked. "Fluke," she said, as Dylan gurgled peacefully over her shoulder.

"Well, do you think you could get a bed in here beside me for a while? After all I've been through, I could certainly do with a break." As she repositioned herself on the bed, Kate winced.

"So how was it?" Leah asked, bluntly. "You know," she nodded downwards and then at Dylan. "Honestly."

"Are you sure you want to know?"

"Of course. I find these things interesting." Leah sat eagerly on one side of the hospital bed.

Kate looked at Olivia, who smiled softly.

"Don't look to me for inspiration. I can barely remember it at this stage."

"So you *do* actually forget – thank God for that. Because I've already told Michael there is no *way* I'm having another one after all that, no bloody way!"

"Oh, come on, it couldn't be that bad, could it?" Leah said, sceptically. "Otherwise no one would *ever* go through it."

Kate gave her a sideways glance. "Not that bad?"

"Well, it couldn't be as bad as they make out in films and television anyway, could it?" Leah laughed. "You said it yourself, Kate. You said you thought the difficulties of pregnancy were completely exaggerated. You took it all in your stride!"

"I was nothing but an idiot who got her comeuppance in the end." Kate replied dryly.

"That bad?" Olivia was sympathetic.

"Worse. If I had had a gun beside me at the time, I would have cheerfully blown my head off."

"No way."

"*Yes, way.*"

"But it couldn't have been *that* bad, not in this day and age surely," Leah was unconvinced. "What about the epidural?"

"As far as I'm concerned, whoever invented that so-called *pain*killer should be taken out and shot. Then he'd know all about pain. It doesn't really kill the pain; it just numbs the intensity."

"Well, that's something surely," Leah replied.

"Not when you've already been suffering for hours on end."

Olivia laughed quietly. "Poor Kate! And you were the one who thought you were ready for anything."

"I *was* ready for anything and I thought I was ready for this. But it was *unbelievable* – really the worst agony imaginable – and by being so bloody blasé about the whole thing beforehand, I reckon the Man Upstairs thought to himself 'Right, this one deserves everything she gets!'"

Leah tittered. "Well, at least you can joke about it now!"

"Oh, don't you be fooled," Kate shook her head. "It was certainly no joking matter. I've always suffered the most horrific period pains and stupidly, *naively*, I thought 'I'm used to this. I can handle this. Don't I already know what I'm dealing with?' Boy, was I kidding myself!" She turned to Leah. "Put it this way, at one stage I felt as though this baby was going to turn me inside out and, if they hadn't cut me, I'm pretty sure he would have."

"Oh, God, Kate, shut up, shut up, *shut up*!" Leah put her hands to her ears, and crossed her legs determinedly.

Olivia laughed. "Yep, I think I remember that feeling."

"And the funny thing is," Kate went on, "Michael arrived in this morning with bits and pieces for the baby and, wait for it – a bunch of bananas. I said to him, 'Why are you bringing me those? The food's great here and anyway I don't even like bananas.' And he said to me, serious as you like, 'Kate, don't you know that bananas are full of potassium and potassium will help your stitches heal more quickly?'"

"Stitches! Oh my God, please, please, stop!" Leah was now crossing her legs even tighter. "I get the message, it was bad, it was bloody bad, you poor thing! Now I've said I feel sorry for you, so can we stop this bloody discussion – please!"

Olivia and Kate laughed out loud, and in that instant, Leah felt much happier and more certain than ever that she and Josh had made a *very* sensible decision.

Chapter 22

Olivia was sure she was being watched. It was a strange sensation really, and something she couldn't quite put her finger on, but she was almost positive of it. She'd felt it the other day when she and Ellie were heading out to visit Kate at the hospital, and she'd had the really weird feeling that someone somewhere was watching her every move.

She didn't like it, not when this area was normally so quiet, and people generally left her alone. She gave a slight glance towards Catherine's house, suddenly feeling guilty and understanding what it must have felt like when she was peeping out her window at them! Olivia grimaced. What did Matt's friend think of their relationship, she wondered.

"She'll be mad about you!" Matt had enthused one evening when Olivia made cautious enquiries about Catherine. But judging by the way Matt spoke about her before, Olivia really wasn't sure if this would be the case.

"She can be quite protective, but only because she has Adam's best interests at heart. She gave up her job to look after him, you know. She managed a fashion boutique in Grafton Street, had been there since school. She supported me so much when Natasha died, and I don't think I can ever let her know how much I appreciate that."

"Wow, she gave up her job to do that for you?" Olivia replied, remembering how tough it was for her in the early days looking after Ellie on her own, and trying to come to terms with the fact that her life had changed utterly. She wondered sometimes if things would have been easier had she not had Ellie to look after. She could have just thrown herself into her work, into helping others and trying not to think about the one she didn't help.

But Catherine, who had no family attachments to Adam, had made a hell of a sacrifice to give up her career in order to stay at home and look after him.

"So, how did she manage to buy here in Cherrytree?" she asked tentatively, not wishing to pry too much. This was a mature and well sought-after estate and houses here wouldn't come cheap.

"I'll admit I helped out," Matt said. "She had a place of her own – a gorgeous apartment in town, but was always saying that she'd love a house – that it would be more appropriate for Adam. I couldn't argue with that – it's been brilliant for him to have a back garden to play in and a bit of space. She got a good sum for her place and I gave her a few quid towards the deposit for this one. Because she's not working, and she had to get a little extra from the bank after the sale of her own, I went guarantor on the mortgage for her." He shrugged. "It's nothing to me and I suppose it was my way of saying thank you."

"You two must be very close," Olivia ventured carefully, wondering why on earth a young attractive woman with the world at her feet had more or less stepped into the role vacated by Matt's wife, at least in terms of looking after Adam and admittedly looking after Matt. He seemed adamant that they were just childhood friends, and their relationship became galvanised even more by the death of Matt's wife. Still, Olivia couldn't help wondering if there was, or ever had been, anything else between them.

"She's great," Matt said, interrupting her thoughts. "She adores Adam, would do anything for him."

"And did you two ever . . . ?" Olivia felt like a heel for even suggesting it when she saw Matt's expression cloud over.

"Of course not," he said sharply. "She was Natasha's best friend."

"Of course." Olivia wasn't sure what that meant, but she suspected that he and Catherine had loved Natasha too much to betray her memory like that.

Still, Olivia had to admit that she found it all very strange, and she wouldn't mind meeting this Catherine, who seemed to have sacrificed quite a lot of her own life to accommodate a simple friendship. Then, she all of a sudden remembered the young guy sneaking – well, in retrospect she had only *imagined* he was sneaking – out of Catherine's house that morning a while back. She was making too much of this – Catherine might be a very good-looking girl who was being supportive to her friend, but she obviously wasn't living like a nun either.

Anyway, Olivia decided now, didn't she do well out of the relationship too – what with her own house in a lovely area, and little to do other than look after a young child? Of course, her life was still her own and no doubt she had plenty of time and opportunity to *have* a life of her own. Olivia was just being silly, and now that she and Matt were a couple, she really should make the effort to get to know Catherine.

And, of course, if Catherine was such a good friend and as lovely and obliging as Matt was saying, then Olivia was sure that the two of them would get on like a house on fire.

Chapter 23

The following Friday evening, Catherine was banging pots and pans around the kitchen as if she was rehearsing for a kitchen-utensil recital. Stupid *bastard*! What was he playing at, inviting *her* over here for dinner? How dare he flaunt the bitch in front of her! Was he toying with her now – was that it? Well, he could go sing – Catherine wasn't going to lie down without a fight – not this time. After all those nights he'd spent crying on her shoulder, telling her that he loved her and didn't know what he would do without her, and then, at the first opportunity, he goes and takes up with some dizzy bitch from across the road!

Catherine couldn't comprehend the hurt she'd felt when Matt didn't seem at all bothered that she was seeing Rory, the manager of the video store.

"I'm so pleased for you," he'd said. "It's not easy to find someone these days and he seems like a nice guy.

Probably worth a few quid too," he added mischievously. Then he went on to say that he had always been concerned that their close friendship might prevent Catherine from finding a partner, that their heavy involvement in one another's lives might be a stumbling block to her independence.

Catherine couldn't believe it – it was as though he was *happy* she'd found someone, almost as though he was now free to go off pursuing other women – women like dumpy Olivia!

How could she have got it so wrong? She'd been so sure that seeing her all dressed up and ready for a night out with some man, someone that wasn't Matt, would make him realise what he was missing. But no, he didn't seem at all bothered about it – in fact, he had collected Adam and without a care in the world had simply toddled off across the road to *her* house. Yes, Rory was a nice enough guy, very charming and very flash with the cash, but really, he had nothing on Matt. Still, she supposed, in her eyes, there wasn't another man alive who could live up to the incomparable Matt.

How could he not see it? How could Matt not realise that they were perfect for one another – that she, Catherine, could give him all the love he needed and more? She didn't presume to replace Natasha, Catherine would *never* dream of that, but since Natasha died she had dedicated her life to helping Matt cope with his grief, helping him and Adam to move on. How could he not see that? How could he not understand that the three of them shared something special – something that could not, or *should* not, be torn apart by some other woman?

Granted, this Olivia seemed to have a lot in common with Matt – she had suffered the death of her own husband and had also raised a child on her own. Was this what attracted Matt to her, she wondered? Was it the fact that he felt some kind of empathy for her situation? Catherine didn't know. All she knew was that she was not going to let some desperate widow from across the road come between her and her happiness. Olivia would soon find out that the course of her and Matt's apparent 'true love' wasn't going to run smooth.

At all.

"Your house is gorgeous, Catherine," Olivia said pleasantly, looking around the living-room. "You have a much better grasp of interior design than I have, I can tell you!" She gave a weak laugh, feeling more nervous about meeting this woman than she cared to admit. She took another gulp from the glass of white wine Matt had put into her hand when she had first arrived, only then realising that, in her nervousness, she was drinking it too fast.

For some reason, Matt had invited her to dinner at Catherine's house tonight, insisting that she loved every opportunity to show off her terrific culinary skills. In truth, Olivia thought, it was weird that Matt would so casually issue an invitation to his friend's house, rather than to his own, but she wasn't about to say anything.

Catherine's taste in clothes wasn't too bad either, she thought, feeling rather self-conscious in her plain attire of jeans and ordinary black woollen jumper compared to Catherine's colourful off-the-shoulder top and flirty short skirt.

Judging by her slim figure and flawlessly applied make-up, Catherine obviously looked after herself, and because of this Olivia couldn't quite put an age on her. She suspected though, that she could be close to her mid-thirties.

"I'm really pleased to meet you," she said, when Catherine didn't make much of a reply to her complimentary remarks about the house.

"Pleased to meet you too," Catherine answered, although there was little warmth in her tone.

She walked immediately into the kitchen and, although she hadn't been asked to, Olivia followed tentatively, hoping that Matt would soon return from settling the kids. Lately, Adam and Ellie had become firm friends, and were largely inseparable. Catherine didn't seem to mind their playing in another room while the adults had dinner.

"Matt has been telling me all about you, and how great you are with Adam," Olivia ventured pleasantly.

Catherine continued busying herself with the dinner preparations as if Olivia wasn't even there.

"To be perfectly honest, I do feel bad about your having to do the cooking." Olivia knew she was babbling but still felt she had to fill the silence. "We could have gone out somewhere to save you all the effort but Matt insisted . . ." She trailed off, wondering what was wrong with Catherine. The way Matt went on, Olivia had thought that the woman wouldn't hear of them having dinner anywhere else!

"Not at all – I enjoy cooking for Matt," Catherine said, with a hint of a smile.

"Well, do you need any help at all?"

"I have everything under control, thanks." Catherine continued opening cupboards and drawers, leaving Olivia standing in the middle of the kitchen like some kind of spare tool.

Again, she wondered what to say next, but luckily didn't have to for much longer as just then Matt reappeared from settling the children.

"How's everything going? Anything I can do?"

Catherine exhaled deeply and wiped her brow with the back of her hand. "If you could finish setting the table, and look after the drinks, it would be a huge help," she said with a grateful sigh.

Great, Olivia thought, piqued that the woman had rejected her offer to help. Now, it looked as though *she* was some ingrate, expecting to be waited on hand and foot!

"I'll set the table if you like," she offered and Matt gave her a warm smile.

"No, no, you go and sit down," Catherine waved her away in the manner of someone swatting a fly. "Matt and I will take care of everything. Matt, why don't you fill up Olivia's glass for her? It's almost empty."

Olivia flushed and did as she was bid, silently annoyed at what was an obvious dig about the wine, and the fact that Catherine had somehow managed to make her look like Lady Muck in front of Matt.

Soon after, dinner was served, and Matt and Catherine joined Olivia at the table.

"Is Adam OK where he is?" Catherine asked, letting her long blonde hair fall loose from its clip and taking a dainty sip from her wineglass. She was one very attractive woman, Olivia thought, feeling downright dowdy sitting alongside her.

"He and Ellie are sitting entranced by some DVD or other," Matt answered, his mouth full.

"Well, as long as they stay entranced until we've finished eating, I'll be happy," Olivia laughed, eager to relax the obvious tension.

Catherine frowned slightly. "Do you let Ellie watch television all the time then, Olivia?"

Olivia tensed, immediately realising that she had said something wrong. Surely the woman wasn't casting aspersions on her parenting skills?

"No, of course not. I merely meant that it would be nice for us all to get to know one another and have a bit of a chat in peace."

"So, Ellie can be a bit disruptive then," Catherine said, spooning cheesy potato gratin onto her plate. The way she said it, it was more of a statement than a question.

"Well no, it's just – as I'm sure you know yourself, kids are kids, and at that age –"

"We don't let Adam away with any of that carry-on, do we, Matt?" Catherine interjected, glancing sideways at him.

"Certainly not." Eyes wide, Matt shook his head. "Adam's generally very well-behaved, but he knows full well that he'd get a good slap on the behind if he started acting up in front of either of us."

Olivia didn't know what to say. Was this turning into a conversation about parental discipline?

"Well, Ellie knows that too, of course, but you know when kids get together . . ." Olivia trailed off as she poured the dregs of the wine bottle into her glass. For a moment there was a strained silence, and then Matt stood up from the table and went to the fridge. *Great,* Olivia thought, mentally kicking herself for taking the last of the wine. *Now I look like a bloody lush!*

"I really can't understand why some parents feel it's wrong to give a child a smack if he or she steps out of line," Catherine said, smiling appreciatively at Matt as he opened the bottle. "Although I suppose, in your case," she went on, "it must be difficult to find a balance, what with your being on your own and all that."

Olivia's heart thudded against her chest. How was she supposed to answer that one?

"I'm sure I'm not the only parent who finds it difficult to find a balance, but of course I have no problem at all with disciplining Ellie when she's bold.

Having said that, I don't need to do it very often because she *is* a good kid and –"

"I suppose television is great for keeping her quiet all the same," Catherine interjected as if Ellie was only good because of this.

"Yes, Ellie does watch quite a lot of telly, doesn't she?" Matt was helping himself to some of Catherine's immaculately prepared roast lamb. The woman had even added a sprig of bloody rosemary to each plate, Olivia noticed. Talk about attention to detail!

"Not really – it's just the few times you've called –"

"I really feel exercise at a young age is so important for a child," Catherine interjected, as if Olivia hadn't spoken. "I take Adam for a good walk in the park most days – time much better spent than sitting on his backside in front of the box. It's habit-forming and hopefully he'll grow up a much healthier child as a result."

Matt smiled. "Catherine's an out-and-out exercise advocate, aren't you?"

"Oh, definitely," she said. "I love a good stint at the gym and I know I'm certainly not going to stay a size ten by sitting on my ass watching *Eastenders*!" She laughed. "And at our age, we *have* to make the effort to look after ourselves, don't you think, Olivia?"

Olivia tried to tell herself that this wasn't a pointed jibe at her very obvious lack of exercise, and the fact that her size-ten days were truly long gone. Yet, her rounded figure never seemed to bother Matt before so . . .

"Of course, but I do think I get enough exercise

running around after Ellie – not to mention all the housework and cleaning up after her." She rolled her eyes amusedly.

"You're right. She *does* sound quite disruptive actually," Catherine said, shaking her head. "And the problem is, Olivia, if you don't nip it in the bud now, things will only get worse."

Olivia could feel the heat rising on her cheeks. "I don't know why you seem to have that impression, Catherine, but honestly, Ellie is –"

Just then Adam burst into the room, his face red and wet with tears. "Daddy, Ellie won' gimme back my Tweenie!" he wailed.

Catherine stood up immediately. "Oh, poor darling, come here," she said, opening her arms towards him. For someone who was such an advocate of hard discipline, Olivia thought, she seemed all too eager to plamause the child.

She stood up too. "Adam, I'm sure Ellie will give you back your toy – where is she?"

Adam pointed towards the room down the hallway, and Olivia, followed closely by Matt, made her way to what was apparently Adam's playroom.

Her eyes widened as she took in the mayhem surrounding her. The floor was covered with toys – popular, expensive toys, the television blared noisily in the background, and poor Ellie was sitting in the corner crying her little heart out.

"He hit me on the head, Mommy," she said, as if heartbroken that her so-called good friend could injure her in any way. "I wanted to play with the Tweenie and he hit me with a Tommy-Truck!"

"Adam, come here, please!" Matt called sternly down the hallway.

"Oh, Ellie, are you sure you two weren't just playing?" Olivia was only too well aware of how kids could exaggerate a situation to their own advantage when adults were involved, and she didn't want to get Adam in trouble. However, a quick examination of Ellie's forehead revealed a red mark and a throbbing bump.

"Adam wouldn't do something like that unless he was severely provoked," she heard Catherine say from the doorway. "He's a very gentle child, and even at playschool has never had any problems with the other children."

"It's fine, Catherine. I'm sure they were just being kids." Olivia knew well that the other woman wasn't offering an apology, but if she didn't try and defuse the situation, she wasn't sure what would come out of her mouth. Catherine had been niggling at her all evening and it was really starting to get to her.

"Well, you really should take her to a specialist or something," Catherine went on. "She obviously has some anger issues."

Olivia tensed. She couldn't believe this!

"With all due respect, Catherine," she said, glancing sideways at Matt for his reaction to the incident. "There are two of them involved in this and, knowing kids of their age, I doubt if either of them are totally blameless."

"You don't honestly believe that Adam hit her for no

apparent reason!" said Catherine. "Look at him – she's obviously upset him just as much." She kissed Adam's temple. "Poor baby, you're OK now."

Olivia couldn't believe what she was hearing. And even worse, what she *wasn't* hearing – from Matt. Catherine was being unbelievably rude, and totally unreasonable – wasn't he going to say anything? Not that Olivia would expect him to take sides against his own son, but she was doing her best to be sensible and objective about her child's involvement in this. Why couldn't he?

Matt shook his head uncertainly. "Ellie must have done something – Adam does seem to be very upset."

At this, Olivia stood up, a tearful Ellie in her arms. "I'm sorry but that's enough," she said. "Ellie and I are not staying here to be insulted like this. We don't know what's happened here, so there's little point in our fighting about it." She went to pass Catherine in the doorway. "Thanks for dinner, Catherine. I'm sorry we didn't get a chance to finish it." She tried her best to sound cordial, but inwardly she was raging.

The other woman gave her a winning smile. "Some other time maybe, perhaps when Ellie has calmed her behaviour a little and –"

"Olivia –" said Matt.

"Goodbye, Matt."

"I'll phone you tomorrow?" he said, following her to the front door.

"Sure."

"Bye, Matt, bye, Adam," Ellie said, waving tearfully

over her mother's shoulder, upset that she and her new friend were fighting.

Olivia closed the front gate behind her. "Come on, Ellie. We'll go home and have some of that nice ice cream Mummy got in the shops yesterday – what do you think?"

"Yay!" Ellie brightened instantly.

Embarrassed by what had happened, and stung at the fact that Matt wasn't prepared to help defuse the situation, Olivia walked slowly back across the green.

So much for friendly neighbours.

And new lovers.

Chapter 24

"She sounds like a right old cow!" Leah gave the house across the way one of her famous laser stares. It was the following afternoon, and Olivia was telling her all about her not-so-cosy dinner with Matt and Catherine.

"It was very strange," Olivia said, having barely slept all night for thinking about it. It had really hurt that Matt hadn't come to her defence. She could have understood it if Adam had been injured, but Ellie was the one with the sore forehead! "The way the two of them carried on, it was as though they were husband and wife," she explained to Leah. "You should have heard the way they talked about how they discipline Adam, and how Catherine loves cooking for him. I was supposed to be there as Matt's guest but as it was I felt like a complete outsider."

Leah wrinkled her nose. "Well, I don't think it's strange at all. In fact, I think it's pretty obvious that

Catherine fancies her good friend Matt, has probably *always* fancied him, and now she doesn't like it that he's taken up with you. She's threatened by you."

Olivia shook her head. "I don't think so. They've been friends for a long time – though Matt did say before that she could be a bit possessive. Anyway, if Catherine does fancy him, I don't know why he *isn't* with her. You saw her before, Leah – she's absolutely gorgeous and she puts the like of me to shame with her slim figure and her glossy hair." Since comforting – no, *gorging* – herself last night with a big bowl of Ben & Jerry's upon her return from Catherine's, Olivia had decided to go on a serious diet.

"Don't be silly – you look just as good as she does, and don't you dare think otherwise," Leah said. "Not every man thinks stick-insects are attractive, you know."

Olivia raised an eyebrow. "Are you serious?"

"Well, if she's so gorgeous and wonderful and such a good cook, why *isn't* he with her then?"

"I really don't know. But up until a couple of weeks ago I was sure they were married, and now I think I understand why." She bit her lip. "It's just typical, isn't it? The first guy to come along in years that I actually like, and now it seems as though it's over before it's even begun."

"Over? Why?"

Olivia explained how Matt had barely tried to prevent her leaving, and how she hadn't heard from him since.

"Ah, I'm probably better off anyway," she said,

although her heart felt empty at the thought of not seeing him again. "It would never work – and, of course, I've got way too much baggage."

"So you still haven't told him then?"

"I didn't have an opportunity, Leah. The kids were around whenever we were together, and then last night we were at Catherine's." She twisted a tendril of hair around her finger. "In a way, I'm glad I did bide my time though. I was obviously wrong about him."

And that was what hurt the most, Olivia thought. She had really believed that Matt was different, that there was something special between them, and she had been willing to give herself up to the possibility that they could have a future together. But after Matt's behaviour last night, it was hard to see how.

"And I can't believe the nerve of the woman implying that you're a bad parent," Leah fumed. "If only she knew!"

"Well, that's another thing," Olivia said. "I'm not too inclined to spill my guts to Matt now, when he already believes I'm irresponsible when it comes to Ellie. What will he think then?"

"I see your point," Leah bit her lip and the two were silent for a moment.

"Well, look, leave it for a while and see what happens," Leah continued. "I'm sure Matt will come to his senses and, if he doesn't, then he wasn't worth it in the first place and –"

The sharp shrill of the doorbell cut off the remainder of her sentence, and Olivia jumped up to answer it.

Matt stood at the doorway, his face drawn and guilty-looking. "Can I come in?" he asked sheepishly.

"If you like," Olivia stepped back to let him pass. "Leah's here," she added and Matt visibly tensed.

Leah jumped up from the sofa. "I'd better get back – I'm going out with Kate tonight!" She picked up her bag and gave Matt a curt nod. "I'll talk to you later, Olivia."

"OK, talk to you soon." Olivia smiled warily at her friend's retreat. She could certainly do with some of Leah's wilful temperament at the moment, she thought, wondering what on earth was coming.

When the two of them were alone, Matt tentatively took one of Olivia's hands in his. "I'm so sorry," he said, and almost instantly Olivia melted. "I should have said something but, to be honest, I didn't know what to do. You must have had a terrible impression of us."

Us? Olivia repeated silently. The way he was talking, you'd swear that he, Catherine and Adam were a package.

"It wasn't what I had expected, that was for sure."

"How's Ellie? I feel so bad about it. In fact, I was so shocked at Adam's behaviour I couldn't think straight. The poor thing must have been in an awful state."

"She was very upset, not so much about the bump, but more so about the fact that she and Adam were fighting."

"I know, and believe me I gave Adam a good talking to afterwards – and a right smack on the bum too," he added.

Then he sat down and ran a hand through his hair. "Whatever I was saying before about discipline, I do think that sometimes I can be too soft on him. But he's all I have left now." He looked at her sadly. "You can understand that surely?"

"Of course, I do," Olivia said, sitting down beside him. "And I understand too that kids will be kids. I was the same with my best friend when we were younger – one minute we were the best of friends and the next we were killing each other. But the parents shouldn't really take sides in these situations, Matt, not when they don't know the facts. Otherwise we'd all end up at each others' throats, and what kind of example is that to be setting the kids?"

"You're so understanding," he said, shaking his head. "I told Catherine that you'd understand but she was sure you'd tell me to go to hell."

Oh? Olivia thought. So now Catherine was reading Olivia's mind and anticipating her reactions, was she? What a strange woman – maybe Leah had been right in thinking that she was jealous of her – jealous of her and Matt.

"I don't think Catherine liked me very much," she said cautiously, not willing to add that the feeling was very definitely mutual.

Matt shook his head. "No, no, it's not like that all. I know she wasn't overly friendly last night but . . . look, you have to understand that Catherine and I are very close – too close maybe, and sometimes, to our detriment. I know she's started seeing some guy now and while I'm delighted – because I worry that with all she does for Adam and me that life is passing her by – I'm also worried and protective of her in the same way that a big brother would worry about his sister. And Catherine is exactly the same with me, possibly more so because of Natasha. She knows what I've been through and she doesn't want me to get hurt."

"I see."

Olivia considered this and decided that, yes, there was certainly a possibility that Catherine would be suspicious of her. A while ago, he didn't know Olivia from Adam (she laughed inwardly at the unintended pun) and then all of a sudden he was involved with her and her daughter. It was only natural that a good friend would be concerned, wasn't it? Still, thinking back on Catherine's behaviour last night, she couldn't get past the sneaking suspicion that Leah might have been right.

Maybe Catherine and Matt *were* unusually close, but wasn't it also possible that in the other woman Olivia could have a serious rival for his affections?

Olivia hoped not, because she really didn't think she could cope with something like that. Not again.

Chapter 25

Leah applied another layer of lipstick and ran a brush through her long dark hair. She'd have to get it cut soon, she decided, spotting tendrils of static broken hair sticking out of the top of her head. She'd been so busy lately she barely had time to eat properly, let alone attend to day-to-day grooming. No wonder her sex life had gone off the boil recently, she thought with a guilty grimace – hairy legs were undoubtedly a huge turn-off! Still, all her late nights and weekends had paid off – the store looked fantastic and business had been incredibly brisk these last few weeks. The launch party and subsequent chocolate-tasting evenings had really paid off.

God, it was so exciting, Leah thought proudly, her very first store and hopefully the first of many! She shook her head, still quite unable to believe that this had really happened. Who would have thought that an ordinary girl from a small village outside Tipperary would end up running a successful chocolate boutique – and in trendy, upmarket, Blackrock of all places! Her old mentor, Anton Belligni, would have been thrilled with her. She really should contact him and tell him how things were going.

The new store was going to send her business into the stratosphere, she was sure of it. Then, after a while, when things had calmed down, maybe she and Josh could think about buying a place of their own, and he wouldn't have to worry too much about being beholden to his father. Things were looking good.

But tonight, she would try her best to put all thoughts of the store out of her mind. Tonight she was going out for dinner with one of her very best friends, and with all that had been going on in both girls' lives lately, she knew that they both really needed it. Having spent so long off the drink while pregnant, she knew Kate was dying for a decent night out.

Checking her appearance once more, Leah idly wondered if Olivia had resolved her little misunderstanding with Matt.

She hoped so. She knew Olivia really liked him and while they might be having a few teething problems, Matt did seem like a very nice guy. And oh, didn't Olivia deserve it! After Peter, Leah was never really sure whether or not her friend would go on to love anyone else. She always hoped she would – after all Olivia was such a loving and generous person that she really ought to have someone special in her life, but

Leah had never expected that her friend would ever meet someone who would live up to the incomparable Peter. Maybe Matt didn't. For the few minutes Leah had spent in his company he seemed an easy, happy-go-lucky kind of guy, but didn't have quite the same magnetism or charisma that Peter had. Still, if he made Olivia happy then that was all that mattered.

Leah grabbed her car keys and, trying her best to stay upright in a pair of spiky heels that would cripple a lesser woman, she raced out the door. She'd told Kate to go all out and dress up to the nines tonight – town wouldn't know what hit it!

Half an hour later, Leah turned into Kate's driveway a little bit faster than she realised and jerked to a stop right behind Michael's black BMV. Whew, she thought with more than a little relief. Michael certainly wouldn't appreciate her slamming into that with her little Fiesta, would he? And really, her car had more than enough dents on it already.

Leah mentally reminded herself to apply once more for her driving test, now that she had a little bit more time on her hands. Although, she thought with a sigh, it would undoubtedly be another complete waste of time.

Only the other day, she'd been trying to manoeuvre out of a tight spot near the shop, and in order to reverse out, had no option but to scratch the paintwork of the Jeep parked alongside her. Leah had left a note on the owner's windscreen, and later had endured a barrage of abuse, which she supposed was justified. It was unfortunate, but at the time there was nothing else she could have done – she had deliveries to make, and in fairness, the Jeep owner was just as much at fault for parking so close alongside her in the first place!

No, she'd have to get her test soon, otherwise her insurance company would just flat out refuse to cover her and her now scratched and sorrowful-looking Fiesta. And that certainly wouldn't do!

Getting out of the car, and having to choose her steps extra carefully on Kate's cobble-lock driveway in her heels and rather clingy chiffon skirt, Leah approached the front door. Unusually, the house looked unkempt from the outside: the flowers hung limply in their hanging baskets, and the front lawn looked as though it hadn't been touched in months. And shock horror, Leah spotted greasy handprints on the sliding doors of the porch. She smiled to herself. Looking after a new baby had obviously affected Kate's normally fastidious housekeeping. Her friend was famous for her compulsive cleaning – a fact that used to annoy Leah no end when the two shared a flat together throughout university.

A very harassed-looking Michael appeared in the doorway.

"Hello!" Leah reached forward and greeted Kate's husband with a hug and a kiss on the cheek. She hadn't seen him in the few weeks since the baby was born, and with his unshaven jaw and the tired, ravaged look in his eyes, he looked equally as unkempt as the house.

"Hi, Leah," Michael returned her greeting with considerably less enthusiasm. "Kate was trying to ring you on the mobile. . ." He trailed off and by his tone Leah knew immediately that their planned girlie night out had hit a snag.

"Let me guess, she's still getting ready," Leah said, with a conspiratorial smile. Despite her apparent devil-may-care attitude, Kate was as fastidious with her appearance as she was with her housekeeping, and Leah knew from experience that it could take her well up to an hour and a half to get dolled up for a night out. Probably more so tonight, Leah thought, imaging her friend cheerfully discarding potential items of clothing, when she hadn't been out in months and hadn't yet shifted the extra baby weight.

"No, it's not that," Michael replied wearily, directing her through to the living-room.

A tired and wrecked-looking Kate was sitting on the couch with a crying Dylan in her arms. Leah couldn't remember ever seeing her looking so dishevelled. She knew that young babies could be disrupting, but because Kate was normally so calm and in control, Leah hadn't expected the chaotic sight that greeted her.

Apart from the baby essentials – nappies, creams and toys that were scattered all over – the room looked as though it hadn't been tidied in years. There were half-empty coffee cups on the floor around the sofa, glasses on the mantelpiece, empty takeaway cartons . . . in all honesty, it looked to Leah like a student flat, a dingy student flat.

This was so out of character for Kate that she felt rather unsettled and instantly guilty. She hadn't seen her friend since that time in the hospital. Thinking that the new parents would need time to enjoy this much-wanted new baby, she had consciously kept out of Kate's hair – not to mention the fact that she too had been up to her eyes at work. She had made all the usual offers to help and 'call me if you need anything' platitudes, but thinking of it now she wondered if she shouldn't have insisted.

"Hey," she said, sitting down alongside Kate on the couch and forcing a smile so as not to betray her unease, "how are you?"

"OK," Kate whispered and immediately, seeming to take his mother's shifting attention as some form of rejection, Dylan screwed up his tiny face and cried – *roared* – even louder.

"*Ssshh, ssshh,* it's OK love. Mummy's here. Mummy's here," Kate soothed, holding him close and rubbing his back in a comforting gesture. "I'm sorry, Leah," she said wearily, "but I think we'll have to call off our night out."

Oh! Leah hadn't expected that. She thought there might be a bit of a delay and that they'd be late getting to the restaurant but . . . .

"Oh, dear, is he sick?" she asked, realising. "Does he have . . ." She racked her brain for the common baby-sickness that Ellie had when she was a baby, "group or something? The poor little thing!" She reached across and touched the baby in a sympathetic gesture.

"I don't know . . . Michael?" Kate's eyes widened

with alarm and she looked to her husband for assistance. "Could Leah be right? Could there be something wrong with him?"

"I'm sure there's nothing wrong with him, Kate." He gave Leah a look that conveyed blatant irritation, before continuing, "He's just tired, that's all."

"But what if there *is* something wrong with him?" Kate's tone hinged on hysterical. "How am I supposed to know? He can't tell me, can he? What if there is something wrong with him, and he needs to go to the hospital or –"

"For God's sake Kate, he's fine! Babies cry, you know that! It's just that this particular baby happens to cry more than most," he added, almost under his breath.

Leah began to feel more than a little uncomfortable and out of place in this family scene. She knew now that her hoped-for pleasant night out, catching up with Kate, wasn't going to happen. She had known that newborn babies could be tough work, and Kate had said that she was dying to let her hair down and get some time to herself.

"Look," Michael continued, his tone more placating, "if you're not going out, and Leah's staying on here, I might head down to the local for one or two, if that's OK?"

"Sure, go ahead," Kate said, with an absent nod, as Dylan's cries began to subside.

"I couldn't possibly leave him like this." Kate turned to Leah, a pleading tone to her voice. "I'd just be worrying and worrying about him all night, and I wouldn't be able to enjoy it. You don't mind, do you?"

Michael didn't seem to mind leaving him, Leah thought uncharitably. Surely, if the baby was that hard going, Kate needed a break too?

"Of course, I don't mind," Leah said, trying to inject some enthusiasm into her voice. This wasn't exactly how she'd envisaged her only night off in weeks but still . . . "Look, why don't you and the baby just lie down there for a quiet moment and I'll get out of your way."

She'd have to ring the restaurant and cancel, she thought, and she felt lousy about that because she'd had to beg for a table in the first place. Shit! If only Kate had rung earlier to let her know the situation, then she could have slung on a pair of tracksuit bottoms and brought a bottle of wine or something.

Although, she thought guiltily, it was hardly fair to expect Kate to worry about putting Leah out, when she was obviously put out about the entire situation as it was – and on top of it, she was probably looking forward to it just as much as Leah, if not more.

Well, if nothing else, Leah thought, removing her trench coat and hanging it over the banister in the hallway, she could give Kate a bit of hand with the tidying-up.

Why the hell wasn't Michael doing it though? As far as she knew Michael was a modern man and, as he and Kate both worked, had no aversion to sharing the housework.

Obviously Kate's priority would now be the baby rather than cleaning the windows, so surely he could muck in that little bit more? Oh, well, she thought, shaking her head. Perhaps the new arrival caused more disruption than they'd imagined. She couldn't imagine it herself. In her and Josh's teeny apartment they could barely stretch to having visitors, let alone giving it all over to the chaos that evidently went hand in hand with a newborn baby. She smiled tightly. There was no fear of that happening.

Removing her shoes, which were already becoming uncomfortable and seemed a little out of place in this domestic situation, Leah went back into the living-room to find Kate lying full stretch on the couch. Seeing Leah about to speak, she put a finger over her lips in a silencing gesture, and indicated gently to Dylan's crib at the other end of the room. She had finally succeeded in calming him then, Leah thought, freezing in mid-movement. Well, at least she and Kate might get to do a bit of catching up anyway. Maybe her friend had a bottle of wine from her pre-mummy days stashed around somewhere and they could crack that open and have a good old giggle and relax a little. It was almost nine o'clock – Dylan would sleep for the rest of night now, surely?

Kate swung her legs onto the ground and carefully – painstakingly – tiptoed to where Leah stood motionless in the doorway.

"You should go," she whispered faintly, while keeping one eye on the baby's crib. "He'll be fine now – I think I have him down until his next feed."

Leah was startled. "Go? I thought I'd stay on for a while, have a bottle of wine or something . . ."

Kate motioned her to the other side of the door and out into the hallway.

"A bottle of *wine*?" she repeated, an edge to her voice. "Jesus, Leah, what kind of a mother would I be if I go off getting pissed with my baby son in the next room? What if he wakes up again and I'm too out of it to see to him properly?"

"I never said anything about getting pissed, Kate." Leah was taken aback at her tone. "I just thought it would be nice for you and me to relax a little, seeing as we're not going out – have a bit of a girlie night in, I suppose." She shrugged, feeling unsure as to what was the right thing to say or do.

"For God's sake, Leah, there's more to life than going out and having silly conversations about handbags and shoes!" Kate whispered loudly, but to Leah it sounded more like an impatient hiss.

Stung, she looked away.

"Look, I'm sorry," Kate sighed, running a hand through her hair. "I'm just not up to it tonight."

"But I wasn't suggesting anything like that, Katie." Leah tried not to betray her upset. "I just thought that with the way things are at the moment, your kicking back and relaxing a little bit might help."

"What? What do you mean 'the way things are at the moment', Leah?" Kate snapped again. "Do you think that just because Dylan was crying tonight that I'm not coping? That I'm not a good mother, is that it?"

"Of course not! Of course, that's not what I meant! Kate, I wouldn't *dream* of suggesting anything like that!" She looked up and seeing Kate's hard expression, realised that whatever she said tonight would probably be the wrong thing.

All of a sudden, she felt terribly guilty. Poor Kate was obviously worn-out and hassled, and most likely all she wanted was an early night while she had the chance. Leah had been silly in suggesting anything else, and she shouldn't really blame Kate for getting frustrated. Leah would be frustrated too if she had been stuck all day and possibly most of the previous night with a screaming baby who couldn't settle, and then, the first second she has to relax, her friend wants her attention.

No, Kate was right. She should leave her alone for tonight, and let her get some much-needed sleep.

"You're right," she said, resting a hand on her friend's arm and getting a weak smile in return. "You're tired, and I'm sure the last thing you need is visitors tonight. I'll go and leave you to it, and perhaps we can arrange another night, when you feel up to it."

She winced, regretting her choice of words as soon as they were out, and Kate's expression instantly hardened.

"I'm not ill, you know," she said touchily. "I just happened to have a bad day with him today – he's usually fine."

"I know that." At this stage, Leah couldn't wait to leave. She picked up her coat from the banister. "Look, get some rest tonight and I'll give you a ring during the week, OK?"

Kate nodded, and Leah thought she spotted a look

of relief on her face as she closed the door behind her.

Despite herself, Leah felt hurt by this. Kate had let her down by not letting her know earlier that she couldn't make their night out. Of course, she could appreciate her friend was tired and weary, but was it necessary for Kate to be so short with her? Leah's only intention tonight had been to help Kate relax, to get her out of the house and back to the real world, albeit temporarily. She had known Kate long enough to be sure that her friend would appreciate that, that she would be grateful for a chance to escape the chaos and regain some sense of normality by getting dressed up and out for a night of good fun and good conversation.

But, obviously, Leah thought, as she got in the car and pulled out of Kate's driveway, she had got it badly wrong.

"What do you think, Josh? Do you think I was being selfish?" Leah asked Josh after he'd returned from yet another late shift at Homecare.

"I wouldn't see it like that," he answered, taking a beer from the fridge. "Kate made the arrangement with you in the first place – it's not as though you just arrived on her doorstep, dressed up to the nines and demanded to be entertained."

Leah bit her lip, recalling Kate's impatience at her suggestion that they stay in with a bottle of wine.

"It was the way she looked at me though – as if I was this brainless shallow idiot."

"I wouldn't make too much of it, Lee – it's probably just a phase she's going through. How old is the kid now – three, four weeks? She's bound to be finding it hard going."

"I know, but I just thought she'd appreciate . . . oh, I don't know," Leah followed him through to the living-room, and then slunk down on the sofa beside him.

"And Michael snaked off to the local, huh?" he said, putting an arm around her. "Looks like fatherhood's getting too much for him already."

Leah had her own opinion on Michael snaking off and leaving Kate holding the baby, but she didn't say anything. She was still reeling from Kate's insinuation that she was shallow. Was she shallow? If shallow meant trying to get a good friend to relax and enjoy herself after having a busy time, well then, call her shallow. OK, so she knew nothing about motherhood and never would, but surely it couldn't be good for either Kate or her baby if she couldn't take time out for herself. Of course, if Dylan was ill, that would be a different story but the child wasn't sick, was he?

If anything, he was just being a baby, crying and looking for attention. She remembered Ellie being the same for Olivia when she was a very young baby. Although she wasn't around at the time, she remembered poor Olivia worrying incessantly about the child, and despite her friend's insistence that she was never going to be one of those mothers who picked up her baby at the first whimper, she wasn't exactly blasé about Ellie's crying either.

That's what she'd do, Leah decided. She'd talk to Olivia and find out how she felt about things when she first had Ellie. Maybe that would shed some light upon Kate's behaviour, and why she seemed rather obsessive about her role as a new mother. She might also ask Olivia to have a bit of a chat with Kate, and maybe Kate might open up to a fellow mother. Unfortunately, Leah couldn't understand what she was going through now and, she thought sadly, she would never understand. But Kate would get over it all and their friendship should be back to normal soon, shouldn't it?

And in the meantime, she thought, cuddling into Josh on the sofa, if Kate wasn't interested in catching up, then she and her boyfriend could certainly do a bit of catching up of their own.

Chapter 26

Ben and Robin stood in their apartment, and looked at one another in awe. Robin picked up and flicked through the glossy pages of one of the proof copies she had just received from the publisher.

Atchoo the Allergic Alligator was now a beautifully illustrated picture book and completely different to the one they had jokingly put together ages before. The basic story remained the same, although Robin had added a few more dramatic adventures before Atchoo finally learns to take his medicine properly, but she decided it was the illustrations that really made the book so impressive.

Bubblegum Press planned to release the books in a series and, in the meantime, Robin had written another three stories in a similar vein, but featuring different animals with different medical conditions. *Hazel the Squirrel* – a story about an unfortunate squirrel with a nut allergy, and a subject very close to Robin's heart, – *Dick the Diabetic Duck* and *Eleanor the Epileptic Elephant*.

Due to the publisher's enthusiasm, and some very well-timed press releases, the *Atchoo* series was gaining a lot of advance publicity. A few weeks earlier, Bubblegum had fallen over themselves in an attempt to issue a press release shortly after the US Health Department published alarmingly high statistics on children's allergies, and the part our disintegrating environment had to play.

They released another after a nationwide outcry when a preschool in Iowa refused an enrolment application from a young boy with a severe peanut allergy. The school wouldn't accept the child on the basis that he would need "significant and continuous attention", something neither the teachers – nor the school's insurance company – were prepared to supply. One teacher gave a highly controversial interview asking why she was "suddenly being asked to practice medicine". The argument prompted clashes between teachers, parents and health lobbyists, and for a solid week the majority of American opinion was split down the middle on the subject. As a result of this opportune media interest, and the associated word-of-mouth, confidence about the forthcoming series was high.

Pre-publication copies of the books had already been distributed to local and governmental health departments, and also to key children's hospitals throughout the state. The response so far had been extremely positive, and the publishers were expecting considerable sales once the book was in stores. The major bookstores – Barnes and Noble, and Borders – had initially dismissed the series as an aid for local health departments, but once the popular chainstore Wal Mart decided to stock the series as a result of the media exposure, they tentatively began making enquiries.

The first book *Atchoo the Allergic Alligator* was due for publication in November, and the others would be published consecutively with a two-monthly interval between each book.

"It seems I'm going to be busy for a while, then," Robin said shaking her head in amazement.

She had met again with Bubblegum recently, and Lucy, the head of PR, had informed her that upon publication they would be doing state, and possibly nationwide TV, radio and newspaper interviews. Although the initial campaign would be focused primarily on *Atchoo*, the release of the other books should sustain interest and hopefully increase the series' profile and momentum. Could Robin make herself available for a couple of weeks around then?

"Of course, I can," Robin enthused. So, she had booked her two weeks' annual leave from Greene & Co, and instead of spending them on holiday in Ontario as she and Ben had planned, she would be spending them touring around New York state, visiting bookstores, radio stations and possibly, some school and health agencies.

It wouldn't be much of a holiday, but Robin didn't mind – in fact, she couldn't wait, and she still couldn't believe that this was actually happening, let alone happening so quickly. At Marla's insistence, she had found herself an agent, a lovely woman called Jessie Logan, who had negotiated her contract and (in Robin's opinion) her completely unwarranted advance – the first part of which was sitting in her bank account until she and Ben found a suitable house. Thanks to the unexpected windfall, they now had a little bit extra to play with, and were hoping to find somewhere quickly – Robin becoming more and more enamoured of the idea of putting down roots as time went by.

She'd been surprised at how much she enjoyed the writing. It wasn't something that she'd thought about all that much before – although her teachers in school had always told her she had a great imagination. Still, she was definitely not one of those people who had always wanted to write. But writing for children, and even better, writing to *help* educate children, be it about allergies or algebra, was different and Robin found that she took to it like a duck to water.

As a result of the publication deal for her *Atchoo* story, she had more than once found herself staring vacantly into space and dreaming up different stories and adventures that might entertain and enthrall young children, when instead she should have been studying budget proposals and checking invoices.

Now, seeing her own words in print for the first time, Robin felt a shiver up her spine. "I think I could get used to this," she said, flopping back onto the sofa, book in hand.

"Well, you'll have to," Ben laughed. "There are still another three books to come."

"No, I mean I could get used to *this*," she said, pointing to the text. "To the writing. I love doing it, but yet I never once considered it before now. Imagine me – a children's writer!"

"But you've got real talent, Robin," he said, sitting down alongside her. "I know you think the illustrations are the most impressive part of the book, but the publishers bought the story, they bought *your* story." He shook his head. "And it is a bloody good story, besides the fact that it's supposed to be educational. It's charming and silly and playful and adults will *love* reading this to their kids. You've got it, Robin – whether you believe it or not, you've got it."

"Ben, I'd love to believe I do have 'it' – whatever that may be – but, to be honest, I don't see how. I don't really know all that much about kids. OK, there's Kirsty, sure, but –"

"And you're so good with her. You're so good with kids in general." He shook his head. "You know it really is such a shame that . . ." Ben quickly trailed off when she flashed him a warning look. "OK, OK, let's not go there now, not at a time like this anyway." He picked up the book and began flicking through it one more time.

"'Let's not go there'," Robin teased, mimicking his accent.

"You brat," he laughed, tickling her. "Don't start going all high and mighty with me, just because you're now a published author!"

Robin giggled and then Ben sat up and once more studied her name on the front cover. "Wow, you're a published author!" he repeated, as if really realising it for the first time. "This calls for a celebration, Robin Matthews, and I'm taking you out to dinner!"

Robin sat up and grinned. "Great, where will we go?" she asked, feeling both excited and nervous about the thoughts of eating out somewhere.

"Chinatown?" Ben suggested with a twinkle in his eye, and Robin threw a cushion at him. "No, seriously, remember that place we went for our anniversary – it was safe enough, wasn't it?"

"Safe but bland and way over-priced," Robin said, remembering.

"Well, as long as the champagne tastes good, I couldn't care less," he said, and Robin wanted to hug him. Poor Ben, it really wasn't fair on him that he had to pick and choose where they ate, and at times like this, it really hit home how lucky she was to have him.

"Champagne sounds great!" she said, getting into the spirit of things. What did it matter what the food tasted like? They were celebrating!

"Well, why don't you go and get ready, and I'll ring for a table," he said, shooing her into the bedroom.

As Robin picked out a suitable outfit for the rather swanky but safe restaurant, she thought again about her little book, and wondered what they'd all make of it at home. She'd told her mother about the publication deal, of course, but her mum, while pleased for her, didn't really understand, and seemed to think that

Robin was printing out and publishing these books herself.

"God knows we could have done with something like that when you were young," Peggy had said. "It's a great idea and, oh, I must say it to that new principal in the primary school – she might take a few off you." She said this as though Robin would be flogging copies out of the boot of her car. "Although," she murmured in afterthought, "the same one is a bit stuck-up in herself and might only want real books."

Robin bit her tongue. "Mum, it's fine, the publishers will be looking after everything and, to be honest, I don't think the books will be available in Ireland anyway. But, of course, I'll send you a copy when it comes out."

"Great," her mother said absently. "Well, best of luck with it anyway."

Once again, Robin was glad that Peggy hadn't asked when she was coming home for a visit. Her mother was good like that, really, and seemed to accept that Robin's life was in New York now. She never made her feel guilty about leaving, and although she'd asked her mother many, many times to come and visit, she had rarely accepted. In a way, it was as though her mother was finally able to have a life of her own, now that she no longer had to worry about Robin.

Robin had always felt guilty about her parents' break-up, and although her mother had never once blamed her directly, it was fairly obvious that Robin's allergy had been the problem. Peggy and Robin's dad, Tom, were on speaking terms these days, but Tom was with someone else now, and there was little likelihood of them getting back together. Anyway, Robin suspected that her mother didn't care. After years of stressing and looking after a sickly child, she was now free to do as she pleased without worry. Why let a man complicate things?

Robin hadn't yet said anything about the book to Leah. She wondered what she and the others – particularly Olivia – would think. Would they be pleased for her? She smiled. They would definitely be surprised anyway, and she could almost imagine Amanda Clarke going apoplectic over the fact that Robin was about to become a published author. Throughout college, Amanda had been convinced that she was the one who would 'make it big', be it in TV, modelling or whatever. Now it seemed as though Robin had pipped her to the post. She grinned, thinking how silly it was to be thinking of getting one over on old school friends, but people like Amanda, who had always been so dismissive about her, deserved it.

She really should tell Leah though. Of course, she'd be delighted for her, although Leah was doing just as well herself these days with her new chocolate boutique. It was nice of her to send Robin and Ben an invite to her big launch night, but there was really never any question of them going – not to a chocolate launch anyway! Leah understood, of course, but at times like that, Robin wondered how long they would be able to keep up the friendship 'for old times' sake'. She had moved on now, moved away from it all, and while she occasionally missed having a solid, dependable friend like Olivia, or someone to go out and have a good giggle with like Leah, she knew that it was inevitable that they would lose touch. Friendships, just like relationships, couldn't really survive long-distance. Robin was certain of that.

Chapter 27

At the weekend, Olivia met Leah in town for some shopping.

Leah had decided that after weeks of ignoring her appearance, her image needed serious sprucing up, and to Olivia's amazement had taken a rare day off from the shop. Olivia, herself, eager to put more effort into her appearance now that she was seeing Matt, was only too happy to accompany her. For once, she had the time too, as Ellie was visiting her grandparents in Galway.

Peter's parents, Teresa and Jim, had always been a great help to her where Ellie was concerned, and they did try to involve themselves in their granddaughter's life as much as possible – trying to make up for the lack of a father, Olivia supposed. But occasionally, Teresa could be a bit interfering, and yesterday morning was one of those times.

"Who's this Matt person Ellie keeps chattering

about?" Olivia's mother-in-law asked her, the suspicion clearly evident in her tone. As they hadn't seen Ellie in some time, they had travelled down to Dublin to collect her and bring her to their house in Galway for the weekend. Teresa hadn't been well apparently, and Olivia had noticed before that her movements were a little bit slower and more measured than usual. She supposed that Teresa was getting on a bit, in the same way they all were, really. So, she was pleased for both Ellie and her grandparents that they'd get the chance to spend some time together. Despite her misgivings about his parents filling Ellie's head with Peter, she knew nevertheless it was important to them all that Peter wouldn't be forgotten. But when Teresa was around, there was no fear of that.

"Matt?" Olivia repeated warily to her mother-in-law.

"Yes – Matt. It's all Matt this and Matt that, and Adam this and Adam that. I gather that Adam must be a young friend of hers, but who is Matt?"

"He's Adam's father." Despite herself, Olivia reddened. It had been years, but still she felt guilty at Peter's mother knowing that she was seeing someone else. She knew that Teresa would no doubt see it as a betrayal. She was right.

"And does Ellie see much of this Matt?" Teresa sniffed disapprovingly. "Do you see much of this Matt?"

Olivia struggled to hold her tongue. She had a good mind to tell Teresa to butt out and mind her own business, that she would see as much of Matt as she liked, but yet she hadn't the heart to. Maybe Teresa was right to be concerned. Ellie had spent all her life without a father – she was bound to be affected by her mother's relationships.

"He's a neighbour, Teresa, and he's a very nice man and a good friend, that's all."

Teresa sighed. "Look, Olivia, far be it from me to stick my nose in your business, but just be careful, won't you? You have to consider Ellie's welfare, and it wouldn't be good for her to have these come-a-day go-a-day men in her life."

Olivia gaped. How dare she? As if Olivia was seeing other men left, right and centre! Matt was the first man, the only man she'd even thought about seeing seriously since Peter – how dare Teresa suggest that her personal life could badly affect Ellie? And it wasn't as though Olivia hadn't considered that – of course, she had – but she and Matt had so much in common, and the children did get on so well . . . most of the time.

Again, she bit her tongue. There was no point in arguing with Teresa over this. The woman had made her point and, as Ellie's grandmother, she did have every right to make it. But she had a bloody cheek all the same, considering!

This weekend though, she was just going to enjoy her bit of free time, and not be worrying about Teresa or indeed Catherine, which, she admitted, was another aspect of this new relationship with Matt Sheridan that was a bit of a worry. What had she let herself in for?

"I just didn't know what to do or say," Leah's confused tones brought Olivia back to the present. She was explaining Kate's behaviour on the night of their planned night out. In the meantime apparently Kate had rung and apologised for letting Leah down.

"She said we'd definitely arrange it again soon, but, to be honest, I don't want to be the one to do the arranging, as I seem to pick my moments!" Leah told Olivia. "But she says Dylan seems fine now, which is great."

"Well, your thirtieth birthday will be coming up soon," Olivia reminded her. "And we'll all be getting together for that. Are you planning on having a big bash for it?"

Leah shook her head. "I don't think so. With all that's been happening lately, I don't think I'd have the energy to organise something. And then of course, it's not all that long since the launch party. I think I might just have a quiet dinner somewhere, just a few of us, that kind of thing."

"Are you sure? It seems a bit dull compared to all that fuss you made for mine – and for Kate's."

Knowing how much Olivia loved Italy and all things Italian, Leah had arranged a special themed party night and booked a full floor at her favourite Italian restaurant. All the guests were invited to dress up as either Roman gladiators or Renaissance artists. Olivia had been totally bowled over upon entering the place, and they all had a wonderful time. For Kate, who wasn't a big party person, and who they all suspected would not appreciate a surprise bash, Leah had arranged a balloon ride for her and Michael over the Wicklow mountains. She was right again. Kate, having got over her initial misgivings about the balloon's safety, had had a fantastic time.

Olivia smiled to herself. Despite her reticence, Leah's birthday might turn out to be a much bigger cause for celebration than she'd expected.

She'd had a conversation with Josh recently, a rather unexpected one, one night at Leah's a little while after the launch party, which led her to suspect that he might be working up to a proposal. Normally jocular, he had been strangely serious, asking questions about Peter and their break-up back in college.

Normally, she wasn't happy to be drawn into conversations about her husband, as it was all still very painful. Yet, being asked about him that night by Josh, who she suspected had his own motives, Olivia didn't mind.

"You loved one another deeply, didn't you? You and Peter, I mean?" he asked her, when Leah was in the kitchen and out of earshot.

"Of course," Olivia said, a little taken aback at his directness.

"But yet, Leah said that you had some problems, back before you two got engaged."

Olivia shifted in her seat. What was he getting at?

"Do you mind if I ask you what changed your mind?"

"My mind?"

Josh scratched his head, equally uncomfortable about raising what was sure to be a difficult subject for her. "About marrying Peter, spending the rest of your life with him – wanting to be with him, no matter what."

Olivia immediately deduced that he was trying to place his feelings about Leah in context. Some men were like that. For years, they could just go along in a relationship, never really questioning their feelings, never really wondering where the relationship was going.

"You mean, why did I change my mind about breaking up with him?"

Josh nodded.

"I just had a case of cold feet," she said shrugging. "The two of us had been together all throughout college, and as far as everyone else, including Peter, was concerned, we would be together for the long term. It's difficult to explain now, but I just felt a bit trapped, I suppose. It seemed as though I was just being swept along, not really thinking about what I really wanted. So, I panicked, and one day I told Peter that I wasn't sure about us any more, that I wanted some time alone to get my head together."

"But it wasn't that simple." Josh stated.

Olivia smiled, remembering. "No, not quite. I had hurt him deeply, more than I realised. I remember him telling me afterwards that he spent those few weeks in a total daze, a fog." It was a feeling Olivia knew well, having had those very same feelings for months after losing Peter, and indeed throughout much of the early days of Ellie's life. The grief had been crippling.

"So, you decided you wanted to spend the rest of your life with him, no matter what," Josh supplied.

She shrugged again. "If you love someone as much as I loved Peter, then the answer had to be yes." She knew then that he was trying to understand why Leah had been so accepting of his not wanting children. He must have been wondering whether she might feel differently at some later stage, despite the fact she insisted she wouldn't. Olivia was glad that he seemed to appreciate the sacrifice his girlfriend had made for him.

Josh sighed. "I hope you don't mind my being so forward like this, Olivia, and I'm sorry to bring up these painful reminders . . ."

"It's fine Josh," she waved him away, "but I suspect you have your own reasons for asking me about this?" She smiled knowingly, and Josh reddened a little.

Then Leah came into the kitchen, and the conversation ended.

It was so obvious that he was going to propose – and very likely for her birthday – but Olivia wasn't about to tell Leah that. She was so pleased for her. The two of them were a great couple, and it would be wonderful to see things work out for them.

"Jesus, Olivia, you have it bad," Leah said, grinning at her and bringing her sharply back to the present.

"What?"

"What?" Leah mimicked. "It's so obvious you might

as well have a banner on your forehead proclaiming 'I am madly in love with Matt Sheridan'. When are we all going to meet him properly by the way? That first time, I barely had a chance to talk to him before you bundled him off! Nervous I might work my charms on him, were you?"

Olivia laughed. Of course, she wanted the others to meet him properly, but despite how well they seemed to be getting on lately, she still wasn't sure. She wasn't sure whether or not she wanted to admit to herself – let alone the others – that she might have a future with him. She couldn't remember the last time she enjoyed herself so much, the last time she had laughed so much with any man other than Peter, the last time she had felt so happy. But, with the strange and definitely disconcerting situation with his friend Catherine, she thought grimly, it was difficult to know at this early stage if she and Matt had any future.

Maybe her mother-in-law was right to be concerned.

"Sometime soon," she said, and then added wickedly, "if Mammy Catherine allows it."

Leah laughed. "Don't mind that one. She might be a good friend, but Matt is a big boy now, and well able to make his own decisions."

"It's weird though, Leah. I'd swear the woman is spying on me. The other day, I called a plumber out to fix my washing machine, and later that evening Matt came over and oh-so-casually asked me if I'd had a visitor. I couldn't believe it! Catherine had obviously told her that some man had been around, and must have been trying to suggest I was having it off with the plumber!"

It had been really strange and rather worrying to think that Catherine was watching her every move. The tables were being well and truly turned, she thought with a grin, remembering her own curtain-twitching.

"Silly bitch obviously has nothing better to be doing," Leah tut-tutted. "Next thing you know she'll have one of those surveillance cameras on you, probably trying to catch you and Matt doing the deed." She shook her head. "Nosy cow – what age is she, for goodness' sake?"

Olivia sat up. "Speaking of cameras, I still have your camcorder. Josh left it in the boot of the car on the night of the launch party." Olivia was designated driver that night, and had driven Josh and Leah home. "I'm sure you're anxious to take a look at it."

"Believe me, there's no rush," Leah drawled. "We might not see that until this time next year. Josh is a disaster – apparently it's a big deal to get it transferred onto tape, and, of course, I can't do it, so . . ."

"Why not just pop it into one of those cassette adaptors? I've got one – I can give it to you if you like."

"Great, I didn't know you could do that. I'll pop over some time and get it off you."

"What about now? We're finished here, aren't we? And seeing as Ellie's off in Galway, it'll be nice and quiet, not to mention there's no risk of her seeing her mother stuff her face on-screen with chocolates and prawn parcels." She groaned, remembering. "I made such a pig of myself that night!"

"It was a great night though, wasn't it?" Leah grinned. "Actually I wouldn't mind taking a look at it, now that you mention it."

"Great. I want to give you back the camcorder anyway. I'd be afraid something might happen to it – Ellie might pick it up or –"

"I don't think it would matter too much," Leah rolled her eyes. "If anything, it would give us an excuse to get a new one. That clunky old thing is useless – it must be one of the earliest models ever made." She stood up. "Yes, I might as well go back with you now. Watch one of the best nights of my life in glorious Technicolor!"

Chapter 28

Leah swung her legs underneath her and got comfortable on Olivia's couch. "This should be interesting."

"You were buzzing that night," Olivia said, putting a bowl of nachos on the table in front of Leah. "You probably don't even remember most of the party."

"It just seems like so long ago!" Leah groaned, fiddling with the remote. "Back then when I was so innocent and thought that the business was mine and mine alone. I hadn't bargained for Amanda Clarke!"

Her hopes that Amanda would lose interest in the business after the launch party had been well and truly dashed and, lately, Leah had had to come to terms with the fact that Amanda was becoming a semi-permanent fixture at Elysium.

Despite all her moaning and groaning about being pregnant, Leah suspected Amanda was actually quite bored, and all the buzz at the chocolate shop was something to get her teeth into. Literally. Amanda was one of those women who decided that being pregnant was the ideal excuse to stop watching her figure, and Leah's creations were now under a state of continuous assault.

Leah didn't mind really – Amanda could be a bit comical in her own way, and some of her antics amused her. No, it was only when Amanda tried to interfere in her business that Leah got annoyed.

"I want to see how they do things in Paris," Amanda had announced casually the other day, during what Leah had thought was one of her many friendly visits.

"Do what over there?" Leah replied absently, thinking that she must have come across some new Parisian waxing method, or some other beauty fad. She held a spoon out for Amanda to taste her new passionfruit sorbet centre, a recipe she had been working on for a while, and which she thought would go particularly well enrobed in dark chocolate and drizzled with a lime-coloured sugar.

Next, to choose what mould to use. Despite her time spent in Belgium, Leah had grown tired of the obligatory seashell mould so often associated with Belgian chocolate, and instead tried to use simple, uncomplicated shapes and let the delicious flavour, rather than the elaborate shapes sell the product.

"The business, of course!" Amanda exclaimed. "This store needs to really stand out, and I'm not sure that what we're doing here is good enough."

"Excuse me?" Leah said, more than a little taken aback. "What we're doing here? We're doing just fine as a matter of fact – stock is flying out the door, and I can't replace it fast enough!" It had all come out a little bit sharper than she'd intended, and Leah had known immediately by Amanda's expression that she'd been wounded by it.

Later that evening she got a call from Andrew.

"Is there any possibility the two of you could come to some kind of agreement?" he asked and Leah's heart sank like a stone. So much for the business being hers and hers alone. So these days, Leah had to get used to having Amanda around to 'help' in the shop, at least until the baby was born.

"I'll bet she was preening and pouting, and practically drooling at the camera all night," Olivia said now, referring to the video.

"Well, as long as she wasn't drooling over the cameraman, I don't mind!" Leah laughed.

"OK, here we go." She pressed play on the VCR remote control, and the images of the party appeared onscreen. "Oh look, there's Kate! Wow, I'd forgotten she was still pregnant then. Doesn't she look great?"

It was true. Kate did look great, much more like her old, happy, smiling, carefree self. Olivia hoped that Kate would soon start to find motherhood a little easier than it was at the moment. It was disconcerting to hear from Leah that she was struggling and unable to admit to herself that she might not be managing.

"And look, there's bloody Amanda again – pretending that she doesn't even know the camera is on her," Leah said, eyes wide in disbelief. Then she let out a little scream. "Oh, Jesus, Olivia, why didn't you tell me that dress made me look like a heifer!"

"What? You didn't look like a heifer. You looked gorgeous!"

"Thank you for trying to make me feel better, but there is no disguising the fact that my backside looks like the back of a bus in that."

"Ah, it's probably that television. I think it could be set on widescreen or something," Olivia argued.

"Oh, I see, so widescreen only affects certain people, does it? It doesn't affect skinnymalinks like Amanda Clarke, then?"

The two of them laughed.

"Josh's camera work isn't too bad actually," Leah commented. "He can be a bit zoom-happy sometimes. Oh look, now he's taking some shots out front – oh my God, I still can't believe that's my store – can you believe it, Olivia, my very own store!"

Olivia smiled at her friend's almost childlike delight. She was thrilled it was all going so well for her. With all the work she'd done, not just now but throughout the years, Leah deserved every bit of her success.

Just then the camera seemed to swerve sharply downwards towards the pavement, and for a few minutes all they could see were the tips of Josh's shoes.

"Typical – and just when I said he was doing so well . . ." Leah trailed off as another pair of feet came into the picture – female feet. With her pretty painted toenails and diamond and silver sandals, the woman must have been a guest at the party.

"Nice shoes," Leah noted, and Olivia had to agree. Whoever the woman was, Josh seemed to know her, and the camera remained pointed at the ground.

"Great, while he's having a chat, the tape was still running. No wonder it ran out so quickly. Trust bloody Josh to make a bags of the video – again! I wonder who he's talking to?" She picked up the remote and hit the volume control.

Josh's voice could clearly be heard. ". . . didn't know you lived around here now."

Then the girl's voice: "Didn't know you were a video-man in your spare time either!"

A flirtatious giggle . . . a male laugh . . . and, instantly, Olivia felt Leah tense.

Right away Olivia knew that something was wrong here. "Here, give me the remote," she said quickly. "We should fast-forward through this. We can't really see anything and –"

"Leave it!" The words sounded like bullets.

"Leah, you shouldn't –"

"I said leave it!"

Her heart pounding, Olivia sat back and waited for what was to come. For Leah's sake, she hoped it wasn't anything to worry about.

Josh's voice. "So how have you been?"

"Great, and you?" Chirpily.

"OK."

"So, what's going on in there?"

Warily. "It's my girlfriend's launch night – she's inside."

A smile in her voice. "I see." The feet turned and

311

pointed towards the store, and Olivia deduced she was trying to get a peek inside. "So you two are still together then."

"Yes, look, Sharon . . ."

"Sharon?" Leah cried, almost to herself.

"You know her?" Olivia asked, vaguely relieved. At least it was someone they both knew and not just some –

"Yes, I know her," Leah answered flatly.

"Well –" Olivia stopped short, as Josh's voice again came all-too-clearly through the TV speakers.

". . . just one night. I didn't mean for it to –"

"Oh, my God!" Leah's face paled, and she put a hand to her mouth.

Olivia's gaze stayed glued to the screen, shocked.

"I know that, Josh. Don't beat yourself up about it. I suppose it was silly of us, really – for old times' sake and all that. Believe me, I didn't expect you to go down on one knee after it." A coquettish laugh. "Anyway, it was fairly obvious you'd go straight back to her."

"Oh, my God," Leah repeated slowly, her eyes wide and sorrowful.

"Look, I'd better go back inside," came Josh's voice. "They're waiting for me . . ."

"No problem. Listen, Josh, it was nice to see you again. And look, don't worry about it. I'm not in the habit of going around trying to wreck other people's relationships. It was one night, no big deal."

"You're sure you weren't angry that I left without saying goodbye?"

"It was fine – I'm a big girl now!" Another laugh,

and a slight movement towards the shopfront. "The thing is . . . I just adore chocolate and this place looks really amazing. Maybe, I should pop in some time and . . . Josh, I'm only joking! God, you should see the look on your face!" She seemed to move back towards him again, as if she was laying a hand on his arm or something. "Really, I'm joking."

Josh now sounded decidedly standoffish. "Right. Look, I'd better go. See you around, Sharon."

"Sure, maybe we might bump into one another again some night."

"Maybe. See you."

Then sudden movement, as the camera swerved, and Josh seemed to walk back inside. Then they heard Kate's voice. "Hey, Josh over there – quickly! Leah's just about to make her speech!"

Then the screen went black for a second, and soon after, another scene opened picturing Leah, beaming and smiling at Josh and his camera, and looking happier than she'd ever been in her life.

Chapter 29

Leah's hands shook as she turned the key in the door to the apartment. She didn't think it was possible to feel such a mix of emotions all at once – fear, anger, loss, there were so many she didn't think she could recognise one from the other.

But as soon as she saw Josh dozing on the sofa, obviously not long back from work, one particular emotion came sharply into focus – betrayal.

Her legs felt like jelly. She didn't know how she was going to deal with this. She had watched a replay of the video three times, and each time things were even clearer. Josh had spent the night with Sharon Whyte, his ex-girlfriend. There was no other explanation, despite Olivia's pleas.

"Leah, you can't just jump to conclusions like this – they could be talking about anything!" her friend had said.

Leah, shocked and bewildered, was clutching a pillow to her as though she would never let go. "Oh, come on, Olivia! 'Just one night?' 'For old times' sake?' What else could they be talking about?"

"Look, go home and talk to Josh about it – show him the tape, and see what he says. Whatever you do, don't accuse him straight out because you could have the complete wrong end of the stick."

"Olivia, I know as my friend that you're only trying to make me feel better, but we're not teenagers here. There could only be one end of the bloody stick!" With that, the tears had come and Leah didn't think she would ever stop crying.

How could she have been so stupid? How could she have been so naïve in thinking that she and Josh were back on course? But of course, he had been so attentive lately, hadn't he? Things had been a bit rough while she was getting the shop set up because they rarely saw one another, but after the opening, it was as though things were better than ever. But that wasn't it, Leah saw now. It wasn't that things were getting back to normal – it was that Josh was feeling guilty about his one-night (who knows, it could have been more?) stand with his ex – a girl Leah had met once briefly, and who seemed nice enough, if a little immature. They had split up because Sharon couldn't come to terms with Josh's decision never to have children, while Leah, good old reliable Leah had. Well, Sharon had the last laugh, didn't she?

Now there was Josh lying indolently on the couch,

oblivious to what was about to come. For one brief second, Leah wished that things hadn't changed; she wished she could go back in time and never have seen that video. But yet, wasn't it better to know now, before she committed herself to a man who wasn't what she thought he was? A man who had the gall to come straight out and tell her that he wasn't the paternal type – who didn't want children, and she could take it or leave it? A man whose decision Leah had spent the last few years trying to justify to friends, family and everyone else who thought she was just being selfish! And all the time, it had never been her decision – it had never been her choice. But she had made that sacrifice, because she was sure that Josh was the one for her, and she knew that sometimes life didn't always work out how you wanted it to. She loved Josh, he loved her and as far as she was concerned, this would be enough.

Until now.

Now, looking at him, Josh Ryan seemed the most insincere, hurtful, selfish bastard Leah had ever come across.

"Wake up!" she cried, throwing a cushion at him, adrenaline pumping through her veins as the anger slowly began to take over. On one hand, she wanted to keep throwing cushions at him all night, on another she wanted him to take her in his arms, give her a perfectly reasonable explanation, and they would both laugh at her silliness.

"Lee? What?" Josh sat up, eyes blinking in the bright light. "What time is it?"

Leah didn't answer, and a sudden calmness seemed to descend upon her as she crossed the room. She took the videotape out of her handbag and put it into the machine.

"What's this?" Josh asked her. "Oh, is it the launch party? Olivia gave back the video then – good. I was thinking of buying one of those new tiny ones for our holidays anyway. Is it any good?"

"Depends on how you look at it," Leah said flatly.

Josh looked at her and grimaced. "Ah no, don't tell me I messed it up again, did I? Shit, Lee, I'm sorry – I probably had one two many glasses of that champers that night – the focus is probably all over the place."

"No, the focus is just fine, Josh. It's the sound that could have done with being a little bit clearer, actually."

"You know what these things are like – with all that music in the background, and people chattering amongst themselves . . . anyway, I told you you should have set up a microphone for your speech. Weren't you hoarse by the end of the night – trying to shout over everyone like that?"

Amazing, Leah thought. He had absolutely no idea, no idea at all he'd been caught. Was he so without a soul or a conscience that he didn't even remember his meeting up with Sharon, that he hadn't been all that bothered about coming face to face with his infidelity that night? Strange how you think you know someone so well and, once the mask had been removed, everything seemed to come sharply into focus.

Speaking of which . . .

"Hey, I think I'm doing all right so far," Josh said, smiling up at her.

Leah was standing there staring at the screen.

"Why are you standing up?" Josh asked. "Come and sit down. I know you've seen this already, but I haven't and . . ."

He trailed off, as automatically he followed her intense gaze back to the TV screen, just as the pair of silver strappy shoes and red toenails came into view. For a few seconds he just stared at the pictures, then at Leah, and when she bent down and increased the volume, and he heard his voice clearly come through, all the blood seemed to drain from his face.

"Oh, Jesus, Leah –"

"Shut up Josh, I'm trying to hear what you're saying. You know, you're right – it *is* almost impossible to make out what people are saying over the music and the crowd. It made much more sense to have a conversation outside. So, how did Sharon enjoy the party? Funnily enough, I didn't see her there."

He looked at her then, and despite Olivia's insistence that there might be a reasonable explanation, one look at his expression told her that there could only be one.

"I'm so sorry," he croaked.

At this, at hearing the admission so simply, so easily, a wave of emotion crashed over Leah, engulfing her in sorrow, disappointment, regret, anger. *I'm so sorry*. In a way, she wished that he would try to deny it, just to give her some hope, even the tiniest bit of hope. But there was no denial. The facts were straightforward. Josh had cheated on her, plain and simple.

"It had nothing to do with you – with us," he was saying, his voice now a sharp contrast to his joviality earlier. "I love you – I still love you. You're the most important thing that's ever –"

"Oh, my God, Josh, this is incredible! I can't believe I'm hearing this! *I'm* the most important thing? You *still love* me? What do you think this is – some poxy TV soap opera? How dare you admit to cheating on me and then have the cheek – the *gall* to say that it had nothing to do with me! Me! Me – who agreed to love and stay with you despite your decision not to ever have children, who put aside my own hopes and desire for a family because I thought I had found someone special! Someone I thought would be enough! How dare you turn around and tell me that it had nothing to do with me!"

"But it's true! It was a stupid situation, a crazy drunken thing. I met Sharon one night in town and –"

Leah cut him off. "Stop it! I don't want to know." But she did, of course, she did, yet at the same time, hearing how it all happened would make it all the more real, and she didn't think she could handle that.

"Oh, God, I had no idea the tape was still running, I had no idea . . ." He put his head in his hands.

"I see. So you would have been quite happy to keep it all a secret, quite happy to keep me in the dark."

"I wanted to tell you but – oh, God, Leah, it was a mistake – a massive mistake."

"Yes, it certainly was." Leah couldn't think of anything else to say to that.

"Lee, you and I were in a bit of rut – you admitted that yourself. You were so wrapped up in getting the shop ready and, don't get me wrong – of course, you were entitled to, but I don't know, we just weren't spending any time together any more. You were totally preoccupied –"

"Oh, I see. So poor little Josh wasn't getting the attention he wanted, the attention he deserved! So instead he decides to get it elsewhere – but not just anyone would do – no, it had to be Sharon! Couldn't you have picked up some stranger from somewhere, Josh, if you wanted it that badly? Why did it have to be someone you knew, for Christ's sake?"

And that was probably the worst part of it. Sharon would always see this as some kind of victory, some sort of childish proof that she could have Josh whenever she wanted him. And how dare he suggest that she was too preoccupied with the shop to give him the attention he deserved. What about the support *she* deserved? She'd been working her backside off trying to get this going – trying to get them the life they wanted. She knew Josh didn't want to spend the rest of his life under his father's thumb, and she had always thought that success in the shop meant that he could scale down a bit, and maybe start doing something for himself. Now, he had gone and ruined it all.

"Love, this is all my fault and I'm not blaming you for one second. I suppose I'm just trying to let you know my state of mind at the time. You have to admit yourself that things weren't great between us a while back."

"But that doesn't give you the right to . . ." She trailed off, shaking her head. Never in her wildest dreams had she imagined this. Somehow she had always thought too much of Josh, had always believed him to be an infinitely decent person, which is why she didn't have to think too much about making the sacrifice of never having children with him. She thought she had found the elusive 'One' and, although things were never going to be exactly as she wanted them, she thought that she had enough. So many people just couldn't be happy; they were so busy searching for perfection that they didn't realise that sometimes the 'One' might not be exactly as they had thought. She loved Josh enough, was sure that he loved her enough too, and there was nothing or no one that could keep them apart.

No one except Sharon apparently.

"Why?" Leah asked now. "Was it really just because our sex life had dwindled? Or was it something more?" She couldn't quite believe that Josh would be so shallow as to throw away everything they had over sex. Yes, things had gone down somewhat but lately, she thought cringing, things had really begun to improve. Had he learnt a few tricks from Sharon then, she wondered, trying desperately to banish unbidden thoughts of them together, what they might have been doing to one another, if Josh nibbled Sharon's ear in the

same way that he nibbled hers, if his hands ran across . . .
Stop it! she warned herself. She would drive herself
mad if she thought about it. "Why did you do it?"

"It was a stupid, stupid mistake," Josh said, and Leah
could see the beginnings of tears behind those large blue
eyes. "I know it sounds like a cliché, everything I say now
is going to sound like a cliché, but, Leah, it's true. At the
time, it had little or nothing to do with us – it was just sex,
drunken pathetic sex, nothing more." He winced and
ran a hand through his hair. "I knew I'd been an idiot
and, believe me, I agonised about telling you for days –
weeks – afterwards but things were finally coming
together with the shop, and you were so happy. I couldn't
just lay it on you like that. I knew it would ruin
everything for you."

"Wow, what did I do to deserve such a thoughtful
boyfriend?" Leah said coldly. "So, first of all, you went
off with that – with *her* because I wasn't paying you
enough attention, and then you decided not to bother
telling me, because you were worried about my *feelings*!
Hell, Josh, do you not think that you've got things a
little backward there?"

"I'm so sorry," he said, again, and this time, there
were actual tears slowly moving down his cheeks.
"Please believe me. I am so, so, sorry. The last thing I
ever wanted to do was hurt you, Leah. I love you so
much you wouldn't believe it."

He reached across for her hand, and it took every
ounce of strength Leah had to move away. She had
never seen Josh cry before, had never seen him so upset.

But as much as the sight moved her, she couldn't let such a simple tactic sway her. That was obviously what he wanted.

"Look, I know you probably won't believe me, but," he sat back on the couch, drained, "I was going to propose to you on the night of the launch party. I had it all planned . . ."

Stop it! Leah raged inwardly, her heart beginning to pound. *Don't do this – don't you dare do this to me!* She had never dared entertain the prospect of marriage to him, and they had never spoken about it before. Josh was as unconventionial as they came, so as much as she loved him, Leah knew she could take nothing for granted. And in all honesty she didn't really care, because they were as good as married anyway.

Now, hearing those words, Leah's heart ached to the core.

"But when I went outside and met . . . met her, well then, I just couldn't," Josh went on. "I couldn't in good conscience go in there and ask you to be my wife, ask you to spend the rest of your life with me. Because I knew then that I didn't deserve you, that I was a weak, spineless, pathetic idiot who didn't know how lucky he was."

Leah finally sat down. She didn't know what to think or what to feel.

"I've blown it, Leah. I know that. I could sit here all night and try and think of a million different excuses, different reasons for why I did it. But there are none. I was an idiot and there's no getting away from it. I let you down. I let *us* down."

"Yes, you did," Leah whispered, and by then she was crying too.

"Look," Josh turned to her, his eyes sorrowful, "I won't insult you any more by trying to explain my way out of it. I made a mess of things, I know that. But you have to believe me when I say that I do love you. Yes, I know you're thinking I have a funny way of showing it, but I know in my heart that it's true. I don't think I can ever make you understand why I did it – I don't know if I understand it myself. But you mean the world to me, Leah. You always will. Our time together has been nothing short of brilliant. You're my best friend."

"Josh, please . . ." Leah couldn't listen to it any more. It was all so final. There was no going back from this. Josh had betrayed her in the worst way. She didn't know what she had expected. She supposed she thought he would beg for her forgiveness, ask to her to try and understand, maybe even blame her a little more.

In a strange way, she respected him for his honesty, his blatant regret for what had happened because it left her with her dignity intact. But she had lost her best friend, she had lost the love of her life, the person with whom she was so sure she would spend the rest of her life.

"I'm sorry," he said again, and before Leah could stop him, he reached across and planted a soft, salty kiss on her lips. "I love you, and you don't deserve this – I'm sorry." With that, he stood up, and walked to the doorway. "I'll stay with Paddy tonight," he said with a haunted look in his eyes.

"Oh. Does he know about . . . ?"

"Of course not – no-one else knows. I wouldn't do that to you. I'll tell him I lost my keys or something . . ." He knew she wouldn't want Paddy knowing what had happened.

"OK." All of a sudden, Leah felt empty, bereft of all feeling for the situation, for Josh, everything.

"I'm sorry," he whispered, before opening the door. "For everything."

Leah heard the apartment door close softly behind him.

"So am I," she whispered, warm tears coursing down her cheeks. "So am I."

Chapter 30

Robin slowly opened her eyes, and groggily lifted her head off the pillow. The incessant shrill of the telephone had woken her out of her deep sleep, and was now piercing her throbbing brain. Which, she supposed, served her right for drinking so much last night. Who the hell could be ringing at this hour, she wondered, her eyes barely focusing on the digits on the alarm-clock. Ben's side of the bed was empty, so Robin deduced he must have already gone out for his morning jog. Catching sight of the time, she groaned. It was eight fifteen, and she was barely in the door after hitting the town in a major way last night with Anna and the girls.

Anna, apparently determined to prove that married life hadn't snuffed her party spirit, and also to celebrate Robin's new publishing 'career' had insisted they visit as many ultra-trendy Village bars as possible. They'd consumed so many tartinis, Martinis and Mojitos throughout the night that after a while, Robin couldn't tell the difference from one drink to another. Afterwards they had gone clubbing, something she hadn't done in ages. It had been a great night, but Robin was paying for it now and, if she had her way, the caller on the other end of the line would end up paying for it too!

"Robin, hey! Good morning!" She sat up as Marla's chirpy tones floated down the line, instantly waking her up. What on earth was her publisher doing ringing her at this hour? "Marla – hi, how are you? Is everything OK?"

"Everything's fine Robin, just fine! Listen, can you come down for a meeting this morning? I couldn't get your agent on the phone, so I haven't had the chance to tell her yet, but – oh, Robin, this is such great news!"

"She's away for a few days," Robin said. "And what's great news?"

Still feeling very bleary, Robin could barely concentrate on the conversation. Somewhere in the distance, she heard the door of the apartment open.

"It's killing me, but I really don't want to say too much on the phone," Marla said. "Just try and get your ass up here as soon as you can – you are not going to believe this!"

With that Marla hung up and Robin was left staring at the phone in bewilderment as Ben came into the room.

"Good morning!" he said mischievously. "*Someone* had a good night out last night!" Then he noticed her bemused expression. "What's up?" he asked. "Who was on the phone?"

Robin rubbed her eyes. "It was the publishers – and to be honest, I'm not too sure what's up," she replied, dragging herself out of the bed, "but, knowing Marla, whatever it is, it'll be worth hearing."

An hour or so later, Robin was wondering if she had actually woken up at all or whether lack of sleep had seriously affected her hearing. "Are you serious?" she asked. Marla had just informed her that translation rights to her little book had been sold in ten different countries.

"It's true," Marla said, her blue eyes shining. "We didn't want to tell you until we had the details worked out, but *Atchoo* will soon be appearing in French, Italian, Russian, German –"

"But it hasn't even gone on sale yet!" Robin blustered. She couldn't believe this.

"Yes, but there's already a massive buzz surrounding it and then, of course –" she paused dramatically, and Robin knew instantly that there was more, "well, we didn't want to say anything until we knew for sure but," Marla took a deep breath, "Nickelodeon have come in for TV rights!"

"What? The children's TV channel?"

"Yes, they want *Atchoo!*" Marla beamed, and Robin knew then that she wasn't really sitting here – she was lying at home in her bed, and her eyes were twitching madly as a result of this wild dream she was having.

"Yes! And we're going to make them pay a fortune

too!" Marla continued. "Gawd, this couldn't have happened at a better time! The book will be in the shops in November and once news of this deal gets out, the book trade will be hammering on our door!" She paced excitedly up and down the room. "Lucy's working on the publicity tour as we speak. I know we agreed two weeks of appearances here, but the ways things are going, this book is going to be massive."

Just then, the aforementioned Lucy, Bubblegum's PR person, entered the room.

"Hi, Robin, great news!" she said, hugging her enthusiastically.

"So, what have we got?" Marla checked her watch impatiently. "I've got a ten thirty, so try and make it quick."

Lucy took a seat alongside Robin, and flicked through some papers.

"Well, Robin, I think you'd better have a chat with your boss and see if he'll give you some more time off –"

"Ha!" Marla interjected. "If I get the big money I want from Nickelodeon, Robin, you might have more time off than you'll ever need!"

"More time off? For what?"

"Well, at the moment, we're in the process of arranging some promotional appearances in Europe – they're going wild about your story, and why you wrote this book in the first place. Seriously, Robin, we seem to have really tapped into a trend here – everyone – be they American, French or German – knows, or has a child who suffers from some kind of allergy. The media are going crazy for it."

"But it's only a simple little story," Robin shook her head. "I just can't understand all this interest, and the book's not even published – it just seems so sudden."

"This is how publishing works, honey," Marla said. "And it'll just as quickly be yesterday's news, so we've got to capitalise on it while we can."

Lucy nodded. "And, while the interest *is* there, we need you to go out and do the PR and the interviews, meet the kids and the parents, tell them about your own experiences." She looked at her notes. "They're going crazy for you in the UK and Ireland, because of the rights hype, and also due to the fact that you're one of their own – you are Irish, aren't you?" she asked, when Robin's face dropped.

"Yes." Robin's heart thudded as she suspected what was coming. Oh, no, she couldn't do this. No way.

"We issued a press release earlier today – and the media, *particularly* in Ireland, are going crazy over it, especially over the Nickelodeon interest. The phones have been ringing all morning since. They really want a piece of you, Robin – school appearances, radio, TV, you name it. So we have to get you over there – and soon!"

Robin's stomach dropped. They couldn't – they *didn't* expect her to go home, did they?

"I'm telling you, from what I've been hearing, you'll be a bit of a national hero over there. I can already see the headlines: *Our very own JK* !"

Marla laughed when Robin eyes widened at this. "Hey, it's not quite Harry Potter, but by the time we're done here, who knows?"

Robin forced a smile. Oh my God, she told herself, please say this isn't happening.

"So, if you could have a chat with your boss, and let us know as soon as possible when, and for how long, you're available," Lucy said. "To begin with, we'll be concentrating mostly on the UK and of course, there'll be a massive campaign in Ireland. Don't worry, we'll make sure you're reimbursed for your time," she added, when Robin looked sick to the stomach at the thought of it all, although not for the reasons her publisher suspected.

"We're really on a roll here, Robin!" Marla enthused. "And with the way things are going, who knows where this will end?"

Chapter 31

Olivia couldn't quite overcome her sense of nagging unease. There she was, nearly forty thousand feet in the air, sitting alongside the man she was almost certainly falling in love with, heading for a romantic weekend away to the Black Sea Coast, and still she couldn't relax.

She couldn't relax because, in four years, it was the first time she had left Ellie. Yes, Ellie had gone to stay with Peter's family many times over the years without her, but this was the first time Olivia had actually left *her* behind.

And the worst part was with whom.

Her own mum and dad were away in Killarney this weekend, Peter's mother wasn't well, poor Leah had enough to cope with, and she wouldn't dream of landing Ellie in on top of a still-hassled Kate. So, when Matt had out of the blue suggested that the two of them head off for a romantic weekend, as far as he was concerned there had been only one option.

"Catherine could take her," he'd suggested while they were discussing whether or not they could avail of seats on the plane his company chartered for property-inspection trips.

"There'll be little or no work, I promise," he said, when Olivia raised an eyebrow at the so-called 'holiday'. "This one is Frank's, and I'll just be going along for the ride. I might have to make one or two phone calls to the builder while I'm there, but other than that, I'm free."

He'd been so excited about it, so eager to show her this wonderful country and to spend some time alone with her, that his enthusiasm was contagious. Olivia wanted to spend time with him too, just the two of them, and – considering that she hadn't had a weekend away, not to mention a foreign holiday, since her honeymoon – she too was eager to go. Still, there was the little matter of a baby-sitter for Ellie.

Matt busily dialled his mobile and, within seconds, Catherine had 'come to the rescue'.

"She'd love to do it," he said, sitting down at Olivia's kitchen table. "She usually looks after Adam when I'm abroad anyway."

The night at Catherine's still fresh in her mind, Olivia almost laughed out loud at the thought of it. Yes, Catherine had apologised and was being, well, quite cordial lately, but still, Olivia couldn't bring herself to trust the woman.

"I don't know, Matt – Ellie doesn't really know her," she said, trying not to betray her real feelings on the subject. Matt tended to be a bit touchy when it came to

Catherine, still believing the sun shone out of her very pert backside, convinced that she was the world's greatest childminder.

"But she'd be with Adam. They'd have a ball! Please, Olivia, it's only for a couple of days."

"Couldn't we leave it until another weekend, maybe? At least until my parents or Peter's are available or –"

"But why – when Catherine has already offered? I think it's very nice of her actually, and she's obviously trying to make amends for that night at dinner."

Olivia bit her tongue. So she should be.

"Look, I've told you already that I'll be too busy to get away once the inspection trips really get going – not to mention that we won't be able to get seats on them for love or money."

This was the problem: Matt would be up to his eyes for the rest of the year, and this might be their only chance to have a bit of time together, without the kids.

On the other hand, Olivia also wanted to be around for Leah, should her friend need her. Although Leah had insisted that as far as she was concerned, she and Josh were finished and there was no going back. Olivia had hardly seen her since, Leah being intent on throwing herself into her work to try and overcome the heartbreak and not at all willing, it seemed, to talk about it.

"I need some space now," she'd told Olivia.

But Olivia wasn't sure. She wasn't sure about leaving Leah, and she was even more unsure about leaving Ellie.

"Matt, I'd really feel better if I knew Ellie would be looked after –"

"Of course, she'll be looked after," Matt insisted, pulling her close to him. "I'm telling you, Catherine would really love to do us the favour, and you know how well Ellie and Adam get on."

"That's true but –"

"It's only three days, seventy-two hours at the most," he said, and Olivia noticed there was a touch of irritation in his tone. She sighed inwardly. To be fair, it *was* good of Catherine to offer, and now by hesitating it looked as though she was being very ungrateful. Still, she had to be sure . . .

"Look, why don't we ask Ellie and see what she thinks," she said, trying to sound brighter than she felt. Blast it, she should cop on to herself and stop sounding like a fussy, overprotective mother. Ellie was four years old and very well behaved. It was true that she adored Adam and would probably jump at the chance of going on her own 'weekend away', even if it was only across the green.

"Yay! Want to go on my holidays!" Ellie skipped around the kitchen when she and Matt put it to her later, and Olivia's heart sank.

"You'll have to stay in Catherine's house and you'll have to be very, very good," she warned, realising that there was no going back now. "As Mummy will be gone away with the keys, you can't come back to your house – you know that, don't you?"

Ellie nodded, her eyes wide with excitement. "Can I play with Adam's toys, Mummy?" she asked, the thought of making lots of noise with Adam's *Bob the Builder* tools appealing to her enormously.

"You'll have to ask Adam first, hon," she said, and groaned inwardly at the arguments that Catherine would no doubt have to defuse. "And you'll have to remember that Adam is being very good to let you stay with him, and you should let him play with your toys too."

"'kay!" Ellie started to suck on her thumb, something Olivia noticed she did more often after her trips to Galway.

"Ellie, don't do that, hon. It's a yucky habit," she scolded. Why her grandparents let her get away with it, Olivia didn't know, but it might have something to do with the fact that Peter had also sucked his thumb when younger, and perhaps they found it endearing. "*And you certainly shouldn't do that in front of Catherine*," she added under her breath, thinking that Catherine, with her apparent obsession with discipline, would be scandalised by it.

In addition to the thumb-sucking, the trips also seemed to be getting more and more frequent, and while Olivia knew she couldn't exactly keep her daughter to herself, she still worried about the influence Peter's parents had on Ellie, especially when, rightly or wrongly, they weren't too enamoured of her mother. Peter's parents had never quite forgiven Olivia for what had happened that day; she knew they blamed her for not being there. And, no matter what Leah said, no matter what all the counsellors in the world said, Olivia knew that they were right.

Still, all she could do to make up for the past was by being a good mother to Ellie, and Olivia knew that sometimes her fixation on this made her seem over-protective.

But who could blame her when it came to Catherine? she thought now, staring out the window at the clouds below. Their first meeting had been an absolute disaster – the woman had more or less implied that Olivia *was* a bad mother, and had blatantly shown that she wasn't too happy about her and Matt's budding relationship. Concern for Matt, my foot! Despite what he said, Olivia still got the feeling that Catherine wasn't all sweetness and light. Hours earlier, when they'd dropped Ellie off at the house before leaving for the airport, Catherine had behaved as though she and Olivia were old friends but . . .

"Olivia, you look stunning in that outfit – it's really slimming on you! Matt, make sure you *do* show her around now, and don't be spending *all* your time in the hotel," she'd said laughing gaily. "Ellie, come inside. I've got some lovely new games for you and Adam in the playroom, and I've got a *very* special place for you to sleep." She ruffled Ellie's flyaway hair. Again, Olivia noticed that she really should get it cut, but the curls were so cute and, once they were gone, they were gone forever.

"And I thought we might all go to the seaside tomorrow, what do you think?" Catherine continued. At this, the children's eyes lit up and, trance-like, they followed her down the hallway without a backward glance, almost like those children in the *Pied Piper* story, Olivia thought, feeling somewhat bereft.

"Now, are you two sure you won't have something

to eat – or a cup of tea before you go?" Catherine went on, fussing over them all like a mother hen, her behaviour the complete opposite of before. Matt refused, citing Friday afternoon traffic as an excuse, but Olivia caught his surreptitious wink, as if to say 'Isn't she wonderful?'.

"Oh, well, I suppose you'd better get going – and, Olivia, try not to worry – Ellie will be fine!" Catherine smiled sweetly. "Look at her playing away there. I'm sure she won't even notice you're gone!"

Olivia smiled just as sweetly back, but she didn't miss the dig. Blast it, why had she agreed to this?

But, as the captain made his airport landing announcement for Burgas airport, Olivia knew that now was way too late to change her mind, and it was pointless even thinking about it. She was thousands of miles away, and although she certainly wouldn't be able to forget, she would have to try and put Catherine and Ellie to the back of her mind. It was only a few days after all. A few days couldn't do any harm, could it?

As soon as they began their taxi journey to the coast only fifteen minutes away from the airport, Olivia immediately understood why Matt was so in love with this country. Somehow, she'd expected austere, grey, ex-communist tower blocks and bleak, barren landscapes, but instead they were surrounded by mountainous lush pine forests and acres and acres of obviously fertile vineyards.

The area reminded Olivia of a trip she and Peter had taken to Tuscany shortly after they were married, back when they had been able to get away at the drop of a hat. She shook her head. Lately she'd been thinking a lot about Peter. She supposed that since meeting someone new, someone for whom she might have strong feelings, it was inevitable that he should be in her thoughts, but she didn't want this to intrude on what should be a special time. This was all about Matt, not about Peter, and there was no point in raking up the past. She hoped that Matt wouldn't want to either.

Very few people, other than her closest friends and family were able to understand the guilt that Olivia carried day after day. Perhaps it was unfair, but for the moment she wasn't quite ready to tell all to Matt. Anyway, this weekend was about getting to know one another, having some fun and hopefully, gaining trust – not for exchanging sad stories.

Matt had told her that the clear mountain air, mineral springs and lush pine forests in Bulgaria made it ideal for holidaymakers seeking something other than just a beach holiday.

"It's great for campers, hill-walkers and health-junkies," he said with a grin. "People are tired of the same old Spanish beach holiday. As you can see, this place has still got loads of rural charm."

"And what about when you're finished building all your apartment blocks?" she challenged, thinking that it would be a shame to blight this gorgeous scenery with high-rise apartment blocks *à la* the Spanish *costas*.

"It won't happen," Matt said, shaking his head defiantly. "They're big on planning regulations here because they're in a position to learn from mistakes elsewhere . . ." He shrugged. "We wouldn't get involved in anything that would be detrimental to the area and, subsequently, to our clients."

"You really are a salesman!" she grinned, giving him a gentle dig. "I suppose that's a popular line for your so-called 'clients'?"

"I might be a salesman but I'm certainly not a dishonest one," he countered. "We do a good job for our clients – they're investing not only a lot of money but a lot of trust in our experience and knowledge. I don't cheat people, Olivia."

"I wasn't implying that you did," she said, surprised at this vehemence at what was supposed to be a throwaway joking remark. Still, property developers – advisors or whatever they called themselves – particularly those involved in foreign property, had been vilified by the media over the years to such an extent that she could understand Matt's frustration at trying to run a genuine business. She resolved not to make any more cracks like that for the duration of this holiday, otherwise their budding romance would be over before it had even begun!

They were booked into a luxurious beach-front hotel, and Olivia hoped that the weekend would be spent lazily sunbathing around the pool, going out for relaxing meals in the evening and, hopefully, she thought with a grin, spending lots of time in bed together. Neither had been with anyone since their own respective spouses and, for Olivia, the first time had been strange, but wonderful. It had taken a bit of getting used to, but Matt was loving and gentle and she enjoyed herself immensely with him.

To her surprise, she didn't think of Peter once when she and Matt were together. It was a strange relief as Olivia had always assumed that when she finally took the huge step of making love with someone else, her husband would completely dominate her thoughts. But no, once her body took over, all memory of Peter was banished, at least for a little while, and she certainly wasn't going to let memories of the past affect this weekend.

The same couldn't be said regarding Ellie though. Olivia swore to herself that she wouldn't obsess over her; she swore that she wouldn't let her worries ruin the break. But it was bloody hard not to, when, as it turned out, Catherine didn't seem too bothered about worrying her.

She rang Catherine's house immediately upon arrival at the hotel, just to let her know that they'd landed safely and to enquire about Ellie.

"Well, she had a right tantrum just after you left, but we calmed her down eventually, didn't we, Adam?" Catherine said breezily, and Olivia could actually feel the guilt stab at her heart. Oh, no . . .

"Was she upset about my leaving?"

Catherine sniffed. "Not really – more upset about the fact that she couldn't get her own way, I think. She and Adam were supposed to be taking turns on the swing this afternoon, but Missy wouldn't let Adam have a go at all."

"Really? That doesn't sound like Ellie."

"And then, she wouldn't eat her dinner. She seems rather fussy about her food actually. I presume you don't feed her takeaways *all* the time?"

Olivia winced. She and Ellie usually had a Chinese takeaway on Friday evenings – it was their little treat. She couldn't see Ellie getting upset over the fact that she wasn't getting it on that particular Friday though, could she?

"Of course not," she told Catherine. "She loves Chinese food, and sometimes we get one at weekends and –"

"Really, Olivia, all those additives aren't good for young children, and Ellie's diet could certainly benefit from some fresh food. It seems she also brought some crisps and sweets in her overnight bag – said you told her she should share them with Adam. Perhaps *I* should have told you that such rubbish is banned in this house."

"Oh!" Olivia didn't know how to answer this. She didn't let Ellie gorge on junk food, of course not, but a little treat now and again wouldn't do any child any harm. And it would have been nice to share with Adam . . .

"Anyway, I confiscated them. She roared for about an hour and a half, but when she realised she wasn't going to get any attention from me, she copped onto herself."

Bloody hell, the nuns at my school had nothing on you!
Olivia wanted to say, but there was no point. Instead
she tried a softly, softly approach.

"I'm sorry, I really didn't realise. I hope she hasn't
been too much trouble –"

"Well, she isn't the easiest child in the world to look
after, that's for sure, but what can you do?"

Olivia felt so guilty she could barely continue the
conversation. A minute or so later, and after listening to
a further bout of complaints about her daughter, she said
goodbye. Jesus! Couldn't the woman wait until Olivia
returned from her supposed weekend 'break' before she
started badmouthing her child? Couldn't she understand
that Ellie didn't know or understand her rules, that she
hadn't outlined anything of the sort when offering to
take care of her? Before dropping her over, Olivia had
phoned to ask if there was anything she should or
shouldn't bring. Catherine had simply told her to bring
Ellie and not to 'be fussing over it'. How could she say
now that Ellie was being deliberately bold?

Blast Matt anyway for convincing her to leave Ellie
for the weekend, blast Catherine for being such a cow!
Her cheeks burning with rage and her heart aching for
her daughter, Olivia let herself into the hotel room.

Matt was unpacking his bag. "Well, how are they?"
he asked.

She bit her lip. "Not so good. Apparently, Ellie is
playing up."

He frowned. "Maybe it mightn't have been fair of
me to rope Catherine into doing it."

Olivia's head snapped up. "What? What do you mean 'rope' her into doing it? I thought she *offered* to take Ellie?"

Matt reddened and immediately Olivia knew the truth.

"I don't believe this, Matt. You told me that Catherine was only too happy to take her. You told me that she would be offended if I didn't take up her 'very kind' offer. I can't believe you tricked me into leaving Ellie with someone who doesn't particularly want her!"

"Olivia, calm down – of course, Catherine wants her – it just takes a bit of getting used to, that's all. And she would have been taking Adam anyway so –"

"But that's not the point! If Catherine's been landed with a baby-sitting job she really doesn't want, then chances are Ellie will have picked up on it. Children aren't stupid, you know!"

"Look, Olivia, it's hardly my fault she's a difficult child, is it?"

Olivia was stunned. She couldn't believe this. "For Christ's sake, Matt, she barely knows the woman!" Hearing her words out loud, Olivia fully realised what she had done. She had left her precious little girl with a woman they barely knew, and one that neither liked all that much, just because she, selfish Olivia, wanted to get away for a dirty weekend with some man! How could she? How could she have been so blind and so stupid to even consider such a thing? Just then, Olivia wanted badly to get out of there, to go back home to her daughter, where she belonged.

"Look, I'm sorry. I didn't mean that like it sounded," Matt said, coming to her side. "I know it was difficult for you leaving her and maybe I shouldn't have forced the issue. But Catherine is great with kids and, given time, I'm sure Ellie will be fine. They're just getting used to one another, that's all. Catherine will sort it out."

Saint Bloody Catherine! Although Catherine wasn't so saintly about leaving them in peace, was she? And the things she was saying about Ellie, well, to her it sounded as though Catherine was deliberately trying to upset their weekend away by worrying her over Ellie's behaviour.

"It's not like Ellie to be throwing tantrums, Matt," she said.

"Look, kids play up sometimes, especially when there are other kids around – I'm sure that's all it is. Tell you what, why don't we go out for dinner now like we planned and I'll give Catherine a ring later to see how they're doing – OK?"

Olivia nodded reluctantly, but there was little else she could do at that stage.

They went for a delicious but ridiculously inexpensive meal on the seafront and, as she studied the menu, Olivia temporarily forgot about Ellie, while wondering how on earth the Bulgarians could possibly make any kind of profit charging prices like those.

"The cost of living is about one fifth of that at home," Matt explained. "It's almost impossible to spend money here. That's why it's growing in popularity as a summer destination – there's real value to be had. As for the drinks, well, let's just say we could drink champagne here the entire weekend and it wouldn't break the bank!" His eyes sparkled mischievously.

Olivia shook her head sadly. "Not tonight, Matt," she said and sighed as she looked out to sea. It was a beautiful place – such a shame she couldn't relax and enjoy it properly.

Matt took the hint and seemed to accept her mind was elsewhere, and they said little else throughout the meal. Eventually, he suggested they head back to the hotel.

"I'll give Catherine a call then and see how they're getting on, OK?"

Olivia nodded. Maybe when he heard his childminder whingeing down the phone he might understand her reticence to go partying!

Back in the hotel room, Matt dialled Catherine's number on his mobile. "Catherine, hi – how's everything going?"

Olivia sat back on the bed and tried to decipher what the other woman might be saying but she couldn't hear anything other than a tinny squeal.

"Oh, no, I'm sure she didn't think that," Matt said, with a little laugh. "No, of course, she was concerned but . . . yes, yes, I'll let her know." He smiled and gave Olivia the thumbs-up. "Catherine, honestly, don't worry about it. You've enough to be thinking about . . . no, no, of course I understand."

Olivia sat up. "What's going on?"

"No problem, I'll make sure I tell her. I'm glad they've calmed down now. Say hello to Adam for me in the morning. OK, talk to you soon . . . we will, bye."

"What did she say?"

Matt scratched his head. "The kids are fine now. They've settled down nicely and they've just gone to bed."

"But what did she say about Ellie?"

"She was quite apologetic actually. Says she felt awful after your phone call and only afterwards it hit her how upsetting it could be for you. She's kicking herself now actually, and is really afraid she's ruined our break. Of course, I told her she was overreacting and that you were fine."

"What?" Catherine knew *exactly* what she was doing – what else would giving out about her daughter's behaviour do other than upset Olivia! And now she was trying to pretend to Matt that it had been unintentional? The calculating cow!

Matt sat down beside her on the bed. "Olivia, everything's fine. She said to tell you to relax and have a great time, that she's got everything under control back there." He reached across and stroked Olivia's cheek. "Does that make you feel better?"

"I suppose so." There was no point in having a huge argument with Matt about it, but it was fairly obvious to her that Catherine had a bit of an agenda. Of course, she didn't feel any better about leaving poor Ellie with her, but what could she do? She was here now.

"Good, because if that doesn't make you feel better,

I'm sure there are other ways . . ." he trailed a finger along Olivia's spine and, moving closer, kissed her softly on her lips.

"I'm sorry, Matt," she said, moving away from him. "I'm tired and at the moment, I can't think about anything other than Ellie."

"But she's fine!" he said, wounded. "Why can't you accept that? Catherine said –"

"Catherine said too much as far as I'm concerned," Olivia said, reaching across and picking up the Patricia Scanlan novel she'd been so happily engrossed in on the plane. Maybe immersing herself in some other misfortunate woman's problems might take her mind off things. "I'm sorry, but I can't do this now."

"Fine." Matt stood up and began to strip off while Olivia did her best to ignore him. Then he got into bed and, turning away from her, reached across and resolutely turned off his bedside lamp.

Olivia sighed inwardly. If Catherine's antics had been a ploy to disrupt their romantic weekend away, then it was one that had worked very well indeed.

Chapter 32

Olivia couldn't comprehend the relief she felt when touching down at Dublin airport. The weekend had improved somewhat after that first night, and after a few more (not-so-upsetting) phone calls to Catherine, Olivia had no choice but to try and make the best of it. Still, for the remainder of the weekend, she and Matt had been somewhat awkward and uncomfortable with one another, and the so-called romantic weekend they'd expected hadn't materialised. She didn't quite know how she felt about this; in fact, she couldn't think about anything other than seeing Ellie.

"I'm sorry you didn't enjoy it, Olivia," Matt said on the journey back from the airport, "but I had no idea you'd find it so hard without Ellie."

"I had no idea, either, to be honest," she said sadly, "but since that first night, I couldn't stop thinking and worrying about her."

"Well, it won't be long until you see her now," he said, reaching across and patting her hand, "and I'm sure she can't wait to see you either."

"The same applies to you and Adam," she said, feeling almost as though a weight had been lifted from her shoulders, now she was back on Irish soil.

He shrugged. "He's used to my being away a lot."

"I suppose." Of course, she had forgotten that Matt too was used to being away from his son, whereas this was the first time she and Ellie had been apart like that. It definitely wasn't an experience she wanted to repeat anytime soon.

Finally they reached Cherrytree Green, and Olivia almost bolted out of the car and up the path to Catherine's house.

"Ah, here are the lovebirds!" Catherine was all smiles as she greeted them at the door. "Did you have a good time?"

"We had a lovely time," Olivia smiled back, unwilling to let the cow know that she had got her way. "But it's nice to be back all the same."

"Well, the kids are out playing in the back garden, not a bother on them. Honestly, Olivia, since that first night, Ellie's a different child! I think once she knew she'd overstepped the mark she learnt her lesson."

Olivia followed her through to the kitchen and out the back door where she could hear children's laughter float through the air. The sound of Ellie's carefree giggle was instantly a balm to her soul.

"As I said, Catherine, it's really not like Ellie to be so

difficult," she said, stepping out into the garden. "I'd imagine she was just getting used to –" She broke off as, at the sound of her mother's voice, Ellie turned and raced towards her, arms outstretched. Olivia's heart lifted. "Hi, darling! I really missed . . . *oh my God!*"

Getting a proper look at Ellie, Olivia stood back stunned. She could hardly believe her eyes.

"What on earth did you do to her *hair*?" she shrieked accusingly at Catherine. Ellie's gorgeous curls had been cut away, and her daughter was now – unbelievably – sporting a blunt fringe!

Catherine looked right back at her, all innocence. "Well, after what happened that first night, I didn't really want to say anything on the phone . . ." She trailed off and glanced at Matt. "You did say she was really upset."

"How dare you?" Olivia couldn't comprehend how angry she felt at that moment. "How *dare* you be so bold as to go and cut my daughter's hair without my permission . . . what the hell were you thinking?"

"Olivia, calm down," Matt began.

"What? I hope for your sake, Matt, that you didn't know about this, because if you did . . . "

Catherine bit her lip. "Maybe I should have said something, but I really didn't want to upset you –"

"Of course, you should have said something! You should have asked for my bloody permission, and if you had, you would know that I would never, *ever* cut the child's hair like that!"

Ellie looked upset. "I'm sorry, Mommy. I didn't

mean it," she said, and her bottom lip began to tremble.

Olivia lifted her up in her arms and kissed her gently on the temple. "It's OK, honey. It wasn't your fault."

"Well, that's the thing," Catherine began, and was Olivia imagining it, or did she say this with a hint of a satisfied smile? "Ellie brought some chewing gum with her and –"

"What? She did *not* bring chewing gum with her, she isn't allowed chewing gum – she knows that!"

Ellie had by now buried her face in her mother's chest, so she couldn't see her expression.

Catherine put a hand on her hip. "Well, she must have got it from somewhere, Olivia, because she came in on Saturday and it was all stuck to her hair. It was everywhere!" She looked at Matt, exasperated. "I combed and combed it but there was no way I could have got it out. In the end I had no choice but to cut it out – there was nothing else I could have done." At this, her eyes sparkled with tears – *feigned* tears. Olivia was convinced of it.

"It's OK, Catherine. I'm sure you did your best," Matt said, putting a hand on her arm.

Olivia felt as though she was in some kind of strange nightmare. Where on earth would Ellie have got chewing gum?

"But why didn't you tell me?" Olivia said. "Why didn't you phone and *ask* me if it was OK to cut it out, if it was OK to cut her lovely hair in this – this grotesque style!" She didn't want to say too much in front of Ellie but she was pretty sure her daughter had no idea what 'grotesque' meant.

"I didn't know what to do. Honestly, I thought and thought about it, but in the end I decided that there was no point in upsetting you again so I just went and did what I thought was best. You didn't see how bad it was, Olivia! The hairdresser said she'd never seen anything so bad. In fairness, I don't know how she managed to save so much of Ellie's hair." At this Catherine burst out crying. "I really didn't know what to do!"

"Oh, Catherine, don't!" Matt put a comforting arm around her shoulders, and Olivia felt like throwing something at him. Why did he always end up taking her side? Could he not see what a terrible thing she'd done? She had no right to make that decision, no right to do something like that without consulting Olivia about it! It would take ages for Ellie's hair to look presentable again, despite the so-called best efforts of the concerned hairdresser!

"Olivia, surely you can understand the position she was in," Matt said. "What was the point of telling you over the phone? What would you have done?"

"I would have got the first plane home, that's what I would have done, Matt! But if I were looking after someone else's child I wouldn't take it upon myself to make such a decision. Her hair is ruined, for goodness' sake!"

"Her hair would have been ruined anyway," Catherine sniffed. "I thought I was doing you a favour by not telling you and ruining your weekend." She looked at Matt. "I knew how much you were looking forward to it."

"I know you did," Matt soothed again and at this Olivia gritted her teeth.

She sighed. "As it happens, I don't agree with you," she said. "But the damage is done now."

"Can we go home now, Mummy?" Ellie pleaded.

Catherine pointed inside. "Her things are in the hallway," she sniffed tearfully.

"Fine."

Without a word of goodbye to either of them, Olivia turned and walked inside. "Yes, we're going home," she answered her daughter, who hugged her even tighter. "Back home where we should be."

Chapter 33

Leah was horrified. "You really should have asked me," she said, when the following day Olivia and the newly coiffed Ellie visited her at the shop. "I would have been delighted to look after her for you, you know that."

"I'm sorry I didn't ask now, but to be honest I didn't want to put you on the spot – you've enough on your plate at the moment." In all the years they'd known one another, she had never seen her friend look so lost, so deflated.

She kicked herself once again for agreeing to go away with Matt when by rights she should have been around for Leah. "By the looks of things, you're still very busy here too." The shop was packed to the gills and Olivia almost had to fight her way through the crowds to get to the kitchen out back. Amanda was out front, flitting around like a butterfly on one wing, and Olivia suspected – spying her casually flicking through a newspaper when there was a queue a mile long – about as much use.

Leah gave a rare smile, the first one Olivia had seen since the split with Josh. "I know, it's great, isn't it? But seriously, you should have asked me to take her. Alan and Amanda could have looked after things here over the weekend, and I certainly could have done with the diversion. I can honestly say too that I wouldn't have cut her hair without asking – not like that anyway," she added, dropping her voice to a whisper. Ellie was out of earshot and incredibly, Olivia thought, seemed to be enjoying all the attention her new hairstyle was getting. Eva had been equally horrified and the previous evening Olivia had to physically stop her mother from marching across the green to "tell that madam exactly what I think of her!".

"But tell me, what happened afterwards?" Leah asked. "What did Matt say?"

Olivia shrugged. "We went straight home, obviously. He called over a while afterwards and, to be honest, he didn't say much other than to reiterate that Catherine had done what she thought was best, and didn't want to upset me by telling me blah, blah, blah!" She rolled her eyes. "The weekend was a disaster, Leah. Bulgaria was wonderful but I was so stressed about Ellie being with that – that *witch*, that I just couldn't relax and enjoy it." She explained how Catherine had – purposefully, she was sure of it – tried to upset her by insinuating that Ellie was being a nightmare.

"I find that very hard to believe." Leah gazed

lovingly at the little girl, who was staring fascinated at the huge blocks of chocolate that had been delivered earlier that day. They lay there like lumps of rock waiting for a talented sculptor to begin work.

"Well, I did too, and, as it turned out, it was *Adam* that was causing problems, not Ellie."

"Oh?"

"Obviously, Ellie knew I was upset about her hair, and she told me that when Catherine took them for a day out at the park, Adam picked up a dirty piece of chewing gum from one of the benches and put it in his mouth."

That wasn't the worst bit, Olivia thought. Back home, Catherine had instantly presumed it was Ellie who had somehow 'sneaked in' the gum. As if Olivia's four-year-old was some kind of underhand smuggler! But as it turned out, it had been Adam who, when finished chewing the delicious flavours of dirt and grime, had taken it out of his mouth and begun playing with it. Hence Ellie's hair.

"Adam gave me the bold bubblegum, Mummy," Ellie'd said, troubled that once again she'd been betrayed by her new friend. "An' it got caught in my curls!"

Leah shook her head. "And the silly cow never even thought to ask if it could be Adam, I suppose."

"Nope. He can do no wrong as far as she's concerned. Don't get me wrong – Adam's a nice child but he's very spoiled, and personally I think he's crying out for his dad's attention. Matt's away a lot, and it's Catherine who looks after him most of the time."

"A regular little family, aren't they?" Leah said sarcastically. "That whole thing with her is really odd, if you ask me."

"You know, I think you might have been right about her having some kind of crush on him," Olivia said, admitting it out loud. She'd been going over and over everything that had happened since she and Matt got together, and it really did seem as though Catherine was doing her level best to try and make things hard for them. "But what should I do? Things are shaky enough between me and Matt as it is, and we've only been together a little while. He can't see any wrong in what she's doing, and he won't hear a word said against her."

"And how do you feel about it all? I mean, despite all this business with Catherine, do you think he's worth pursuing?"

"To be honest, I don't know where I stand with him, let alone how I feel. We tiptoed around one another at the weekend – it was hardly the love-in that we'd planned."

Leah looked sideways at her. "So you haven't bared your soul yet, as such?"

"With the way things are going, I don't feel confident enough, Leah. I had hoped to broach the subject at the weekend but then . . ." She shook her head. "Anyway, I'm not sure if this thing we have is actually *going* anywhere, so why put myself through it? Why 'bare my soul' as you put it, to someone I'm not sure of?"

Leah nodded. "Maybe it *is* best if you don't say anything for a while. See how he deals with this

Catherine situation first. But if he stays around, you might have to get used to the idea of having *her* around too."

"God help us then!" Olivia laughed, although it wasn't at all funny. "So, have you spoken to Josh since?" she asked, tentatively changing the subject and instantly a shadow crossed her friend's pretty face.

"I'm seeing him tomorrow," Leah admitted, almost shyly, as if she didn't want anyone to think that she was being weak. "He's phoned the apartment every day since, but it's been hard . . ." She trailed off, a catch in her voice.

"I know it is." Olivia touched her gently on the arm. "Still, I think you're doing the right thing by meeting him. You two still have some things to talk about, I'm sure."

"Yeah, mostly about how he should take the rest of his stuff out of the apartment and get out of my life for good!" Leah said vehemently, but Olivia could see the sorrow in her eyes. "I don't want to talk about – about *her*," she added, and her expression grew hard. "I just don't want to know. You won't believe this, but I dreamt last night that Sharon ended up getting pregnant as a result of that night." She gave a broken laugh. "It would be just my luck if she *did* and, despite all his bullshit, Josh was consumed with joy, and the two of them and their spawn ended up living happily ever after!"

Olivia didn't want to admit that this particular thought had crossed her mind too. Sometimes, life had a way of coming back to bite you in the rear like that.

MELISSA HILL

"Don't be silly," she said. "Look, just go and meet him and keep an open mind about what he has to say."

"I suppose." Leah didn't look at all enamoured of the prospect. "I might need a shoulder to cry on afterwards though."

Olivia grimaced. "We're invited to Kate's tomorrow night though, aren't we?"

Leah rolled her eyes. "I'd forgotten about that."

"Does she know about you and Josh?"

"No, I didn't want to say anything yet, because I know exactly what she'd say. And let's face it, she'd probably want to hunt Josh down and kill him."

Olivia nodded. As they both knew only too well, Kate was fiercely unforgiving about any wrongdoings towards her friends.

"Well, I suppose you could always leave it, but I think I'd better go. It was nice of her to invite me and I've hardly seen her since she had the baby –"

"No, no, I will go. It's not ideal, but at the same time, she'll have to know eventually. I hope she's in the mood for vino this time though." Leah raised a tiny grin. "Something tells me I'll need to drown my sorrows."

"Well, look, there's no point in you driving then. Why don't you call over to me beforehand, and we'll both go from my place. Mum's taking Ellie for me, and from what I can make out, is determined to do a patch-up job on her hair." She grimaced. "Not sure it's such a good idea but what can I do? It has to be better than –"

"Girls, girls!" Just then Amanda burst through the door and cut short the remainder of Olivia's sentence.

360

Typically dramatic, she was flushed and seemed to be waving a newspaper over her head. "You have just *got* to read this!"

"Let me guess," Leah drawled. "Whistles are having a mid-season sale?"

Amanda shook her head impatiently, as she flicked through the pages. "Nope, even better. It's last Saturday's paper actually, and I would have missed it only . . . oh, where has it gone?"

"What is it?" Olivia asked, and then she and Leah gawped in unison as they caught sight of Robin staring back at them from the *Weekend Lifestyle* section of the *Independent*, the headline overhead proclaiming: *Nuts about Robin – Irishwoman Takes US Publishing World by Storm*.

"Publishing world . . . *what*?" Olivia asked, looking at the others. "I didn't know Robin had written anything!"

"Neither did I," Leah said, and by her tone, Olivia knew she was hurt at being kept in the dark. She and Robin normally shared everything and Olivia knew that Leah had told Robin about her and Josh's recent split. So why hadn't Robin said anything about this?

"Well, according to the paper she's being paid a fortune for writing these dinky little picture books," Amanda said, only too happy to fill them in. "About children's illnesses, apparently."

"Illnesses?" Olivia repeated. "What kind of illnesses?"

Amanda tut-tutted. "Honestly, Olivia, I would have thought you of all people should know!" She shook her head. "Aren't they always saying that you should write about what you know and, by the looks of things," she added, eyes widening, "Robin's making a nice little career for herself by doing exactly that."

"You don't mean . . . ?" Olivia's sentence trailed off as she scanned the article. As she tried to read the words, she felt as though a firework had just gone off in her stomach. Robin writing stories . . .

Leah, who had by then read the article from beginning to end, looked up from the newspaper. "She has," she confirmed, astonishment written all over her face. "Robin's written some book about allergies – children's allergies – and now it's being made into a cartoon or a TV series, or something."

Olivia looked at her in disbelief. "You're not serious."

"I know!" Amanda cried. "Believe me, Robin was the *last* one of us I'd have expected to do something like that!" She put a hand on her hip. "I'm a bit annoyed, to be honest – I had hoped to try my hand at one of those pregnancy manuals. But now it seems freaky old Robin has beaten me to it! Lucky cow, I bet she'll get to go on TV and everything!"

"That's not all," Leah said. "It says here she'll be doing a promotional tour here shortly! I can't *believe* she kept quiet about this. I'm always asking her when she's coming home!"

Olivia said nothing. She was still coming to terms with the fact that Robin had written not just a book – but a book for and about children. What did Robin

362

know about children? What advice did she have to give to anyone about looking after an allergy-prone child? Granted, she had the experience of her own childhood but still . . .

"So, she's finally coming home, then," Amanda said. She shook her head wistfully. "Imagine, all the old gang together again." At this, Leah nudged her. "Oh, except for Peter, of course. Sorry, Olivia," she added hurriedly, but Olivia didn't even notice.

She was too busy wondering what would happen when Robin returned home, and when their paths crossed – as Olivia was certain they would – what would the two old friends have to say to one another?

Chapter 34

From her bedroom window the following day, Catherine watched them giggling and laughing with one another outside Olivia's house like they were a couple of teenagers. Tears sprang to her eyes. She was losing Matt, she knew it.

Despite what Matt had described as their 'disastrous' weekend away, despite all the hullabaloo about Ellie's hair, they still seemed crazy about one another. If Matt had thought of taking Catherine away for a weekend with him, it would have been far from disastrous. Olivia didn't know how lucky she was that he kept going back to her, despite her carry-on.

And talk about being overprotective! Jeez, the woman was close to obsessed with that child! Catherine supposed it was because she'd been widowed, and Ellie was all she had in the world, but still! If Olivia wasn't careful, her daughter would grow up terribly spoiled.

Not that she was a bad kid, Catherine thought, a little guiltily. Ellie *had* taken some time to settle on Friday, but she'd over-exaggerated when she told Olivia her daughter had had a tantrum. She was very good-natured really, and Catherine felt bad about using her to try and upset her mother's new romance.

Matt seemed fascinated by Olivia, though – it was as though he felt some sort of kinship with her, simply because they were both widowed. Catherine felt what lately had been an all-too-familiar sense of panic. What if Olivia and Matt and their respective children started playing happy families? What would happen to her if they all lived happily ever after?

Yesterday, after Olivia had gone off in a strop over Ellie's new haircut, she'd quizzed Matt about the woman's husband, and how and when he'd died. She'd been naturally curious about it, but more importantly, she wanted to find out if the two had had the heart-to-heart over the weekend that Matt expected.

But to Catherine's utter delight, it turned out they hadn't shared any stories, past or otherwise.

"She was totally preoccupied with getting home to Ellie," he said, over the hearty meal she'd prepared for him. "The time wasn't right. I told her a little bit about Natasha, but she seems very hesitant to talk about Peter. All I know is that he was her first love, they'd been together since their college days and she presumed they'd be together forever." He shrugged. "Obviously, things didn't turn out that way. I'd imagine she's finds it hard to let go."

"It must be very difficult for her," Catherine said, using her most compassionate tone. "Matt, I know you like her a lot, and she seems a lovely woman but . . ." She faltered, as if unsure how to say it. "Olivia might not yet be ready to move on. If she's still not over her dead husband, well, you could be in for a very difficult time." She patted him on the hand. "And as far as I'm concerned you've been through enough already these past few years. Don't bog yourself down in a relationship that might not be going anywhere." Her heart thudded as she waited for his reply.

"I know what you're saying, and you're right to be concerned – it's just . . ." Matt's expression softened and his eyes took on a faraway look, "she's the one woman, the *only* woman since Natasha to make my heart beat faster." He gave a short laugh, while Catherine desperately tried to keep her sympathetic smile from slipping. "God, that sounds like something from a cheesy romantic film!"

"Well, I'm glad you said that and not me," she teased, although in truth she felt sick to her stomach.

"Seriously, Catherine, I want to stick with this – I think it could be something special. She's wonderful, Ellie's great and, more importantly, Adam seems to really like both of them."

"Yes, but, Matt, do you think it's a good idea to have the children so involved at this early stage? If things don't go according to plan then it will be very difficult for them."

Matt stroked his chin. "Of course, I've considered

that too, but something in my gut tells me that things *will* work out between me and Olivia – and for the better. Just think, Catherine," he said, his eyes shining with pleasure, "Adam might finally have the mother figure he's had to do without for so long and –" he broke off, when he saw her crestfallen expression. "Oh, of course, I didn't mean it that way, and you've been great with him – the best, but it's not quite the same thing, is it?"

This time, Catherine couldn't hide her true feelings. Whatever about losing Matt, she couldn't bear to lose Adam too. She loved that little kid with all her heart. "I know it's not the same," she protested. "But I love him as much as any mother could!"

"I know you do and I'm very sorry. I didn't mean that like it sounded. You're wonderful to him. You're wonderful to us. As I keep telling Olivia, we just couldn't have coped without you."

Have coped? What the hell did that mean? she wondered.

Now, seeing how well those two were getting on, and how determined Matt seemed to make it work with Olivia, she would have to work harder to make sure that Matt and Adam didn't discard her like some old piece of furniture. For the past few years, she'd made those two the centre of her life.

And she wasn't going to give them up without a fight.

Later that afternoon, Catherine decided to pop down to the small corner shop at the entrance to the estate. She rarely shopped there, preferring to get a full grocery shop in the larger Tesco further up the road, but today she had an ulterior motive. In the few times she'd been here since moving, mostly popping in for milk or after a day out with Adam, she'd realised that the shop's proprietor was a bit of a gossip. Catherine hoped that today the woman would be in fine fettle.

To her delight, the small shop was empty and the shopkeeper, Molly, gave her a friendly wave. "Warm outside today, isn't it?" she said, rolling her eyes and fanning her face.

Catherine gave her a winning smile. "It certainly is. I'm painting my dining-room at the moment, but it's hard to keep going in this heat."

Molly leaned forward, her eyes shining with interest. "Oh, are you living locally?"

"Yes, on the Green – number seventeen? I've been there a few months and it doesn't need a lot of work, but still, you have to make it your own."

"Of course, you bought Eileen Kavanagh's place, didn't you?" She made a half-hearted sign of the cross. "God rest her, she was a lovely woman."

"So I believe."

"Yes, I thought I'd seen you in here before. You moved in just before Easter, wasn't it?"

Wow, you don't miss a trick, do you? Catherine thought to herself.

All the better.

She nodded. "It's a lovely area, and very quiet, but at the same time, it can be hard to get to know people."

"Oh, I wouldn't worry to much about that, pet. Given time you'll know everyone, although in fairness most of them keep themselves to themselves up there on the Green. They're all a lot older than you too, of course – I can't see stuffy old bridge parties being your thing!" She laughed gaily before supposedly adding as afterthought. "So, you're up there on your own then?"

"Single white female, that's me!" Catherine agreed, with a self-effacing grin.

"Ah, I can understand then why you might find it lonely. No man on the scene at all?"

Wow, Catherine thought, this one really goes in for the kill!

"Unfortunately, no. All the good ones are either married or gay, and the rest aren't worth bothering about – not the ones I meet anyway!"

Molly laughed along, but then her eyes grew serious. "I suppose you have to be careful these days too, don't you? What with all these stories you read in the papers."

The bell on the door went, and both women looked up as another customer came in. Molly smiled a greeting, but obviously didn't know her, and the customer made her way towards the back of the shop.

"Absolutely," Catherine answered, pleased that it wasn't a local. "And in a way, that's why I'd like to get to know a few more people around here – you know, just so they can keep an eye if needs be."

"Well, you know me now!" the older woman laughed and extended a hand. "Although we haven't been properly introduced. I'm Molly Cronin."

"Catherine Duffy," she said, shaking Molly's hand with enthusiasm. "Although, now that I think of it," she added, as if just remembering, "I do know one person on the green, although not very well really. Do you know Olivia Gallagher?"

"Of course, I do! Wasn't I one of the first people Olivia met when she moved into the area? She's a dote, so she is! And, of course, I suppose she was a bit like yourself – you know, a single woman, no husband or boyfriend to look after her."

Catherine held her breath and waited for her to continue.

Molly shook her head sadly and then lowered her voice slightly. "Poor thing, she's a lovely girl and in my opinion she deserves a nice romance, so she does."

"Well, I really don't know her all that well. She's a little bit shy and I didn't want to ask, but I guessed she lost her husband . . ." She let the sentence trail off in the hope that Molly would take the bait.

The older woman looked pained. "Yes, it was a terrible thing, a terrible tragedy altogether. She often pops in here with the little one to get flowers for the grave, and it would break your heart seeing the two of them head off – Ellie with her little pictures and everything . . ." She trailed off, a sorrowful expression on her face.

"A tragedy?"

"Yes." Molly recovered from her momentary lapse,

and went on to fill Catherine in on the situation with added gusto. "Oh, it happened before she moved here, and Olivia doesn't say much about it, but reading between the lines . . ."

"Between the lines?" Catherine made a mental effort to stop behaving like a demented parrot.

Molly leaned forward and gave a quick glance towards the back of the shop, apparently not wanting to be overheard, but unable to resist passing on the rest. "Apparently, she's somehow to blame for what happened to her husband. He had a turn and she wasn't there to help him. You do know she used to be a vet but, of course, she had to give it all up when the child was born. I think she does a bit now and again though for the Animal Centre up around Enniskerry."

"Yes. But you said he had a turn? Like a heart attack?" Now Catherine too was leaning forward. "He died of a heart attack?"

"Supposedly – and him only a young man. Isn't it terrible? But according to that Trudy one who lives near her – and who, if you ask me is an awful motor-mouth –" she added disapprovingly, "Olivia is still cut up with guilt about it because she wasn't there to help him."

"But how was that her fault?"

"It happened at home, not above in the Green, mind, I think it was somewhere over in Shankill, but anyway, the way I heard it, that day she was supposed to be home early, but she was called out on some emergency, and she was late back. Apparently, if she'd been back a bit earlier she might have been in time to help him."

"But that still doesn't explain why she blames herself for it." Catherine was thinking out loud. "He could have had a heart attack at any time."

"That's what I thought, but sure, who knows how people deal with these things? Obviously the poor crature felt she should have been there and, if she was, then she might have saved him, and all the rest of it. It's a very big if, but if that's how she feels, then God love her, that's how she feels." Molly blessed herself again.

Catherine nodded absently.

"And, of course, wasn't it ten times worse because, apparently, hadn't she only just found out that they were going to have a baby? They'd been trying for years, seemingly," she added authoritatively.

"How awful," Catherine murmured, although her mind was elsewhere. "You say the neighbour told you all this?"

Molly reddened. "Well, no, not all of it . . . I mean, I know Olivia well, of course, but some things you don't ask straight out. No, Trudy let slip a few things, and a lot of it I figured out for myself."

"Oh." So it was just tittle-tattle, gossip and nothing more, Catherine thought.

Still, she had shed some light on why Olivia was still so obsessed by her husband – because she rightly or wrongly blamed herself for his death. And oh, wouldn't Matt just love to try and help her through that? He was soft as marshmallows at times, and the fact that Olivia was carrying this so-called burden of guilt would probably make the silly sap fall for her even more!

"The poor thing," Catherine said, plastering a compassionate smile on her face. "Now I understand why she can be so shy and mysterious sometimes."

"Yes, she can be like that – oh, hello love, that'll be ten-fifty," Molly's tone changed expertly as the customer approached the counter to pay for a bottle of red wine. "Do you need a bag for it?" she asked, all pleasantries.

"No, thanks, it'll be fine." The customer, seemingly realising she was interrupting something, gave them both an apologetic smile. Molly reddened a little, and then stood back slightly from the counter as if remembering herself.

When the woman had collected her change and left the store, Molly turned again to Catherine. "Now, you won't tell her about our little chat, will you?" she said, backtracking slightly. "I'd hate Olivia to think I was talking about her behind her back. She's a lovely girl, and a good customer and normally I wouldn't say a word but . . ."

"My lips are sealed," Catherine soothed. "And sure, you only told me because you know I'm anxious to make friends, isn't that it?"

"That's exactly it," Molly agreed, apparently satisfied with this idea. "And if you two are going to be friends, it was only fair to fill you in on Olivia's background, just so you wouldn't put your foot in it or anything. I think you two might be just what the other needs actually – you both could go out hunting for men together, maybe!"

"Maybe," Catherine said with a smile, before

adding, "Of course, I'd hate myself for Olivia to think.
was –"

"Don't worry about that. Sure if she asks, I'll let on I
hardly know you," Molly said with a maternal smile.
"Although, now you're a bit more settled, I do hope
we'll see a lot more of you from now on."

Oh, you'll see plenty of me, don't worry, Catherine
thought to herself, as she smiled and said goodbye to
Molly. *I'm not going anywhere just yet.*

Chapter 35

As she walked toward Olivia's house, Leah clutched the bottle of wine as if it was Catherine's devious little neck, hardly able to believe her ears.

Her friend had been right – that woman was poison! How dare she and that old hag of a shopkeeper discuss Olivia like that! How dare they presume to gossip about her past!

Leah had a good mind to go back to that shop and let the two of them know exactly who she was *and* exactly what she'd like to do with them!

Bloody hell! Was nothing sacred in this godforsaken country any more? A place where everyone seemed to know everything about everyone else, and if they didn't, they'd bloody well make it up! She knew that Olivia had moved to this area after the tragedy in the hope that she could get away from the sympathetic looks and the well-meaning but overbearing neighbours in her old estate. She was always saying that she loved living in Cherrytree Green because it was anonymous and private and the residents were mature enough not to want to poke their noses into everyone else's business. She remembered how Olivia had been annoyed with herself for all her 'curtain-twitching' when she first met Matt.

How wrong had poor Olivia been! Catherine, it seemed, would stop at nothing to get at her supposed good friend Matt's new love, and as for that Molly one – well, she was a right little telegraph pole, wasn't she?

Leah took a deep breath. Now to decide whether or not she should tell Olivia about it. She didn't want to upset her friend, but at the same time she didn't want her to be taken in any more by her supposed friendly local shopkeeper.

Local scandalmonger, more like, she thought with a scowl, recalling the rubbish the woman had been spouting. The bloody nerve of her! Avidly spreading *her own* interpretation of what had happened around the neighbourhood! How many people had she already told – of all things – that Olivia was responsible or at least blamed herself for Peter's death? Leah had a good mind to go back and set those two right!

But no, she decided then, let them think what they liked, especially that Catherine one. Let Catherine slip herself up, and then Matt would know exactly what kind of woman he was dealing with. Olivia had already admitted that she didn't yet trust Matt enough to tell him the full story, and – much as she'd love to – Leah certainly wasn't going to be the one to put his so-called 'best friend' straight.

Catherine could make her own mistakes, and only she would be the loser in the end.

Chapter 36

Matt had been at the house when Leah arrived, and he and Olivia were all smiles and seemed to be getting on well again, despite their disastrous weekend. There was no point in disrupting their peace of mind again by saying anything, Leah reassured herself – it was stupid mindless gossip, and she didn't want Olivia upset.

One of them like that was enough.

She was silent on the way over to Kate's in the car and grateful that Olivia allowed her to be – obviously conscious of the fact that she had a lot on her mind, and also of the fact that Ellie was in the backseat being dropped off at her granny's.

Leah had met Josh that afternoon. She had agreed to meet him on neutral ground – in a café near the apartment – and it was amazing, she thought, how calmly and maturely she was managing their break-up. There was no going back, she had told him, no second chances. He hadn't said much, but she had been shocked upon seeing him. His eyes were bloodshot, his face pale, and he looked as though he hadn't slept in weeks. She'd tried desperately not to let his appearance get to her. Somehow, the calm, mature, adult way they were dealing with the situation made things much harder. In some ways, she longed to have a screaming match with him, hoped he would act like the typical cheating bastard by begging for her forgiveness and swearing that he would never do it again. But Josh didn't do that. He seemed to calmly accept that their relationship was probably over, but kept telling her that he would go along with whatever she wanted to do. "Whatever makes you happy," he had said, and Leah thought mournfully that it would be a long time before anything made her happy again.

In the time that followed the viewing of the videotape and Josh's admission, she had thrown herself into work at the shop, experimenting with different flavours, different textures and producing way more fresh chocolate than could possibly be sold.

She sighed inwardly. She wasn't particularly looking forward to this get-together at Kate's house tonight. The invitation had been issued ages ago, and much as she needed to get away from her own company and her own thoughts, she wasn't sure that a night with the neurotically maternal Kate would do her any good.

But when Leah and Olivia reached the house, Kate seemed in flying form.

"Dylan's fast asleep!" she said gleefully upon their

arrival and, despite her own heavy heart, Leah was gladdened to see Kate looking much better.

This time at least she was fully dressed, although clearly she wasn't yet back to herself, the shapeless tracksuit hanging off her rakish frame. By contrast, and in an effort to make herself feel better, Leah's hair was freshly styled, and she was wearing a bright multi-coloured Pucci-style top over blue jeans. Blast it, she'd thought, she might as well look as though she was coping.

"Come through," Kate said, leading them through to the kitchen, which, normally spotless and uncluttered, had now been taken over completely by baby-related appliances and paraphernalia. There were Babygros drying on the radiator, stacks of Milupa lined against the wall, a whole vat of Johnson's baby powder on the counter-top, and enough nappies to cover every baby born in Ireland for the next twenty years. Who'd have thought babies needed so much? Leah thought, eyes widening as she tried to take it all in.

She sighed deeply, not sure if she was able for this tonight. Olivia looked at her, a silent question in her eyes.

Kate didn't seem to notice. "Now, I thought I'd get Dylan down much earlier," she twittered, "and I completely underestimated how long it would take to get dinner organised. So, if you two don't mind, do you think we could order Thai or Chinese or something?"

"Fine by me," Leah said easily, and took a seat at the table alongside Olivia.

"Me too."

"Great! Now where did I put that menu – although at this stage Michael and I know it almost off by heart and . . ." She stopped, only then sensing the atmosphere. "What's wrong?"

"Josh and I have broken up," Leah said, as calmly as she could muster. "But look, I just wanted to let you know, and I don't want my problems to get you all down. I came here tonight to try and forget about it – so Kate, don't look like that."

"But – but, when did this happen? More to the point *what* happened?" Kate spluttered, sitting down alongside her. "No, hold on – don't tell me anything yet – I'll open a bottle first."

As Kate rummaged in the fridge, Olivia gave Leah's hand a reassuring squeeze. Leah obviously didn't want to have to relive the whole scenario by telling Kate, but it was clear she didn't have much of a choice.

"The stupid bastard!" Kate exclaimed, when Leah explained about the videotape. "How could he?"

"He made a mistake. Kate. Anyone can do that," Olivia said, a note of warning in her tone.

"A mistake!" said Kate incredulously. "He went and did the dirt on Leah with his ex-girlfriend! What, did he forget which woman he was actually with at the time?"

"It wasn't like that," Leah shook her head. "Things had been a bit funny between us, before. We hadn't been getting on all that well, and I was up to ninety trying to prepare for the opening and –"

"I'm sorry, Leah, but I sincerely hope you're not

blaming yourself for this," Kate interjected. "*He*'s the one that did the dirt."

"I know that, Kate, and thanks very much for reminding me!" Leah said through gritted teeth. "But the truth is, I might well have contributed to the fact the relationship wasn't going well." And this was true. As much as she'd love to blame it all on Josh, as much as she could blame it all on Josh, Leah had to admit that she wasn't exactly guiltless in the entire scenario.

Olivia spoke carefully. "Leah, as much as I would love to choke Josh Ryan at the moment, I'm inclined to agree with you. You were very preoccupied. You told me yourself that you thought things were a bit stale."

"Oh, for goodness' sake, I don't believe what I'm hearing here! Have all those romantic novels you two read gone and fried your brains, or what? Leah, Josh *cheated* on you! Please don't go down the road of thinking that it might have been 'all your fault'. He's a grown man, not some immature schoolboy! He has to take responsibility for his own actions. Why do women in these situations always blame themselves?"

"Jesus, Kate, I'm not just a woman in a 'situation' – I'm your friend. And it might be very easy for you to see him as just another 'cheating bastard' but I've spent nearly two years of my life with this man. I love him and I know that, despite what he's done, he loves me."

Kate shook her head. "I don't believe this. Surely you're not saying that you're thinking of taking him back, are you?"

"It's not that simple, Kate," Olivia said. Then she turned to Leah. "He admitted it right away, didn't he? There were no grand denials or lies?"

Leah nodded. "He didn't have to – I knew by the look on his face when he saw the tape. But, the weird thing was, Kate, he didn't even ask me to forgive him, or anything like that. He just came right out and admitted that he'd messed up. He was in an awful state. And today, today was the same. I just think now that maybe I made some mistakes too."

Unmoved, Kate shook her head. "Try and put yourself in his position. Would you have done the same thing? Would you, supposedly so in love with Josh, have gone out one night, got totally plastered and ended up with some bloke you knew in college or something?"

"Well, now that you say it, Kate, I really can't say whether I would or I wouldn't have! The thing about being drunk is that you're not really yourself – you don't really know what you would or wouldn't do in that state!" She tried not to sound so touchy but Kate's callous attitude was getting to her.

"Oh, for goodness' sake!"

"Kate, I don't know, OK? You're not in this situation, so it's easy for you to sit here and judge. I can't say categorically that no matter how drunk I was, or no matter what situation I was in, I would never, ever cheat on Josh. Things aren't that simple!" Sick of Kate's prodding, by now her voice was shaking with anger.

Leah didn't need Kate to point out Josh's betrayal: she was trying her best to make sense of all of this, was trying to come to terms with how, if he loved her, Josh could cheat on her.

It was a bloody mistake coming here tonight, she thought. Kate could only ever see things in black and white – for her, grey just didn't exist in any colour chart! Yet things weren't always black and white – rarely if ever.

Olivia broke the silence. "Everyone has moments of madness and can do things they wouldn't normally dream of doing. Some people aren't as strong as you are, Kate. I think that, yes, Josh did make a big mistake but he's well aware of it."

"There's something else," Leah said, refusing to look at Kate. "He told me that the night of the launch party, he was planning to propose." She paused, trying to blink back the tears. It was this admission that had got to her the most. "But once he met up with her he . . ."

"Changed his mind?" Kate cut in and, seeing how much her remark stung, softened her tone. "Look, I'm sorry – I'm not trying to hurt you intentionally here. But even you have to admit that it was a bit convenient of him to mention this when he was looking for forgiveness."

"That's where you're wrong. Josh never once asked me for forgiveness; he never once tried to explain his guilt away. All he asked was that I understand that he loves me and that he made a big mistake. He seemed to accept that he had messed things up and he didn't ask me to take him back."

People did make mistakes, didn't they? And didn't some couples go on after infidelity? Didn't they work even harder as a result? Didn't they forgive and forget?

She looked at Olivia for some assistance. "Surely you can understand why I'm feeling like this?"

Olivia nodded. "From what you're telling us, I think Josh behaved pretty admirably since – OK, besides the fact that he cheated on you," she added, seeing Kate shake her head in exasperation. "But at the end of the day, you're the one that knows him best. You said before that you feel like you know him inside out. Do you believe that he is genuinely sorry for what has happened? Do you believe him when he says that he loves you, that he's always loved you and that he simply made a mistake? Do you think you can forgive and forget?"

Leah was silent for a moment. Those were the questions she'd been asking herself these last few days and she knew in her heart of hearts that her answer was of utmost importance.

"Do you think you can forgive him?" Olivia asked again.

It took Leah an age to speak. Then . . .

"I don't know . . . I . . . think so," she answered hoarsely.

"Oh, come on!" Kate put her head in her hands in blatant disbelief. "Olivia's hardly the best person to be giving advice, is she?"

Leah frowned. "Kate, that's not fair – this is about me."

In fairness, Olivia didn't seem too disturbed by Kate's comment, but as she turned to answer, Leah noticed her hands were tightly clasped together.

"Despite what you might think, Kate," Olivia said,

her tone measured and calm, "I have no problems with forgiveness – in fact, I think it's good for the soul. Leah's entitled to ask my opinion and I'm entitled to give it."

Kate sniffed, annoyed at what she perceived as her friends' weakness. "You two are unbelievable! Is there anything you *wouldn't* forgive, Olivia? Oh, and speaking of which, I see our old buddy Robin is finally returning to the fold too, fresh from making money out of other people's problems. Typical, wouldn't you say? Here's an idea, Leah. Why don't you ask *Robin* how to deal with this? I'm sure she'd only be too delighted to give you advice – before, of course, turning around and stabbing you in the back!"

Olivia shook her head sadly. "I really thought that motherhood might soften you up a bit, Kate, but no, you're the same unforgiving, grudge-bearer you've always been, aren't you?"

"What? I've only ever tried to stick up for you two – can't you see that?"

Leah looked at her. Kate just couldn't comprehend that sometimes people made mistakes, that it was inevitable, human nature, a simple fact of life. "It's not your fight, Kate – it was never your fight. We're not in college any more, and things are bad enough without your judgmental attitude."

"I can't help it if I don't like to see my friends get walked over!"

Leah tried to speak evenly – otherwise she knew Kate would really go off on them. "I know that, but unfortunately you can't impose your will on your friends, and you certainly can't fight our battles for us either."

"But Josh really let you down . . ." Kate slumped further in her chair.

"I know he let me down, but I let him down too. Can't you understand that? That's why I'm so confused. That's why I can't trust my own feelings on the subject." Her expression softened. "But Kate, when I ask for advice, I'm looking for advice, not recrimination."

"Recrima wha'?" Kate said, but she seemed to have calmed down a little. "Look, I'm sorry. I just care about you, and I hate to see you upset." She glanced at Olivia. "You too."

"It's OK. In a way I can understand what you're saying. But you can't keep harping back to the past and really, Kate, that crack about Robin was uncalled for."

"What? I can't believe you sometimes! How long are you going to keep defending her, forgiving her for turning out to be the most selfish, disloyal, unfeeling –"

"She was thousands of miles away," Olivia interjected calmly. "It would have been impossible –"

"It's not too impossible for her to come home to promote her crappy book though, is it? Such a bloody cheek! And yet she wouldn't dream of coming home for something as unimportant and inconsequential as a funeral!"

"That was all a long time ago," Olivia said, "and *I've* forgotten all about it – *I've* let it go, so why can't you?"

"Because I just can't!" Kate cried, and Leah was

taken aback by how strongly she felt about it – still. "I can't forgive her for that! So much for our grand reunion, so much for figuring out what would happen to one another! We all know what happened to Robin, so good at playing the shy innocent in college – the one we all had to look out for because of her and her blasted peanut allergy!"

"Jesus, don't you think that maybe Robin's suffered too?" Leah asked. "When was the last time you spoke to her? What – five, six years?"

"I have nothing to say to her, not now, not ever and certainly not when she comes over here on her 'rub our noses in it' tour!"

"Kate, that's crazy," Olivia said, laying a soothing hand on her arm. "You shouldn't carry that kind of hate around with you. There's no point. Robin is Robin and," she shrugged, "I'm sure she has her own regrets about not coming back that time. Anyway, that's not why we're here. There's no point in getting upset and arguing amongst ourselves over what Robin should or shouldn't have done. It's in the past. And we have to let it go."

Still, Leah wondered then, as she listened to her friend trying to convince Kate to forgive and forget, would Olivia – the strongest and most magnanimous person she had ever known – be so willing to do that herself, once she came face to face with Robin again?

Chapter 37

It had been seven long years since she'd seen the place, and still Robin didn't miss it. Too many bad memories, she supposed, looking tentatively around the Arrivals area of Dublin airport. Too many painful reminders of everything that had gone wrong in her life since university, and not enough positives to balance things out. Still, it would have been nice to have had the time to go home to Waterford this weekend, she thought, but because this would be a very short stay, her mum was travelling up on the train to visit her.

Now, Robin wondered, how could anyone – after just arriving from a country thousands of miles away – possibly be expected to come up with a one-euro coin? Robin had never even seen a bloody euro, let alone be able to magic one up for the blasted luggage trolley! She gritted her teeth and tried to quell the growing frustration coupled with a deep-seated sense of anxiety. Typical bloody Ireland!

Then she took a deep breath. Oh, get a grip! she told herself. It's not the misfortunate currency's fault you're feeling like this, is it?

Having obtained the obligatory shin-bashing from the golf-club brigade at the carousel, which really helped her mood, Robin eventually claimed her luggage and made her way through customs. She paused slightly before coming through to the Arrivals area. Would she recognise anyone? Worse – would anyone recognise *her*? Oh, come off it! she admonished herself again. Who do you think you are – Madonna? Of course no-one would recognise her – no one knew she was here yet, did they?

Two weeks ago, Leah had been on the phone giving her hell for not letting her know.

"I can't believe you wouldn't tell me something like this!" she'd said, and by her tone Robin knew that she was genuinely hurt. She felt bad about not telling her, but it was all happening so fast, and around the time of the Nickelodeon deal, Leah had emailed Robin, informing her that she'd just broken up with Josh.

"Oh, Leah, of course, I wanted to tell you, but I didn't think it would be right for me to say: 'You know, I'm very sorry that your heart is broken and that you're going through hell – but I really have to tell you that I've just landed myself a major publishing deal.' What would you have done?"

To her surprise, Leah laughed. "I see your point. And sorry for being such a Moany Minnie."

"Oh for goodness' sake, how many times did I moan down the phone to you over the years?"

"Well, plenty, now that you say it, but not since you met Ben. How are things going there by the way?"

Again, Robin wasn't quite sure what to say. Surely the last thing Leah needed to hear was that she and Ben were planning on buying a house and settling down. Particularly when, not too long ago, Leah and her boyfriend had been making the very same plans.

"He's fine," was all she said.

"And is he coming home with you? Oh, I really can't believe you're coming back!"

Robin couldn't quite bring herself to match her excitement. "No – he has to work – not to mention the fact that this trip has been sprung on us a bit."

"'*Robin takes publishing world by storm*', eh?"

"Believe me, Leah, I'm as stunned by all the fuss as you are."

"So when *are* you coming home then?"

Robin hesitated. She'd have to see her – she *wanted* to see her, but if seeing Leah meant seeing the others, well . . .

"It isn't finalised but probably soon. They want to 'strike while the iron's hot', or some such."

Leah chuckled. "Poor Amanda is inconsolable that you'll be appearing on TV. You do know that's her life-long dream, don't you?"

Robin nodded, remembering. "Well, she could go on instead if she likes. A rabbit caught in the headlights will have nothing on me!" Her heart sank as once again it hit home to her how close and involved in one another's lives her old college friends still seemed to be.

"You'll be great."

"So," Robin tried to make her voice sound casual, but her heart was hammering, "have the others heard about all this or –?"

"Of course, they've heard about it – it's the best bit of gossip we've had in years!" Leah enthused. "Amanda's green with envy obviously, but she did say to pass on her congratulations. Olivia's pleased for you, and Kate, well, of course Kate's delighted too." She hid it well but nevertheless Robin picked up on Leah's hesitation. She wasn't too surprised. True to form, Kate had obviously never forgiven her for not returning home for the funeral.

"And, Olivia – how's she doin'?" Robin asked carefully. "You know, I never did get round to ringing her, I have her number somewhere but –"

"How's she *doin'*?'" Leah mimicked in an exaggerated New York drawl. "You sound like Tony Soprano. And you're telling me that Ballyhooley *Ben* lost his accent?"

"It's Ballymoney actually, and believe me, that's nothing compared to him."

"Mmm, we'll see about that when you come home," Leah replied and again, Robin's heart plummeted. "But yes, Olivia's '*doin*' fine. Very fine, actually." Robin could hear the smile in her voice. "She's starting seeing this lovely guy, Matt. It's early days but he's a dote, and they seem really well suited. He's a single parent too."

Robin was so stunned by this she could barely speak. "Really?" she answered, afraid that Leah might notice. She really didn't think Olivia would ever –

"Yeah, I know what you're thinking. I honestly

didn't think she'd find anyone else after Peter either. But it's been years now and – time to move on, I suppose."

"Well, good on her," But Robin was still amazed. Olivia adored Peter – there had never been anyone else other than him, and she clearly remembered her vowing that there never would be. This Matt must be pretty special.

"But I'm sure you'll meet them all again soon," Leah said airily.

"Well, I hope so but the schedule is pretty hectic, and I might not have much time . . ." Robin left it at that, unwilling to make any concrete arrangements to see Leah, let alone 'them all'.

Now, sitting in a taxi and heading towards her city-centre hotel, Robin wondered what lay ahead. She thought back to the last time they had all been together, just days before graduation, back before they went out into the big bad world, and everything went a little crazy. They had been so confident, so cheerful, so optimistic about life. They all knew where they were going, and what they wanted to do, and despite their petty little differences, were so sure that they would honour their reunion, so sure that the friendship would stay the same forever.

Didn't any of them, Robin thought, feeling a curious mixture of sadness and regret as they drove along O'Connell Street, realise how silly and naïve they had been?

Chapter 38

The morning of her thirtieth birthday was bright and sunny, and Leah tried her utmost to feel the same. Thanks to Olivia's insistence that she mark the occasion in some small way, she was actually starting to look forward to the celebrations the following night. She'd booked a table at her favourite Thai restaurant, and was anticipating a nice cosy dinner with Olivia, Kate and their respective partners. Josh, the previous week, had moved all his belongings out of the apartment, and Leah was beginning to come to terms with the fact that it was well and truly over.

So, it might not have been the best idea to invite some loved-up couples when all it would do is painfully highlight her single status, but blast it, it would do her good to get out and have a laugh with her friends. Thirty was a landmark birthday after all, and despite the fact that she hadn't had all that much to celebrate lately, she was damned if she was going to let it pass without event.

"Not true," Olivia had said defiantly when Leah was bemoaning the fact the other day. "What about Elysium? Isn't your talent and your success something to celebrate?"

Ever the optimist, Olivia was right. Yes, her love-life was a disaster, but at least she still had her dream. *But at what cost?* the little voice inside piped up and, instantly, something tightened in Leah's stomach. She waved the thought away and went back to getting out this morning's batch of white-chocolate-and blueberry specials. *Think positive!*

Just before lunchtime, the telephone rang.

"Lee, don't kill me but I think I'm going to have to give the dinner a miss tomorrow night." On the other end of the phone, Kate's pleading tone was palpable.

"What? Why?" Leah was taken aback. "What's going on?"

"Well, it's Dylan," Kate answered. "He's running a bit of a fever and I'm afraid to leave him, just in case."

"Oh!" OK, Leah thought, trying to be rational. A sick child was a decent excuse for crying off on your heartbroken friend's only hope of a social life – a good excuse actually. But without Kate and Michael, she couldn't possibly expect Olivia and poor Matt to baby-sit her on her birthday. That would be pathetic. Then she thought of something.

"But what about Michael?" she asked reasonably. "Couldn't he keep an eye on him tomorrow night? And surely he will have improved by then?" Problem solved, she thought. Actually, a girls-only night was probably a better idea. Then again, considering that their last two attempts at a girls-only night had ended badly, the first with Kate cancelling, and the second with the three of them arguing, it might not be the best idea after all.

But there was a silence on the other end of the phone and, instantly, Leah realised she had said the wrong thing, although she wasn't exactly sure what.

"I wouldn't be able to enjoy it, Leah," Kate said shortly. "Perhaps he will be better by then but I'd still be worrying about him all night."

Disappointment coursed through Leah as she tried desperately to see things from her friend's point of view but failed miserably. It wasn't as though it was a competition or anything – after all, she was Kate's friend, but Dylan was her son and Leah would never expect Kate to choose her over him. Yet, Kate had been the very one to admit that he wasn't exactly at death's door, that he was just 'running a bit of a fever' – so why all the drama? Michael could keep an eye on him – after all, he was equally responsible for Dylan's welfare, wasn't he?

"I'm sorry, Leah, you know how it is." As far as Kate was concerned the conversation was over. The choice had been made. Broken-hearted friend, baby with a slight fever? No contest.

"Yes, I do." She tried to keep the almost unbearable disappointment out of her voice. She'd be there for Kate, wouldn't she? In fact, she had been there for Kate, many times over the years, helping her nurse every broken heart, letting her cry on her shoulder and then going out and getting rip-roaring drunk in order to forget about which 'him' happened to be the problem. Did motherhood mean that was the end of all that then?

"Well, look . . . have a really good night, and we'll meet up soon – for dinner or something, OK?" Kate said absently.

"Sure." Leah was so hurt she could hardly speak. She couldn't believe that it had happened again with Kate. What was happening to her? She knew having children changed your life, but did it change it to the point where you no longer cared about your friends?

"Obviously," Andrew said, when he rang that afternoon to wish her a happy birthday and Leah told him what Kate had said. "It isn't the first time Kate's cried off like that, is it?"

"No." Kate had also missed a recent outing in town, giving some other life or death situation with Dylan as an excuse. "I just don't understand it. I'm trying to see things from Kate's point of view but, to be honest, I'm finding it difficult." She bit her lip. "You'd think, what with being stuck on her own all day every day with the child that she'd love the opportunity to let her hair down."

"I'm bloody sorry that we can't go either, Leah. But being so close to time, Amanda is as crabby as anything and –"

"Oh, don't be silly, I wouldn't expect you to come," she answered.

"I suppose children do change things all right," Andrew went on, referring to Kate.

"I know," said Leah. "It's just that, out of all people, Kate was the last one I would have pegged for a fussy old mammy. It just isn't like her. God be with the days when we used to get thrown out of pubs for dancing on tables," despite her heavy heart, she giggled, "or getting caught by the guards for tipping cows."

"Tipping cows? What the fuck . . . ?"

Leah giggled. "Oh, never mind!"

"No, tell me!"

"Well, it's something you do in the dead of night – usually on the way home from the pub. You go into a field of sleeping cattle, simply give them a little nudge and . . . hey presto! Easy as you like, they topple over onto the ground!"

"And isn't that a little unfair to the misfortunate cows?"

"I know – but when you've a few drinks in you, it's the most hilarious thing ever." Leah shook her head. "But we're from the country, remember?"

"Ah, yes, culchies – they really are a breed in themselves," Andrew teased.

Leah raised a smile, remembering her and Kate's young, free and single days. It hurt deeply that Kate was unwilling to make the effort, not just for her birthday, but for her sake. Still Kate had responsibilities now and she couldn't just take off and . . .

Suddenly it hit Leah that she was the only one of the old gang left that was alone, truly alone. Kate had her family, Amanda and Andrew were about to have their first baby, Olivia had Ellie and now she had Matt, and if things went well – which she hoped they would – they were as good as a family too. The realisation stung, and all of a sudden, Leah wanted Josh badly. She wanted the security of not having to depend on tearing her friends away from their families to entertain her, to keep her from going crazy, to keep her from feeling lonely.

Yet, being lonely wasn't a good enough reason to go back, was it? Despite Olivia's insistence that it was always possible to forgive and forget, and despite Leah's admission at Kate's that she might be able to forgive Josh, deep down she really didn't think she'd have it in her. She would always be watching, wondering, worrying . . .

But, Leah thought, as she said goodbye to yet another happily attached friend, maybe that was better than being alone.

Later that evening, she was discussing something with Alan, when, outside the store, Leah caught sight of something that had to be an apparition. The features were the same, the hair was the same but a little longer, but this girl was way too stylish and way too confident to be the same.

"Oh my God, *Robin!*" she cried, racing outside. "It really *is* you, isn't it?"

Robin smiled nervously. "Hi, I was going to phone, but I didn't have the number and I wasn't sure . . ." She trailed off, as Leah reached forward and engulfed her in a huge hug.

"I can't believe you're actually here!" Tears sprang to

Leah's eyes. She had known Robin was coming home, of course, but at the same time, it didn't seem real. After all these years, after all this time . . . she couldn't comprehend how great it was to see her again.

"I know. It's strange for me too. The city's changed quite a bit since I was last here." Robin raised an eyebrow. "What's with that big flagpole on O'Connell Street?"

Leah laughed. "Now, now. The Spire is a very important Dublin landmark – a symbol of growth and optimism." She rolled her eyes. "Not quite the Chrysler building, is it?"

"No, not quite," Robin grinned.

"When did you get in? Where are you staying? Are you here for long and . . . oh, for goodness' sake, listen to me rabbiting on! Come inside. I have to stay and work late this evening unfortunately, otherwise we could go for a drink. Don't worry," she added, when Robin looked slightly wary. "There's nothing dangerous in there. The chocolates are all behind glass or boxed up. Everything else is safely locked away out back."

"I'm sorry. I didn't mean –"

"Don't be silly. It's fine. Actually, I'm in discussion at the moment with my suppliers about introducing some nut-free and diabetic chocolate. It's amazing. Years ago you were the only sufferer I knew – these days I'm getting non-stop enquiries."

Robin smiled. "We're a pain in the butt, aren't we?"

"Not at all!" Leah led the way through the shop, anxious to show off her little empire to this new, stylish and mature Robin. As it was teatime there was a bit of a lull in custom, so they could at least have a bit of an uninterrupted chat.

"I'm impressed!" Robin said, checking out Leah's elaborate displays. "These look good enough to make me want to take a chance!"

"Ah, I wouldn't recommend it," Leah grimaced, before adding wickedly, "Then again, if you really want to die happy . . ."

The two girls laughed.

Leah proudly introduced her old friend to Alan, and then continued with their discussions about the following day. Not long afterwards, Alan went home and they were on their own.

"So where are you staying?"

Robin smiled, as if a little embarrassed. "They put me up in the Westin. It's fabulous, Leah – way too good for me. Irish hotels have come a long way since I left, I can tell you!"

"Well, you're hot property now – a famous author and all that."

"I'm not a famous author. To be honest, I'm not even an author. I just got lucky and happened to be in the right place at the right time, that's all."

"That's hardly true. You were always good at stringing words together, Robin. In college, you were always the one with the interesting theories and subject matter. Professor Hughes was mad about you."

"Perhaps." Robin wasn't convinced, and then Leah realised that her friend hadn't changed that much after all – she was still the same reticent and insecure Robin she'd always been. This was strangely comforting.

"So, what about you?" Robin asked. "Are you and Josh still –"

Leah's face clouded. "Yes, but I don't want thoughts of that idiot to bring me down. Things are bad enough as it – hey!" she broke off, remembering. "I was cheesed off earlier, because Kate cried off from my birthday dinner and –"

"That's right, you're thirty today, aren't you? Don't worry, I hadn't forgotten. It's just with this jet-lag I'm not sure what day I have. Happy Birthday!"

"But you'll come out tomorrow night, won't you?" Leah asked, pleased that they'd have something to celebrate after all.

Robin paused slightly before answering. "I suppose so." But she looked a little worried. "Who else is . . . ?"

"Don't worry. It won't be a big deal – I don't have that many friends, unfortunately! No, it'll just be you, me, Olivia and Matt –" She broke off, remembering that there would be some awkwardness between Olivia and Robin after their prolonged lack of contact. She hurried on to cover up the pause, "Ben's not with you, is he?"

"No, but are you sure –?"

"The problem is, I've booked Thai, which I know will be a problem for you, so –"

"Oh, don't worry about that, honestly. It's your birthday – you should go where you want."

"You don't seriously think it matters to me where we eat, do you? Robin, I haven't seen you in years! And with all this success with your book, this is as much a celebration for you as it is for me!" She reached under the counter-top for the telephone directory. "Now, I'll just make some enquiries and see what we can get."

"Are you sure? I feel awful about this, Leah – it's your night and now you have to go and rearrange things for me."

"I said don't be silly," Leah said, tucking the handset under her chin as she dialled. "You'd do the same for me, wouldn't you?"

After a few failed attempts, she finally located a suitable restaurant, a nice place near the seafront in Dun Laoghaire, which would be a bit of a trek for Robin, but handy for Leah and Olivia.

"So what are your plans for the weekend?" Leah asked. "I'm taking the day off tomorrow, so if you want to do some shopping or anything . . ."

"Well, Mum's coming up to visit at some stage and I'm doing – I think it's called TV3 –" she looked at Leah for confirmation, "on Monday morning at eight." She groaned. "But tomorrow, I only have a couple of newspaper interviews before lunch, and after that I'm free."

"Great! Let me know what time and I'll pop in to town and meet you at the hotel." She hugged Robin once more, thrilled to see her again. "The Westin, eh?" she laughed. "Haven't you come a long way!"

"Robin's back?" said Olivia. So, she'd finally come home after all this time.

"Yes, and she's coming out for my birthday dinner

tomorrow night," Leah announced on the other end of the telephone line. Then she paused. "Do you mind? The invite had come out of my mouth before I had a chance to really think about it – and I know it might be a little awkward after all this time but –"

"No, don't be silly. It'll be great to see her." Olivia tried her best to sound enthusiastic. .

"Brilliant," Leah said, sounding relieved. "It will give us all a chance to catch up and have a good chat. Oh and by the way, I had to change the restaurant because of Robin, but this one will be nearer to us." She gave Olivia directions. "She looks amazing, Olivia!"

"I'm sure she does." Olivia didn't want to think about how amazing Robin looked. She was still trying to come to terms with the fact that after seven years of little or no contact, she would see her old friend again in less than twenty-four hours.

Just then Olivia was sorely tempted to make some pathetic excuse and pull out. But she couldn't do that now, could she? Not when Kate had already let Leah down and she'd been so upset about that. No, it wouldn't be fair. She'd just have to bite the bullet and go with it. And Matt was really looking forward to it – he'd been eager to meet her friends properly for some time.

Still, what on earth would he make of Robin?

Chapter 39

On her return to the hotel from Leah's, Robin sat in the taxi deep in thought. She stared out the window, hardly seeing the places and landmarks of this city that had once been so familiar to her.

Should she do it? she wondered. Should she do it while she was here – while she had the chance?

But what if she bumped into Olivia? Although that was highly unlikely. Robin doubted very much that Olivia would do twenty-four-hour vigils at the place, but still . . .

But there was also the possibility that someone else could notice her and then mention it Olivia, so should she –

Oh, for goodness' sake, Robin, admonished herself, after seven years in Manhattan you'd think you'd know better! This is Dublin, not some tiny little village!

Of course, no one would recognise her, and even if

she was seen, it was very unlikely it would get back to Olivia. She didn't live around there any more now, did she?

Feeling a sudden burst of nervous energy, Robin sat forward.

It was now or never and she had to do it. She would never forgive herself otherwise.

"I'm sorry, I've changed my mind. Can you take me to Shankill instead, please?"

The taxi-driver looked at her as though she was mad. "Love, it's late-night shopping and we're on the outskirts of town – it'll take us a good hour to get all the way back out there."

"I know and I'm sorry," Robin replied, "but I really need to go back."

"Your money, pet." He shrugged and went to do a U-turn.

"Thank you." Robin said nothing more for the rest of the journey, as she tried to convince herself she was doing the right thing. Then, about forty-five minutes later, they reached the turn-off for Shankill.

The taxi-driver tapped his steering wheel to the beat of the music on the radio, not having any idea that he was echoing the quick tempo of Robin's heart.

"So whereabouts will I drop you, love?" he asked when they entered the village.

Robin's heart fluttered as though it was struggling to keep beating. "Shanganagh, please," she replied, her voice heavy with emotion, "Shanganagh Cemetery."

Chapter 40

"Hello, Robin." Olivia's voice was calm and neutral as she approached the table. She reached across to give her old friend a hug. "It's good to see you again."

"Good to see you too." Robin half-stood up from her chair and returned the brief embrace. Olivia's greeting was warm but, still, Robin wasn't sure what to think or how to behave. Her friend had aged, as had the rest of them, but as always Olivia possessed an air of calm serenity which somehow never seemed to falter.

Not even now.

"Matt, you know Leah, of course, and this is another friend, Robin," Olivia said by way of introduction. "We were all in college together, and Robin's just back from New York. Remember, I told you about the children's book she wrote?"

"Hi, Leah, Happy Birthday!" Matt waved a greeting. "Pleased to meet you, Robin, and congratulations on your book." He sat down across from Leah, leaving Olivia sitting directly across from Robin. "New York's a great city. Have you lived there long?"

"Seven years," Robin told him.

"And do you get home much? Although I don't know why you'd want to," he added amiably. "Dublin's great, but the Big Apple is in a different league I think!"

"Well, this is actually my first time home since I left," she replied, trying not to make eye contact with Olivia.

"Oh!" Matt couldn't hide his surprise. "Oh, well, living in a great place like that, I suppose I can't blame you."

"Doesn't she look fantastic, Olivia?" Leah, was saying, already well tipsy on the wine she was drinking. She'd had a few drinks in the apartment before they went out, and had already knocked back two champagne cocktails before the others arrived. Robin suspected her friend was out to get well and truly blotto tonight.

"She certainly does," Olivia answered. "I love your dress, Robin, and you've really kept your figure too. Typical! Now, if I wore something like that I'd look like Ten Ton Tessie." She laughed gaily, but to Robin there was something a little forced about it.

"Thanks, you look great too."

"Robin, I think you and I both know that dieting was never my forte! I still have the old ice-cream weakness," she added conspiratorially.

"Don't be silly. You look great," Matt said, looking up from his menu.

"Love must definitely be blind then," Olivia laughed and rolled her eyes.

"Women!" Matt said, exasperated. "Remind me again why I agreed to come here tonight."

All of a sudden Robin wished she *hadn't* come. Olivia was being way too nice to her and behaving as if she didn't have a care in the world. Well, maybe she didn't. She was a bit taken aback at how easy and comfortable she and Matt seemed to be with one another. She supposed she was so used to seeing Olivia with Peter that it seemed sort of strange. Then again, Peter wasn't around any more, was he, so why shouldn't Olivia move on with someone else?

Thinking of her last-minute visit to the graveyard yesterday, Robin shivered, ashamed. After all Olivia had been through, she deserved to be happy.

"So, things are going well in New York?" Olivia asked her. "Great news about your book, although I must admit it was a bit of a surprise. I didn't know you were writing."

Robin was almost embarrassed discussing this with her. It felt as though she'd let her down somehow. "It's all a little bit out of the blue for me too," she said. "I have a niece, well, she's not exactly my niece, she's Ben's niece but she's asthmatic and –"

"Ben'ssh her cutie boyfriend," Leah interjected, her voice slightly slurred.

Olivia looked at Leah. "Slow down a bit there, you – we haven't even started eating yet," she admonished teasingly.

"It's my birthday and I'll get pisshed if I want to!" Leah laughed back, her tone giddy.

Matt topped up his wineglass. "Leah, if you can't have a few to celebrate reaching the big 3-0, sure when can you?"

"Cheers, Matt!" Leah clinked glasses with him, pleased she had a drinking partner in crime. She waylaid a waiter passing their table. "Can we get three more Bellinis here, please?"

"I'm almost sorry I'm driving," Olivia said, grinning at Robin. "We're obviously in for a good night!"

Robin smiled back uncomfortably. Another cocktail sounded good, because at that moment, she wasn't sure how to continue this one-to-one conversation with Olivia. She wished Leah would get involved a bit more, but her friend was too busy knocking back cocktails and chattering with Matt.

"So, you've put down roots in New York now, as such?" Olivia asked her.

"I suppose so. I like it there, and we have some good friends, although it's not quite the same as . . ." Robin paused, embarrassed. Why had she said that? She was the one who had gone off to America and lost all contact. As far as they were concerned she couldn't care less. Why would Olivia of all people believe her when she admitted she missed her old friends?

"I know what you mean," Olivia said, as if sensing her discomfort. "When you're so far away from home, I'm sure the grass can sometimes appear greener."

Just then, the waiter came to take their order and as usual, Robin stiffened, dreading the drawn-out exchange to come and the usual accompanying frustrated looks.

"Hi," she said, when he stood beside her, her complexion reddening slightly. "I'd just like to let you know that I suffer from a severe peanut allergy, and I'll need to ask you a couple of questions about this menu. If I eat something with peanuts in it, I might die." She smiled hesitantly at him, eager to get it over with.

To her amazement, the waiter smiled back. "That's no problem, madam. My youngest suffers from the same thing. I know how careful you have to be."

"Thank you," Robin couldn't comprehend the relief she felt. As the waiter went through the menu with her, she saw Matt watching her with interest.

"It must be tough," he said, when the waiter had left the table. "Not everyone is as accommodating as that, I'd imagine."

Robin nodded. "That was rare, to be honest. Usually when I'm somewhere I haven't been before, they get very annoyed and frustrated. I don't blame them, but it's hard when you're made to feel like an over-hysterical fusspot. People just don't realise, that's all."

Olivia smiled tightly. "It's probably much easier in New York too. With so many more sufferers, I'm sure they're well geared up for that kind of thing."

Again, Robin wished she wouldn't be so nice to her. She almost wished she'd be frosty, uncommunicative, anything but the understanding, sympathetic Olivia she'd always been. After all these years, after everything that had happened, it just didn't seem right.

"It is, when you know where to go. But, there are always risks." She turned to Leah, anxious to change the subject. "Are you OK there, Leah? You've downed most of that bottle of wine yourself!"

"Why shouldssn't I?" Leah slurred, her eyes glazed. "When issh my birthday?"

Olivia caught Matt's eye. "Tell you what," she said to Leah, "why don't we just have water with the meal and then later we'll have some champagne."

"Champagne!" Leah sat up straight. "I love champagne!"

Sensing now that her drinking was a little bit more than just celebratory, Matt swiftly removed the bottle of wine and hid it under the table. He and Olivia exchanged worried looks. Robin was worried too. Leah was getting way too drunk way too fast.

"Where'sh the wine gone?"

"Don't worry, he'll be back with more in a minute," Olivia soothed. "Oh, look, here's our starters."

Leah took a huge gulp of the water, and the table was quiet for some time while they ate.

Robin took only tiny bites of her food, the discomfort of the reunion with Olivia making her lose her appetite. Despite Olivia's best attempts at being off-hand and friendly, there was a real tension between them. She would have to say something, but not here, not now and certainly not on poor Leah's birthday. Anyway there were also certain things that Robin wanted, no, *needed* to ask.

The conversation became a little stilted and awkward once the introductions, and what could be considered their attempts at catching up, were out of the way. Matt kept up some chit-chat during the main course, which lightened the tone a little, but Robin was finding it very hard to relax and even harder to find things to talk about.

She wasn't sure whether she should enquire about Olivia's daughter as she had never seen the child, and hadn't exactly been all that supportive when she was born. Mentioning Ellie might only bring it all back to Olivia, and simply highlight how terrible a friend Robin had been. She decided instead to concentrate on safer ground. "So how's Kate getting on?" she asked. "Does motherhood suit her?"

"Kate told me and Olivia that she thinks you're a bitssh, Robin!" Leah blurted, in a drunken, childlike tone. "But I think she's a bitssh, so there!" She'd been drinking water during the meal, but everything she'd had beforehand was obviously still very much in her system.

Matt looked visibly uncomfortable, and Olivia looked as though she wanted the ground to open up and swallow her. "Leah, don't be silly," she said. "I know you're upset that Kate couldn't come tonight but –"

"She wassh alwayssh horrible to you, Robin, wasshn't she?" Leah went on as though Olivia hadn't even spoken. "She was a bitssh to you, when we all knew it wasshn't your fault."

"Leah, it's OK," Robin began, "I don't mind. Oh, look, here's the waiter – let's order dessert!"

Leah shook her head exaggeratedly. "I told her it wasshn't your fault that you couldn't come home, but she didn't believe me!" All of a sudden, she looked distraught. "It wasshn't your fault, Robin, I know that, but Olivia didn't want me to tell her. Sshure you didn't?" She reached across and grabbed Olivia tightly by the hand. Then she reached for Robin. "You two are my bessht friends, my bessht friends, I want you to know that."

Matt stood up, evidently deciding it might be a good idea to give them some time alone. "I just remembered I have to phone Frank," he said, taking out his mobile and waving it in front of the others as if to demonstrate.

"That'ssh OK, Matt. That'ssh fine. You're my bessht friend, too," Leah giggled at his retreat.

Olivia caught Robin's eye. "Forget about dessert. I think it's time we got you home, Leah," she said.

Leah's eyes widened. "Home? Will Josh be there?" she asked in a child-like voice.

"No, honey, Josh is probably fast asleep in bed," Olivia soothed, obviously not knowing what to say. "Maybe you might see him tomorrow."

Leah sniffed, as if remembering. "I won't sshee him tomorrow – sshtupid bastard!"

Now she was making a scene, and Robin knew they had to get her out of there as soon as possible.

"I'll take her back in a taxi, if you like," Robin offered, after Olivia hurriedly paid the bill and the three of them joined Matt outside.

"It's OK. I'm driving," Olivia replied quickly. "Can I give you a lift back to the hotel?"

"No, that's fine. You guys go on – I can get a taxi."

"Don't be silly," Matt piped up. "Sure, it could take you forever to get one here, and once we've got Leah settled, it'll only take us a few minutes to drop you into town."

If Olivia was annoyed that he'd persisted, she didn't show it.

"No, really, I'll be fine."

"Olivia, tell her."

Olivia spoke quietly. "Robin, it's no problem, although it might be a while before we get Leah sorted. She's very drunk and I don't particularly want to leave her on her own."

"I could stay with her," Robin suggested. As tomorrow was Sunday, her time was her own, and the next item on her publicity itinerary wasn't until Monday. "I could keep an eye on her, make sure she doesn't get sick or anything."

"That mightn't be a bad idea," Matt said. "At least then you wouldn't have to worry about her, Olivia."

She nodded. "OK, let's get Leah to the car."

Sitting in the back seat alongside Robin, Leah wouldn't stay still. Nor, to Robin's discomfort, would she stay quiet. It was as if once the air hit her, she got another – giddier – lease of life.

"You know, I knew you two would be friendssh again. I just knew it! Thissh has been the best birthday ever – we're *all* friendssh again now – and don't worry about Kate. I'll deal with Kate – she'll come round, Robin, and it wasshn't her fault that she didn't know. She just thought you were being horrible to Olivia, by not coming home that time, but *I* knew you weren't being horrible, Robin. *I* undersshtood why you didn't come, and so did Olivia, didn't you? We knew that you jussht –"

"How's the shop going, Leah?" Matt asked.

"Fine, Matt, thanks very mussh for asking. You should come in and visit me soon – I'll give you a free chocolate!"

"I'd like that – do you have any Turkish delights?"

"No, but I'll do some sshpecially for you, if you like!" She giggled and whispered to Robin. "He'ssh very nice, isn't he, Robin? Nicer than bloody Josh anyway, and do you know sshomething? I think he's nicer than Peter too. There, I said it! He's nicer than Peter because Matt would never, *ever* –"

"Oh, is one of these yours, Leah?" Robin asked, as Olivia slowed and turned into the entrance of an apartment block, hoping and praying that Leah would stop chattering. She was covering some potentially dangerous ground here, and it could be very uncomfortable and embarrassing for Olivia if they let her keep going. Olivia and Matt hadn't been together all that long, so chances were he hadn't a clue what Leah was going on about. Robin doubted that Olivia would find it that easy to open up to someone that soon.

"Yep, that's mine, sshee that one up there? Josh didn't care, but I wanted one with a balcony." She sniffed, and suddenly her mood changed. "I have the balcony all to myself now." She turned to Robin. "Why did he do it, Robin? Why did he break my heart like that? I gave up ssho much for him – I told him it didn't matter that he

416

didn't want shhildren – if he didn't want them, well then, that was fine, but then he goes and sshleeps with someone else. Why, Robin?"

"I don't know, honey." Robin knew that poor Matt was mortified. She was mortified for him and equally mortified for Olivia – and indeed for poor Leah when and if she remembered all that she'd been saying tonight. She was sure that Matt didn't know the half of it. After tonight, there was a very good chance he wouldn't want to know. She caught Olivia's eye in the rear-view mirror and gave her a sympathetic smile.

But, true to form, Olivia seemed much more worried about Leah than Matt's apparent discomfort. She stopped the car and, having rummaged through Leah's bag, got the keys to her apartment and let them in. She went on ahead to open the door and, as best he could, Matt helped Robin support poor drunken Leah as they made their way up the steps to her apartment. He gave her an embarrassed smile. "The poor crature – I'm sure she'll suffer in the morning."

"She certainly will," Robin agreed, relieved that they'd finally reached Leah's apartment. She followed Olivia through to her friend's bedroom. The two were silent as they helped her undress, Leah mumbling all the time. "I knew we'd all be friendssh again."

When Leah was safely tucked up in the bed, the two women joined Matt in the living-room.

"Is she asleep?" he asked, his face concerned, but also, luckily, a little amused by the situation.

Olivia nodded. "I think she'll be OK now." She

turned to Robin. "Will the couch be OK for you? I think she has some spare blankets in the hotpress –"

"I'll be fine – I'll find them," Robin interjected. "Look, it's late, and you two need to get back. I'll keep an eye on her, honestly."

"Are you sure you don't want us to – ?"

"No, I'll be fine."

Robin walked them both to the door, unable to understand why she felt so sad, and desperate to say something. But yet it wasn't sadness, she decided, trying to read Olivia's expression as she lost her nerve and said nothing other than goodbye. It was guilt, wasn't it?

"So are you staying long or . . . ?" Olivia ventured cautiously.

Robin shook her head. "No, I'm off to the UK on Tuesday, so I don't know if I –"

"I see," Olivia nodded. "Well, the very best of luck with everything. I'll be sure to pick up a copy for Ellie."

"Thank you." Robin didn't know what else to say, but still she knew that there was much, much more.

Matt gave her a quick kiss goodnight on the cheek. "Good night, Robin – it was great meeting you. Good luck with the book and sure, we might see you again soon."

"Bye, Matt, thanks."

Closing the door softly behind them, Robin could clearly understand why Olivia was involved with him. He was similar to Ben in a way – considerate, loyal, unselfish. They were both very lucky, but the big difference was that Olivia deserved someone like that in her life; she deserved someone who cared enough about her to understand her loyalty to her friends.

The fact that Robin, with all her faults, didn't deserve a man like that was obvious, and something that, tonight, all Leah's babblings had brought home even more.

Chapter 41

Olivia was mostly silent on the way back home in the car, her thoughts scattered as she kept going over the evening.

She'd handled it well, she thought. She'd been polite, friendly and gracious – despite the fact that she had felt totally uncomfortable throughout, and especially towards the end with all Leah's gibberish.

Robin had been initially subdued and, Olivia thought, definitely uncomfortable too, but seemed to come out of herself after a while. With Leah getting so drunk, they had no choice but to slip into their old roles of looking after one another. Poor Leah, she would really suffer tomorrow, in more ways than one. Olivia knew that she'd feel awful about her drunken chattering, especially in front of Matt, although, in fairness, he had seemed to take it all with customary good humour.

She sighed inwardly. Seeing Robin tonight really brought it home to her that she'd have to let Matt into her confidence soon. It wasn't fair otherwise. They'd been getting on extremely well lately and, luckily, Catherine seemed to be staying out of the way. Whatever problems she'd had with Olivia at the beginning, be it concern or jealousy, at least she seemed to have come to terms with it now. Matt had mentioned before that she was seeing some guy – probably the one that Olivia had seen at the house that morning a while back – so perhaps these days she was more interested in her own budding romance than about Matt's new relationship. Olivia really hoped Catherine had laid off her and Matt for good, as she knew she couldn't cope with the hassle and strain of it all. What was the point? She liked Matt – in fairness, a good deal more than just liked – but at the same time she knew that if the situation with Catherine became unbearable then she would have no choice but to end their relationship. Olivia had spent years pining over the loss of one man, one relationship, and she was determined never to let another man affect her life or indeed her sanity the way Peter had. No, this time Olivia was in control.

"Are you OK?" Matt asked softly.

Olivia jumped. She'd almost forgotten he was there.

"Yes, I'm fine. I'm just thinking about Leah, that's all. I've never seen her like that, Matt, and it worries me. She's always been great at convincing everyone that she's coping, that she's getting on with it. Stupidly, I took that at face value, when I should have known that she was really suffering." She shook her head. "I'm her best friend – how could I not have known?"

"Look, I don't know Leah very well, but she does strike me as the type of girl who likes her independence. Yes, she's upset over this guy now and she's having a tough time of it, but that's only natural."

"I know, but I've never seen her so out of control."

"It was her birthday – a big occasion and he wasn't there to share it with her. Of course, it would affect her – it would affect anyone! I remember after Natasha died I went completely off the rails on what would have been our fifth wedding anniversary. I couldn't cope. I drank solidly the whole day long, trying to shut out the pain and the memories. It was a nightmare."

"I know." Olivia did know, but unfortunately she never had the luxury of going off and getting blotto whenever a meaningful birthday or anniversary came round to mock and remind her of all that she had lost. She had Ellie to look after.

Still, looking at it from that point of view, it did explain why Leah seemed so out of it. This time last month, her life was wonderful – she'd achieved her lifetime ambition, she had a man who loved her, and the promise of an exciting future. Now, things were looking a whole lot different and, while her professional life still looked promising, her personal life was in tatters. Olivia felt for her, and made a mental note to be there as much as she could for her over the next while, seeing as Kate didn't seem to be prepared to do the same thing. She knew Leah was suffering over that too. Once Kate became pregnant and now, since she had her baby, the friendship was slowly but surely slipping away.

Matt looked sideways at her. "Robin seems nice."

Olivia stiffened. "She is," was all she said.

"There's a bit of history between you two then?" It was a statement rather than a question.

She shrugged, not really wanting to get into it just then. "We were close in uni, but we lost touch when Robin moved to the States."

"So, tonight really was your first time seeing one another in what – seven years? And you didn't keep up contact in the meantime?" Matt was amazed. "No wonder there was tension."

"Did you think there was?" Olivia was worried now. She thought she'd played it to perfection. Was Matt now saying that she'd failed?

"Well, I thought she seemed a bit edgy, but I could have been imagining it." He seemed to pause intentionally, before adding "So, Leah, in her own way, was hoping to be peacemaker then?"

"Peacemaker?"

"Well, I didn't really understand most of her gibberish, but she kept repeating that stuff about you all being friends again and how this Kate thinks Robin's a 'bitssh'," he mimicked good-humouredly. Then his tone grew more serious. "It doesn't take a genius to work out that she wasn't there for you when Peter died." Matt shook his head. "That must have been tough. Or . . ." he hesitated, "is there more than that to it? Did Robin do something even more –"

423

"What? What are you saying?" Olivia cried, then slammed down on the brakes and swerved as a car pulled out of a parking-place on her left. She had all but hit it.

"He was indicating," said Matt mildly.

Olivia didn't answer. It was as though every muscle, every tendon in her body had all at once tensed to breaking-point, and she felt as though a herd of horses had just trampled over her stomach.

Staring rigidly at the road ahead, her pulse still racing, she scrambled to sort out her thoughts. But how could she explain it all here – in the car, while she was supposed to be concentrating on her driving? Still, she had to say something now, didn't she? Otherwise. . .

"Matt," she began then. "Matt, that's not –"

Just then Matt's mobile shrilled loudly, and the remaining words died on Olivia's lips.

He glanced at her apologetically, as he recognised the number displayed.

"Hello, Catherine," he said, with an edge to his tone.

Olivia exhaled loudly.

"Hi, yes, we're just on our way back – what? You're kidding – shit!"

She glanced away from the road briefly, a question in her eyes.

Matt looked worried. "Well, did you call the doctor? What did he say? Good, well, look, I'll be back in say, ten minutes or so, OK? And try not to worry, I'm sure it'll be fine but . . . Tell him I'm on my way, won't you? Right, right, see you soon – bye."

"What's happened?" For a split second, Olivia wondered if she'd been wrong about Catherine coming to terms with their relationship, but by the anxious look on Matt's face she knew the woman wasn't being dramatic just to try and ruin yet another night out.

His voice was fraught. "It's Adam. He has a fever and she thinks it might be meningitis."

"Oh, no!" Olivia had a similar scare with Ellie one time and it was horrific. "Is there a rash? Did she try the glass test?"

"I don't know. It was hard to make out what she was saying, she sounded so distraught."

"Look, I know it's impossible, but try not to worry – we'll be there soon." Instantly she increased the pressure on the accelerator. "Matt, it could be well be something small."

"I know, I know, but I just want to be there now." He turned away and looked quickly out the window, but as he did, Olivia thought she saw the glistening of tears in his eyes. "I don't know what I'd do if I lost him too, Olivia," he said in a broken voice, and her heart went out to him. "I really don't know what I'd do."

Olivia didn't know what to say. All she knew was that her own problems would have to take a back seat for a while.

At the moment, there were far more important things to worry about.

Chapter 42

Andrew Clarke sat in the Arrivals area at Dublin airport, bored out of his trolley. This had almost been as bad as the wait outside the delivery room last night. Although at least he was outside, and not inside with all the screaming and thrashing around and stuff. He really wasn't the kind of fella who could deal with all that sort of thing.

But Amanda had done well and apparently eighteen hours' labour was a common enough thing. Andrew grimaced and once again thanked his lucky stars that he'd been born a man. How did women do it? All that pushing and shoving and blood and goo – surely it wasn't natural? Surely, the human species had advanced far enough along the evolutionary chain to come up with some better way of reproduction than that sort of primal carry-on? Although, he thought, grinning to himself, the reproduction part being primal wasn't really all that much of a problem; it was trying to get the finished product out that caused all the hassle.

But, after it all, he was now the proud father of a tiny little girl who as yet had no name. The child had been born at 4am that morning and Amanda was still dithering over names. Andrew dreaded the final decision. Yesterday, before her waters broke, she'd been talking about naming the child, 'Manchester'.

"It's original and classy and the great thing is it would suit either a girl or a boy, wouldn't it?" she'd said, full of enthusiasm. All Andrew could think about was the hiding the child – male or female – would get all its life from football fans.

Amanda was thrilled it had turned out to be a girl. She thought she was 'beautiful'. Andrew thought she was nice enough but, in all honesty, right after the birth she just looked like a small, shrivelled sausage with arms and legs.

He'd often wondered why it was that, out of the entire animal kingdom, human offspring were the only ones that didn't look cute at birth. Look at baby elephants, lion-cubs, puppies and the like – wouldn't you run away with them in a second? But the tiny prune-faced object lying in the hospital alongside his wife at the moment was very far removed from that.

He checked his watch. Jesus, were Amanda's parents ever going to emerge from that bloody flight? The eleven-thirty Aer Lingus flight from London had landed a good half an hour ago and still there was no sign. Amanda's mother was probably fussing over her luggage and no doubt redoing herself up to the nines in the Ladies'. Amanda's vanity was nothing compared to

Mummy Langan's. Although, Andrew thought chuckling, these days the woman was a bit rough-looking and needed as much Polyfilla as she could get!

His stomach growled with the hunger, and he was just about to pop down to the Sandwich Bar near the bookshop, when a glut of passengers with Aer Lingus tags on their bags came through arrivals. There must have been some delay with the luggage then, Andrew thought, deciding that he'd better be here when Mummy and Daddy Langan did come through or there'd be Holy War.

He could always grab something on the way back to the hospital anyway. Luckily, he was one of those people who couldn't hear much when his jaws were moving, so he'd be spared the worst of Mummy L's annoying high-pitched rants about how the flight was delayed, and the luggage was lost, and how the air-hostesses had some cheek because they didn't kiss her fat feckin' arse.

He began scanning the faces of the passengers, just in case his in-laws had changed at all since the last time he'd seen them, which in Andrew's opinion wasn't long enough ago. Just then, he stiffened as he thought he caught sight of a familiar face, a face he knew well, but hadn't seen in a very long time. It couldn't be, could it? Andrew blinked and looked again like they always did in the movies. He almost went to wave but then, he thought, no, he was wrong it couldn't possibly be . . . it feckin *was*!

Should he go over and say hello and . . . shit, no, there was no time, because there were the Langans waving condescendingly at him, and pointing to their bags.

As if he was some thick hotel porter or something, Andrew thought, irritated, as he approached them.

"Hello there! Did you have a good flight?" Andrew asked, kissing Mummy L on the cheek and almost retching at the whiff of her probably expensive, but definitely manky, perfume.

"Don't talk to me!" Amanda's mother waved a dismissive arm. "Don't talk to me about that flight. People just don't know a *thing* about customer service these days. Can you believe that they actually tried to charge me for a glass of Perrier? How tacky!"

Andrew decided there was no point in asking if the two stingy feckers had anything to eat – no doubt Mummy would have gone apoplectic at the thoughts of paying five or six euro for a chicken sandwich. Good, that meant they'd have to get something on the way to the hospital. His stomach growled approvingly.

"Well, you're here now and you'll be glad to know that Amanda's doing fine and really looking forward to seeing you," he said, slightly annoyed that they hadn't even bothered to ask.

"Andrew, the only thing I'll be glad to know is that the car is parked close by and ready to take us away from this poor excuse for a cowshed!"

Andrew picked up the bags and followed them out to the carpark. He sighed deeply. It was going to be a long journey back to the hospital.

Olivia sat in her kitchen, waiting impatiently for news

of Adam. She hadn't heard a thing from Matt since he and Catherine had gone to the hospital the night before, so she had no idea if Adam was still in danger. She was reluctant to call Matt's mobile, feeling somehow it was not a time to intrude – it would probably be switched off anyway if he were in the hospital – and she was even more reluctant to call Catherine at her house. She had phoned Crumlin Children's Hospital earlier that morning, but because she wasn't family they wouldn't give her any information about his condition. She had expected nothing more anyway.

At around midday, she got a call from Leah. The poor thing was dreadfully upset and embarrassed about her behaviour the night before.

"I made such an idiot of myself," she wailed, mortified. "Matt must think I'm an unbalanced lunatic!"

"Don't be silly. Of course he doesn't think that," Olivia said, and went on to explain that Leah's behaviour was the last thing on Matt's mind at the moment.

"Give him my best regards when you hear from him, won't you?" Leah said. "Oh, and while I think of it, I got a call from Andrew first thing this morning. He's the reason I'm up out of bed, actually. Amanda had a baby girl early this morning."

"Oh, that's great news!" Despite her own concerns, she felt pleased for Amanda.

"Yeah, apparently it wasn't pretty, and Amanda threatened the midwife with litigation if she kept forcing her to push like that, but it all worked out in the end."

Olivia forced a smile at the image of princess-like Amanda going through hard labour. That would have been some sight. Then she thought of something.

"Is Robin still there?" she asked, trying to sound casual.

"No, I made her go back to the hotel this morning. I felt awful about her having to sleep on my lumpy couch when she should have been relaxing in sumptuous luxury. She knew me and my hangover wouldn't be much company today, but I'm meeting her again before she heads off to London." She paused slightly, and Olivia knew what was coming. "Olivia, how can you ever forgive me? I just wasn't thinking straight. I really didn't mean to drag everything up like that. It must have been hard enough for you as it was, seeing her again."

"No, it wasn't too bad actually." She forced a small laugh. "But it was unfortunate that you mentioned Kate."

"I know!" Leah groaned again. "I spent much of this morning trying to convince her that Kate didn't know any better, but I think I'd said more than enough at that stage." Her voice dropped slightly. "I know she found it tough too – last night, I mean."

"I know that. That's why I tried to make it as easy as possible for her."

"You're a good person, Olivia, and a good friend."

"I don't know about that, but, as you know, I've never felt there was much point in holding a grudge. As it turned out, I wasn't exactly blameless myself."

431

"Well, look, I'm very sorry if I made it uncomfortable for you," Leah said softly.

"Don't be silly – we were bound to come face to face at some stage and, if anything, it gave us something to talk about, didn't it?" she replied, trying to keep her voice light. "Anyway, you should go back to bed and try and sleep that hangover off."

"I think I'll have to," Leah moaned. "At the moment I feel like my head is about to split in two. But let me know what happens with little Adam, will you? And try not to worry."

"I will – and I won't." She went to say something else but hesitated. "Talk to you soon."

"You too, bye."

Olivia hung up, realising that just then she'd been about to ask something else about Robin. Try as she might, she couldn't stop thinking about it, as she'd thought about it many times before. After all these years, surely they had more to say to one another. Didn't Robin have any questions? Didn't she wonder about any of it? Had it been that easy for her to shut them all out of her life?

Or was it that Robin simply didn't give a damn?

Robin sat in her hotel room, trying to decide what to do until her mum arrived that evening. She had nothing on today, and there had been no point in staying any longer at Leah's. The poor thing was in bits, and not just with her hangover. She'd apologised over and over again, trying to convince Robin that Kate simply didn't know better and that she'd always been unnecessarily harsh on her.

Robin didn't care what Kate thought. She'd had her reasons for staying away. Olivia knew that and, in fairness, had somehow seemed to understand it.

But why? Why was it so easy for Olivia to forgive her? Why had she always made excuses for her? Why hadn't she gone beserk when Robin had let her down like that? Many times over the years Robin had tried to imagine what she would have done in Olivia's situation. She didn't think she could forgive and go on as if nothing had happened, like Olivia had. Olivia had been so calm, so friendly last night at dinner that it was almost unreal.

She checked the time – it was just after one pm – just after eight am New York time. She should catch Ben before he left for his morning jog. Ben religiously went for a jog every morning, even on Sundays.

"Hey! How's it all going over there?" Ben's friendly voice cheered her up instantly, but at the same time made her miss him even more.

"It's OK, a bit tiring though. The journalists just ask the same questions over and over again. They don't really need to talk to me – all they need to do is copy everything directly from the press release."

"Get out of that – I'll bet you're loving all the attention!" he laughed.

She raised a smile. "Well, I'll admit I did enjoy the first TV one, apart from the dreadful make-up."

"I hope you kept me a recording – I'm dying to find out if you come across like you have an American twang!"

"No – that would be you," Robin teased him.

"So what else is going on over there? Did you get a chance to see your mum or your friends? What about Leah?"

"I'm meeting Mum this evening, and I was out with Leah last night for her birthday."

"Great – I'm glad you got the chance to meet up, although I hope you didn't bump into any old flames or anything?"

Robin smiled sadly. If only he knew.

"No."

Then she heard their apartment intercom ringing in the background.

"Shit, that's probably Dave! He's tagging along this morning. The poor guy is desperate to get rid of his love-handles!"

"I'd better go too. I'm on the hotel phone, so I'm sure it's costing me a fortune."

"Bill it to the publishers!" he said with a laugh. "Look, give me a call when you get to London. I wish I could have gone with you, Robin – I think I'm more excited about this than you are!"

She smiled. "I'll be home soon and I promise I'll tell you all about it. In the meantime, you'd better let poor Dave in before those love-handles get any worse."

"OK, I'm going, I'm going! Love ya lots and tell your mum I said hello, OK? Bye." With that, Ben hung up.

Robin replaced the receiver feeling bereft. Ben seemed so far away and in all honesty she felt lost in this place. She missed him desperately, much more than she'd expected. He really was the most important person in her life now, the only one who trusted her and loved her for what she was. And yet she'd always been so unwilling to yield fully to that, to accept his love for her at face value – or to risk telling him about her past. Robin supposed it was because she'd never been really able to convince herself that she was worth loving. After the mistakes she'd made in the past, why should she deserve it? The last man she'd given herself to fully had made that all too clear. He'd abandoned her at her most vulnerable and had robbed her not only of her self-esteem, but of everything that was important. He'd robbed her of her friendships.

Coming home had been hard, and although Robin had always known deep down that she'd have to do it eventually, visiting the graveyard the other day had been even harder. But still she had to do it.

She'd felt like an interloper standing there, reading the so familiar but yet equally alien name inscribed on the headstone. It was all so surreal. She noticed how well Olivia was taking care of the grave; it was obviously regularly attended, and she'd recently left some fresh flowers. She saw what must have been little Ellie's contribution of some childish paintings of a house and some happy-looking people, a happy family. At this, a lump came to Robin's throat as she realised that she really didn't belong there; she had no right to

435

be there, just as she had no right to be at the funeral all those years ago. Not a single day had gone by for Robin without a sense of aching regret, regret for not being there and regret for what had gone before. Kate thought she knew it all, but in fact she had no idea.

No idea how desperately difficult it was for Robin to come home and say goodbye to someone she too had loved deeply, but never had any right to.

Catherine sat in her favourite spot by the front window, unable to concentrate on anything other than Matt and Adam at the hospital. He'd sent her away earlier this morning, telling her to go home and get some sleep.

But Catherine couldn't sleep, not when the most important people in her life were in trouble. She didn't know what she would do if anything happened to Adam. And she knew Matt wouldn't be able to cope with losing him either, after all he'd suffered after Natasha.

Catherine sighed guiltily. She'd been a fool to think that she could keep Matt all to herself. He didn't love her. He never had. He was in love with Olivia now, and there was nothing she could do to change that. And now, with all that had happened in the last twelve hours, she didn't know if she wanted to any more.

Matt was going through a very tough time just now, and Olivia had obviously had a tough time of it too, losing her husband and blaming herself for his death. It must have been hard enough to deal with the loss, let alone feel as though she'd contributed to it. Catherine shook her head. Maybe, in a strange way, taking on the burden of guilt for her husband's death was Olivia's way of coping with her grief – in the same way that Catherine tried to cope with her unrequited love for Matt by transferring hate and suspicion onto Olivia.

And that was it, wasn't it, she thought, the severity of Adam's illness mellowing her senses and letting her see it all in a new perspective. Matt didn't love her, at least not in the way she wanted him to. He loved Olivia, and why shouldn't he? Take away the jealousy and she supposed Olivia was a nice enough woman, although she had nothing on Natasha. But Catherine knew that no one would ever replace Natasha in Matt's eyes – not Olivia, and certainly not her. Natasha simply couldn't be replaced, no matter how much she believed it, no matter how hard she tried. But nevertheless he had fallen for Olivia – she made him happy and maybe the two of them deserved that. They had both been through enough.

Maybe she should just let Olivia and Matt get on with it and she should get on with her own life. She'd get over Matt, eventually – she had no other choice. And Rory from the video shop wasn't the worst either, was he? What had started out as a little fling had gradually become something more, and only recently, Rory had said something about taking their relationship 'to the next level', whatever that meant. He was crazy about her, and although she had convinced herself she was only using him to get to Matt, deep down she did enjoy his company. And in all honesty, he was a pretty decent prospect for a girl like her; he had more than a few quid in the bank, and a very nice house over in Glenageary. So, Catherine decided, catching sight of a car rounding the corner at one of the entrances to the green, maybe she should just forget about Matt once and for all, and concentrate her energies on nabbing Rory before he went in search of someone closer to his own age.

The car stopped outside Olivia's house and a tall, dark and – from what she could make out – attractive man, got out. He paused outside the house for a moment, as if unsure whether or not he had the right address.

But no, Catherine decided, shifting her position to get a better view, it wasn't that. It was more like he was hesitating, pausing for breath, making sure he knew what he was doing before he went any further. Then, feeling more than a little silly, she shook her head. God, her imagination really did run away with her sometimes! The poor guy was probably nothing other than a salesman.

But by the look of utter horror on Olivia's face when she opened the door to him, Catherine knew that this man wasn't just a salesman.

Chapter 43

"What are you doing here?" she asked, her voice a low whisper, her face white with shock.

He looked nervously at her, his features soft, his expression grave. "I wanted to see you. I'm sorry, I know I shouldn't but –" he ran a hand through his hair, through those locks that just then she ached to touch. "I . . . I *needed* to see you."

Why did he have to come here now – today? When she was feeling terrible and even worse, she thought, *looking* terrible. Her hair was unwashed and still matted from the night before, and she knew she hadn't bothered removing her make-up. She'd barely dressed herself this morning – her mind had been completely elsewhere, and she just didn't have the energy.

"Can we talk? Please?" he asked.

She bit her lip, trying desperately not to just launch herself into his arms, which she knew in her current state of mind she could so easily do. He looked tired and drained, devoid of spirit. He looked . . . vulnerable.

And he was obviously suffering too.

"Can I come in? Just for a minute or two, and I'll understand if you don't want to, but . . ."

He looked directly into her eyes then, and her stomach leapt with the old familiar sense of longing. "I miss you so much, Leah."

She knew she shouldn't, she had to be strong, but it was so hard. "Josh, we've been through this before. There's nothing more to say." Her voice sounded strange and alien, even to her.

"I know that, and I know you're probably still very angry with me, but Leah . . . I just can't explain how sorry I am." His voice was thick with emotion. "I made the biggest mistake of my life, I know that. But I also know that I love you."

"Josh, don't . . ." Leah didn't want to hear this, yet at the same time she *did* want to hear it. These last few weeks she could barely sleep or eat for thinking about it, for thinking about him, and how much she missed him too. And last night had been especially hard, which is why she'd ended up drinking so much. She'd hoped that getting really drunk would numb the pain and the emptiness she felt without him.

Still, no matter how much she loved him and missed him, Josh had done something unforgivable – Leah had to remember that. There was no going back.

Her mind firmly set, she decided that she'd listen to what he had to say, but that was it. Definitely.

Maybe . . .

"Look, it's OK if you don't want to let me in. But I don't want to say what I have to say out here. This is between us, just the two of us."

"Josh, it would have been just the two of us, if you hadn't gone off with some slapper," she shot back, the reminder of his betrayal giving her the strength she needed.

"I know that," he said contritely. "And I've suffered over that too, as much as you have – if not more," he added, when he saw her expression.

Leah sighed. "Come in then," she said, going inside and expecting him to follow her.

Josh quietly closed the door behind him. "Happy Birthday, by the way," he said with a hesitant smile, taking in all her birthday cards on the mantelpiece.

"Thank you for the flowers." Leah indicated the lush bouquet on the coffee table. She'd been all at once annoyed and touched that he'd sent them, touched because he hadn't forgotten, and annoyed that he'd had the cheek.

"I wasn't sure . . ." he shrugged.

The two of them sat at opposite ends of the room, Josh in 'his' armchair, and Leah curled up on the couch and under the blankets Robin had used only a few hours earlier. They served as some kind of comfort, some kind of barrier if necessary.

"Leah . . ." Again, Josh ran a hand through his hair, as if unsure where to begin. "I don't really know where to start, so I suppose I'll just come right out and say it. I know I fucked up big-time."

She said nothing, assuming that he expected her to agree, to move the conversation along. She wasn't doing him any favours.

"That 'thing' I did – was one of the lowest moments in my life. I was disgusted with myself for letting you down, for letting myself down, for risking all that we had because I was feeling left out. That's exactly how I felt, Lee," he said, when she raised an eyebrow. "I felt left out of everything, thought that you didn't want me to share all the great things that were going on in your life." She opened her mouth to say something, but he stopped her. "Before you say anything, yes, I know it was stupid. It was stupid and immature and pathetic but it was the way I felt. I never liked that Andrew Clarke. You know that."

"I do know that, but I could never understand why. Andrew never did anything to you. Actually, he likes you. He thinks you and I are well suited."

"Does he now?" Josh sniffed.

"Yes, he does," Leah heard her voice rise an octave, "and I'm not going over this again with you, Josh. Don't you dare try and tell me that you went back to your ex for a night of passion, just because you couldn't handle your own stupid jealousy!"

"Lee, calm down, that wasn't it," he soothed. "In a way it *was* jealousy I suppose, but not the kind you think. With one flick of his expensive Parker pen, Clarke gave you everything you wanted. I couldn't do that. I'm just my dad's dogsbody, probably always will be, and as a result I felt threatened, useless, all the stupid things I never thought I'd feel. I felt it was *my* place to look after you, to support you in your dream. But he came along with his fat bloody cheque book and blew me out of the water."

"It wasn't like that, Josh. *I* approached Andrew for investment. Granted it was a stupid drunken conversation, which at the time I thought wouldn't amount to anything, but it did. And I'm grateful for that. You said yourself that Elysium is my dream. How could I have turned down that opportunity?"

"I never expected you to, but I also didn't expect you to be so gung-ho about it. You threw yourself into it without a second thought, and all of a sudden it was Andrew this and Andrew that. Suddenly he was the most important part of your life and I felt unbelievably threatened."

"Threatened? By an old friend who is, incidentally, married to another old friend?"

"Like I said – it wasn't like that. I didn't think there was anything going on between you two, but I couldn't really express how I felt about it. You threw yourself into setting up the shop and didn't seem to want me involved in any of it. Instead of telling you how I felt, I just kept niggling you about the business being more important than I was. I know you began to resent me and probably not just for that."

"What do you mean?"

"Leah, I know you want a child of your own, that you've always wanted one. Despite what you said to me about my being enough for you. I know you were affected by Kate's pregnancy and, despite what you think, I understood how difficult it must have been seeing it all happen for her, all the time knowing that it might never happen for you.

"That's not fair. I made that decision long ago and it was *our* decision. Kate's pregnancy shook me a little, but that's because she's changed, not because I have." In a way, he was right, but Leah wasn't going to allow this to be all about her.

"Well, with everything that was going on, I became confused. After a while, I began to wonder what you were doing with me. I couldn't help you with your business, I couldn't give you what you wanted. I was a total failure."

"Josh, I'm sorry, but this smacks of feeling sorry for yourself."

"I know it does, and in a way, it is. But the thing is, over the last few weeks, I've come to realise how stupid I've been, and how wrong I was to deny you the chance of becoming a mother." He sat forward. "Leah, I know you probably can't even consider it at the moment, but if you could possibly think about having me back, then I'd like to have a baby."

Leah blinked, and instantly her heart tightened. "What? Are you serious?"

"Yes, I know it would take a bit of getting used to, but I know you and I could make a go of it and –"

Never in a million years did she expect this from him, and despite the fact that Josh was now offering her everything she wanted, offering her the chance to start over, strangely, the idea just saddened her. "Josh, you're delusional! You think that you can just waltz in here, tell me you're very sorry for being unfaithful, but not to worry, sure a child of our own will make it all right! What planet are you on?"

"I know we'd have some work to do, but –"

"*Some* work? Josh, it's too late. There's no trust any more. And yes, maybe I did play a part in pushing you away and making you feel inadequate, but that doesn't mean that you had any right to jump into bed with the first available person!"

"I know that, but, Leah, surely we can work on it? I love you. Doesn't that mean anything?"

"It didn't mean much when you were with her, did it?" she said in a broken voice. She turned away, willing away the tears that were threatening.

Josh moved across to sit beside her on the sofa. "Leah, I messed up – I know that, I knew it straight away. I wanted to tell you, but I knew you'd never forgive me and I didn't want you to think badly of me." He touched her hand. "I wish I could make you understand how sorry I am."

"I'm sure you are, but that doesn't mean much now."

"Don't you think we could work through it, Lee?" he said, his voice soft and hopeful. "It would be a shame to throw away all that we have."

"Josh, if we don't have trust, then we have nothing."

"But we can work on that, surely? Look, I know it might be hard for you to believe me at the moment, but

I know *I* can do it. I love you more than anyone – you're the best thing that's ever happened to me. You're my best friend, my life, all the usual clichés but they're clichés because they're true. I know I want to spend the rest of my life with you, even more now that I know what it's like to be without you. I know too that you made a big sacrifice to be with me, but what I'm saying now is – if you want – that that doesn't have to be the case any more. I'm willing to give it a go if you are." He smiled at Leah then, and amazingly uttered the very words she would have been elated to hear not all that long ago. "Let's settle down and buy a place of our own – let's get married and, yes, let's have kids. We could have a great life, Leah, I know we could. And I'm almost certain that we can get through this. People do, don't they? If they really love one another, then they can get through anything."

Leah's head spun. It was so tempting, so tempting just to throw her arms around him and agree that yes, they could do it, and yes, they could have a great life. He was telling her everything she so badly wanted to hear. But she knew in her heart and soul that she just couldn't forget what he'd done that easily.

She shook her head, and she could actually feel the tightness in her heart as she said the words. "I'm sorry, Josh, but I know I can't do that." She tried desperately to keep her voice even. "It's over."

"You don't really mean that."

"I do," she replied, trying to sound more determined that she felt. "And I'm sorry, but I think you should go."

"Leah, please, just give me one more chance. I know we could make it work. I'm sure of it. Just one more chance."

"I can't, Josh – it's too late." Leah stood up and, legs shaking like jelly, moved across the room and opened the door. She stood back, appealing to him once more to leave. Josh stared at her, as if unable to believe that she was really serious. "Please," she asked again.

After a few long moments, Josh acquiesced. "I'm sorry, Leah. Really I am."

"I know." Leah refused to meet his eyes, painfully aware that this really was the end. Every inch of her ached with sadness. "Goodbye, Josh."

She closed the door behind him, shutting him out of her home and out of her life.

As much as she still loved him, and as tempting as it was to take him up on all he promised, she knew she just couldn't do it. She couldn't handle his infidelity, the fact that he had broken her trust. She wasn't one of those people who could just pick up the pieces and move on. She wasn't strong enough to be one of those people who could forgive and forget.

She just wasn't Olivia.

Chapter 44

Earlier that afternoon, in order to take her mind off things, Olivia had decided to tidy out the garden shed. It was a job that was way overdue, and one that she'd been putting off for ages. But as the house was spick and span, the ironing up to date and the shopping done, she couldn't think of anything else to do other than fret over the situation with Robin, and worry about Adam. Not to mention fretting over Matt's surprising comments last night on the way home.

Ellie was at her mother's, Eva having decided that Olivia should be free to go to hospital should Matt need her. Olivia had tried his mobile a number of times since, but it was switched to messages, and still she'd heard nothing. Despite what they said about no news being good news she didn't think it was appropriate in this case. Surely Matt would know she'd be on tenterhooks, wondering whether or not Adam was suffering from meningitis? At one stage, she'd been so desperate for something concrete, she'd almost called over to Catherine's house. But an idiotic sense of pride stopped her doing that, as she suspected that Catherine would feel some sense of superiority at the fact that Matt hadn't been in touch.

She was in the process of dumping some ancient congealed paint-brushes and tins into a black refuse sack, when the doorbell rang.

Matt! She raced back into the house, forgetting to remove her rubber gloves in her haste to get to the door – and hopefully for him to put her out of her misery once and for all. With any luck, all would be well with Adam, and then she could have a good long chat with Matt and finally let him into her confidence about her marriage to Peter.

But when she opened the door, Olivia's world spun on a three-hundred-and-sixty degree axis.

"Hello, Olivia," her visitor said with an unsure smile.

She was so stunned it felt like a couple of hours before she could get the words out. "What – what are you doing here?" she whispered eventually, her head dizzy with shock.

He shook his head apologetically. "I'm sorry. I know I should have called first. But my flight got in around lunch-time and I was really anxious to get here so –"

"But what are you doing here?" she asked again. "What do you want?"

"What do I want? Olivia, surely you must know –"

Somewhere nearby she heard a car door slam.

"He's OK, Olivia!" came Matt's relieved-sounding

voice over the air. Then the sound of his footsteps on the path outside. "It wasn't meningitis at all, thank God – it was just some reaction to – oh, I'm sorry . . . excuse me . . ." Matt's voice trailed off as he approached the doorway. He looked at the other man and grinned apologetically. "Sorry to interrupt, but I had to let her know."

"That's wonderful news!" Olivia barely heard the sound of her own voice, so strong was the sound of her heartbeat thudding against her ribcage, so intense were the feelings of anxiety, confusion and – and out-and-out panic.

What on earth was she going to say?

She saw that Matt was looking unsurely from her to the other man, obviously waiting for an introduction, or some explanation as to why she was acting so strangely. And unfortunately, Olivia would have to give him one – one that she knew he wouldn't be expecting.

She tried to clear her throat, to clear her mind and get some hold on her senses. How – knowing full well that Matt had somehow got it all wrong – was she going to explain this? How?

Olivia willed her heart to slow down, willed her nerves to settle a little. She began to speak slowly, hoping to soften the blow somewhat.

"This is Matt Sheridan, a good friend of mine," she said, her voice hoarse and her hands shaking as she made the introduction.

Then, she turned and looked directly at a smiling Matt.

"Matt, this is Peter – my husband."

Chapter 45

It was as though every drop of blood had all at once drained from Matt's face.

"What?" he said staring at Olivia, his expression a mixture of shock and confusion, "What the hell is going on here?"

Olivia scrambled to explain. "I'm sorry, Matt. I know you thought otherwise, but I only realised that last night when you said you thought he was –"

Peter spoke to his wife as if Matt wasn't even there. "Olivia, obviously this is a bad time, so maybe I should –"

"Will somebody please explain to me what the *fuck* is going on here?" Matt said, his voice rising a few octaves. He glared at her. "I thought your husband was dead! You *told* me your husband was dead!"

Olivia floundered. She had never seen him so angry, but yet she could completely understand why. "Matt, I never told you that," she began, her words slow and deliberate, as if she were trying to explain something complicated to a child. Yet at the same time, her heartbeat was galloping. "I never told you *anything* like that. I know I haven't been exactly forthcoming where Peter was concerned but I never, *ever* said –"

"Hold on a goddamn second! You *told* me you were a widow, that you'd brought Ellie up on your own, that you didn't know how you'd have coped without her. You didn't like to talk about it, you said – it was too painful. No wonder it was bloody painful – the geezer was still around!"

Peter stepped forward. "Look, mate, I've no idea who you are, but I don't think you've any right to talk to –"

"Peter, stop, please!" Olivia felt as though she'd landed on another planet. What was Matt saying? She'd *never* told him that she was widowed or that Peter was dead – she'd barely said anything at all about him because it *was* too painful! Where had he got that idea? Granted he knew she was married, and that she and Ellie now lived on their own, but surely he couldn't have made the huge leap to the notion that Peter was dead, could he? She had told him she was separated, hadn't she? Because why else would he have come to her house that time telling her he had feelings for her? Her head spun as she tried to remember all the conversations they'd had about her and her marriage, tried to figure out how she might have misled him. But in her heart of hearts she knew she hadn't misled him. Granted, she'd been evasive, but he must have come up with the assumption that she was widowed all by himself!

Still, at that moment, Olivia desperately wished that she hadn't been so reticent, so unwilling to let him into her confidence. Now it looked as though she'd deliberately misinformed him, although where he got the idea that Peter was dead she still couldn't understand . . .

"Matt, please come inside and let's talk about this. I don't know why you thought that, and I never, ever tried to mislead you." She ran a hand through her hair. What a total mess! She should have explained straightaway last night, but then he was so upset after Catherine's phone call, she hadn't had the opportunity and . . . oh, God, what was she going to do? Her thoughts and emotions were so confused just then that she couldn't think crooked, let alone straight.

"Look, Matt, Peter and I separated many years ago, but we haven't yet divorced and . . ." She trailed off, as the thought struck her. "Is that why you're here?" she asked Peter, feeling an odd combination of relief and disappointment. "For the divorce?"

"I don't fucking believe this!" Matt was saying as he marched back down the path. "I don't believe what I'm hearing, what I'm seeing! I thought you were special, Olivia. I thought you and I had something. But you're nothing but a lying trollop!"

"Hey, watch it!" Peter called after his retreating back, but Matt was already in the driver's seat of the car. He started the Volvo and revved the engine ferociously before driving off. Olivia watched him speed off towards the main road. Strange, she thought absently, that he didn't go straight to Catherine's.

"Olivia," Peter's strange but yet weirdly familiar voice brought her sharply back to the present, "can I come in? I think you and I need to talk."

She looked at Peter's face then, a face so familiar it was as though she'd never been apart from him. Then, with no clue or idea as to what he was doing here, Olivia stood back from the doorway and let her husband – the man whose return she'd dreamed about for five long years – into her house and back into her life.

Olivia stared into those expressive eyes she had once known and loved so well. "Why now, Peter? What do you want from me – from us?"

"I didn't plan for it to happen this way, believe me," he answered softly. "I was going to call first – I know I should have called first, but when I landed in Dublin airport this morning, I couldn't not come."

"But what are you doing back in Ireland in the first place? Oh," she said, the realisation hitting her, "it's your mum, isn't it?" She knew that Teresa wasn't well, but Olivia had never in her wildest dreams imagined that Peter would come back all the way from Australia just because his mother was feeling out of sorts.

"Did she tell you she's suffering from Parkinson's?" he asked, and instantly Olivia felt guilty.

"No, no, she never said." Teresa had never opened her mouth. Olivia had noticed her slowing down, of course, in the same way that her own parents were showing signs of getting on in years, but she had never once suspected that it could be anything more serious. Suddenly she felt guilty for all the nasty thoughts she'd been thinking about Teresa lately. Suddenly her insistence on spending more time with Ellie made sense.

So, Peter was home for Mummy then. Nothing to do with the wife and child he'd so cruelly discarded years ago. Then again, why did she think it could be any different?

"She's getting progressively worse and the treatment she's on doesn't seem to be having much of an effect." He studied her. "But I'd been thinking about contacting you for a while, Olivia."

"Then why didn't you? Why didn't you let me know that you were coming back to Ireland at least – let alone turning up unannounced on my doorstep? Jesus, Peter, never mind me, but how did you think Ellie would react to you turning up out of the blue like this?"

"Do you . . . do you really think Ellie would know me?" he asked unsurely.

"Of course, she'd know you – she has photographs in her bedroom, and your parents make doubly sure to show her pictures of you every time she visits. What they don't tell her is that her father was so upset with me that he decided not to bother about her!"

"That's not true – of course, I bothered about her. Of

course, I cared about her. But these last few years been hard, Olivia. Being away from you was the only way I could see things more clearly, you know that."

"And you had to go to the other end of the world to see things more clearly?" she said, his reference to wanting to 'stay away from her' cutting her deeply. He still blamed her then. "This is crazy, Peter."

"Is Ellie here?" He looked nervously around the room, and his eyes rested on a framed photograph of her on the mantelpiece. It was a professional photograph Olivia had commissioned a few months back, on Ellie's fourth birthday. She was grinning happily at the camera, the gap in her teeth unmistakeable and charming. Olivia followed his gaze and instantly folded her arms protectively across her chest.

"She's at my mum's," she replied shortly, offering up a relieved prayer that Ellie wasn't here when Peter arrived. "So, four years and a few birthday and Christmas cards later, you think you're entitled to just pop in and see her – without so much as a phone call beforehand? How dare you, Peter?"

"I know, I'm sorry, but I just thought –"

"You thought you could waltz in here after abandoning her – abandoning *us* like you did!"

"Look, I didn't think I *would* come here, and certainly not so soon. I'm sorry but I just wasn't thinking straight. I'm tired and jet-lagged and worried about Mum and . . ." he trailed off. "Being back here again is a huge thing for me, Olivia – surely you can understand that."

She did understand, but still couldn't forgive the casual way he had just turned up on her doorstep. Then she thought of something. "How did you know where to find us? You sent the cards to your mother's and I never gave you this address, so how did you know how to get here?" Although, as soon as she'd asked, Olivia thought she knew the answer.

She was right.

"Mum told me where you were, but she also told me to leave it for a while before getting in touch. She knew it wouldn't be easy for you, but at the same time, I think she knew I'd want to see you two eventually."

"And you thought *I'd* feel the same, I suppose?" Olivia was so angered by this she could hardly think straight. Who did the Gallaghers think they were, playing with her feelings like that? With all Teresa's snide remarks about Matt and her so-called 'concern' for Ellie's welfare! She was just making sure that if Peter *did* decide to come home, he'd still have a ready-made family there waiting for him! How heartless could a person be? "You thought *I'd* be sitting patiently at home, waiting for you to change your mind, to decide that you did love us after all – was that it?"

The problem was – only a few months earlier, Olivia *had* been hoping the same thing. She'd been waiting for him to return, waiting for him to forgive her, hoping that they might eventually be a family again. But that was before, and now, try as she might, she couldn't concentrate properly on the sheer magnitude of his actually being here. She was too concerned about Matt and the mess she had made of it all by being secretive, by trying to protect herself.

Peter sighed deeply. "I'm sorry. This was a mistake. I should have called first. I should have at least told you –"

"Yes, you should."

He hesitated a little. "I know this probably isn't the right time but . . . you're looking really well, Olivia. And it *is* good to see you." At this, he flashed his best Colgate smile, those teeth seeming even whiter against his Australian tan.

Amazingly, in all the years she'd known this man, this was the very first time that Olivia could see through the compliment for what it was. It was an attempt to control her, to get his own way, to soften her up a bit. She had always thought Peter was charming, had always thought she was lucky to find a husband who was so respectful and considerate not just to her, but to other women also. Only now did it strike her that he was simply a weak, selfish bastard. Absence didn't quite make the heart grow fonder – in this case, it made it insightful. But, she thought, that wasn't the whole story, was it? Her feelings, or lack of them, for Peter now, had more to do with Matt, than her finally realising how spineless and pathetic Peter had been in taking off and leaving her and Ellie. She could, perhaps, understand why he had abandoned her, but there was no excuse for his selfish rejection of Ellie.

All of a sudden, Olivia didn't care that Peter was back, or about what Peter did or didn't want.

"I'm sorry, Peter, but I can't do this now. Ellie will be

home soon, and I don't want you here when she returns. I have a life of my own – *Ellie* and I have a life, one that you're not part of, that you haven't ever been part of. I know you had your reasons for leaving but, to be honest, I think I've done my penance and suffered enough over the years. What you seemed to forget so easily was that it was hard for me too, yet I didn't have the luxury of taking off to 'get over it'. I had a child to raise."

"I know." To his credit, Peter looked shamefaced.

"Yet, you didn't care about my suffering, did you? You just believed what you wanted to believe – that I had come home late intentionally, that I didn't care about the consequences, that I should have been there." She shook her head, unwilling to relive the pain and the guilt all over again, especially in front of him. "But I just lost track of time." At this her voice broke and she closed her eyes briefly, the pain almost too strong to bear.

"I know."

"And yet you couldn't see that at the time. You kept thinking that I had done it on purpose – as some kind of revenge, for God's sake! That was never *ever* the case!"

Peter nodded with heavy emotion. "I know, but I had no other way of getting my head around it. No matter what you say, there was always some resentment there, Olivia – you admitted that once yourself."

"Yes, but the resentment was towards *you* – couldn't you ever see that?"

Peter said nothing and for a long time husband and wife just stood there in silence, painful memories hanging heavily between them.

Eventually, Olivia shook her head. "Peter, I'm sorry but I don't want to get into this now. Maybe we can arrange something later, but you can't just turn up at the door like this. Matt, the man that called just now, he's very important to me and I have a lot to explain."

"I see." His hands in his pockets, Peter began to head towards the door.

"No, you don't see!" Olivia followed him out to the hallway. "You don't have a bloody clue how hard these last few years have been for me, and finally, when I get a chance at happiness, you turn up and ruin it all."

"That was never my intention," Peter said, stepping out onto the front path. He turned to look at her. "I never wanted to upset you, Olivia – I just wanted to see my daughter."

She nodded. "Well, Teresa has my number. If you're still in Dublin, phone me later maybe – when I've had a chance to prepare Ellie," she added pointedly.

"Thanks, I appreciate that and I would like to speak to you before I go up to Galway if I could." Peter paused slightly as he turned to leave. "Look, I'm sorry for surprising you like I did. I hope I didn't mess things up with you and that – that guy. I didn't mean to do that – I didn't even know you *were* with someone. I mean, Mum didn't say . . ." He trailed off, slightly uncomfortable with the admission. "In fact, I'm in another relationship now too – with an Australian girl."

"Good for you." Olivia suddenly realised she didn't care any more. She'd always suspected that he might have found someone else – after all, it was a long time – but now she decided she just didn't care about Peter, his new relationship, or even the fact that he'd finally come home. At that moment, all she cared about was Matt.

She had to explain why she hadn't told him everything about her marriage before now. Maybe she *could* understand why he thought that Peter had died, but yet . . . Olivia's head thudded, her brain unable to cope with the enormity of all that was happening.

If only she'd told him everything from the beginning. But she couldn't have done that though, could she? She had to make sure she trusted Matt beforehand, trusted him enough to tell him the truth. Otherwise, he wouldn't understand.

Just like Peter hadn't understood.

Chapter 46

"Catherine, I really need your help,"

She was stony-faced. "I don't know where he is."

"His mobile is switched off, and he's not answering at home. Please, I really need to talk to him."

"I'm sure you do."

"It's very important."

"I'd imagine it is."

"Catherine, please!"

She sighed. "Look, I don't know what's going on between you two. All I know is that Matt is very annoyed. I presume it might have something to do with that man at your house a while ago?"

"My husband, yes."

Catherine's eyes widened. "Jesus, no wonder he's upset!"

Olivia didn't have the energy to try and explain; she needed to save that for Matt.

"I know he's here. Can you ask him to come out and talk to me, please?"

He must have gone straight back to the hospital after leaving her house, as Olivia hadn't been able to reach him at home, and then, some time after Peter left, she finally spotted his car outside Catherine's.

"I don't know if he'll want to talk to you. He certainly doesn't want to talk to me."

"Catherine." Both women turned towards the voice in the hallway. "It's OK. Come in, Olivia," Matt said quietly. "We might as well get this over and done with."

Catherine stood back to let her in, and the three of them stood silently in the hallway. Eventually Catherine spoke. "I'm heading off to visit Adam now anyway," she said, her voice low and gentler than Olivia had ever heard it.

"He was asking for you earlier," Matt said, his hard expression softening somewhat.

Olivia waited until the front door closed behind Catherine before speaking.

She smiled warily. "Matt, I don't know what to say."

"Neither do I."

He went into the front room, obviously expecting her to follow him. Olivia obliged and sat nervously on the edge of Catherine's leather sofa, Matt sitting on an armchair nearby.

"It was only when you mentioned something about Peter's funeral last night that I realised you thought he was dead," she began, her voice slow and nervous. "And I really was about to correct you when Catherine rang about Adam and –"

"But I've *always* thought that," Matt interjected, shaking his head. "The woman in the corner shop told me that you moved here after your husband died."

Olivia's eyes widened, surprised at this. "Molly actually *said* that?"

"Yes. I felt a bit uncomfortable about her telling me actually, as I didn't really know you well at the time, and I hate those gossipy types."

But – but Molly didn't know anything, *nobody* in Cherrytree Green knew anything – Olivia had made sure of that. It was the only way she could live in peace, knowing that she'd have none of the pitying smiles and sympathetic looks she'd had in her old estate! She'd never said a word. How the hell had Molly come up with that scenario?

But then, Olivia realised that her insistence on maintaining her privacy had simply made her prime fodder for local gossip. Thinking of it now, she recalled her neighbour Trudy being quite intrusive in her questions when she was on her way to the graveyard one day, although Olivia hadn't told her much.

And, of course, Trudy and Molly were bosom buddies, so between the two of them they'd taken two and two and come up with fifty! She shook her head, unable to take it all in herself, never mind try and explain all to Matt. Granted she'd never been all that happy to call herself separated as she'd always hoped that someday Peter would return. But yet, she had no idea that all this time her neighbours thought she was a widow. What an absolute mess! Why did they think that when . . .

But just then it clicked. Just then, Olivia thought she knew exactly why her neighbours had made such an assumption. She turned to Matt.

"Matt, I moved here after Peter and I separated, not long after Ellie was born."

"But why did she think –"

"I'm not one hundred per cent sure myself actually, but it might have something to do with my visits to the graveyard," she said, realising that this had to be the most likely scenario. "When they don't have all the pieces of a puzzle, some people like to try and make the most obvious parts fit." She sighed. "But I wasn't visiting Peter there."

A very long silence hung between them. Eventually, Matt spoke.

"Who – who *were* you visiting then?" he asked.

Olivia's eyes filled with tears and she tightly grasped her hands together. "Our son. Peter and I lost a toddler, a little boy. His death was the reason we split up." Her voice began to shake.

Matt leant across and put a comforting hand on her knee. "Olivia, I'm sorry. I just assumed Ellie was your first child."

Olivia took a deep breath before continuing. "She is, but she isn't – *wasn't* – Peter's first."

He waited for her to elaborate.

"Peter had a little . . . romance many years ago, just before we married, actually. He and I had split up at the time."

"Oh."

"It was my own fault because I'd initiated the break-up in the first place, and we only found out about the other girl's pregnancy once we'd made up and become engaged. I was devastated, naturally, but I was madly in love with Peter and in the middle of making plans for our wedding." She paused slightly, before continuing. "Eventually, I just resolved to get over it, and get on with it." She shrugged. "I agreed to take on the child as my own."

"So you and Peter looked after him?" Matt was confused. "But what about the mother?"

Olivia shook her head. "She didn't want him. As far as she was concerned it was a one-night stand. Peter discovered that she was going to have an abortion, but neither of us would stand for that. So we offered to adopt Jake – that was his name, Jake," she said, smiling sadly.

"And she let you?"

"As I said, she didn't really want a baby. She hadn't long left college and she wanted to go and do her own thing. I expect she felt guilty about the fact that Peter had a fiancée then too, and she didn't want to rock the boat, as such. She had no problem with letting us adopt him."

"But she told him about the baby?"

"No, we heard about that from another source. It was good that we did actually, otherwise the poor thing might not have had a chance."

"You were never going to let that happen anyway," he said.

"No, despite the fact that little Jake would always be

a reminder that Peter had been with somebody else. But, as I said, I couldn't blame Peter. I couldn't blame her. I could only blame myself. Right after graduation, I panicked and one day out of the blue I told Peter that our relationship was stifling me. I told him I didn't want to be with him any more. Matt, you have to understand that Peter and I had been together for years then, and as far as everyone else was concerned it was inevitable that we'd get married and be together forever. They used to call us the Golden Couple. But after college, things changed. I felt terrified, smothered, tied down – it's hard to explain really. But after some time apart, and some space to determine how I really felt, I decided that I did want to be with him after all."

"But in the meantime, he was so upset that he shagged someone else? Doesn't sound like such a nice guy to me," Matt said sardonically.

"I can see why you'd think that," she said, "but it wasn't quite like that. This girl was comforting Peter, they'd been drinking and, well, you know yourself. There was nothing between them." At least, that's what Olivia had always tried to convince herself – if she hadn't, she knew she wouldn't have been able to go ahead with the wedding, let alone the rest of it.

"So you took on the baby, and the mother didn't mind. That must have been tough on you all the same."

She shrugged. "I thought about it a lot, but once I'd made the decision that was it. And he was Peter's, so as far as I was concerned he was as good as mine. Still, he was a sickly child and sometimes frustrating to look after. I think . . . well, I *know* that Peter sometimes thought I resented Jake because he wasn't mine, but that was never the case – it was just that he was difficult to take care of."

"Catherine told me before that she heard you blamed yourself for your husband's death." He shook his head. "But it must have been that you blamed yourself for the *child*'s death. Why? How did it happen?"

"As I said, he was a sickly child and needed a lot of looking after. We had one very tough year when he started going to a crèche – we were so fearful about entrusting him to anybody because he really needed to be watched almost every hour of the day. The carers at the crèche knew the situation, of course, and did their part – and all went well for a while." She paused, her face bleak, then continued with obvious difficulty. "Peter and I had a system going, whereby we kept in close contact during the day . . . to ensure one of us would always be there to pick him up in the evenings, whatever emergency might overtake either of us at work . . ." She trailed off, the memory of it all so clear in her mind. "To this day, I still wonder why I went back to work at all, why I didn't just stay at home and look after him full-time, but we felt that we could manage – stupidly *I* felt that we could manage. I thought it wouldn't be good to smother him just because he was difficult, that having him interact with other children would be good for his development."

"So, the day he died, you were late collecting him from the crèche?"

"I wasn't just late, Matt – I completely forgot. I lost track of time . . . we had an emergency at the Centre, and it took a lot longer than expected, and in the middle of it all, I forgot to tell Peter I'd be late and . . ." her voice shook, "when I realised the time, naturally I panicked. But for some reason, I couldn't get Peter on the phone, and no one in the crèche was answering . . . So I just jumped in the car, and to this day I don't know how I managed to drive home at all, because I knew. Deep down I just *knew* that something had happened, and when I came back and saw the ambulance there . . ." her words trailed off softly. "I had gone by the crèche on the way, but everything was locked up, and they were all gone"

"So what happened? Why didn't the crèche wait for you, or even try to contact you?" Matt asked, frowning.

"One of the other mothers, Deirdre – she didn't know us all that well, she was a newcomer to the estate – she lived down the road from us and she offered to take him home. The crèche would have normally phoned me or Peter to ask, but there was a part-timer on that day who didn't know any better. So she let him off with the other mother, without consulting with the other carer there, thinking she was doing us a favour. Like Deirdre thought she was doing us a favour. Deirdre brought Jake back to her house with her little boy and gave them both something to eat. She didn't know any better, and she tried her best but . . ." She stopped, unable to keep going, the pain of it all just too much.

"He choked on something?" Matt supplied gently. "Olivia, that was just an accident. It wasn't your fault."

"He didn't choke, Matt. He had allergies, and he needed medication, *specialist* medication that only someone with experience could give him. Poor Deirdre didn't know what to do – she rang her doctor but it was too late." Olivia looked at him. "My next door neighbour Cora tried to ring me, but stupidly, I had forgotten to bring my mobile, so instead she phoned my mother. But it was too late by that time anyway." She paused again to try and steady herself. "He died because I wasn't there to collect him, Matt, and when it all went wrong, I wasn't there to help."

Peter had been furious, wanting to blame her, the crèche, poor Deirdre anyone. But ultimately Olivia knew it had been all her fault.

She paused for a moment and Matt let her, giving her the chance to collect herself.

"Within a few minutes of eating a sandwich Deirdre gave him he went into shock and then into a coma. He died before the ambulance came."

"I'm sorry, Olivia."

"Of course, afterwards Peter blamed me, even more than I blamed myself. He accused me of being resentful towards Jake, of being resentful of the fact that he wasn't mine, that he was a reminder of what Peter had done. That wasn't the case – I loved him just as much as if he had been mine. Yes, it was difficult living with the peanut allergy, but . . ."

"A *peanut* allergy?" Matt repeated. "Like your friend

470

Robin's?" He shook his head. "Wow, I didn't realise it was so widespread these days!"

Olivia said nothing more – she just sat there, waiting.

Matt was still talking. "Coincidental, isn't it? I mean, what are the chances of . . ."

Then he trailed off, as hearing the words out loud, the realisation hit him.

Olivia knew she didn't have to explain anything more. "It was no coincidence, Matt," she confirmed quietly. "Robin was Jake's mother."

Chapter 47

She'd never meant for it to happen, but it did. She'd never meant to betray her best friend, never meant to fall head over heels for Peter Gallagher but she did, from the very first moment Robin laid eyes on him.

He'd known it too, way back then, on the first night Olivia asked her around for dinner, not long after the episode in the cafeteria. She remembered the way he watched her, the way he followed her with his eyes, and yet all the time continued to be nothing other than charming and gracious to his girlfriend's new friend. How he made light of 'saving her life' that day.

"But you did, Peter," Olivia had insisted. "If you hadn't helped with the shot, she might have died."

"Ah, sure it's all in a day's work," he'd said, laughing it off, but still those watchful eyes were focused on her every movement. It was disconcerting, but strangely exciting.

At least it was for a while, until Robin began spending more and more time with Olivia and her diverse group of friends, some of whom, like Leah and Andrew welcomed her into the fold like she'd been around forever and others, like Amanda, who viewed Robin's unobtrusive persona and reasonably attractive looks with suspicion. And she'd never been one hundred per cent sure how Kate felt about her.

Not to mention the fact that they all seemed to find her nut allergy freakishly bewildering. But she and Leah in particular seemed to hit it off very well, the fact that the other girl seemed to be as unlucky in love as Robin helping form an instant bond.

When they were all together, Peter's behaviour was even more disconcerting, as Robin watched him play devoted boyfriend to Olivia and often wondered if she'd been imagining it all. Feeling an absolute heel for even thinking for a second that her new friend's boyfriend was giving her the eye, Robin resolved to cop on to herself and stop imagining things.

But one night after a few drinks, Peter confirmed her suspicions. "You know there's something between us, don't you?" he'd said, slurring slightly. "Something special – a connection."

"I don't know . . . I'm not sure what you're talking about," Robin said, precarious exhilaration stirring inside her as she realised exactly what he was saying.

But it was wrong, very wrong and she'd been stupid and naïve. In retrospect, she should have confided in Olivia straightaway, but she hadn't known her all that long, and she didn't want her to think badly of her boyfriend, or of Robin. And nothing had actually happened, had it? It was just the drink talking.

Still, Robin couldn't help but be even more aware of Peter after that, disconcertingly aware. And the problem was she really liked Olivia and had come to like her even more as time went on. It was an uncomfortable situation and yet one that Robin could do nothing about. She was like a moth drawn to Peter's flame; she knew he could be dangerous and yet she couldn't resist getting closer.

And then, after graduation, when out of the blue Olivia decided to break up with Peter, Robin had a chance.

She remembered the absolute joy she felt when Olivia told her how trapped she was feeling, how she wasn't sure if she wanted to head straight for 'happily ever after' with Peter. "We've been together for as long as I can remember. But who's to say he's the right one for me?" she'd said one day. "Who's to say that I won't wake up in ten years' time and decide that I should have played the field a bit more? I'm just not sure any more, Robin. I love him, but I don't know if I love him enough to commit to him for the rest of my life."

"So what are you going to do?"

"I'm going to suggest a break," she said defiantly. "A real break, not just something for the sake of it. I'm going to tell Peter exactly what I told you, that I'm not sure."

"But what if he takes it badly?" Robin asked, feeling

a whirlwind of emotions at the thought of it all. She felt bad that Olivia was so confused and even worse for thinking about how this might benefit her. Maybe after a while, when Olivia and Peter had fully decided that they no longer wanted to be together, then maybe she and Peter could give it a try. The thought of it excited her more than she cared to imagine. Maybe she and Peter were meant to be.

"If he takes it badly, then he takes it badly. But there's nothing I can do about that, Robin. There's little point in our going on with the relationship if I'm feeling like this. Anyway, I think Peter will understand. He's known me for a long time now, and he knows I wouldn't do something like this without thinking seriously about it."

But Peter didn't understand. In fact, Peter went crazy. He couldn't come to terms with the fact that Olivia had finished with him. He was continuing his training in a city-centre hospital but was so distraught by her leaving that he was turfed out within a few weeks. Olivia didn't want to speak to him, assuming that the more they thrashed it out, the harder it would be to make a clean break. Some time afterwards, she started a job as a veterinarian assistant in a practice in South Dublin, and had little time to concern herself with Peter's feelings.

A few months passed and soon they had all gone their separate ways, Kate to her new job as a trainee accountant, Leah to France to continue her chef's training, Andrew to work on his new data-provider software, while Amanda, well . . . Amanda went to work on getting Andrew to marry her.

And in the meantime, Robin made sure she was there for Peter. Although she tried to convince herself she was acting just as a friend, as a shoulder to cry on, she knew it was much more than that. She was hoping that Peter would eventually realise that Olivia didn't need him, that he could go on without her, that there was someone else waiting for him, right in front of his eyes.

And after a while, she did convince him, after a while he managed to forget about Olivia, and come to terms with the fact that she was getting on with her life, and he would have to do the same.

So, one night, after Robin casually suggested making him dinner, it happened.

"Dinner – ugh? What will you give me, baked beans on toast?" Peter joked. At that stage, he was almost back to his best.

"I'll have you know that I'm a great cook and I know a lot about food," she shot back, feigning annoyance. "You know how careful I am about what I put in my mouth."

"Remind me never to force anything on you then," he quipped back, making her embarrassingly aware of her unintentional double-entendre.

But from that moment on, the flirting began, and it didn't stop until, two bottles of wine later, she and Peter ended up in bed together. For Robin it was everything she'd ever imagined. He was passionate and loving and, best of all, he was no longer Olivia's. The fact that he was with her meant that he was finally over Olivia, didn't it? It meant that the two of them had a future now.

And Olivia wouldn't mind, would she? At that stage, it had been over between her and Peter for some time.

"I'd rather not say anything just yet," Peter said, the following morning, when Robin raised the thorny subject of Olivia.

"But I'd hate her to find out from anyone else, and I'd also hate for her to think we were carrying on behind her back."

"She won't think that," he'd said and was, Robin thought, considerably less playful over breakfast. "But we should give it some time all the same."

Robin agreed, but was confident that Olivia wouldn't mind. In fact, she had met her for lunch the week before and she hadn't mentioned Peter once. No, Olivia was over Peter, Robin was sure of it.

Which is why it came as a major shock to her when, two weeks later, Olivia and Peter were back together and telling the world how much they'd missed one another and that they planned to get married the following year.

Robin was devastated. By then she'd fallen heavily for Peter, believing their passionate night together was the start of something special, sure that, by her own choice, Olivia was fully out of the picture.

So, she tried her best to smile and say all the right

things when her friend proudly displayed her stunning engagement ring, and asked her opinion on wedding dresses. Ironically, she and Robin had become even closer at this stage, as Leah had gone abroad and Kate wasn't so good at keeping up the friendship.

So, Robin had to come to terms with the fact that what she had thought was a budding relationship with Peter was nothing other than a stop-gap – something to keep him occupied until Olivia changed her mind.

But, when a few weeks later, Robin began throwing up in the mornings and feeling tired and listless at work, she realised that their one-night stand could have devastating consequences – for everyone.

She didn't know what to do. How could she support a baby? She was barely out of college, had just begun working as a junior in a small finance company, not to mention the fact that the baby's father happened to be making plans for happily ever after with her best friend!

So, racked with guilt and unable to come to any other conclusion, Robin went to the student union office at the university and asked for help. A single phone call later, she was booked into a clinic in London. It was only by pure chance that Leah phoned one night for a chat, anxious to tell Robin about a gorgeous man she had met in Paris. "He's a chocolatier," she'd explained giddily. "How perfect is that?"

Robin laughed along with her, trying her best to sound enthusiastic but almost instantly Leah picked up on it.

"What's the matter?" she asked. "The last time I spoke to you, you were in great form. In fact, I wondered if you hadn't found someone yourself."

"I did, but it's over," Robin stated flatly.

"It was Peter, wasn't it?" Leah said, typically direct.

"What? How did you –?"

"Come on, Robin, every time I phone he's either there or you're talking about what he said or did the last time you spoke to him. I know you two got close when he and Olivia split up, and I know that since they got engaged, you've been a long streak of misery. What are you going to do?"

And then Robin blurted it all out: how being in love with Peter was the least of her worries, how she'd betrayed her friend, and had quite possibly ruined her life.

"I can't keep it," she told Leah. "It's all arranged."

"You have to tell him," Leah tried to convince her. "Don't do this alone."

"What else can I do? I've just started with the job – it's a junior position with bad pay and little prospects. How can I possibly bring a young baby up on my own? Olivia is bound to suspect something – she knows I haven't been seeing anyone, and the timing is too obvious. Not to mention that I've been trying to avoid her since I found out they were back together."

It had all seemed so bleak, so desperate then, and the only way out it seemed was to take the baby out of the equation. Robin was shocked and dismayed at what she had been reduced to. At college, she and Olivia were always signing up for those pro-life demonstrations and rallies. The two of them had spent many an afternoon on Dame Street in front of those graphic photos of aborted foetuses looking for signatures from passers-by. It seemed so easy to be idealistic or moralistic about 'choice' when the choice wasn't yours to make. Things seemed so much simpler in college, in that cosy little cocoon where you and your little student societies could all play at politics and play at real life. But outside the walls of UCD, outside that structured framework of right and reason, it was all very different.

There hadn't been a day since that Robin didn't think about how close she had come to doing something so awful.

"You don't have to do that," Leah advised. "You should tell Peter – it's his responsibility too."

"But Olivia would hate me," Robin whispered sadly.

And Olivia did for a while. She knew that. She hated the fact that Robin's unborn baby had thrown a huge shadow over her new life with Peter. Unbeknownst to Robin, but ostensibly for her own good, Leah had approached Peter and let him know what was happening. All of a sudden, Olivia and Peter were there for Robin, and made it known in no uncertain terms that aborting the child was the last thing she should do, that there was no need. After a few months of trying to come to terms with it, the two of them, but especially Olivia, had been wonderful to Robin and had helped her through the remainder of her pregnancy. Which made Robin feel even guiltier for messing up her own and her friend's life so spectacularly, but also helped her with her next decision.

Long after they had persuaded her to keep the baby, and just before the child was born, Robin knew exactly what she had to do. One day she broached the subject with Olivia.

"I don't want this baby, you know that," she said, when they were alone in her tiny bedsit. "I never wanted it." Her heart hammered guiltily as she lied through her teeth. Of course, she wanted the baby. Granted not in these circumstances, but still this little life inside her was precious – and hers.

"Don't say that. You're just nervous about the birth," Olivia said, dismissing her.

"I mean it," she persisted. "I don't want it. If you and Peter hadn't convinced me to keep it, you know I would have gone through with the abortion. I'm not a maternal person." Robin grasped at this and tried to convince herself that she really *wasn't* maternal, but with each passing day as she felt this new life growing inside her, she came to love it more and more. It would be torture, but Robin knew she had caused enough misery. And she also knew she had to try and make amends.

"Robin, you'll be fine," Olivia said, but every time Robin looked at her, she could see the sadness and disappointment in Olivia's eyes. She couldn't put her through this, put her through trying to pretend that everything would be OK, that they could continue as friends. It just wasn't fair.

"So, I was thinking that maybe you and Peter might

take it . . ." she went on, trying to make her voice sound casual, as if she was talking about a second-hand TV set, although once she'd uttered that simple remark, Robin felt as though she'd already lost a part of herself.

"What?"

"The baby. I was hoping that you might take it. That's if you'd like to," she said, just catching the expression of hope on Olivia's face. "Look, you two are getting married, and I know it's not ideal, but you've always said you'd like a family." She tried to shrug off-handedly. "I know it might not be how you imagined but . . . chances are I'll have to give it up anyway."

For a long moment, Olivia was silent. "Let me talk to Peter about it," she said.

And that was it. Decision made. Robin tried not to think too much about it after that, although inside her heart ached. She made herself imagine that it was Peter and Olivia's baby then, that it wasn't and would never be hers. And by rights it *should* be their baby. Robin had no claims on Peter, or on their relationship. She knew that. She had made a stupid mistake but at least this could be a way of making up for it somewhat.

So, by the time the baby was born slightly prematurely, Robin had almost convinced herself that she didn't feel anything for the tiny little thing in the incubator, baby Jake Gallagher. Olivia had picked the name, at Robin's insistence.

When a few days later, Robin returned from the maternity hospital – lonely and bereft after giving up her special baby – and found that the financial controller's job she'd applied for in the States was hers and that the company would sponsor her visa, she resolved to move on, to try and forget what she had done, and get on with her life. She'd be better off away from Ireland, she thought sorrowfully, away from everyone and everything – away from all the trouble she'd caused.

And Olivia, Peter and little Jake would be much better off without her.

Chapter 48

The following morning, Robin gave another interview about her children's books on breakfast television.

The bubbly blonde presenter was doing her best to relax her, but Robin just couldn't feel relaxed. The last few days had been torturous, and she just didn't feel like spending all this time gabbing on and promoting her stupid book. It all seemed so shallow and inconsequential, considering.

There hadn't been a single day in her life since giving him up that she hadn't thought of Jake, but especially after meeting Olivia the other night, Robin could think of little else, and the pain and guilt was all-consuming. Now, she just wanted to go home, home to New York, home to Ben and away from all the hurt and regret that being in Ireland had caused.

The presenter asked her another question. "The publishers believe that these stories won't just entertain, but will really help the children and the parents of allergy sufferers," she asked. "Do you feel that your own experiences as a nut-allergy sufferer helped you understand better than most the problems associated with these conditions?"

Robin sat forward, deciding she'd better just get it over and done with. "Yes, and it can be tough as an adult living with the condition, but at least I'm old enough to be able to take responsibility for myself." She paused. "I do know it's a lot harder for parents. The reason the book came about in the first place was because I saw how hard my partner's sister found it with her little girl, who suffers from asthma and hayfever. In a city like New York, especially in the summer time, it's very difficult. And of course, she's now school-going age, so it's even more worrying for her mother."

"I can imagine," the presenter nodded sympathetically. "So the book did have an effect on your partner's niece?"

"Yes, it did, but I think it had even more of an effect on her mother – but you have to remember this was all unintentional. I have no idea what it's like to look after a child with a medical condition, I don't know how it must feel to live permanently in a state of potential emergency." She stopped then, her heart thudding against her chest as she realised what she had just admitted. She did have no idea, no idea at all of what Sarah really had to go through. Or Olivia.

"Yes, it's not something most of us experience, thank God. So, your sister-in-law brought the book to the attention of the publishers?" The presenter glanced almost imperceptibly at Robin's left hand.

"No –" Robin went on to explain how she and Ben had provided their own crude booklets for the school and that one of the parents worked on the production team for Bubblegum Press.

"And then Nickelodeon got in on the act with their big money deal. It's such an amazing story," the presenter was shaking her head in awe. "And you never wanted to be a writer before then?"

"Not really. To be honest, I feel a little guilty about that. I'm sure there are thousands of people out there who could have done a better job on these books than I did."

"Yes, but you're the one who had the experience. You know how to put the message across."

"Perhaps," Robin shrugged self-consciously.

"So, as a result of your series, hundreds, if not thousands of parents around the world should be helped by giving their children a copy of your book. Congratulations, Robin. I'm sure every parent watching who has a child suffering from such a condition will be very grateful to you." The presenter smiled then, as if to wrap up the slot, but Robin shook her head.

"I don't know about that," she continued, her voice softer and less assured. "I had a friend, a good friend, who sacrificed a lot to look after a nut-allergic child like me. It didn't just affect her life; it affected her marriage."

"Oh, so more experiences to draw from then!" The

presenter tried to keep the tone light. "But I'm sure it's difficult."

"The thing is," Robin went on, the reunion with Olivia, the visit to the graveyard, all of it, really hitting her then, "I never really understood how much it had affected her. To be honest, I didn't want to understand. I was too busy getting on with my own life."

And that was true, she admitted. She had been so intent on getting over her own pain, her own loss, that she hadn't really thought about Olivia and what she must have gone through. Jake wouldn't have been easy to raise, and the fact that he was a constant reminder of what Peter and Robin had done would have been doubly hard for her friend. All of a sudden Robin realised that she had been even more selfish that she'd imagined.

She looked away and her eyes shone with tears. "That's why I feel there should be more help given to the parents of children with allergies, diabetes, etc. People seem to think that keeping children away from the food in question is the answer. But it isn't. The way of life has to change and the pressure is enormous. I didn't really understand that."

Yet she didn't want to understand it, she thought. She was too wrapped up in her own problems, in her own regrets.

"I see, well, thanks –" Again the presenter tried to wrap things up.

"But she's the most kind-hearted, unselfish person I've ever known, and I know she did her very best for the child."

"Did?"

Robin's head snapped up then, almost as if remembering where she was. "Yes," she said sadly. "My friend's son died from his allergy." Robin's eyes sparkled under the bright studio lights, and just then the presenter realised that this bit wasn't on the press release.

"Oh, dear – I didn't know it could get that serious . . ." Her gaze flickered fearfully to the production crew. Now she was concerned, not just for Robin, but for the fact that this slot was running *way* over time

But at this stage Robin was in full flow, as everything seemed to overwhelm her all at once, her grief for Jake, for Peter and for the friendship that she had lost. "Yes, but I think – I mean, I *know* my friend always blamed herself for that, and she shouldn't have. She was a fantastic mother and she did her best, more than her best for him. It was a tragedy, but one that was always possible until he learned to look after himself. But in the meantime, there was no one better than Oli – than my friend – to take care of him. She did that to the best of her ability – no one could have done any better."

And that was true too. Despite the fact that Jake was lost to both of them, Robin knew deep down that Olivia had done her best for him, something that she herself could never claim.

"But you wish you could have helped more?" the presenter prompted.

She paused, unsure how to word this. "Yes, I should have helped, and I hope she can forgive me for that."

The presenter nodded again. "I'm sure your friend is thrilled you decided to write a book about it."

"I'm not so sure about that," Robin answered sadly, and a little too cryptically for the presenter's liking.

"Robin, thank you very much for sharing that with us, and thank you for coming on the show," she interjected while she had the chance. "Robin's first book is called *Atchoo the Allergic Alligator* and will be in shops in November, just in time for Christmas!" She turned to Robin. "Best of luck with it all."

"Thank you," Robin nodded uncomfortably.

With a winning smile, the reporter turned to face the camera. "Right, now we'll go over to the newsroom for an update and next up, our vet spot where we'll explain how *you* can really communicate with *your* pet!"

The telephone rang, and Leah put down her coffee mug and muted the TV.

"Did you see that?" Kate asked snidely. "Who the hell does she think she is?"

Leah groaned. "Oh, leave it out, Kate, will you?" she said, sick to the teeth of Kate's constant sniping and bad humour. "She was just answering the woman's questions."

"What would she know about it? 'There should be more support' indeed! She wasn't exactly that supportive of poor Olivia when her child *died*, was she? No, she was too busy living it up in New York!"

Leah shook her head "Kate, I'm sorry – you're my

friend and I love you, but lately you've turned into an almighty pain in the arse!"

Silence at the other end.

"Look, Kate, what's with all the Robin-bashing? You weren't close to Olivia back then either. What's it got to do with you?"

To her amazement, her friend began to cry. "I don't know!" she wailed. "I don't know what's wrong with me lately. I'm angry at Michael, at Dylan, at Robin, at everything! I'm sorry for not going out for your birthday – I know you probably hate me now but I'm sorry!"

"Oh, you silly goose!" Leah couldn't help but smile. "I know you'll make it up to me."

Kate sniffed again. "I want you to be Dylan's godmother. Now it's OK if you say no, because I know it might be hard and –"

"I'd love to." Leah was touched.

"Would you?"

"Yes, it would be an honour."

"Thanks." Another sniff. "I didn't know if you would want to after me being such a bitch about Josh. But you know it's only because I care about you," she said mournfully.

"Kate, listen to yourself – you sound like a right moan!"

"I do, don't I?" Kate answered, as if just realising it then.

"Yes, you do!" Leah said, amused. She supposed she'd been unfair to her really, giving out about her not making an effort any more. It was pretty obvious that the root of Kate's suffering was severe baby blues.

And Leah had just the cure for that. "Look, I have to go into the shop this morning, but I'll pop over later for lunch and a natter, OK?"

"OK," Kate sniffled again, and Leah grinned.

"And then afterwards, you get Dylan organised, and we'll go to the hospital and visit Amanda and the new arrival. Apparently, the slice and dice never happened," she added wickedly.

Almost instantly, the sniffling stopped. "What? She went through with the whole thing – properly?"

"Yep. Apparently her timing must have been all wrong, 'cos when she went in, she was too far gone to do a Caesarean. Her waters had broken and everything. *And*, listen to this, Andrew said she was *also* too far gone to get the epidural." Poor Amanda, Leah thought.

"Oh my God, I can't miss this!" She was sounding much more like the old Kate. "Don't you *dare* go to the hospital without me – I want to hear every detail!"

"Now, are you sure you're feeling up to it?"

"Never better, now that I know little Miss Perfect had to go through what I went through!"

With a slight grin at the thought of their visit, Leah replaced the receiver, and began to get ready for work.

It was weird, she thought a while later, driving towards the shop, but today she was feeling really fantastic. It was as though finally coming to terms with the fact that she and Josh weren't getting back together had been an epiphany for her. Although then again, she thought with a smile, it could be that lovely feeling you get the day immediately after an almighty hangover. Nevertheless, it was onwards and upwards from now on, she decided. No more feeling sorry for herself about Josh and her lack of a relationship. No more feeling cheated just because her best friend didn't have as much time for her any more. Today was the first day of the rest of her life and all that.

Beeeep! Beeeep!

Leah slammed on the brakes as a huge Mercedes headed towards her from the right and she realised that she didn't actually *have* the right of way on the roundabout. *Eeek!* The rest of her life mightn't last all that long if she carried on driving like this, she thought, smiling her apology at the retreating motorist.

Well, to mark her new-found freedom, Leah decided there and then that she was going to learn to drive. Properly. For the first time in her life, she was going to take some lessons. Then she might at least have a hope of passing the blasted test.

And, she thought, turning onto Blackrock's main street, and glancing adoringly at the Elysium shop-front, she was going to enjoy being proprietor of the best bloody chocolate boutique in Dublin!

Chapter 49

"Robin? Hi, it's Olivia."

"Olivia?" Sitting in her hotel room, Robin was lost for words. What did she want? Did she want to have a go at her? Was Olivia mad, annoyed, upset – what?

"I was wondering, if you don't have anything else on, do you fancy meeting for a coffee, later?" Olivia asked pleasantly. "We didn't really get a chance to talk the other night."

Inwardly Robin was petrified. "I don't have anything else until tomorrow, and I'd love to," she said, before she could change her mind.

"Great, would around two o'clock suit? I'll meet you at your hotel if you like – it's the Westin, isn't it, I think Leah said?"

"It is and, yes, that would be fine."

"OK, see you then."

And Olivia rang off, leaving Robin feeling shocked

and bewildered, not just at the call but at the possible reason behind it.

At two on the dot, Olivia was standing at reception. "How are you?" she said with a smile. "I saw your interview this morning. I thought it was very interesting."

"You did?" For some reason, Robin hadn't considered that Olivia might be watching. She was so used to all the different networks back home in the States that she thought it would be a blink-and-miss performance. But then of course, Ireland had only a few homegrown TV stations, and apparently only one did breakfast TV, so there was *every* chance Olivia would be watching. Shit – did she say too much? Robin knew she shouldn't have gone on like that. It was stupid really, but once she started talking about it she just couldn't stop and –

"So where would you like to go?" Olivia asked.

"Well, we could go up to Grafton Street if you like," Robin answered hesitantly. "But there is a beautiful tea-room here. It has a glass roof and it's very relaxing."

"Why not? I'm sure it'll be better than fighting for a table in one of those postage-stamp places, anyway," she said, and Robin realised that this time the warmth wasn't forced. Something had changed about Olivia since Saturday; Robin was sure of it.

But when they were seated in the hotel's Atrium Lounge, and she found out what, Robin nearly spat out her tea.

"He did *what?*" she all but shrieked, forgetting that with the tall ceiling and the glass surroundings, every loud word uttered was echoed right back through the room.

Olivia had just told her about Peter's visit. Later, after she had spoken to Matt, she had met with Peter locally, and he had explained that he wanted to arrange their divorce.

"And how do you feel about that?" Robin asked, feeling a little surreal talking to her so easily like this, as though all those years had never happened.

"Not so good, but there's something else," she said, leaning forward. "You know I always blamed myself for . . ." she paused slightly, "well, for not looking after Jake properly, for not being there when he died."

"I've always thought you were crazy for thinking that," Robin said. "And when Leah told me how you felt about it, so many times I wanted to pick up the phone and tell you never to feel that way, that it was pointless. But I wasn't sure if it was my place to say anything. I didn't know if you'd want to hear something like that from me." Not to mention that it had taken Robin a very long time to come to terms with the tragedy herself.

Olivia sighed. "I always wondered if maybe you blamed me a little bit too, if you thought that maybe I didn't make enough of an effort with him. Peter used to accuse me of being resentful, but, Robin, that was never the case. I did do my best for him. I know it wasn't enough but –"

"Olivia, I never once thought that," Robin reassured

her, although inwardly her heart ached. "I knew you'd look after him. There was nobody better."

"Peter didn't think so though," Olivia said. "He was so angry and so accusing." Her hands shook as she spooned sugar into the tea. "For some reason, I always believed that he'd forgive me, that he'd come to terms with it all and that, when he did, he'd come back to me and Ellie and we'd be a family again." She shook her head. "I know it was stupid, but I'd forgiven him so much, we'd been through so much – sorry," she broke off then, remembering.

But Robin understood perfectly. Olivia *had* forgiven Peter a lot, too much maybe.

"I thought it was only a matter of time, a couple of weeks maybe. Still when the weeks turned into months and the months turned into years . . . well, you know how it is. Eventually I began to let go, to try and move on with my life. Ellie was happy enough anyway getting birthday cards and the odd phone call every now and again. I also suspected he might have had somebody else at that stage, so I suppose I had no choice but to try and let go."

"And then of course, you met Matt."

"Yes," Olivia smiled. "Then I met Matt and I realised just what I'd been missing. Strangely, I began to notice all the things that were lacking in Peter. Matt's a great father and he's really good with Ellie. He's gentle, considerate and when I'm with him it's only me, you know? He isn't checking out the blonde at the bar or the brunette with the nice legs like Peter used to. It's just me."

"I know exactly what you mean. In a way, that's what attracted me to Ben. Peter was always so unpredictable whereas Ben is simple, uncomplicated, straightforward. From day one, I knew where I stood."

"But – does he know? About Jake?" Olivia asked hesitantly.

Robin flushed. "No. I haven't told him. It hasn't been necessary . . . up to now. But, he's loving and supportive and I hope he'll understand . . . when I do. He's not selfish like Peter was. Sorry, Olivia, I know you probably don't need to hear that."

"That's no problem. Anyway, I know well that Peter has hidden depths and not just emotionally," Olivia said scathingly. "He's divorcing me because he and his Australian 'friend', Joanna, plan on getting married 'after five long years together'. He told me this the other night and it was definitely a little slip of the tongue on his part."

Robin looked at her, suspecting that Olivia was waiting for a reaction. "I don't get it," she said.

"Robin, he's been seeing this woman for *five* years. They worked together at the hospital here – I think she was a nurse or something, and they were obviously seeing one another around the time Jake died. Yesterday Peter finally admitted that, yes, he had been cheating on me." She paused for breath, before continuing. "And on the day Jake died, Peter wasn't working late, Robin. He wasn't working at all. He was away somewhere screwing this Joanna."

Robin almost dropped her cup into her lap. "*What?*"

"That's why he was so angry, so upset back then. He went crazy, crazy over the fact that I hadn't been there. In a way, I could understand his rage. But the problem was, it wasn't me at all he was angry with – it was himself! He realised what he'd done, and what the consequences were. Of course, he couldn't admit to it back then, so after a while the easiest thing to do was to take off to Australia with her and pretend that he'd left because he couldn't face me, because he blamed me. But thinking back on it now, all the signs were there. He was stressed, always tired, and a little distant, but stupidly, I just assumed he was working too hard." She smiled tightly. "I remember being quite worried about him actually, worried that all the late nights and stress at work were affecting his health. That day, the day I was – late home, I'd been on at Peter to get himself seen to. Little did I know that he'd take me at my word," she finished sardonically.

Robin couldn't comprehend how she felt upon hearing this. How selfish could a man be? How could he let them all think that Olivia had been the one at fault? Hadn't he put her through enough? "The stupid bastard!"

Olivia smiled sadly. "I know. But in a strange way, it's a relief to find that out now – it's a weight off my mind if you like. Now I know that it wasn't just my fault."

"But yet he let you think that!"

"It was Peter's way of getting out of a difficult situation, Robin. Our marriage was under pressure with Jake, there's no point in our pretending otherwise, and I'm not saying that to get at you. I'm simply stating a fact."

Robin cringed with guilt, even though she knew Olivia genuinely wasn't trying to get at her. But there was no denying that what she'd done had damaged Peter and Olivia's relationship – for good. Despite the fact that she'd been so sure that giving up the baby was the best thing to do for them, the best way to repair the wrong and let them all get on with their lives. Now, Robin ached with regret to think that her decision might well have been the wrong one.

"I knew he was unhappy, but yet I loved him desperately, so I thought that if we had a child of our own it would be different," Olivia went on. "Yet, I think I knew in the back of my mind that we weren't going to make it." She gave a watery smile. "Then, when Jake died, I knew it was all over. I had no choice but to accept the blame for his death and for the fact that Peter was leaving me. What else could I have done?"

"But you were pregnant and grieving, and I just can't believe he let you think that for so long? How dare he?"

Olivia shook her head. "Robin, you and I both know that Peter isn't exactly the upstanding guy he pretends to be."

Robin nodded, realizing that Peter had betrayed them both, not just after university, but many times since and in many different ways.

"And then, immediately after the funeral, he told me he needed some time alone to get over it all. I never saw him again – until yesterday. "

Robin gulped slightly at the mention of the funeral.

"I couldn't go," she whispered softly, her voice frail. "I toyed with it for a long time, but in the end, I thought it better that I didn't go. It wasn't my place to."

Olivia laid a gentle hand on hers. "You would have been welcome to come, but I understood. I knew it would be difficult for you."

Robin almost couldn't grasp her friend's depth of feeling, her wonderful strength. Even then, at the height of her own grief, Olivia was still able to make allowances for her.

"I'd always thought you'd hate me for it."

"Look, of course, it would be difficult for you, having to pretend concern for me and trying to hide your own feelings. And again, I also worried that you might blame me. After all, you trusted me to look after him, and look what happened."

Robin looked at her friend then, and hoped Olivia truly understood what she was trying to say. "Olivia, all I've ever done is admire you, and I'll be forever grateful for what you did for me back then. I'm just so sorry that I didn't return the favour, that I wasn't there for you when you were struggling to bring him up."

Olivia smiled, and her eyes twinkled. "I know, I found that out this morning – on TV of all places."

Robin grimaced, remembering. "The poor woman must have felt like a priest in the confession box. She didn't know where to look." And in a way, it was almost like a confession, a release of all the confusion, guilt and regret that Robin had been feeling all these years. The longer she stayed away, she'd thought, the easier it would be. But she'd been wrong. There was so much she hadn't understood, so much she hadn't *wanted* to understand about Olivia's situation. She'd been too consumed with her own grief.

But here now sitting with her friend, Robin felt as though a huge weight had been lifted off her shoulders.

"Well, I'm glad you said something." Olivia paused slightly, as if she was unsure whether or not she should continue. "Robin, I can appreciate how tough it must have been giving him up, but at the same time I couldn't figure out why you didn't want to ask about him."

Robin knew exactly what she meant. She wanted to know why Robin didn't seem interested in knowing about Jake and what he was like as a child, what her son, her baby was like. Olivia had never asked that Robin stay out of his life; in fact, she had been insistent that moving to America so soon after the birth was the wrong thing to do. She had been willing to share with Robin not only Jake, but also the heavy burden of coming to terms with giving him up. She was and had always been a true friend, yet Robin – and to her own detriment she knew now – had willingly abandoned that friendship.

"I did want to," she whispered softly. "In fact, all throughout this visit, I was desperate to ask you. But yet, I couldn't forget that it would be difficult for you, and you and I had grown apart and there never seemed to be a right time or place." She looked at her. "The other night, after dropping Leah home, I was sorely tempted to ask you to stay on too."

Olivia smiled. "Well, with the way Leah was that night, we might not have got a word in edgeways," she said, lightening the tone.

"How is she about the Josh thing – really?" Robin asked. "I tried to talk to her about it the next morning, but she was very hung-over."

"I think she'll be OK. You know Leah as well as I do – she's tough and she'll get through it. And it might be good for her in the end. It wasn't fair of him to deny her the right to a family like that."

Although it wasn't directed at her, the remark stung. Robin had been guilty of doing just that where Ben was concerned. She knew he was desperate to settle down and start a family and, yet, she was denying him that because of her own reticence about bringing up a child that needed more care and attention than normal, because of her guilt at abandoning one years before.

But that was it, wasn't it? It just needed that little bit more attention, something that she was sure Ben would give effortlessly. He would be a wonderful father. Still, the root of Robin's problems was that she didn't know what kind of a mother *she'd* be. She'd already given up a baby – who was to say she even deserved the chance to have another?

"And what about you?" Olivia asked then. "You've been with this Ben a while now, haven't you?"

"Yes." Robin smiled once more at the thought of it. "He's great. I'm very lucky to have him – more than I realised."

"I'm pleased for you, Robin," Olivia said. "You

didn't deserve to get mixed up with a bastard like Peter – neither of us did, to be honest."

Robin looked at her. Peter had done a terrible thing letting her take the blame all this time when he had been off with some other woman. Again, she realised that Olivia had suffered a lot more than any of them over this. And yes, even more than Robin herself. Olivia had been betrayed many times over and in the end had wrongly been left carrying the guilt.

"He wasn't always that bad, you know, and he loved you very much."

Olivia shook her head sadly. "He loved the idea of me, Robin. He got a hell of a shock when we split up because he didn't see it coming. He just liked the idea of his being in control, and when I pulled the plug he was blindsided."

"Maybe, but that never excused what *I* did." She thought of the mess she had made of their friendship.

"You just fell for the same things that I did, his smile, his charm, and that so-called little-boy-lost routine. Peter was always very skilled at making women fall for him." Olivia was looking at things a lot more clearly now. "I think I might have known it at the time, but I didn't want to admit it. It was easier to think that you two just had a drunken fling, but I don't think it was quite like that."

Robin simply nodded. She didn't really want to get into that night with Olivia – it wasn't fair to her.

"Anyway," Olivia sighed, "he's out of both of our lives now and, to be honest, I think we're the better for it!" She grinned. "He can have his bloody divorce and good riddance! Although, in fairness, he was great with Jake."

There was silence for a long moment, as both women were lost in their own thoughts, neither knowing quite what to say next.

Then Olivia reached into her bag, took something out and laid it on her lap. She looked speculatively at Robin.

"I brought some photographs – of Jake," she said carefully, and Robin's heart leapt with nerves, anticipation, she wasn't quite sure what. "I was planning on sending you one on each birthday, but you were so insistent that you didn't want to know . . ."

Her stomach fluttered. "You were right – back then, it would only have made things harder." She paused, and stared at the small photo-album on her friend's lap. Then she smiled. "But I'd love to see them now." And she realised that she meant it.

"I hoped you would," Olivia said, smiling too.

She laid the photo album on the table, and they both moved their chairs closer around it. Then the two friends sat side by side as Olivia slowly turned the first page.

Chapter 50

Poor Amanda lay deathlike on the bed, looking tired and worn-out, although Leah could see that her make-up had been carefully applied, and her hair was freshly washed.

"Hello, Mummy Clarke!" she said, and Amanda's eyes opened wide with delight when she saw her two visitors.

"Hi!" she said sitting up easily, and then, as if remembering, her face contorted into a grimace worthy of a day-time-soap actress. "Ah, I'm sorry," she whispered fraily, "but I'm still very sore!"

"You poor thing," Kate soothed, but Leah could hear the sadistic pleasure in her tone. "So it wasn't as beautiful an experience as you'd imagined?"

"Kate there is nothing beautiful about any of it, as you well know," she said huffily. "I can't understand how they honestly think there's anything natural about all that huffing and puffing and pushing and, oh, don't get me started!"

"You did it though, didn't you?" Leah said, looking in awe at the tiny pink bundle in the crib beside the bed. "And she's beautiful!"

"Just like her mum!" Andrew bellowed, upon entering the room. He leant over Amanda and gave her a delicate kiss on the forehead.

"Mmm, stay away from me, you – it's all *your* fault I'm here in the first place," Amanda groaned, looking thoroughly peeved. "And that's another thing that's totally unfair," she said, addressing Kate, as if by magic the two of them were now best friends, 'sisters of labour' and all that. "Why do they let men in the delivery room with video cameras? Honestly! Throughout the entire gruesome and hellish experience I didn't see Andrew for dust, and then when it was all over and I'm lying in the bed looking like *The Wreck of the Hesperus*, with my hair matted to my forehead and my face drenched with sweat, he arrives in with the video camera!"

Leah smiled at the mention of a video camera, and realised that it didn't hurt her quite so much any more. She wasn't over Josh, but she was on her way and she knew she'd get through it. The thought cheered her immensely.

"Just think, you'll be able to look back on it in years to come and little – little, hey, did you pick a name for her yet?" Kate asked.

Andrew and Amanda's eyes met and a secret smile passed between them. "Yes, we're going to call her Lulu," Amanda confirmed.

"*Aww!*" Leah and Kate said in unison.

"Sorry, we missed that – what are you calling her?" Olivia said from the doorway. And to Leah's total amazement and delight, standing behind her was Robin.

"Come in, come in – Robin!" Andrew grinned, surprised. "It's great to see you!"

"Thanks," Robin smiled shyly around the room. She and Kate looked at one another warily, but eventually Kate smiled too.

"Well, I must admit, I didn't expect this many visitors!" Amanda said, although Leah could tell she was delighted that so many of her friends had seen fit to visit her. Then she looked around. "Me, Andrew, Leah, Kate, Olivia, Robin – it's almost like a reunion!"

"Like the reunion that never was?" Kate said sardonically. "I told you all it was a stupid idea but, of course, you had to insist, and you were all so sure, and then I said . . ."

Leah stood back and looked around at the faces of her friends, the faces of the people she knew would help her get through the difficult times ahead.

She and Kate had had it out over lunch, and she knew now that Kate had been afraid to ask for help with Dylan, because she worried Leah might feel obliged. She also worried that Leah would find it difficult, knowing well that Leah had made a huge sacrifice for Josh, and not wanting to shove her own motherhood in her face.

Obviously Robin and Olivia had had a few things out too, and now the two of them looked relaxed and easy with one another. It was wonderful.

Amanda had the new baby in her arms now, and she and Andrew were looking from their daughter back to one another with such love and pride that Leah knew that motherhood – *parent*hood – was an experience she didn't want to miss, she didn't want to sacrifice.

She smiled inwardly. God knows who the misfortunate father would be but . . .

"My, don't you have a lot of friends, Mrs Clarke!" A nurse came in on her rounds and smiled graciously at them all.

Amanda beamed. "Yes, I suppose I do," she said proudly.

"Well, give me that camera of yours, Mr Clarke," the nurse said to Andrew, "and I'll get a photograph."

"You don't mind?"

"Of course not – this kind of thing doesn't happen every day, and I know what it can be like. By the next time you lot get together it could be ages."

"Thanks – I appreciate that."

They all gathered round the bed, and just then Leah realised that this *was* a reunion of sorts, and although they were missing the one that had scattered them apart, they had gained one who it seemed had somehow brought them together again.

It was as though this was a new chapter, a new beginning – for all of them.

Six happy faces looked into the camera and smiled.

The other one just yawned.

Epilogue

pLeah took a deep breath and tried to calm herself. This was easily the most terrifying experience of her life. Worse than starting her business, worse than opening the shop, even worse than breaking up with Josh!

She pulled into the kerb, trying her best not to drive up onto . . . *oops*, she'd done it anyway. This wouldn't be a good start.

Leah turned off the ignition, and glanced in her rear-view mirror. Where the hell was this bloody driving instructor? He'd told her seven pm – it was now well after two minutes past!

While she waited, Leah impatiently tapped the steering wheel. She switched on the radio. Whoever he was, he'd better not tell her that she couldn't have the radio on while driving. Leah had to have the radio on – it kept her mind off things – and if she didn't have it on in the background she'd definitely crash the car.

Then Leah suddenly realised that maybe that was why she *shouldn't* have the music on. It *did* take her mind off things. Only the other morning, she'd been on her way back from Olivia's, and was laughing at something Ray D'Arcy was saying on air and what did she do? Completely miss the turn-off for her way home!

It had been all hours by the time she got back to the apartment, having to drive for ages around the one-way system before turning back around again. Not that she minded much, she thought with a smile. Olivia and she had a great chat, and it was wonderful to see her so happy, carefree and comfortable with Matt. They were great together and Peter was well and truly out of her life now. They had drawn up plans for their divorce, Peter had applied for full residency in Australia, and Olivia and Ellie were finally free to move on.

In fact, all her friends seemed happy with themselves lately. Back in the States, Robin and Ben had finally found their dream house and were making plans to move in shortly. Her little book had done well upon publication, and there were high hopes for the subsequent releases.

Leah suspected that an engagement might be on the cards for them soon too as, upon her return to New York, Robin had told Ben everything about her past.

"I think he might have suspected something like that anyway," she'd told Leah shortly afterwards. "He knew I was running away from something back home. But he's fine about it, and we're going to talk seriously about where we go from here."

Leah suspected that Robin would be at her happiest staying in New York. She had a good lifestyle there and, indeed, it was probably the best place for someone like her to live successfully with her allergy. Leah too had booked her long-awaited and well-earned holiday, and was due to visit Robin and Ben in the new house soon. She couldn't wait.

Amanda, to everyone's surprise, had taken to motherhood like a duck to water and incredibly was being a huge help to Kate! This in turn was helping Kate to grow more confident with Dylan, and by comparing notes with Amanda she didn't feel so isolated.

Leah was so busy thinking about how well things had turned out for her friends, that she almost didn't hear the sharp tapping at the driver's window.

She looked up and saw what had to be one of the youngest, but *cutest* driving instructors she had ever seen. Why the hell hadn't she done this ages ago? Leah thought with a grin, opening the car door and getting out. A little bit of flirtation would definitely be on the cards here.

"Leah, is it?" the instructor asked.

"That's me!" she answered, eyeing him unashamedly as he walked round the car, and then sat into the passenger seat.

"I'm Ian. Sorry I'm a little late," he said but Leah barely heard him. She was too busy trying not to stare. Look at those stunning dark eyes, those huge hands, and that smile – Jeez! George Clooney had nothing on this guy! And, dare she say it, he was even more attractive than Josh.

"So is this your first lesson?" he asked, with a friendly smile.

Leah quickly stopped staring and resolved to concentrate on the task in hand.

"Yes, it is my first lesson and, to be honest, I'm a bit of a disaster. I've failed my test three times in a row now, and although I try my best, I know I'm a crap driver, and I just want to say that you have a big job ahead of you because I will never, *ever*, be able to pass this bloody test." She couldn't resist a coquettish flick of her dark hair.

"Don't be so defeatist," he said, shrugging. "I've taught lots of different kinds of drivers over the years, some good, some bad and some downright terrifying!"

Leah groaned. She was definitely in the latter category. "I can imagine!"

"But," Ian continued, and Leah tried her best not to stare at that undeniably sexy mouth, "when it comes to any pupil, no matter how good or how bad, we driving instructors have a little saying about the driving test."

"Yeah, and what's that?" Leah asked, thinking that she didn't care a jot about the test, but she couldn't wait to get going on the lessons – especially now.

Ian looked at her sideways, and winked. "Never say never."

THE END

Published by Poolbeg.com

Something you should know

MELISSA HILL

Just when everything was going so well for Jenny and
Mike, Roan Williams had to come back into
their lives.

Four years earlier, while her friends Tessa, Gerry,
Karen and Shane were falling in love and heading for
happy ever after, love-rat Roan had broken Jenny's
heart and completely shattered her life.

Harbouring a terrible lie, Jenny had struggled
to pick up the pieces of her life, but if Roan was going
to be around, the truth would have to come out.

It would ruin everything but Mike had
a right to know . . .

ISBN 1-84223-161-8

Published by Poolbeg.com

Not what you think

MELISSA HILL

**Good friends are there through thick and thin
– or are they?**

Laura Fanning has the wonderful Neil, talent to burn and her
brand-new jewellery design company.

Her best-friend Nicola Peters has independence, a job she loves,
her own home, great friends and the lovely Ken.

Glamorous and successful Helen Jackson has legs to die for,
a killer wardrobe, a thriving career and her cute daughter Kerry.

Social climber Chloe Fallon is marrying the gorgeous Dan Hunt
and planning the wedding of the year.

But all is not what it seems. Under the surface Laura struggles to
live up to her parents' impossible expectations, Nicola is coping
with a life-changing event, Helen resents Kerry for putting an
end to her love life and Chloe wants to know why Dan is being
so mysterious about his divorce.

When times get tough you find out who your friends really are.

ISBN 1–84223–170–7